WATER FAERIES

JAIME LEE MOYER   KAREN L. ABRAHAMSON

GRAYSON TOWLER   DAYLE A. DERMATIS

THEA HUTCHESON   JAMIE FERGUSON

ANTHEA SHARP   BRENDA CARRE   ALETHEA KONTIS

LOUISA SWANN   BRIGID COLLINS

DEANNA KNIPPLING   LINDA JORDAN   DEB LOGAN

SHARON KAE REAMER

Edited by
JAMIE FERGUSON

BLACKBIRD
PUBLISHING

COPYRIGHT

On a rock by the shore sits a mermaid fair
Dreaming of her lost lover as she combs her hair

Kelpies, and selkies, and the great snakes of the sea
All stop and listen as she sings of a love never to be

For the sailor she saved from those dark, storm-tossed
*   waves*
Got back on his ship, and sailed away

Now the mermaid's alone, with broken-hearted dreams
And far, far away the sailor stares out at the sea

CONTENTS

INTRODUCTION

The fourth volume in the series *A Procession of Faeries*, *Water Faeries* contains stories about sirens, kelpies, mermaids, sea monsters, naiads, and other magical water creatures.

What if the Loch Ness monster is more than a myth?

Where did the Lady of the Lake go after leaving Avalon?

Can a mermaid ever truly leave the sea, and follow her lover to land?

This collection includes fifteen tales about sirens, kelpies, mermaids, sea monsters, naiads, and other enchanted creatures of the water.

Enjoy the magic and wonder of these watery tales of Faerie!

—Jamie Ferguson
Editor

OCEAN DAUGHTERS

JAIME LEE MOYER

S ix coins—all the money I had left in the world.

I let them fall, copper and silver discs shining against a rum-colored cloth. Madame Kasa scooped them into her long-fingered hand, claiming payment before I had time to change my mind. Her eyes were blue, not with the brightness of summer skies, but dusky as storm-tossed waves. Flickering candles and smoky oil-lamp light darkened them to shadows in a rouged and powdered face.

"I can't tell you what to do, Lina. I look for signposts of what you might try, nothing else." Candlelight glinted off a dozen jet buttons on the front of her dress, painted ghost-shadows on the wallpaper behind her. She shook her head, gold earrings jangling. "And I can't promise anything you try will bring Ilya back. I don't think you can."

The chair wobbled as I sat, but was still stronger than my knees. She stared at me, measuring, and I didn't turn away. "Sailors tell stories of men returned by the sea. I have to try."

"So be it." Her lips shone red against white teeth. A smile, even one given freely, did nothing to lift my spirits. "The tea water will take a moment or two to boil."

Most of the village women thought telling fortunes a pretense for what Madame Kasa really was—a painted whore. I didn't understand why. Seers were respected on the plains and the foothills of home, consulted for the best time to plant crops and when to gather the herds for winter.

I'd not been born with the smell of seaweed on the wind, or raised with the keening gossip of gulls in my ears. There was much about living in a seaside village I didn't understand. People here whispered when I walked past, greeted me with pity in their eyes. Their pity had little to do with my grief.

The scent of jasmine and gardenia filled the room as Madame Kasa fetched cups, brewed tea, and carried the pot to the table. My head spun with perfume and fear. Fear that Ilya would never return was a sharp-edged panic that cut deeper with each passing day. Madame Kasa set a cup in front of me and took her seat again.

"Give me your hand, Lina." She touched my palm, tracing a line with one crimson nail from my wrist to my marriage ring. "How long have you known about the child?"

"Why do you—" She frowned and I took back the lie. "A week before Ilya disappeared I thought maybe I'm right, maybe this time it's true. The midwife says if all goes well the baby will be born midwinter."

"All will be well." Madame Kasa patted my hand. "The birth won't be easy, but not too hard as these things go. A girl, healthy and strong as her mother. Drink your tea. It's hot, so take care."

A daughter, a child I'd not be afraid to hold close. I'd dreamed of having a girl, but not dared hope. All men wanted sons to work the boats and follow them to the sea, while mothers feared losing son and husband both. Ilya was no different, but he'd love a daughter too, I felt sure of it. There'd be other children, sons, once he came home.

The cup was china, shiny white and painted with tiny yellow roses. My teeth rattled against the rim as I gulped too hot tea. I worried about the cup breaking, spilling liquid and leaves across the table, and losing this chance.

"That's enough." Madame Kasa took the cup, cradling it in both hands. "Now we'll see."

Twice she swirled tea puddled in the bottom of the cup, coating the sides with sodden black leaves. Twice she twisted the cup in her hands and started again, mouth set in concentration.

She sighed, the sound almost lost in the clink of china coming to rest on a saucer. "Staring longer won't change what I see or tell me if any good will come of it. Wear your widow's weeds to petition the sea. Go at sunrise and stand where the waves rush in to foam round your ankles. Don't wade any further or Mother Ocean may decide to claim you too."

I fingered my marriage ring. "How do I petition the sea? What do I offer?"

She gathered the cups; mine thick with leaves already shriveling as they dried, hers still full of untasted tea. The bead curtain over the opening to her small kitchen swayed as she pushed through. After she rinsed the cups clean and came back to me, the curtain swayed again.

"Speak from your heart and the words will come. Whether any will hear and answer I can't say." Madame Kasa opened her front door, dismissing me. "Think carefully about what you're willing to offer, Lina. You've not been married long and you could go home, back to the plains. If you stay there are other men in the village to make a life with. Not all of them steal from the sea."

"Ilya never stole!" I put hands over my belly, trying to shield our daughter from hearing. Salt scented air rushed in the open door, ruffled my hair and made me shiver. All sailors paid the tithe to Mother Ocean, a fair exchange for the fish they pulled from the sea. Trinkets mostly, adornments for her daughters.

"I helped him buy mirrors and combs." Tears filled my eyes, but I wouldn't let them fall. "I was with him! And I chose the best fruits at market, near as fine as if picked from my mother's trees. He paid the tithe."

She watched me, blue eyes steady on mine. "As you say, Lina. Come see me when you've gotten your answer."

"I've no more coin to pay you." Shame burned in my cheeks, but I'd not slink away. "The six I gave are the last."

"Not everything is measured in stacks of copper and silver." Madame Kasa smiled. "Sharing a meal is a good time to share a tale. Come see me and don't fret about payment."

The door closed with a soft click. My reflection stared back at me from the curtained window, worn and too thin. I turned toward home and food and rest.

I'd need strength to face the sea.

The walk from house to sand wasn't long and the streets far from empty. Men hurried toward boats rocking on mooring lines, eager to catch the outgoing tide and make the most of daylight hours. Clouds of pipe-smoke rose from some of the boats, wind carrying the sweet smell far from the docks. Bachelor boats, the women called them, full of men who couldn't bear to be off the water long. A few paced the decks, waiting impatiently for married sons or brothers, before getting underway.

Women waved from doorways or made their own way to market. They'd buy what they couldn't grow in garden patches, bake the day's bread, and gather in the late afternoon to stand vigil on the beach. Children would play, mothers gossip in the shade of lean-tos open to the sea, and young wives learned to patiently wait for the first glimpse of sails silhouetted against the sunset.

That was my life not so long ago. I wanted it back.

Wind filled sun-bleached sails, and the boats raced for the horizon, while men on deck sang to call fish from the bottom of the bay. Ilya told me that fishing songs were passed from father to son, and each family had its own. The songs were very old, stretching back to the time men first took to the sea, and no one alive understood the words. Fisherman's magic, he'd called them, easy to lose if a man didn't respect the sea.

I left shoes and stockings inside a lean-to, dry and safe. Sand whispered between my toes, chanting *go back, go back*. The first caress of waves, and a touch of foam, drowned the whisper in a roar of water.

"Ocean mother, I beg of you, tell me how to find my man. I've more need of him than you." Speaking from the heart was easy; choosing the right words to convince the sea was hard. I shouted, trying to be heard over the ocean's song. "Please listen! Send Ilya home where he belongs."

Sand hissed and slid, tugging me toward the depths. The waves, so soft at first, became iron fists seeking to pull me under. I felt the ocean's hunger for the salt locked in my blood, and for the tiny daughter swimming inside me, grow stronger as my footing melted away.

"No! You'll not have her too." I backpedaled, finding strength enough to break the sea's hold. Dry sand crusted the hem of my mourning dress. I stumbled over a castle built under a mother's watchful eye, and knew I'd reached safety. No joy came with the thought, only the certainty the sea mocked me.

I dropped to the sand, breathing hard, and not wanting to believe I saw mermaids bobbing to the surface. One swam closer, riding a wave. Half out of water she still moved with grace, twisting to sit with her tail curved around her.

Men told tales of mermaids glimpsed from the boats and their great beauty, of sailors carried in a mermaid's arms from a floundering ship to safety. They spoke of the rainbow shimmer of scales on breasts, and soft kisses that haunted a man's dreams, pretending their wives wouldn't hear. All the older men told stories about nights on deck locked in the arms of ocean daughters. I'd thought it strange. The women all knew, shrugging my questions away when I'd asked if I should worry.

I could well believe all I'd heard given the creature confronting me. What men never spoke of was the cruelty in a mermaid's smile, and the glimmer of hate in sea-green eyes. Perhaps fishermen never saw.

"Since you won't swim with us, I came to you. You have my mother's attention. Most women don't have the courage to challenge the sea." Her words were a song, each one a melody of restless waves and foaming sand. Scales glistened on the side of her neck, the top of bare breasts. Rainbow shimmers rippled down her belly to a darker place on her tail. She saw my red-faced stare and laughed. "Make your plea and be quick about it."

My mourning veil blew into my face, and I pulled the comb from my hair, dropping the hated black lace to the sand. "Send Ilya back to me. I beg you."

The mermaid raked her fingers through long green-black hair, paying me little heed.

I went to my knees. "Please, let him come home! You've no use for him, and our daughter needs a father."

She looked up at that, sharp-eyed and searching for weakness. "A daughter deserves better than a father who steals from the sea. Find another man."

Madame Kasa had said much the same, but my faith was blind and strong. "Ilya told me he paid the tithe. He wouldn't lie to me."

The coldness of the depths was in her smile now. Knowing that men looked on such creatures with desire baffled me.

"And yet my mother sought to make him answer for his thievery. You still smell of land and rock and not belonging, but know this to be true. Mother Ocean doesn't send her daughters to pluck innocent men from the decks. Think on that and if he's worth any bargain you might make." She slid backward into the surf, holding motionless as waves crashed against her. "Make an offering to the sea, something that means much to you. Tithe a daughter for a thief if you truly want your man back. You'll have my mother's answer by morning."

She swam back to her sisters, more fish than woman. The five mermaids waiting for her flipped tails in the air like a pod of dolphins and dove below the surface. She paused before following, rising high in the water to stare at me. There was nothing kind in her gaze.

"What can I offer the sea in exchange for your father? I've little to trade and less I'm willing to part with." I rested a hand on my belly, already talking to my child as if she heard. "I won't let her have you."

Not even for Ilya. I didn't say the words, wouldn't say them so our daughter could hear.

That didn't make them any less true.

I sat near my shoes at the edge of the lean-to, out of reach of questing waves and the shimmer of wet sand. The sea waited patiently.

Morning moved into afternoon and I'd not chosen. I heard voices —mothers and children, babes in arms and old women hobbling with canes—coming to the beach to wait for the boats' return.

The youngest of the wives, my friends only days ago, nodded but didn't speak. Widow's weeds and a tear-streaked face made me an unwelcome reminder that not all men came home at sunset. Older wives spared a glance of sympathy and continued on to an empty lean-to. Only the grannies sat near me, some widowed before I was born.

8

Children paid me little mind. I'd never watched them before, too close to a child myself while thinking myself grown. Knowing I'd soon be a mother changed that as well. I noticed how young daughters raced to the edge of the water, fearless and fierce in their game of tag with the waves. Small boys gathered in clumps to dig holes and build sand castles, or pile rocks into towers. Girls roamed free while their brothers never strayed too far from a mother's side.

One of the widowed grandmothers, Madame Bana, patted my arm, comforting and drawing my attention both in her touch. "Why are you here, Lina? It's too soon. Go home where it's quiet, and you're not forced to remember. Rest is what you need if the baby is to grow strong."

I didn't think to wonder how she knew. A grannie knowing I was pregnant was the least strange thing in this day. "I came to make an offering to the sea, and plead with her to return my husband. I want Ilya home again."

The older women sighed as one. Madame Bana's wrinkled hand clamped tight on my arm. "Go home, Lina. The sea never relinquishes the men she claims. No offering you can make will win Ilya back."

"I don't believe that. She sent her daughters to hear my plea." I pulled free gently, respect for age preventing me from yanking away as I wanted. "A mermaid said I'd have her mother's answer by morning. I won't leave until I know. I can't."

"The answer will be the same, and you'll still be alone." The widow who spoke from the back of the lean-to watched the sea, grey hair escaping pins and mouth twisted in bitterness. "It's time you learned men use pretty baubles to buy favor with all women, not just the sea's daughters. Be smarter the second time and choose a man who respects Mother Ocean. A live man warming your back on cold nights is better than a dead one lying at the bottom of the sea."

Tears taste of salt. I licked them from my lips, cool as sea-spray, wiped others still warm on my sleeve.

"Leave the girl be, Estella." White haired and frail, Madame

Tolane was the oldest and seldom spoke. "Men lie and women believe them. Her hope will be gone soon enough."

The widows grew silent for a time. When they spoke again it was of grandchildren, the new fabric in the weaver's shop, and the ills of old age. I listened to their talk, these women who'd lost husbands to the sea so long ago, hoping for an inkling of why the men were taken, why none of them returned.

Listening, among the talk of the small things, for a reason why the widows sat vigil each day if they had no hope.

Sails appeared on the horizon, sharp-edged white against apricot-tinged clouds. Mothers called children back to them, gathered sons and daughters reluctant to leave their play. The older women left me to hobble up the slope away from the sea. Not one said farewell, or spared a backward glance.

A tow-haired little boy pulled free from his mother and ran to me. Unsmiling and solemn, he offered a sprig of sea pinks clutched in a tiny fist. I wiped away fresh tears and took the gift. Big blue eyes watched me, curious and unafraid.

I held the sprig to my nose, and inhaled the sweet scent. They smelled like flowers from my mother's summer gardens, far from the sea. I missed my mother, missed green and growing things, and the smell of roses on the breeze. "Thank you, little one. I like pretty flowers."

He didn't say a word, too young or too puzzled by a strange woman crying to answer. His mother smiled and shrugged, tugging him toward home.

I saw the fishing boats land, and the scramble to tie lines to moorings. Men shouted on the docks, crude jokes and laughter tossed back and forth between boats. Friends tried to outdo each other, bragging of the size of their catch, boasting of the welcome their wives would give them. Their banter went on until the fish were piled in baskets on the sun-weathered planks of the pier, ready to be carried to the icehouse for the night.

The chant started soon after; singsong and rolling, like waves beneath the boats. One by one, men walked to the end of the pier or leaned over their boat's side. Distance swallowed the sound of small splashes, men thanking the sea for her bounty with gifts from the land: flowers and sweet fruits, wooden combs, trinkets of polished glass and stone. A tiny bit of profit from the catch returned as payment for what they'd taken.

A few men, very few, busied themselves with carrying fish to the icehouse, disappearing until the others finished their chant. No one said a word when these men emerged for the walk from dock to home. They joked and talked as the rest, but I'd not seen them pay the tithe, I was sure of it. The other fishermen had to know as well.

Perhaps everyone in the village knew some men stole from the sea. All but a woman rooted in the stillness of the soil; a woman who missed the scent of roses.

Doubt chipped at my faith. I rested hands on my belly, wishing to hold the daughter swimming in the ocean inside me. "I don't want to believe your father lied to us, little one. I don't want to believe Ilya earned his fate."

The sun began to slip under the horizon, and still I sat undecided. Clouds deepened to orange and red, the sky to indigo. I stood and twisted my marriage ring from my finger, toes sinking in sun-warmed sand as I strode to the water's edge.

"This ring means much to me!" I threw my ring into the seething surf, threw anger at lies and silence and pleas for mercy into the wind. "Send Ilya back to us so my daughter will have a father. I know more of the land than men of the sea, more treasures to offer they'd never dream of! I'll pay your tithe each day for the fish he caught. You have my promise!"

My ring sank without a splash. I waited, knowing my answer wouldn't be swift, but hoping for some sign I was heard. When none came I moved back to sit at the front of the lean-to.

The tide turned, gliding out with a whispered hiss of waves. Crabs crawled from their burrows, scuttling across wet sand awash in moonbeams. The margin between land and sea grew wider with each surge of surf and measured retreat.

Stars peeked from behind thin clouds. I searched for the shapes and patterns my mother taught me, dredged up names from memories. My daughter would learn about the stars from me, pass on their names and stories to her daughter. I'd learned from my father as well —how to sharpen a knife, what knots held a horse tight to a post— but he'd no time for stories. Mothers and fathers taught different things. I wanted my daughter to know both.

The last light went out on the bachelor boats. Barking dogs and crying babes hushed, the final notes of lullabies fading as lamps were blown out in the houses facing the harbor. Silence settled over the village and the beach, broken only by the nighttime song of the sea.

I curled up on the sand, head pillowed on my arm. The night was warm, the wind gentle enough not to carry a chill; sleep beckoned, whispering promises. All I need do was close my eyes.

Mermaids gathered on the harbor wall to comb their hair. They laughed and chatted in a language I didn't understand, happy for reasons I'd never know. Dolphins racing a ship knew that joy, reveled in the same freedom.

Sirens sang from the rocks. Their songs planted love of the sea in men's hearts, luring them back to the boats with the rising of each sun. I listened to the ocean's daughters, unsure what was real or a dream.

The little girl playing tag with the waves was a dream, but I knew her, knew I'd name her Miriam. Nose dotted with freckles and hair the soft brown of summer hares, my daughter raced the surf, fierce and fearless. I called and she ran to me, laughing and happy. Miriam threw her arms around my neck and held tight, her weight in my arms a welcome burden.

But this wasn't her time. Not yet.

～

I woke to bright skies. Lacey clouds softened the blue, while gulls cried and keened, swooping above the waves. They followed the boats, ready to feast on bait and what they scavenged from the nets.

The lead boats were already far out on the bay. Others followed behind, beads on a string stretching to the horizon.

Hundreds of shells sat on the sandy beach, a bride's marriage ring cupped in each one. My answer.

"Men lie and women believe them." I put a hand over my belly where my daughter slept, safe in dark waters. "Don't be afraid, small one, you're not alone. I'll teach you to be strong."

I left the rings for the widows to find. They deserved an answer too.

ABOUT THE AUTHOR

Jaime Lee Moyer is a writer of Fantasy and Science Fiction, herder of cats, occasional poet, and maker of tangible things. Her first novel, *Delia's Shadow*, was published by Tor Books, and won the 2009 Literary Award for Fiction, administrated by Thurber House and funded by the Columbus Arts Council. Two sequels, *A Barricade In Hell* and *Against A Brightening Sky*, were also published by Tor. Her new novel, *Brightfall*, will be out from Jo Fletcher Books on September 5, 2019.

She writes a lot. She reads as much as she can.

Find out more about Jaime at:
jaimeleemoyer.com

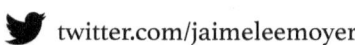 twitter.com/jaimeleemoyer

bookbub.com/authors/jaime-lee-moyer

pinterest.com/jaimeleemoyer

THE LADY OF ASHUELOT

KAREN L. ABRAHAMSON

The Greyhound bus's grumble brought Gwen's head up from her hammering. She peered out from the sweltering blacksmith shop into the cool October sunshine where the hillsides clung to the red of the New Hampshire fall. Something at the bus caught her eye.

A turn of head, a lift of chin, a cutting movement of hand.

Lancelot.

Gwen's hammer fell, her loving creation and the landscape forgotten. The stroke broke the delicate leaf she'd fashioned. The coal burned sour in her nostrils. She stepped around the anvil to the door.

It couldn't be.

But he stood apart from the tourists, come on a day-trip to see the Ashuelot covered bridge. He carried a simple over-the-shoulder bag as if used to traveling light and his dark hair fell back from his temples and hooked behind his ears, meeting the collar of his white tee-shirt and leather jacket.

He surveyed the town of 40 run-down colonial houses strung along the road like antique pearls, then headed towards Gwen's place and the blue sign at her gate '*Ironwork and Oddities: Gallery and Bed and Breakfast*'. His walk swayed like someone who had ridden horses for too many years.

Lancelot, she was sure.

Gwen rubbed her stomach. She stepped out the door still wearing her leather apron and stood next to a barrel of pink-blossomed impatiens.

He looked almost the same as when she'd last seen him, except for the small pot belly that rode over the top of his snug low-slung jeans. Almost the same as when he'd tried to father a child for their King. As when he'd ridden away with a promise to return.

She'd learned later he said that to all the girls. And she was a woman now, though the bitterness of her barrenness still rode her.

She crossed her arms and leaned against the doorframe. "Hello Lance. What'd'you want?"

"Gwen? Little Gwen?" He rubbed his eyes and started past the peeling picket fence and up the gravel driveway. "Is it really you?"

"I haven't changed that much," she said dryly and flicked at a piece of long fair hair she'd sucked on as she worked. She looked down at herself.

Well maybe she had changed. She had muscles now, from years of forge work. She had scars and singed hairs on her hands from the spattering clinker and metal. Instead of long gowns and fur she wore jeans and a tee-shirt that were stained with salt marks and sweat.

Lance stopped a pace from her and looked her up and down. "Still a beauty."

Gwen rolled her eyes. "Cut the crap. What do you want?"

Lance stepped up to her. "Aren't you going to greet me? Aren't you even a little happy to see an old friend?" He placed his hands on her shoulders and pulled her into a hug. "God, Gwen, you feel good. I've been looking for you for ages."

Gwen stiffened in his arms, even as the scent of him – riding leather and man-sweat – filled her nostrils and set her knees to shaking. For ages. For ages she'd waited for him. Through the early middle ages, and the late, and the renaissance, and the age of enlightenment. When she'd finally become tired of waiting she'd emigrated and had taken up a new life here.

"You never looked too hard, because I was right where you left me. Then I decided I'd waited long enough. I came here with the Lady of the Lake."

"She's here?" He set her away from him. His gaze flickered.

Gwen nodded and swallowed at the surge of jealousy. Another of Lance's conquests, cast off when he'd had what he wanted. The Lady had been thrown over for Gwen. It had been a point of contention between the two women for centuries, but they'd resolved it lately. The two of them - aging, single women - needed each other. They didn't need Lance destroying that gentle peace.

"So one more time, Lance. What is it you want?"

He gave her an innocent look – the same look he'd had when he seduced her behind her husband's back. "Nothing, Gwen. Only to see you and spend some time. Old time's sake and all that." He lightly stroked her cheek with his finger.

She jerked away. "Get thrown over by someone? If you're looking for comfort, you won't find it here."

Lance looked at her and finally sighed. "You're not the girl I used to know."

"And thank God for that."

"I just wanted to see you. To talk. Maybe to ask for your help. Things are changing in Britannia. It's time for the King to return."

Gwen swayed. She looked into the shed where the breath of the old vacuum cleaner gave life to the forge and her loving leaf creation lay destroyed on the anvil. "Wait a moment."

The King return? She went inside and turned off the vacuum. The air stilled. Only the coal fire burned and she shoveled the burning coals into a heap, the other fuel away from the flame. The heat in the shed dissipated. She picked up the warped metal leaf and felt a familiar sadness as she tossed it into the heap of scrap in the corner. Then she hung up her apron, splashed water onto her face from the bucket by the forge, and stepped back out to Lance.

In the sunlight, his dark hair gleamed silver at the temples. Age had found him too, but the crags of his face were the same. And his eyes. And his hands. She'd always remembered his hands.

He looked past her into the shed. "What's with the smithy? I never would have figured you'd get into that."

She glanced over her shoulder. The coal-bed still glowed, waiting for air to bring it to life. So like the very earth that burgeoned with creation given the right care. Or a woman's womb with the gift of seed. At least that was what the ancient Alchemists had said.

"It's creative," she said, not telling of the need it filled. She led him past the lines of day lilies still blooming even this late in the fall, to the guest house she had bought when she came to the town. Now its white paint had grayed and the tourists came less frequently to this backwater stretch of highway.

In her kitchen of worn linoleum and white cupboards chipped with time, she waved him to a chair at the table and turned to the sink to put the kettle on for tea. "So tell me." She glanced at him.

Lance had thrown his jacket on the back of his chair. His biceps filled his shirt sleeves, stretching the fabric.

She pulled her gaze away when she caught herself staring at his hands.

"It's the legend, Gwen. Britain is in need."

She stayed silent. The whole world was in need. The Lady's powers had faded so that even Britain was laid bare and only this small town still nestled in her protection – and even then her power needed help.

"Britain needs Arthur to unite the people. Right now the Scots want to separate. The Welsh are making noises. And at home the people fragment. They care about their country, sure, but they and the government are at odds. The leaders are making bad choices. We're going to war for all the wrong reasons. We need a King – someone to lead us – someone strong the people can have faith in."

"And you want Arthur." She turned back to him and leaned against the counter. "The man who couldn't even stop his wife from having an affair. The man you cuckolded. You want him to save you."

"Us, Gwen. We need him to save us."

"I don't live in Britain anymore."

"His influence could save the world."

She shook her head. "No one would believe. No one would follow."

"They would if he had the sword."

The room stilled except for the kettle's whistle. Gwen poured hot water over teabags into two mugs, trying to stop her trembling. She handed one mug to Lance and hauled a carton of milk from the fridge and a box of sugar cubes from a cupboard near the sink.

The sword. The sword they were all bound to through their oaths to Arthur. The sword of star-iron that through Merlin's magic sustained – still sustained - the heart of the Court of Camelot.

She looked out back to the garden she and the Lady had built when the other woman had still been healthy. They had warded each corner in the ancient ways, to make the soil fecund, to keep blight away. Tall bamboo filled the back corner, tall iris leaves and lily stood in front of that. Low beds of marigold and begonia and purple alyssum gave color. Ivy trailed over old stone and iron trellises.

But the plants were fading. All of them turned brown at the edges from the strange weather of the summer. She didn't want to see them die.

In one corner a terra cotta face peered out from between leaves of sumac blazing red with fall. It was a face the Lady had made when she still worked in clay; a mask, made from memory, of the only man the Lady had ever truly loved.

Lancelot.

"I need you to give me the sword, Gwen. He left it with you."

She shook her head, still gazing into the garden. "I don't have it." Her gaze trailed up the hillside to the forest – those trees and plants faded, too, though at least the Lady's magic slowed the process.

Lance came to her, the tea forgotten. He turned her to him and looked into her eyes. "But you showed it to me when he died. You showed me the sword. We need its power."

"Use other star-iron and make a new sword. Have Merlin work his magic with that." She glared at him, met his gaze unflinching.

"It's gone, Gwen. The other star-iron's been swept from Britain's shores, stolen as implements – sold as artifacts. And none hold the same power as the sword. Merlin placed too much power in it. We need it."

She looked away. "I buried it with Arthur. I don't have it."

"Well it isn't with him now."

She pulled away, thinking of the dark cave she and Merlin had found. "You've been to his tomb?"

Lance nodded. He caught her hand and led her to the table, placed the cup of tea in her hand and Gwen realized she was cold, so cold. Cold as Arthur had been at his death. Cold as she had been at the sadness he showed at her betrayal. Cold as the earth she and Merlin buried him in. "Merlin. He sent you."

Lance nodded. "He's gotten too old to travel and he doesn't like planes. If man were meant to fly... and all that."

Gwen looked away. All these men and their swords. They came

and they took and they rode away. Warriors raped and pillaged and cut and hacked and it was the women who paid. The women who gave themselves up for their babes. And the land left barren as their wombs. Why couldn't man spend his strength sustaining? Her hand went unconsciously to her belly, her gaze to the hillside out the window.

But Merlin... he at least she'd thought understood the needs of life, of the land, of the world.

Instead he'd sent this... man... across the world to reclaim that which she and the Lady had hidden. That which held so much power to do basic good.

"I can't help you."

Lance's gaze scanned her face and he grabbed his bag. "Then I guess I'd better go talk to the Lady." He stood and turned toward the door.

Gwen slopped tea over herself as she scrambled after him. "No! She doesn't like visitors." She grabbed his hand and halted him at the door, surprised at the strength she had – that it actually stopped him. When they first had known each other he could have pulled away as easily as a bee off a blossom. Now his wrist stayed in her callused grip even as a tremor ran up her arm.

He looked at her hand and then up at her. "I have to ask her. Merlin expects it. She and the sword are linked. She'll know where it is."

Gwen studied him. The face she had swooned over, had betrayed her husband for. It showed signs of years of decadence, and yet the heroic line of his chin, of his brow, still took her breath away. Should she help him? Return the sword?

"Let me talk to her." She released him when he nodded and left her tea cup on the table, untouched. Outside she stood panting by the door and the huge planters of amber-colored chrysanthemums. The house was too hot with him there. There were still too many things she felt – like begging him to tell her why he left. Like telling him she still ached for him at night.

But she was stronger than that now. She understood about men.

Since Lancelot she'd tried taking other lovers but they'd left her as well. Left her alone, childless, until she learned that was all she would ever be. She looked up at the hillsides. So she'd come here.

She hurried down the street towards the old covered bridge that crossed the Ashuelot River. On both sides of the river the hills rose, laced with the broad-leafed trees that so reminded her of England's greenwood. Not like the mangy hillsides she'd seen elsewhere. So far the Lady's fading power had kept the loggers from discovering this small corner.

So far.

The river ran swift, the carcass of a huge oak lay stopped by rocks before its branches could tear the bridge out. She hurried across to the small house that stood on the far side of the water.

It sat low against the forest, its yard overgrown, a line of fallen picket fence lying amongst the tall grass, a low line of twigs still resplendent with bits of fall foliage replacing the boundary around the property. The trees and bushes inside the boundary still blushed, leaving the hillsides brown in comparison.

The powers of the Lady had drawn further inward.

She stepped over the line of foliage into cooler air and hurried to the door, knocked once and stepped inside. "My Lady?" she called.

The house ticked silently around her, light streaming through the windows in long dusty cords, cobwebs formed at the junctions of the walls. A line of wilted wildflowers trailed down the hallway towards the kitchen.

Gwen followed them. "My Lady?"

The kitchen was empty, the faucet dripping over dirty dishes in the sink. Gwen left the house, knowing where the other woman would be. Where she always waited when she went missing from the house.

Gwen turned back to the bridge and found the narrow, slippery path down to the river's edge. Tall oak and beech leaned over the trail. Birch leaves, tinged golden, shivered in a light wind and fluttered to the water. A sugar maple blushed just downriver.

She clambered down to the water and then edged along the tall grass and stones toward the bridge. At its base a smooth stone slicked into the water.

Kids used it to fish from.

The Lady used it to contemplate her waters.

She sat huddled there, her long silver hair wild over her shoulders, her slight frame hunched over her knees as she laced the fingers of her left hand in the water. She wore a faded blue housedress. Light reflections dappled a face aged by years of effort to protect the land.

"My Lady?"

The other woman looked up from her contemplation of the water. Her delicate features showed a light tracery of lines. Her wide blue eyes showed signs of crying. "They called me a troll," she whispered.

"What?" Gwen shook her head.

"The children. They wanted to fish and I wanted to sit. They said I'm like an old troll. Then they laughed and ran away."

Gwen clambered out onto the stone and sat down beside the other woman, placing her arm around her shoulders. "It's alright, My Lady. They're young. They just don't understand how you need the water."

"But they hurt my feelings." The Lady gazed at Gwen with innocent eyes.

Gwen smoothed the other woman's hair back from her face. "Children can be cruel, My Lady."

The Lady pulled away. "I don't like it here anymore. I want to go home."

Gwen closed her eyes. How could she tell her that the home she remembered wasn't there anymore? Too many years had passed. The lake the Lady recalled was surrounded by houses now. Coal dust darkened the sky – or it had when they had come here. There was no place for a beautiful woman to bathe naked under clear stars.

The years had not been kind to the Lady. She had drifted mentally until she lived childlike, with Gwen's care. Gwen brought her food. Gwen cleared the snow in the winter. Gwen made sure the other woman was safe, her gas furnace working, that the lady did not try to feed it wood.

"We can't go home. I've explained it to you."

The Lady pressed her lips into a line. Her body stiffened and she half-turned away.

Gwen caught the other woman's hand, all the while questioning whether she should she do this. "But someone came today. From the old country. He wants to see you."

"A man came? For me?" The Lady's eyes sparked with interest.

Gwen nodded, feeling sorrow at her lie, at the Lady's eagerness. Once a long line of suitors sought the Lady. No longer. She was lost as the stuff of her legend. They both were. The difference was Gwen was glad to be lost from the notoriety, while the Lady missed her people, her land. The island kingdom she had gentled and maintained.

Gwen grasped the other woman's hand. "He wants the sword, My Lady." Gwen saw the momentary confusion in the other woman's eyes. "Arthur's sword. You still have it?"

The Lady's face glowed as remembrance flowed in. "Of course. It's safely in the soil where its magic can do the most good." She gestured into the water at the base of the stone. "There. Its star-iron helps me feed the land."

Gwen looked through the moving current and saw the dim outline of the grip and cross-guard. The sword had enough power to keep the Court of Camelot alive and also to help the Lady in her labors.

The Lady suddenly scrambled to her knees. "Who is this man? Who has come?" Her voice was eager. She smoothed her hair back from her face.

Gwen looked into the water. "Lancelot."

The word fell like a stone into water. Silence filled the space between the two women. Finally, the Lady breathed: "He has come for me."

Gwen jerked upright from her contemplation of Lance's face, of the feelings his arrival had stirred in her.

The lady had already scrambled to her feet, had leapt back to land to push through the low brush along the river path. "He has come for me."

She ran her fingers through her hair. "He has come. Oh, he has come." She ran her palms over her face, then down over the tattered housedress she wore, then pushed up the river bank towards her house. "He can't see me like this. I've got to bathe and dress."

Her voice floated back to Gwen, who sighed. She pushed herself up and followed the other woman. Somehow Gwen had to make the Lady understand what would happen if the sword went back to Arthur.

In the house the Lady ran her bath, steaming water filling the rust-stained porcelain. The Lady pulled the dress off her shoulders, letting it drop like a flower petal to the cold tile. Her body had wilted with the years, as her power wasted with her distance from her lake and her waters. Still, her emanations had held Ashuelot as the lovely, small town it was.

And when her power had dwindled too far the sword had helped.

"My Lady, please." Gwen gently touched the other woman's bare shoulder. Hard bone poked through aging flesh. "Lance has come for the sword. He wants to take it away from us. He wants it to wake Arthur, to bring his power back. He thinks Arthur can save Britain from itself."

The Lady shook her head. She faced the mirror, tilting her head to catch the light, pushing her hair over her ears. "Rose water will help. He always liked the scent. And oils for my hair. How could I have let it get so wild?" She ran her palm down over her cheek and frowned. "But what is this?" She leaned in closer to examine the lines around her eyes. "No," she whispered. "It can't be."

"My Lady," Gwen tried to interrupt the other woman's ministrations. The room filled with steam, and sweat ran between Gwen's breasts. She wanted out of here, hated seeing the changes in this once powerful woman. But the Lady hadn't been the same since Lancelot. Would Lance change that now? The Lady needed to be warned. "He wants the sword, My Lady. Only the sword."

The other woman shook her head as she wiped steam off the mirror. "A fabrication. An excuse to see me. Tell him to come tomorrow." She looked into the mirror. "I'll be ready then." She leaned in closer. "Surely I will," she whispered.

Gwen left for the cool fall air in the Lady's front yard. She inhaled and sighed. Lance couldn't love the Lady. He had left her for Gwen. Perhaps he'd really come for Gwen?

She snorted and shook her head before heading home. She just wanted the man gone. If Lance came down to see the Lady she, Gwen, would come with him and make sure he left after not getting what he wanted. They needed the sword here.

She'd comfort the Lady afterwards.

At home she found Lancelot had moved into one of the rooms on the second floor. As if that wasn't bad enough he'd chosen a room next to her own and had taken a shower, leaving damp footprints for her to follow across the hardwood floors.

The door to his room was open; he stood with his back to her, his hips draped in a towel, late afternoon light staining his skin golden.

Gwen's face flushed as he turned to her, as the blood flowed to her head. Even with the slight pot belly he was beautiful – as beautiful as she remembered.

"Gwen." He came to her as she stood stunned in the doorway. She hadn't expected him to move in, hadn't expected to see him like this, didn't expect it when he leaned in and placed a kiss on her lips. He pulled back slightly. "Did you see her?"

She looked into his eyes and felt herself falling – again. Nodding, she swallowed. What was this hold he had over her, this need she had for him?

"She says you can come tomorrow."

"And the sword?"

"She knows where it is."

"Then she'll give it to me." He caught Gwen's upper arms. "That's good. The sword will give us Arthur back and Arthur will give us back our power, our destiny. Britain will be great again." He paced around the room, Gwen still standing in the door, still trying to find the strength to move, to leave.

"It has been too long we've let the rest of the world overrun us.

Too long since we were a great people. The power of the sword will complete us and give us back our greatest leader." He paced and he fumed and he spoke of Britain and its power and the greatness and respect they would command in this world that had become.

"But..." Gwen started. She blinked, trying to bring her thoughts into focus. "But the sword's power is creation. Britain already exists. And the sword can't undo what has already been done."

Lance turned back to her. "That may be what the ancient smithies thought as they placed that iron into their furnaces, but we know better. We know the strength of that sword. Excalibur was made for one reason, to lead warriors, to lead a country, to lead a world."

He came to her, caught her in his arms. "Don't you see, Gwen, we're the stuff of legends. People cry out for us and the dreams we raise. With the sword we can rally our people. We can be great, you can be great, instead of lost in this backwater town."

He looked deep into her eyes. "God, Gwen. Think what we had. Think what we could have again."

And he kissed her. Kissed her so hard she lost all sense of where she was, of the time, of her age, of what she had learned as a woman, of how the sword could do more than raise a country to greatness. She was a girl again and Lancelot wanted her. Lancelot her beloved.

He pulled her into the bedroom and to the bed, heat blooming in her body.

It was dark when she woke in a tangle of sheets, Lancelot's arm draped over her breasts, her long hair caught under his shoulders. The air was cool in the room and Lance's body was hot. The golden glow she'd felt at his touch seared away as she stared up at the ceiling trying to understand what had happened. What she had done. She studied Lance's profile in the starlight through the window.

He was still elegant and strong, but he wasn't for her. She didn't even love him. Not the way the Lady did.

The Lady.

Gwen sat up, pushing Lance away, ignoring the pull of her hair, the way Lance spoke to her in his sleep.

What had she done?

She looked down at her naked body, muscled under her breasts, flat abdomen. She'd stepped away from men all these years, determined to make her own way, to be strong, not to be caught by the need for another. Certainly not to betray a friend. She rubbed her face, tried to push away the sickness she felt, the sense of his hands.

She pushed the covers off and stood, the wood floor cold under her feet, the air chilling her. She crossed her arms and looked at the man on the bed.

The Lady's face, her excitement and hope, filled Gwen's mind.

Gwen left the site of her betrayal at a run; gathering up her clothes, she ran down the hall. In the bathroom she showered, scrubbing herself, but still felt unclean. Then she pulled on clothing that still smelled of forge smoke and sweat. At least that was honest, not the scent of sex on her fingers.

She pulled on her work boots on the front porch, inhaling deep gasps of leaf-scented air. Night blanketed Ashuelot. The moon had set. The river's rush placed a lulling pall across the town. The cicadas and crickets layered their songs on the air. No traffic traveled this backwater bit of highway 119.

She headed for the small house by the covered bridge, her footfall clumping across the hollow structure. At the Lady's house she tried the door.

Unlocked as all doors were unlocked in this peaceful town. She pushed inside. The Lady slept little, usually worked, humming, in her kitchen.

But no song came from the back of the house. The building ticked around Gwen like a clock. The air smelled of metal. "My Lady?" Gwen called softly.

She stepped further down the hall.

"My Lady?"

Could the other woman have gone to the river? Perhaps to get the sword?

Gwen turned to check the river edge when a small sound caught her attention. Something like the sound of insect wings against a window. She stopped, listened, then followed the sound towards the

Lady's bedroom, past it, to the bathroom where light seeped under the door.

Gwen pushed the door open and stopped.

The lady lay in the tub in a sea of red, her hands resting palm-up, like lilies in the lake where she had first lived. Her head shook as she lay there; her hair whispered cross the tiles.

She looked up at Gwen and smiled.

"My God! What have you done?"

Gwen fell on her knees by the tub, pulled the Lady's arms free of water. Blood oozed from the numerous cuts up her forearms.

Scrambling to her feet, Gwen rummaged the medicine cabinet for bandages. She wrapped the woman's arms tight then ran for the phone and dialed 911. Then she went back to the Lady to wait.

"Why, My Lady? Why?"

The other woman shook her head, her long hair spread in wet spider silk across her brow and shoulders. She gazed up at Gwen, her eyes filled with tears that would once have sent a man to quest.

"Look at me, friend. How could Lancelot love me? How could he even stand to look at me?" Her gaze shifted to the mirror and her voice fell to a whisper. "I saw. How could I face him like this?"

"Then you should have said something to me. I'd have told him to go. I'd have told him you didn't want to see him."

The lady shook her head slightly. "I love him. I would have had his child." Her eyes closed and she slumped in the tub. In the night came the wail of the ambulance.

Daylight stained the east when Gwen returned to Ashuelot. The Lady slept in the hospital, but she had lost so much blood no one knew if she would live. To live takes will. To live takes a reason and a belief in your own strength, your own worth. The Lady, it seemed had lost both. No wonder her power had faded.

Gwen stood at the roadside and looked up at the hills blushed with fall and the sunrise. The air smelled of leaves souring on the branches and of snow to come. Gwen's hands brushed her belly, rested there.

If the Lady died, this place, this haven they had come to, would be bare to depredations of the world. It would have no protection.

Except the sword. And Gwen herself.

But Lancelot would take Excalibur if he found it and the land would be at the mercy of man - could become barren as the desolate cities she had escaped. She could not let that happen.

She checked her watch. Lance had always been an early riser. She had to do whatever she was going to do.

She started for the river.

It ran deep and cold under the bridge and its spray chilled her. She balanced out onto the Lady's flat rock and looked down into the water. The first light of day glanced off the surface, hiding the treasure there.

She plunged her hand into the water, down, down into the depths until her shoulder touched the water and her t-shirt was soaked.

Her fingers closed on the ornate grip, on the jeweled cross. She yanked upwards and the sword came free from its hold in the riverbed. The water seemed to part around it. The sunlight caught on its edges, on the water dripping down her arm. Her breath caught in her throat.

It was a beautiful thing. This thing formed of star iron mined in the ancient days of the world, the same star iron the ancients worshipped as the seed that gave life to the world. She held it up to the flame of sunlight and wished for other choices.

When she pulled the sword back down to her side it was as if a light went out. She hurried back to her house and looked up at Lancelot's window, still dark. The man was no longer the vigorous lover of his youth, just as she was no longer the girl smitten with a fair warrior's attentions.

She ducked around to her workshop, shoveled coal onto the embers of yesterday's flame and turned the vacuum on. Soon flames bit at the coal, caught and heated the inside of the forge. Soon the heat filled the shop. She buckled on her apron.

Gwen closed her eyes.

She gripped the sword, then plunged it into the heat.

The metal sang at the contact. The sword was not intended for this treatment. The sword had been made as an icon for all time. But that was in another time. A man's world. A world of warriors and courtly love and manners and kingdoms.

Now there was just the world and it needed the seed of star-iron far more than it needed another sword.

The metal glowed. She used her tongs to turn the sword in the flame. Let it heat evenly. She could show the blade at least that respect.

When the metal was white-hot she drew it forth. She set a wedge in the anvil top and laid the blade across it. She picked up the hammer and hefted it in her grasp.

Her muscles tensed as she raised it. As she let it fall.

Metal rang against metal as the hammer broke the blade's back across the wedge. Sparks flew across the room, against her leather apron, against her cheek. Pain, pain as the metal sang.

Years fell on Gwen's shoulders.

She lifted the hammer again and let it fall. The tip of the sword broke free and the blade's music stopped. From the house came the sound of screaming.

She shifted the broken sword so another section lay across the wedge. Hammered again, and felt age press on her. Her hair silvered and went brittle against her shoulders. She had to do this. She had to last. Each blow, each section of the sword destroyed the power that had held all of them in the hearts of legend.

In a tomb somewhere Arthur withered away.

Merlin would feel his powers drain.

But in return the metal, freed from its form, could feed this place, the land, and preserve it.

At least that would do good.

When she had severed the blade into four she left the shop. Her back bent under the weight of the pieces in her carry bag. Arthritis nipped at her knees and hips. But she was not finished.

She ignored Lance when he tried to stop her, his spindly arms and legs no match for her determination.

"What have you done? What have you done?" he cried as she left him in the driveway and went up to the hills.

What indeed, she thought as she struggled through the forest to the farthest point she could walk that day. Undone a dream. Defiled a legend.

Still, when she stood on the first hilltop and looked out across the land, she knew had acted rightly. The rich hills rolled away in folds of trees, small farmsteads, the winding threads of streams and rivers. To the west the Connecticut River unwound toward the sea.

Light filtered down through the trees and placed golden filigree on the soil. A squirrel chattered at her from the trees and a tanager flashed its scarlet tail and flew away. So much life.

She dug in her bag and pulled out one section of Excalibur, then held it up to the sky. The sunlight seemed to flow into the metal and down her arm.

She bent and plunged the metal into the soil. Streaks of lightening flashed across the tree roots, across the soil and the metal hummed. She looked out across the land at the three other hilltops she had chosen.

When she was done it would be a garden, this place her dying body and the star iron would preserve.

Better one garden, than men united by a sword.

She smiled to herself and all her years of barrenness fell away.

ABOUT THE AUTHOR

Karen L. Abrahamson is a well-traveled writer who has explored cultures and countries around the world but British Columbia, Canada is her favorite place to come back to. She is the author of literary, mystery, romantic and fantasy fiction including the highly regarded Cartographer fantasy series. She lives on the west coast of Canada with two Bengal cats that aren't quite as well traveled as she is.

When she isn't writing she can be found with a camera and backpack in fabulous locations around the world.

Find out more about Karen at:
karenlabrahamson.com

f facebook.com/karenlabrahamson

g goodreads.com/karenabrahamson

BB bookbub.com/authors/karen-l-abrahamson

THE BEST DISGUISES

GRAYSON TOWLER

"You're serious?" Lucky asked me, his eyes going wide. "You're going after the Loch Ness Monster?"

I leaned against the workbench and grinned. "Yep."

His dark hair fanned out as he shook his head and laughed. "Oh, Moira! Don't get me wrong, I love the idea! But it won't look very good on your scientific résumé."

"Hey, you're the only one I've told," I said, then took a cautious look around to make sure nobody was in the equipment lab with us. I definitely didn't want any of my fellow marine biology colleagues to overhear this. "You said you can keep a secret."

Lucky Bundy had a wicked smile and eyes that looked like they could see through a vault door. "I'm very good at secrets," he said. "And other things. I'm *very* good at other things." His grin widened as his gaze traveled over me.

"Ach, you know you're not my type," I said, letting my native Scottish brogue out of the bag, as I always did when he tried to flirt with me.

"I could wear a dress," he said, fluttering his eyelids and puckering his lips. "I make a very pretty girl."

Swap the tie-die T-shirt for a blouse and I could almost see it, with Lucky's fine features and wide, dark eyes. "Leave off, you troublemaker," I said with a grin. "I'm here for your gear, not your smart mouth." Technically, the gear belonged to UC Santa Cruz, but Lucky pretty much ran the workshop where all the field research equipment was kept. He was kind of possessive about it.

He dropped the flirty face and made a gimme motion. "Let's see the forms."

I handed over my recently obtained approval forms. The field where I'd been asked to fill out my reason for the requested gear simply read "Graduate project, Scotland."

Lucky raised an eyebrow at my paperwork. "You got approved with *that*?"

I whistled innocently. It helped to know which professors could be bribed with a bit of peat whiskey.

"Well, I guess it's all on the up and up," he said. "One custom fishfinder and one hot-rod submersible camera drone, coming right up."

I waited as Lucky rooted around amongst the vast array of boxy machines, scuba equipment, and other waterproof scientific gizmos stored at the Long Marine Lab. I had some good history with the fish finder sonar and the drone. Lucky had worked his technical wizardry on both of them, and they'd helped me complete my research project on sardine populations in Monterey Bay.

Maybe that's not the sort of project that gets national headlines, but it had made a difference. I presented conclusive evidence of chemical contamination in the area leaking from a landfill, which had degraded the sardines' ability to reproduce. In the end, the State of California took action, and now those humble little sardines might have a snowball's chance in Hell of bouncing back from the over-fishing.

That's about as good as it gets for us marine biologists.

To top it off, a women's philanthropy group was so impressed by my wee contribution to saving the world that I ended up with an unexpected but very welcome chunk of prize money.

I'd offered to share some of that prize with Lucky, but he'd refused. So after using most of the cash to pay down my student debt, I'd had a fair bit left over to do something on my own.

Which is how I ended up being able to self-fund a research trip to Loch Ness.

Lucky hauled out the wooden crates containing my gear. "This is some of my best work," he said. "You take good care of these babies."

"I will," I promised. The gear really was good stuff. Lucky had an MIT-worthy brain, but seemed content to slum it here at Santa Cruz —which, let's face it, is not famous for its engineering department. Said he liked the surfing.

He frowned at the boxes, tapping his finger on his pointed chin. "Still... Moira, you know this has been tried. There've been research teams up and down Loch Ness looking for anything that ought to be extinct swimming around in there."

"They haven't had gear like yours, have they?" I said. "Besides, I've got another secret weapon those other lads didn't."

He locked eyes with me. "You mean the fact that you're a magician."

"Aye," I said. "That."

Well, it's true. I *am* a magician.

This is not a fact I share often. "Magician" to most people means pulling rabbits out of hats on stage, which is not what I do. Even here in Santa Cruz, where you can barely chuck a crystal pyramid without hitting a Wiccan or a pagan, not many people get what magick (with the "k") is about. I have yet to run into a person who says, "Oh, you must mean hermetic esotericism, the ancient practice of mysticism that traces its roots all the way back to ancient Egypt."

Depending on where you fall on the spirituality spectrum, you might think of magick as kind of like meditation or yoga, and that's partially right. Or like a religion like Wicca, where you do lots of old pagan rituals and spells, which is also sort of right. Or a kind of New Age thing like in *The Secret* for wishing your way to a happy life, which is not entirely untrue but also doesn't do magick justice.

Or you might call it a load of old mince practiced by superstitious nutters, which is what most of my academic colleagues would say.

While Santa Cruz prides itself on tolerance, you're still supposed to leave religious or spiritual stuff at the door of any kind of science department. More's the pity, because magick and science are not all that different. Both are about seeing the world clearly, testing and experimenting, and getting to the truth. Just so happens my experience of truth veers into territory most of my colleagues in the marine biology department would never accept.

Hey, if I'd become a quantum physicist, I think I'd pretty much fit right in.

Though I don't go around chanting incantations where the PhDs can hear me, I make use of my art in my work. I used it in my sardine project. In the morning, I sat in a pentagram and called in spiritual help to find the schools of fish, and in the afternoon I found the schools of fish. I dreamed about what to look for in the chemical analysis of the fatty tissue of the sardine. And I invoked every archangel in the Qaballah to make sure my evidence found its way to the right people in government so they'd move quickly to contain the contamination I'd found.

I don't cast Hollywood spells with high-budget CGI effects, but I get results.

And maybe I could get results at Loch Ness, too.

I hoped so. This expedition was personal in a way that even my sardine project wasn't.

Lucky's the only one in my scientist life I talk to about mystical stuff. He takes it seriously too. Like now, he wasn't rolling his eyes at the idea I might magick up an encounter with the Loch Ness Monster.

"Well, magick might just make a difference," he said. "You got a plan?"

I hesitated. I could talk to Lucky about magick... but I'd never gone beyond a certain threshold of weird. Not with him, not with any of my pagan friends, and not even with my hard-ass occult teacher— and yes, I did go to school for magick.

But Lucky had never made fun of my magick talk before. I figured I could trust him.

I leaned forward, my voice dropping. "What if Nessie's not what everybody thinks she is?"

"What, you mean not a dinosaur?" he asked. "Then what is she?"

I decided not to point out that plesiosaurs weren't actually dinosaurs. "I think she's a water faerie."

Lucky said nothing. His blank expression could've flummoxed a poker champion.

"A shape-shifter," I said, the words now gushing out all on their own. "That's why there's no consistent description of her. And why the scientists never spot her. Faeries want nothing to do with people who don't respect them enough to even believe in them, yeah? Only if I can convince her to come to me..." I trailed off.

He tilted his head slightly, considering me with those dark, unblinking eyes. "Where'd you get this idea?"

All of a sudden, I felt like I'd swallowed a handful of moths. I tried for a casual shrug. "Just came to me, that's all," I lied.

Charms and incantations were one thing in the pagan community. Even faeries were okay, so long as you treated them as sort of non-corporeal nature spirits. But if you started talking about faeries like they were something you could pick up on sonar or capture in a photo, even the New Agers started to back away and look for the nearest exit.

I had my reasons to believe in faeries, and in Nessie. Only now I worried I'd finally exceeded Lucky's weirdness threshold. The thought that he might start to give me the condescending "Mad Moira" treatment I'd endured through most of high school made me more anxious than I cared to admit.

Finally, Lucky spoke. "Give me a sec, Moira," he said. Then he trotted off and disappeared into the little office connected to the warehouse.

I fidgeted with a splinter on the drone's crate, my overactive imagination suggesting he'd gone to get a tranq gun.

Instead, he came back with a little green object about the size of a tennis ball. He held it out to me, a bundle of something wrapped up in broad leaves, tied with a thin golden thread. I took it and sniffed in a sweet, heady aroma. "Is this rum cake?" I asked, knowing that wasn't quite right. I caught a hint of some deeper scent... something like meat.

He shrugged. "Recipe from the old country. Supposed to be a faerie lure."

I blinked. "Like, bait?" Then I frowned. "I'm not trying to hook her or anything."

Lucky let out a sharp laugh. "Not that you could with this!" He tugged at the string binding the bundle shut, pulling out a length of the gold thread. It was absurdly flimsy stuff—any respectable fish could break it just by breathing on it. "Nah, just toss this out there and let it float. Who knows? If your theory's right, it might even tempt Nessie."

A dozen questions bubbled up in my mind. Was he having me

on? Why did he keep faerie bait around? And what "old country" did he mean? Lucky never talked about his past, except when he was obviously spinning a yarn.

But he also didn't like people who pried, and I could respect that. Maybe when I got back he'd tell me more. Especially if I had pictures of Nessie to share.

I tucked the faerie lure into my purse. "Thanks, Lucky. Gimme a hand out to the car with these crates? Your babies here have a long trip in front of 'em."

~

The reason I know Nessie is a faerie is I'd met her.

Late in the summer right after I turned nine years old, Mom took me to Loch Ness for a long holiday—just the two of us, with Dad working overseas at the time. We stayed in a little village called Inverfarigaig, where the river runs into the middle of the loch. Mom spent most of her time reading, which suited me fine. I spent my days fooling around on the shore.

That was me, crazy about water even back then.

I was shivering along merrily as I waded rib-deep into the cold loch, walking carefully with my bare feet clinging to the slick pebbles, and trying to figure out if I'd really seen a lamprey or just another stick. Then I heard a splash.

Well, I instantly thought about the monster, didn't I? Anyone would. Dare you to find a kid who visits the loch and doesn't peer at every ripple on the water hoping for a glimpse of the fabled Nessie. Most adults do the same.

So of course I whipped around to where I heard the splash... and damned if there wasn't a reptilian face staring down at me from the top of a tall, slick neck.

Okay, so a normal kid might've screamed or bolted. But honestly, if she was some kind of plesiosaur, she was a fish eater. Small head on a long neck, great for gulping down your average trout, but never something big as a human, even a child. I knew that much even at nine.

Maybe I was a weird kid.

Point being, I didn't feel a lick of fear. I just stared up at that grey, streamlined face, with its startlingly blue eyes, and said, "You're real!"

Then she lowered her head down on that amazing serpentine neck, and she did something even more surprising than showing up. She *spoke*.

"Of course I'm real," Nessie said.

She didn't move her mouth, and I don't think she actually spoke out loud. But I heard the voice in my head all the same, soft and musical and full of gentle humor. Not a monster's voice at all. She sounded like a friend.

I remember shivering. Nessie noticed. "Are you afraid?" she asked.

"No," I said. "The water's just cold."

That made her laugh. "Not to me!"

I reached out, slowly so as not to startle her. I was afraid if I touched her she might vanish like a soap bubble. But she didn't mind when my fingers brushed the silky-smooth skin of her muzzle. It felt more like touching a dolphin than a fish. My whole body hummed with joy.

"Everyone says you aren't real," I said.

"Yes, I know," she said. "Rude, isn't it? That's why I don't show myself to just anyone."

"What if someone sees you when you come up to breathe?" I asked. Little geek that I was, I knew plesiosaurs were air-breathers. I'd read all about them before coming to Loch Ness.

"I don't have to look like this if I don't want to," she said in that lyrical voice of hers.

Now that stumped me. "Huh?"

Suddenly she pulled away. Her smooth flesh flowed like water, and in an instant I was looking at a salmon almost as long as me. The fish splashed merrily as it swam around me. I pivoted to follow its movement, my eyes bugging out.

"I can look like this," Nessie's voice came in my head. Then the fish did a barrel-roll, and suddenly it became a log. "Or this," she said, still circling me. The log rolled itself over, and then she became a big eel. "Or like this."

She circled me and kept changing, swimming for a few seconds in each new body before rolling over to become something else. Nessie became a sturgeon, a rubber duck, a sea lion, a big wave, and then a shark. That last one actually did scare me into letting out a whimper.

Nessie rolled over again, and this time she was a mermaid. She took my hands, and my fear melted away. She had hair like sea grass and skin like a pearl, and she smelled like clean surf and sunshine. Her eyes, blue like the purest glacial water, made her the most beautiful thing I'd ever seen.

"Don't be afraid," she said—her mouth still didn't form words, but her smile lit me up from the inside. "What's your name?"

"I'm Moira," I said. "Moira Kerr. What's yours?"

At that, her lovely brows knit and she looked puzzled. "Hmm. You know, the best disguises are so good that you sometimes forget who you really are."

I didn't understand that. "Can I call you Nessie?" I asked.

The confusion cleared in her perfect blue eyes, and she gave me that dazzling smile again. "Yes. I like being Nessie."

We played together all that holiday, Nessie and me. Things feel like forever when you're a kid, but looking back at the calendar I realize we had less than a fortnight. I still dream about the games and stories we shared in those magical days.

And it wasn't like I hid it. I told Mom about Nessie, and she seemed happy to hear all about it, though Nessie never would introduce herself. Only when it came time to pack up and I cried about leaving Nessie, Mom got cross with me, and I realized she'd just been humoring me the whole time.

I never told anyone else.

I knew what they'd say. Childhood memories aren't reliable, are they? Imaginative kid like me, playing on her own one summer and cooking up stories of the Loch Ness Monster in her head. Not exactly what you'd call credible witness testimony.

Deep down, I knew going back wasn't going to change anybody else's mind. If Nessie did let me get a photo of her, it'd just go into the pile with all the other debunked monster sightings. I'd get laughed out of my career if I tried to publish.

Besides, even if I got a selfie video of me and Nessie sharing a coffee with Elvis and Amelia Earhart, nobody would believe *what* she really is. The serious scientists can't swallow the idea of a plesiosaur descendent swimming around in the modern world. Try to tell them I've got evidence of a water faerie, and they'll tattoo the scarlet letter "W" for "woo-woo" right smack on my face.

Nah, this trip really was never for the evidence, in spite of what I told Lucky.

With all the study I've put into magick, I've had some pretty amazing experiences—but nothing to match what happened spontaneously that summer in Inverfarigaig, when Nessie appeared to me from the depths of that dark, cold water.

Yet some part of me wonders if it all really happened, and I cannot stand that doubt. I'd kept my silence about Nessie because I couldn't bear to face the skepticism, the disbelief. My memory of her was so clear, yet also fragile as a dewdrop.

I couldn't be sure if I could trust one childhood memory. Even if the magician in me said it was true, the scientist wanted more evidence. So that's what I was going to Loch Ness to get.

Nessie had been my *friend*.

All I wanted to do was see her again.

E ven though I hadn't been back for the better part of a decade, Scotland still felt like home. We'd moved to the States when I was sixteen, but Dad's work kept us on the move and we'd never settled in anywhere. The moment I stepped off the plane in Edinburgh the ground felt more solid—like the earth was older and deeper.

Inverfarigaig hadn't changed much. It was barely a town at all, just a handful of homes for foresters and fishers, along with a couple tourist hotels mostly for folk coming to try their luck catching a glimpse of the monster. Humans only had a toehold in the scrappy forests along Loch Ness shore. Most directions you looked, you'd see a wild land not much different than it'd been thousands of years ago.

I liked it that way.

To make the best use of my limited budget, I'd decided to rent a small fishing boat. Tour boats were more expensive, especially if you wanted to ride without a bunch of other passengers gumming up the air with their gab. I'd been pleased with my ingenuity in finding a local fisherman willing to take me out alone with my borrowed gear and my secret semi-scientific mission.

I was a bit less pleased when I met him, though.

"Tor Hardvor," said the big man on the little spur of land that passed for a pier. He extended a beefy hand, and with the other failed to stifle a burp that smelled like stale beer.

"Moira Kerr," I said. His fingers felt like wood pegs wrapped in rough leather.

"Okay," he said, swaying very slightly as he looked me over. "Good to meet you."

He looked the part of a local, with his rusty hair and a beard any hipster would kill for, but that accent marked him as an import from somewhere on the continent. German, maybe? I'm rubbish with accents.

And he was a *big* guy. Shoulders like a linebacker, his t-shirt stretched so tight over his chest I could see the outline of some cross-shaped necklace underneath. Plus he'd been drinking. Obviously.

When you're a lone woman about to get on a boat with a strange man, it pays to think about certain things. In my case, I thought about my obsidian knife.

I had a couple of ceremonial knives in my magick kit, actually. The silver one I used mostly for things stirring and marking out circles in the earth. It couldn't actually cut anything tougher than a biscuit. But the obsidian knife... that had a four inch blade with an edge so sharp it made a surgical scalpel look like a spoon. In the worst case scenario, it would be my best option.

Not that Tor was putting off a threat vibe. Sure, he took his look at me like most guys did, but he didn't give me a leer or any of that shite. Still, with a fella that big, it seemed like I'd be wise to keep the obsidian knife close at hand. Just in case.

There was an upside to having such a big guide. Tor loaded up the crates I'd been struggling with the entire trip like they were filled with whipped cream instead of chunky metal scientific instruments. And he was a gentleman about helping me onto the boat.

Tor's fishing boat had the odd name of *Goat's Tooth,* and it looked like it had seen a lot of years on the water. Still, at least he kept it clean, and it had a nice flat aft deck right on the water where I could set up with all my gear.

Once we were on the water and moving with the gentle rhythm of the lake, I felt myself relax. Tor drank a lot and didn't talk much, but he seemed okay. He even helped me unpack my gear.

"This is all for finding monster, yes?" he asked as he hauled out Lucky's drone. The submersible was all smooth white and Star Trek-curves, looking bizarrely out of place on this rustic boat on a nearly-empty loch.

"It's for finding evidence of whatever's out there," I said in my responsible scientist voice.

"Everyone is looking for monster," Tor said.

I gave him a small smile. "I suppose so. You ever seen it?"

His face clouded over, and he frowned out at the tranquil waters. "Long ago. I saw...something." He shook his head like an ox throwing off flies, then shrugged at me. "Probably just too much to drink."

"Maybe so," I said, not knowing what to think. I knew Nessie was out there, but didn't know much about her standards of who she'd reveal herself to, other than nine-year old girls. Would Tor's presence keep her away?

And did my old magical friend even remember me?

～

I had five days at Loch Ness in my budget. Four days into my search, and I was starting to feel the leaden disappointment in my gut might drag me right through the bottom of *Goat's Tooth.*

Most people don't know it, but Loch Ness is huge. On the map you can see it stretches halfway across Scotland, but even that doesn't give you the full story. Loch Ness is so deep that it holds more water than all the lakes in England and Wales combined. Searching that territory for one specific organism was not the sort of job one scientist in a fishing boat could hope to achieve in five days or five months, even if that critter wasn't a shape-changing water faerie.

I'd never deluded myself into thinking I could find Nessie through sheer legwork. My hope had been that she'd find me.

Every morning before dawn, I'd set up my pentagram in my little room in the Monster Lodge, chanting and praying to actualize the outcome I wanted to achieve. I brought my charms and my talismans onto Tor's boat, and focused my will through them even as I kept my eyes on the fish finder and drone camera. Every evening after chugging around the loch with nothing to show, I came home to my pentagram, lit my candles, and went through my magickal rituals yet again before bed.

I focused my dreams on finding Nessie, and spent the nights tossing and turning as I plunged through dark depths, searching for my childhood friend.

I'm here, I called to her in every way I knew how. *I've come back.*

Not sure which possibility hurt more—that she couldn't hear me, or that she could, but chose not to come.

I did my best not to give up. I had another day left to go. Magick of the sort I was trying responds best to confidence and serenity, not desperation and despair. So I meditated away my fears and went through my morning ceremony with all the glowing, positive energy I could muster.

The weather answered my efforts with the sort of rain my mom calls a "pish-oot."

Thunder rolled across the long lake, rising and falling in a nearly continuous rumble. I wiped the rain from my eyes and peered at the drone controls, seeing pretty much nothing but dense murk through the camera.

Tor laughed as the thunder hit a crescendo. "I love this weather!" he shouted. Runnels of water splattered down from his beard onto his soaked T-shirt. Guess he didn't believe in parkas.

"Yeah, it's the best," I said.

He may have missed the deadpan, because he smiled at me like we were kindred spirits. "Most tourists would run for shore right now!"

"You don't get far as a marine biologist if you're afraid of the damp," I said, mustering the tattered remains of my pride.

He roared with laughter at that, and the thunder seemed to laugh with him.

At least someone was having a good time. I squinted out over the loch, but couldn't make out the shoreline on either side through the rain. We might've been in the middle of the sea. Crap weather for spotting monsters.

Of course, if Nessie really was a shape changer, she might have floated by as a log or a fish a hundred times. I had no way of knowing.

I stared glumly into the glowing screens of the fish finder and the remote drone's camera feed, trying not to think of all the depressing stories about children growing up and losing their imaginary friends. Maybe I shouldn't have even brought the equipment along. Whatever luck this gear had brought me in Monterey Bay, it wasn't doing me any good on this expedition.

"What is this thing?" Tor asked. I turned and saw him holding up Lucky's "faerie lure" by its thin thread, staring at it like a mesmerist's pendulum.

"Just a bit of bait," I said.

Of course I'd tried Lucky's faerie lure, for all the good it had done. In order to make sure only Nessie could get the lure, I'd perched the package up on the gunwale at the stern, where something with a long neck could easily pop up and snatch it, if she so desired. No takers.

Tor swayed like he was tipsy, grinning hugely. I'd seen this guy knock back a dozen cans of stout every day without batting an eye, but now it was like he'd gotten drunk off the foul weather. "You are marine biologist, not fisherman," he said. "Bait is no use on boat. It goes in water!"

And with that, he chucked it over the edge, still holding onto the thread.

"No!" I said, but a thrum of thunder drowned out my words. In the water, any damned fish might eat the lure.

As I wondered whether it was worth the trouble to try to reel the lure back in, my eye caught something moving on the screen of the drone remote.

I wiped off the drops of rain and bent over to get a better look. The drone's camera could barely penetrate more than a meter in the murk of the loch's water, which made the thing pretty much useless. But something moved through the tiny region illuminated by the headlamp now. Something grey and slick...and big.

Sturgeon? They were the biggest things in the loch, far as I knew, and could get to be almost four meters long. But my heart pounded hard, and my magick intuition told me that was no fish gliding past my little camera drone.

"Tor!" I said and turned his way, meaning to ask if he'd seen anything.

He stood at the stern of the boat, his back to me, his fist clenched tight. Rainwater drops on the thread made the tiny strand visible—it was taut as a violin string, leading straight into the water.

That was weird. The flimsy thread should have snapped under any kind of pressure.

"Tor?" I called again, but he didn't seem to hear me. I moved closer to get a better look at his face.

The raw fury in his eyes nearly sent me tumbling over the side.

Lightning flashed, casting Tor into sharp relief. The sky had darkened in the last few minutes, and when the flash illuminated my companion he looked even more immense than before. The seams of his waterlogged shirt split under bulging muscles.

A wild beeping erupted from my fish finder. I turned and saw the reading on the sonar display flashing something that simply couldn't be true. For a moment I thought the thing was reading the lake bottom and interpreting it as a fish, but that was impossible.

Either that gizmo had blown a fuse, or something *enormous* was in the water with us.

The boat gave a sudden lurch, and I tumbled to the deck with a loud yelp. Freezing water splashed over me. Something was pulling the boat backward. The blunt stern kicked up frothing masses of water as *Goat's Tooth* traveled the opposite direction she was meant to.

I was eye-level with Tor's boots, and saw him braced against the gunwale as whatever was on the other end of the thread hauled us backward through the water. Lightning lit up the world again, and Tor let out a loud grunt. Then his boots smashed straight through the deck.

I screamed, afraid for a moment he'd be dragged right through the boat into the depths.

Instead, his feet seemed to catch on something underwater. A massive shudder shot through the boat, and suddenly we were no longer moving.

I scrambled to my feet, my mouth hanging wide open, my limbs trembling with terror and cold. Tor's legs had grown thick as tree trunks, and he seemed to tower a whole meter over my head even with his legs buried past his knees into the planks... but still, what was he bracing on? It couldn't be the bottom of the loch. The lake bed was about 200 meters down from here.

"Tor!" I shrieked—my voice sounded half-mad even to me. I flung myself at him and tugged with all my might on the arm holding the thread. I might as well have been trying to pull down a redwood. "What's happening?"

He didn't even notice me. Instead, he ripped away the tattered remains of his t-shirt with his free hand. The necklace I'd seen before rested in a tangle of rust-red chest hair.

It wasn't a cross. It was a hammer.

The braided leather cord snapped as Tor took his hammer in hand. In an eyeblink, the tiny weapon grew to something like a giant sledgehammer with a short handle. Lightning flashed and danced through the clouds as Tor raised the weapon to the sky.

"I have you!" he bellowed over the waters. "After all these years, I have you now!"

Thunder rocked the world he spoke, but it didn't drown him out. Instead it amplified his words, as if the sky itself spoke in Tor's voice. The sound hit me like a blow, and I couldn't hear my own scream.

Tor's arm flexed like a tectonic plate under my grasp, and he hauled on the thread.

I looked out over the water and saw something my mind couldn't comprehend.

I'd seen great white sharks. I'd been in the water with humpbacks and grey whales. I'd even been on a zodiac pacing a blue whale, the biggest creature Mother Earth has ever produced.

The monster rising from the lake could've swallowed a blue whale in a single bite.

My stomach did a flip, and I lost my lunch over the side. It wasn't just fear—the reek coming from the monster was rotting fish and poison and pure evil rolled into one. Though the creature was mostly just a monumental black shape against the lightning-streaked sky, I could see its vast reptilian jaws part to reveal snake fangs. They dripped with some hideous green venom that sizzled and foamed as it cascaded into the water.

The towering silhouette wrenched itself to and fro, but it couldn't break free. The thread was stronger than the roots of a mountain. And Tor? He was a gnat next to this beast, yet somehow his strength still held it fast.

Streaks of lightning blasted down into the sky and into the hammer. Hot wind battered me as the head of the weapon glowed like the heart of a star.

In that searing light, I saw the monster's eye—blue as the pure water in a glacial lake.

That thing was *Nessie*...and she was afraid.

Tor let out a battle cry that sent waves blasting out in every direction from the boat, and reared back with his blazing hammer.

My heart took over where my brain had long since stopped working. With numb fingers, I reached beneath my parka and grasped the handle of my obsidian knife. I let out my own battle cry—inaudible through the thunder and Tor's bellow, but it tore at my throat all the same—and swept my deadly-keen knife at the thread.

The blade bounced off the tiny strand.

Wild panic shot through every inch of me. I was neck deep in magic like I'd ever imagined. Terrifying, ancient, powerful beyond measure. I wasn't prepared. My little skills and paltry training were nothing, *nothing* in the face of these powers.

But I was the only magician here.

And I'd be damned if I let a pair of ancient beings wreck my world with their battle if I could help it.

"I am not helpless!" I shouted, though I could barely hear my own voice over the roar of raging thunder and sizzling lightning. "I am *a magician!*" I reared back with the knife, mentally uttered a prayer to every goddess and spirit and angel who would help me, and focused everything I had in me on the microscopic edge of volcanic glass.

My knife slashed down, and the thread split with a snap and burst of golden light.

Suddenly, we were back on a quiet lake. The sky was grey, not black, and a gentle rain came down instead of an apocalyptic thunderstorm. The quiet was so shocking I fell over.

Tor stood on the deck. His feet no longer stuck through the planks—the deck of the *Goat's Tooth* was back to its old grubby self. Tor's shirt once again covered his torso, looking only a bit worse for wear. In one hand, he held his necklace with its little hammer charm, and in the other was the last bit of Lucky's thread.

He looked down at me. For a moment, I saw an echo of that terrible rage smoldering in his eyes, and I was sure he was going to chuck me over the side.

I let out a strangled sound and clutched my knife to my chest.

Then he shook his head, and the last shadow of that other self melted away. He was just Tor again, a big and amiable fisherman with a bushy red beard.

He looked down at the deck, and seemed surprised to be standing in a finger's depth of water.

"Have we sprung leak?" he asked.

I looked down. There were no holes in the floorboards that trunk-sized legs could fit through, but there were some suspicious dents that had buckled the planks.

"I think so." I was still breathing hard and my hands shook, but my voice sounded more or less like my own.

Tor ran his hand through his hair and looked embarrassed. "I am so sorry," he said, putting the necklace back on in an unconscious way. "I will get electric pump." He splashed his foot around and shook his head. "We need to head back for repairs. Sorry."

"That's okay," I said. "I'm ready to go."

While Tor slouched off to the cabin to retrieve his pump, I looked out over the stern of the boat and across the waters of Loch Ness.

A long, serpentine head poked up out of the water.

As I watched, the head shifted. A beautiful mermaid stared at me, her green hair slick and bright, and those blue eyes visible even from far away like tiny diamonds.

Nessie waved at me and flashed a smile. I raised a feeble hand and waved back.

She spoke to me then. Not in words, like I remembered as a girl, just straight emotions beamed from her heart to mine.

Gratitude. Relief. Joy. I couldn't sort which feelings were hers and which were mine. And that didn't matter. She wasn't the monster Tor had been so set on killing anymore. She was *my* Nessie again.

Behind me, I heard Tor's boots splashing back toward me. Nessie flipped and dove. I caught one last glimpse of her tail, and then disappeared.

❧

"So," Lucky said as he checked over the crates, "did you find anything?"

The memory of that strange encounter on Loch Ness still burned bright in my mind, every detail clear as if it had happened just a minute ago. I suppressed a shudder as I considered my answer.

I'm up on my pagan lore. I know the Norse legends about Jörmungandr, the Midgard Serpent, a dragon so long that its coils encircled the Earth. I know that the thunder god, Thor, is sworn to kill the serpent... and that their battle will usher in Ragnarok, the end of the world.

I also know there's one troublesome fella in the Norse myths keen on making that happen. And his name sounds an awful lot like "Lucky."

"Nah," I said. I patted the drone box—I'd wiped its video record after I'd made a copy. The drone didn't catch anything conclusive before it had crapped out. Any responsible scientist would probably say the big shape that had passed before the camera was an over-grown sturgeon. "Thanks for the help, though."

He shrugged, not even seeming a bit disappointed. "Oh well," he said with his friendly smile. "Better luck next time."

I wondered if even he knew what he'd been setting me up for. Would the world really have ended if I hadn't cut that thread? I didn't know, but I figured it was best all around if we never found out.

Like Nessie had once told me, the best disguises are so good that you sometimes forget who you really are. Maybe Lucky could be content as a brilliant engineer-surfer instead of dangerous trickster. Maybe Tor was happier as a fisherman.

One thing I did know. Nessie would rather stay Nessie. And that was plenty good enough for me.

"It's okay," I said. "I think I was lucky enough."

ABOUT THE AUTHOR

Grayson Towler is the author of *The Dragon Waking* (Albert Whitman & Co., 2016), along with many published works of short fiction. He is an editor of speculative fiction for ElectricSpec magazine, and is a marketing writer and editor of non-fiction for Sounds True. He is also an illustrator, and writes and illustrates the urban fantasy comic, Thunderstruck. He and his wife, Candi, live in a house owned by three relatively benevolent cats in Longmont, Colorado.

Find out more about Grayson at:
graysontowler.com

facebook.com/GraysonTowler

goodreads.com/14396228.Grayson_Towler

bookbub.com/authors/grayson-towler

I SING A SONG OF MOURNING

DAYLE A. DERMATIS

"Whore!"

His hand cracked against her cheek.

"Trollop!"

Against the other cheek. The dark bitter taste of blood scraped along her tongue.

"I'll not have you cuckold me, you bitch's whelp!" His face blazed with fury.

In the three years since her father had sent her into this marriage, she had never seen her husband smile.

The fire beside them popped suddenly, spitting sparks up the chimney. Selene set her chin defiantly, an attempt to mask the deep apprehension that raked within her. She saw the subtle flicker in Balfour's eyes, and knew he knew her fear.

"I have not been unfaithful to you, husband," she said, keeping her voice even, though she knew the truth was no defense against him. The heat from the fire sent a trickle of moisture down her face. A drop caught in the corner of her mouth, salt stinging the split flesh.

"Liar." His voice was level now, quiet. She suppressed a shiver. She preferred his shouting, his thoughts blurred by anger, to this deceivingly calm tone he used when his mind was whip-clear, calculating. He jerked his head at the men flanking her. "Take her to the docks and put her in the *Lady Luck*." His mouth twisted in a gross parody of a grin at the irony. "I'll be down shortly."

"Is that what you'll do, my lord?" she asked as the men seized her, their fingers pinching into her upper arms. "Abandon me on the mainland?"

He had started to turn away; now he turned back. "Oh no, my lady," he said, seeping condescension. "Twill be much, much worse than that."

~

They were anchored near Sailor's Folly when Selene realized what he meant. Before the channel islands were settled and the treacherous narrow channel well-mapped, there had been a tragic number of shipwrecks. Sailor's Folly was less an island than a lump of bare rock thrusting from the waves. Sailors would clamber up upon it and await rescue, not realizing that when the tide came in, their tiny haven would desert them beneath the waves.

She couldn't even find the strength to scream; it was all she could do to huddle in the bottom of the yawning skiff, skirts stained with her own vomit, terror wrapping around her tighter and tighter until she thought she would suffocate. That her breathing would be soon choked by the water clung in her mind.

She had always feared this more than anything. Feared it since she was three years old and her mother had fallen in the pond and hit her head. Selene had tried to help her, but her own skirts dragged her down, down into the icy depths. Her mother's footman had pulled her from the depths just in time, though she was left motherless. In her frequent nightmares he failed, and wet weedy tendrils pulled her down forever.

She had been stunned with dread on her wedding day when, essentially sold to Lord Balfour, her new husband had sailed her to their island home.

Unable to leave the prisonous island since, she had thought the day she did leave would be joyful.

The skiff scraped gently on the rock. The men reached down to lift her. Though her legs were unsteady, unseaworthy, Selene shook off their grasp and stood. She would refuse Balfour his pleasure at seeing her cower and cringe with fear.

Back straight, she stepped carefully to the front of the small boat, no easy feat because her knees trembled at every movement. At the prow, she gathered her skirts and began to step over. The toe of her slipper caught the rope ring.

A hand at her elbow steadied her. "Careful, my lady," the young oarsman warned politely.

"Thank you, Kendrick," she said clearly. "We couldn't have me pitching into the ocean and drowning before my time, now could we?"

He flushed and looked away. Poor Kendrick. Selene doubted any of the men relished the task at hand. But they were loyal enough to Balfour, and unwilling to risk their lives for someone who amounted to no more than their lord's property.

Her quaking legs would no longer hold her, and she sank onto the rock as the skiff pulled away. Balfour was the only one who looked back. He said nothing, but heartless triumph gleamed in his eyes. She wondered inconsequentially who he thought she had dallied with. Solicitous Kendrick? The chamberlain? A visiting nobleman?

It wouldn't matter to Balfour that she were innocent. Now, the only thing that mattered was that he had won, and sentenced her to the cruelest death he could.

She suffocated her screams until the ship was out of range, then found herself unable to voice her terror any louder than a whimper. The sun's fire pressed lower on the horizon, soon to be extinguished by the greedy waves. Opposite, the rising moon heralded the coming high tide, and the same greedy waves cracked against Sailor's Folly, hissing laughter.

The moon: her namesake, and a conspirator in her death.

The sea encroached on her tiny haven, and Selene scrambled to the highest point, knowing the action's futility. The water pressed nearer, higher. Sobbing, Selene tucked her feet beneath her skirts, out of range of the soaking fingers that sought to pull her from her tiny perch, drag her down, down. She wished she had the strength to stand and leap into the depths, to grasp her fate instead of hopelessly denying it. But fear was an anchor around her neck, and she was moored in her paralyzed state.

The waves spat up tendrils of seaweed that curled and twined at the hem of her skirts like green witch hair. Dizzy with terror, Selene began to believe that it *was* hair, that some denizen of the deep rose out of the angry waves...

But then someone did surge from the water to lounge against the rock, with hair not of slimy strands of seaweed but of soft sea foam. Selene pressed her eyes shut, sure that the vision heralded her death.

"Why are you here?"

Selene caught her lip between her teeth, reopening the wound from Balfour's slap. The sharp tang of blood mixed with the spray of salty water, the pain bright and biting.

The sudden shock of hurt surprised her, made her realize she wasn't yet dead. She opened her eyes. The apparition remained, watching her curiously with eyes as dark as the ocean depths. Foam-white hair splashed down across her shoulders, and pearl-smooth breasts shimmered through the fall. Her lower half was hidden beneath the water, but Selene thought she glimpsed a spreading of glistening green at her waist when the water lapped briefly away.

The water... Though the tide should have been turning Sailor's Folly to a seat of doom, the waves no longer encroached upon Selene's tenuous haven. That was impossible, as impossible as the mythical creature facing her, something that could not possibly exist. The Siren—for that's what she appeared to be—was a tale born from the mouths of hapless sailors unwilling to admit their errors.

A cool hand gently touched Selene's wrist.

"Yes, I am real," the Siren said. "I see the doubt in your eyes, shadowed only by your great fear. Tell me, why are you here?"

"Judged falsely by my husband, I have been sentenced to die here," Selene answered. Then, laughing bitterly, "And you are no more than a hallucination borne from my fear."

Amusement hinted around the Siren's mouth, though concern still lingered.

"No, lady, I am very real." She took Selene's hand and pressed it to her breast; Selene felt moist flesh beneath her palm, foam-light hair caressing her wrist.

She jerked her hand away.

"Real, then, and a scourge to any man who sails the seas," she spat.

Humor and sadness warred in the mer-grey eyes. "Not so, lady. A scourge only to those men whose very nature brings it upon themselves."

A sharp outcropping of rock gnawed at Selene's leg, but she had nowhere to move, no way to shift—and, now, little use for comfort. Before she could bring a question to voice, the Siren explained.

"The scourge of which you speak is only one of two songs that we may sing," she said. Beneath the wavelaps, her scaled tail twitched. "Yes, our strain may entice men to their doom against the rocks. Those men who chance to survive carry the warning to others. But we sing another song, one of vigilance, to warn your sailors of dangerous reefs and deadly shoals."

"So you toy with them," Selene said with horror. "Some you save, some you destroy, depending on your whim."

"Not whim, not capricious choice," the Siren protested. "Among you there are men who are evil, are there not? Such as your own husband, lady, who would leave you here to perish."

Selene, tasting bile again, could only nod.

"Those are the men for whom we sing of death. For the others we sing a warning, sing to guide their ships *away* from harm."

The sun slipped farther, and a wind skimmed the darkening swells. Selene shivered beneath her damp clothes. The Siren seemed stilled in thought; then, abruptly, she held out her hand.

"Come with me."

Selene shrank away, and the Siren's gaze softened.

"Sister, I cannot hold back the waves much longer," she said gently. "When I leave here, you will drown. If you come with me, you will be safe."

She was right, of course, about the drowning. Selene took one last glance at the angry water churning around Sailor's Folly, and closed her eyes.

A tug on her hand, and the water rushed up and around. Selene opened her mouth to scream and the brackish water clogged the air...

Black depths, and then, nothing.

Salt stung her nose as she awoke to a sibilant murmur of voices. Above, the sky looked like the underbelly of the sea, blue-black and swimming with tiny bright fish-stars.

"Drink." A curved shell was placed in her hands, and she sipped the cool clear liquid, washing away the puckering taste of seawater.

Around a small dark pool lounged the Sirens, seven of them, tails lazily stirring the depths. Beyond them, rock walls rose up to enclose the pool in its own bowl. Selene realized she could barely hear the ocean, only a muffled pounding somewhere without.

She couldn't remember a time when she had been far enough away to not feel the persistent throb.

The Siren who had found her beckoned her closer, and Selene pulled herself to the creature's side. The Siren gently began combing her hair, a gesture so ordinary that for a brief moment, Selene forgot.

Then the Siren spoke again, her voice low and melodious and colder than the ice that rimmed the windows of Balfour's stark island keep in winter.

"Do you hate him, Selene?"

Selene grappled with the surge of truth she had suppressed so long, that now rose spitting poison like a serpent as she remembered the sadistic delight in his eyes at her fate. "Yes."

The Siren never paused in the comforting stroking of her hair. From the corner of her eye, Selene saw the flash of pearl.

"I told you of our songs," the Siren said. "We have talked, and we have agreed: we will teach you the songs, if you wish."

The sight of delight in Balfour's eyes changed to terror as *Lady Luck* splintered, screaming in agony, on Sailor's Folly.

Selene's answer was swift, unhesitating.

~

The Sirens served her the songs and she hungrily fed on the power like a starved child. When she was full, they took her hands and led her down through the pool, down below their secret island home, and through the sea to Sailor's Folly. Her rage boiled the water, kept her conscious.

Her senses inhumanly sharp now, she heard *Lady Luck*'s sails crackling in the brisk wind before the ship was even in view. With eyes farseeing, she watched the lookout scramble down the rope ladder, in his haste the telescope tumbling from his grasp to shatter on the deck below.

Above, a seabird lazily banked on a current of air, then suddenly swung away, retreating from the scene below.

Selene waited until another telescope was found and Balfour angrily—she could easily hear his curses—snatched it from the sailor's hand and yanked it to his eye. His face contorted with shock, then suspicion. She saw him shake his head, denying what he saw as a trick of sunlight on the water. Fearful murmurs of "ghost" floated across the waves, counterpointed by Balfour's shouted commands to turn. Did he think his crew would mutiny if he ordered them to continue forward?

She smiled, the dark bitter taste of revenge scraping along her tongue.

Then she began to sing.

The seductive melody wafted across the waves, borne on the breeze. Words too old to remember whispered hither to the sailors, and they paused, and turned, listened, saw. The murmurs changed. She called to them sweetly, promising whatever each most wished to hear; called to them in the voice of the woman loved or the desire sought. Slowly, each stumbled to work on the sails, adjusting them not to turn the ship, but to move swifter toward the source of the summoning song.

Only Balfour remained on the deck, wooden, staring, his crotch stained dark with terror. Selene made sure he heard the song clearest of all.

The ship creaked nearer to the rocks beneath the waves that surrounded Sailor's Folly. Slowly, it approached the place where it had anchored and she had been thrown in the skiff and rowed to her doom.

Selene let her gaze roam around the *Lady Luck* as if memorizing its lines and contents one last time before they shattered and were claimed by the sea. The men, their posts forgotten, strained toward the visions just out of reach. Behind Balfour, the wind blew the shaggy hair into Kendrick's eyes, but he made no notice.

Kendrick.

She remembered his gentle hand on her arm, his courteous words. With her new sight she could see the smooth planes of his face, and realized he was barely older than she had been when her father had wed her to Balfour. So young...and so blameless.

Her breath struggled, trapped beneath the sudden choke of her heart in her chest.

"Among you there are men who are evil, are there not?" the Siren had said. *"Those are the men for whom we sing of death."*

Balfour was evil—oh, so evil. But what of Kendrick? What of the other sailors? Among them were those who were cruel and unkind, evil, but not all. What of the others?

"For the others we sing a warning, sing to guide their ships away from harm."

The prow of the ship was nearly to the dooming sunken reef; the figurehead stared sightlessly ahead, unable to give alert.

Selene changed her song.

No longer seductive, now she cried a warning; on the melody a portrait of the killing reef. Shaken from their trance, the sailors leapt to action, pulling the sails to catch the wind and sweep them from danger. Kendrick wrapped callused hands around a rope and called hoarsely as he hauled. Only Balfour still stood unmoving, watching her, still desperately denying as she had denied her own fate earlier.

For the briefest moment, her voice faltered. But she knew not all should die for what he had done, and her song swelled anew. Selene turned her mind to the song and the ship's safety, and it was moments again, as *Lady Luck* sailed from danger, that she looked again.

Their ship protected, the sailors now converged on their captain. Across the water Selene felt their anger at what he had done to his lady, their horror...and their revenge, completing what she could not.

A body, dark and hard, dangled slowly in the wind.

Waves lapped against Sailor's Folly. The song faded away, and

Selene found herself recoiling from the hissing sea. Then the sea foam became the hair of the Siren and her sisters.

"The choice was yours," the Siren said.

"I don't want the choice," Selene said. "Who am I to decide who lives or dies? Not all men are wholly evil, or wholly good. It's not for me to decide what their fate will be."

"That, too, is your choice," the Siren said. "But if you will not become one of us, still you need not die. We will make you a sea-creature, then, and you may live out your life in peace."

Selene glanced at the green waves and felt the world shift beneath her. She saw her mother's face, pale and cold and splashed with water from Selene's hair as the child knelt over her.

"What, then?" the Siren asked.

Selene lifted her face, felt the rare warm sun on her skin and the cool breeze lift her tangled hair. To be free of the sea...

Though could she ever be truly free, so far away from the throbbing life of the world?

The Siren smiled. "Of course, my sister. Our blessings are with you." She and the others began to chant, swirling the power from the sea and up into the air. Selene raised her arms, closed her eyes.

With a joyous cry, the seabird lifted into the wind's current, grey feathers flashing in the light. Flight was a gift, a blessing, and the bird plunged into exhilarated flight.

Below, the sea foam crested and surged. In the distance, a ship sailed away.

ABOUT THE AUTHOR

Hailed as "one of the best writers working today" by bestselling author Dean Wesley Smith, Dayle A. Dermatis is the author or coauthor of many novels (including urban fantasies *Ghosted* and *Shaded*) and more than a hundred short stories in multiple genres appearing in such venues as *Fiction River*, *Alfred Hitchcock's Mystery Magazine*, and DAW Books.

She is the mastermind behind the Uncollected Anthology project, and her short fiction has been lauded in year's best anthologies in erotica, mystery, and horror.

Find out more about Dayle at:
dayledermatis.com

facebook.com/dayledermatis

twitter.com/dayledermatis

goodreads.com/DayleDermatis

bookbub.com/authors/dayle-a-dermatis

COMING INTO THE
IRON AGE

THEA HUTCHESON

Mneme perched on a tree branch off of the acropolis and peered out from behind a pine cone, watching the Christians riot in front of Dionysus' temple.

The early evening breeze carried the smell of the burning pitch torches they carried. They intended to loot the graceful marble temple and destroy the sacred space, including her sanctuary, killing anyone they happened to find.

When Zeus had faded, people still continued to honor the other deities. Because Mneme was one of the original muses, and associated with the water that flowed when Pegasus stamped his foot at sacred Helicon, many people still respected her. But these Christians were restless under Emperor Theodosius I, and he ignored their poor behavior.

Dionysus had been a graceful and thoughtful god, and Mneme had traveled with him as he taught people to cultivate the grapes. She treasured the many conversations she'd shared with him over meals of nectar and ambrosia. She hoped he had found safety wherever he had fled to.

All the old gods were scattered now, either stamped into oblivion or hiding in some foreign country. Some had tried to acquire new followings; the rest had faded into obscurity, eking out a meager living in this new age of iron.

She hoped the satyrs and maenads had escaped as well. Futile fury burned in her breast at these Christians' disrespectful and boorish behavior.

"Mneme, are you okay?"

She jumped and nearly fell off the branch. Her heart thumped, even as she realized it was only Komonus, a satyr. His long ears swiveled as he glanced through the branches from her to the frenzy in front of the temple. He flicked his tail at the flies that fled from the smoky breeze. His obsidian black eyes reflected flecks of the sunset.

He was the descendent of her milk brother, Krotos. Eupheme, Krotos' mother, had nursed her and her two sisters after they had appeared in one of the springs Pegasus created when he landed on the crown of Mount Helikon. The four of them, satyr and muses, could have been true siblings, carrying the same olive skin and black hair.

She turned away from him as a great shout went up. A whooshing column of smoke and fire roared up into the sky from the temple.

The people poured out of the burning building into the streets, spilling amphorae of wine as they poured it into goblets while chanting prayers to their new god, Jesus.

"Smart of you to shrink to your tiny aspect and hide in the tree. I only found you because I followed your scent," Komonus said. He hefted his pack. "All I have is two skins of wine, two hares, my pipe, and my bow." He also had an erection, but that was not surprising because satyrs were known for their incessant joyous sexuality, and Mneme ignored it knowing it would fade. Probably.

Bitterly, Mneme said, "I'm fine. I only managed to bring this small bag." She gestured at the leather pack leaning against the tree trunk. It held a change of clothing, a silver cup, an oil lamp and a bit of oil, a pouch of coins that had been tossed in her fountain, and small vial of nectar.

The thought of the Christians pawing through her things and defiling her sacred fountain at the other end of the acropolis made her fury spike. The breeze turned stiff, gathering the moisture that precipitated in response to her anger.

"We can go to Mount Helikon," he said. "We'll go far up into the trees and find a comfortable place near your holy springs."

She wondered if she would see her sisters, Melete and Aioide, again. Just for a moment she realized she would miss the mortals coming to her for prophecies, for advice, to bask in her strength. But they had their Jesus now. Why would they need a muse?

She shuddered to think of what the Christians would do to her if they caught her. She should go east instead of to the mountain. There were still mortals there who would welcome her.

But some of the divine never adjusted. Could she?

Only time would tell. In the meantime, she could pass for human, but Komonus would have to cover his ears and tail. He hadn't mentioned clothes, so she would have to find him some before they ventured too far.

"Very well," she said. "I will find you a tunic and a himation in the morning."

"Come now, with me," he said. "I have a blind just outside of town."

Komonus held his hand up and she stepped into it. She could change size to match his and make her way behind him, but his forestry skills surpassed hers and they needed every bit of cunning they could muster. He sat her on his shoulder and she nestled against the base of his ear, holding on to a hank of hair.

He moaned softly in pleasure, and Mneme sighed sadly. This was not the time for pleasure. Her fury spiked sharper and the air grew moister, creating tiny droplets on the tips of the needles.

He lifted her bag and slunk away from the shouting crowd, blending into the long shadows of the buildings as easily as if he slipped invisibly through a forest.

As soon as they had left the town behind, she breathed a sigh of relief. His camp nestled in a hollow surrounded by trees and brush. He lifted her off his shoulder and set her on the ground before spreading fresh rushes from the pile at the edge of his small camp. After he pulled out the oil lamp from her pack, he set the pack down, and she sat on it.

Using a flint, he started a small fire to one side of the blind, and then lit the lamp. He stared at her over the flickering flame, his eyes reflecting the light, his erection tenting his loin cloth.

"Not now my friend," Mneme said. "I couldn't give you the attention you deserve."

He sighed. "You're right, but you know the danger is exciting."

"Only until they catch us. You're far too loud in your pleasure."

He laughed and she joined in.

A breeze blew, rustling the branches, and a bird called sleepily. Komonus rummaged in his pack and pulled out a skinned hare which he cut in half, spitted, and set to cooking.

The Earth exhaled and Mneme breathed in the sacred nectar, refreshing herself.

After he ate, he settled into the rushes, pulled several fir branches over himself, and closed his eyes.

Mneme curled up in his neck. Soon his snores filled the hollow, and she found a fork in a low bush to settle into and covered herself with leaves. Owls called softly from the trees and she heard mice rustle in the underbrush. She had missed the sounds of life the natural world while she lived at the temple.

She admitted to herself that she grown soft and protected. The time of the gods had ended and she had only her innate smarts and the gifts that water gave her. Would it be enough?

~

The next morning Mneme woke, shimmied down out of the bush, and stripped off her clothes. The sun felt good on her skin and she stretched like a temple cat, transforming into her full size.

Reaching quietly around Komonus, she retrieved her pack and put her tiny clothing away. Once she'd put on her woolen robe, she added the short tunic with red trim over that, and wrapped a bright yellow himation around her shoulders to ward off the early morning chill.

A handful of coins would buy clothing for Komonus, some grapes, and bread if she haggled wisely.

It would take a few days of walking to go from Mount Cithaeron, where the temple was, to Mount Helikon. And then they would have to climb up the mountain and search for somewhere to settle. She could go all the way to the springs, but she hated the idea of leaving Man behind.

She brushed her hands over her face and obscured her divinity beneath a mortal mask. Mneme was not a public figure, but a steady stream of supplicants had come to the temple seeking prophecies or inspiration, and someone might recognize her.

Picking her way back through the trees, she climbed the final stairs up to the acropolis, passing men and women wearing smoke-scented clothes. Many of them were smudged with ash, and a few with blood.

Her heart pounded in her chest and she tried to not meet anyone's eyes as she reached the terrace. The shops sat along the far end. Slaves worked to clean up the mess from last night, sweeping and scrubbing the mosaic tiles. The design detailed wine cultivation, ending with a bacchanalia at the foot of the temple.

The statue of Dionysus that had graced the far end of the portico lay smashed, pieces strewn across the porch and down the stairs. The wine god's smooth face seemed stricken with grief.

She looked away and slipped through clots of dazed pilgrims discussing what to do since their destination had been burned and pillaged. Some of others in the square were Christians, hung over after their orgy of destruction last night. The residents who made their lives serving the temple and those that visited it stood to the sides, shaking their heads and, sometimes, their fists.

The shops had been spared, and she walked quickly across the terrace toward them. A man lurched into her and she sidestepped him, but he grabbed her by the arm. "Hey, you one of those non-believers?" He shook her arm, yanking it.

He wore the short-sleeved woolen tunic of a Roman soldier, and had a sword tucked in a leather scabbard. The soldiers had stood by and watched as the Christians destroyed the temple last night.

If he had been so rude as to touch her in her sanctuary, she would have punished him, calling water to drown him where he stood. But she was not in her temple. She was not revered anymore. She was actually in great danger if he discovered that she was divine.

"Oh, no, good sir. I am a believer." She kept her eyes and her head lowered in respect.

He looked down at her and squeezed her arm painfully. "Where's your husband?"

She froze like a hare at night, pinned by one of Komonus' lanterns. "I, I have no husband, sir."

"Then who is your guardian?"

Anger boiled up in her chest pushing fear out. Yes, the law required women of affluence to have male oversight. And everyday women often lived their own lives. But she was a muse, a divine being who had no master, no need for oversight. And for him to appoint himself the arbiter of behavior was the height of hubris. She flushed with anger, even as she strove for calm.

"My brother, sir. He is waiting for me to bring him food and a tisane."

She extended her senses surreptitiously to see if there was any water nearby that she could use as he considered her words. But a small group of people had stopped to watch and anything she could do with water now would be too obvious.

"Please, sir, he's waiting."

He let go of her arm with a disgusted sound. As she scurried away, humiliated, she wondered why he was so angry. She wondered if he had adopted Christianity. Many soldiers had accepted Jesus after Mithras had faded away. If this man had, did Jesus not bring him comfort? What about the Christ's teachings of kindness and mercy? Perhaps he had a hangover and vented his discomfort on her. Or he simply hated women and needed to see them subdued.

Mneme wasted no time in heading for the shops while chewing on her thoughts. Her hands shook and her belly roiled as the anger suffused her. A pot boiled over in a small food cart in response, and a woman cried out, her hand scalded.

Chagrined, Mneme tried to let her anger go so she didn't hurt anyone else. Perhaps it would be best to find a solitary place far away from mortals and gods alike where she could live in peace. Ignoring the pain at the idea of abandoning artists and craftspeople who relied on her, she made her way through the shops, quickly buying sandals, a woolen chiton, a red himation with a yellow embroidered edging, a coil of leather cord, and a length of linen Komonus could use to cover his head.

Mneme turned the corner and made her way down an alley

where she bought a basket to carry everything, and then she found a food merchant selling grapes and flatbread fresh from the ovens.

Carrying her purchases, she slipped away from the acropolis on the far side and then crept through the trees until she could make her way to the camp. Komonus had left, probably scouting the traffic on the temple road, and she fidgeted, repacking her bag and slipping some of the coins into her waistband.

"Are you ready?"

She whirled quickly, her heart nearly leaping from her chest. "Don't do that."

He tchhed and shook his head. "You need to rediscover your forestry skills. I know Krotos taught you forest craft. And I have seen you move in the forest. This is life and death, Mneme. Being immortal means nothing to these Christians, and there are brigands on the road who would find you—and me—amusing."

She nodded. He spoke the truth. Krotos had taught her and her sisters how to hunt. Although she had no interest in hunting, she had learned how to move silently, how to read signs, how to track.

He flicked his ears as flies bit them. She handed him the clothes and he took them, curling his lip in distaste.

"I know I need to wear them," he said. "But I don't have to like it."

He used the cord to tie his tail to his leg, then slipped the tunic over his head. Mneme wrapped the linen around his head so that his ears were covered. He adjusted it so that he could hear and scratched his head through the turban.

"As soon as we can leave the road and go back into the forest," he said, pulling on the sandals. "This is all coming off."

She hoisted her pack as he gestured her to follow. They left the forest and surreptitiously joined the acropolis trail. A steady stream of people headed away down the mountain, some of them singing and chanting and joking as they went, the rest trying to stay well away from those people, keeping their heads down, their voices hushed.

~

A pollo drove his chariot across the vault of the sky and the heat rose. Periodic breezes brought scents of the flowers and trees and hot people, along with the food and wine they shared as they rested off the side of the trail.

The path was smooth and, in some places, paved with limestone and scattered with goat and sheep droppings. Niches for offerings and statues dotted the way. Puffs of dust rose as the train of people made their way down the mountain, and Mneme was soon dusty.

When Komonus allowed them to stop and rest, she sat in the shade of a maenad statue, drank from the skin he offered, and surreptitiously pulled moisture from the air onto a small kerchief, which she used to lave her face.

The man who had stopped her on the acropolis earlier stared at them as he walked past. Mneme modestly lowered her eyes and watched from under her brows as he walked on, paused, then turned back to look at them again, his hand on the pommel of his sword.

"This is your brother?" he asked loudly. "He's a satyr, if I ever saw one. A filthy, godless creature."

All of the people near them stopped. Komonus rose, pulling Mneme up with him. "When I tell you, run for the trees," he said softly.

But Mneme stood tall. She remembered prideful men from her time with Dionysus. She was a muse, and satyrs had taught mortals the finer points of hunting when they were still scavenging after lions. She and Komonus were worthy of respect.

She understood mob mentality from watching the maenads, but she could also defend herself if pressed. Twisting her hands, she sought the moisture in the air, pulled it together. Even the clouds responded, tightening into dark gray masses above them.

The man strode up to them. Komonus pushed her behind him.

"You," the soldier said, poking at the satyr's chest. "Your depraved forebear, Pan, died when Jesus was born. And Zeus is gone, deserting his temples. Where are you going, unholy creature?"

People began to murmur.

Mneme wished Dionysus was here. He always excelled at defusing tense situations. He would throw his arm around the soldier, offer a cup of wine. And if that failed, he'd cause ivy and vines to grow around the man.

She had no such talents, but she could wield water as a weapon.

"Good day to you sir," Komonus said. "We are all pilgrims on this road. We have no argument with you. In Jesus' name, peace be to you."

This infuriated the man, and he raised his hand and struck. Komonus dodged the blow, but the turban was knocked askew.

The people gathered closer, their expressions of awe and horror causing others to notice and join them. Mneme's heart began to pound.

"Now, Mneme, run."

Galvanized, she went around the statue, flicking her hand as she went, releasing all the moisture she had bidden. The sudden downpour turned into a squall and everyone sought cover.

She took advantage of the confusion and ran for the trees. Someone grabbed her hand. At first, she thought it must be Komonus, but it was the man holding her wrist. She twisted, but he held on tightly.

Anger twisted up with fear and she used a move Krotos had taught her as a child, stepping toward the man and under his arm so that he would have to bend his arm awkwardly or turn. He chose turning and, as he did, she tripped him. Her arm slipped from his grasp as he fell to the muddy ground.

She ran, seeking out the darkest shadows to hide her. Komonus joined her and led her quietly through forest. Soon the hubbub died away. They made their way down the mountain parallel to the trail.

As Apollo's sun chariot slid down toward the underworld, Komonus tapped her on the arm and gestured her to the right.

She followed him through the underbrush until he came to a grouping of six trees hemmed in by brush. She stopped, stripped her damp clothes off quickly, and hung them up to finish drying.

Komonus removed his clothing, exposing his phallus. He brushed his hand over its hardness as his eyebrows waggled an invitation. She wished she could go into his arms. The pleasure would release her pent up fury and shame. But they were still close to the road, and the soldier could seek them out.

"If he was so angry to see us together on the road, imagine his disgust to see us coupling."

"I could be quick," he said with another leer.

She laughed. "Quick as the day is long."

"It will be night soon."

Mneme gave him a quick kiss and shook her head sadly. She brushed her hands over her face, removing the mortal mask, and shrank to her smallest size. The space he had found was cozy, and she felt safe as she made her way through the brush.

It was perfect. Enough room for Komonus and a small fire. The vegetation would screen them from any casual observation, and predators would not bother with them.

In another day they would be down the mountain, and three days later reach Mount Helikon. Then they could start searching for a place to settle in. But she hadn't been back for several hundred years. Things changed.

Komonus squatted on his hams. "Stay here. I'll gather wood and some fir branches to cover me while I sleep."

She wanted to help, but he didn't need her and would move faster without her. She sighed. The good times of the age of gods was gone. She wondered if there would ever be more good times, and what they might look like in this new age.

The Earth's exhalations were generous here, and she caught the nectar in her hands and drank until she was full. Komonus returned and she grew tall enough to help him arrange twigs and branches for a fire. He soon had a small blaze going, and skinned the two hares he had caught during his outing. He covered one in a length of cloth, and spitted the other after he wrapped the offal in the skin and laid it over the fire.

The scent of the offering brought her closer. She wondered if any of the gods enjoyed this gift anymore.

What kind of a life could she make for herself in this changing world? Who would need her encouragement?

She stared across the fire, and her eyes grew misty. The smoke swirled in the twilight, and Komonus' eyes reflected the flames, turning them into blazing rubies. She seemed to fall through them into another fire-lit camp.

The fire crackled. She smelled roasting fowl, caught a hint of spring water and heard it murmuring to itself as it fell over the verge and raced across rocks. She glanced up to see Hera's spray of milk filling the sky with a pale, numinous glow. Movement caught her eye, and she turned to see forms cavorting in the camp's flickering light beneath the star strewn sky.

A figure raised his hand, one finger impossibly long as it pointed sharply at another figure who writhed on the ground. As Mneme watched, the figure brought his finger down to the other's chest, and then looked slowly over to her.

She stared into its bright, hungry eyes, its mouth filled with shining teeth that promised to rend her flesh, to laugh as the ichor in her veins ran out into the ground like an offering to forgotten gods.

She found herself crouching just outside the light of the fire, half hidden in the brush of their camp, her heart pounding as Komonus stood over her.

"Mneme," he said gently, holding out a hand.

She stared at it for a long moment, tracing the shape of it, recognizing his palm, and the face of her friend.

"Mneme, come out, have some wine, let me hold you."

She took his hand and allowed the satyr to draw her out of the brush and bring her back to the fire. He poured some wine in her cup and she drank obediently. When she began to shiver, he pulled the rabbit out of the flames and wrapped his arms around her. His erection rose between them. She shifted away. She needed comfort, not pleasure, in this moment.

"What prophecy did you see, Mneme? What frightened you so?"

She tried to parse the vision, see past the fear it had engendered. The camp she'd seen had been larger, so it wasn't here, wasn't now.

She looked upward and saw the gloaming just settling over the forest. It had been full night in the vision from the thick swirl of stars in the sky.

So, not now. The horror of what she saw wouldn't happen tonight.

That didn't help. She understood how the supplicants felt when she told them something in the future. There was no other hint of when the vision she had seen would take place and she would have to wait, knowing it would come and she could do nothing.

"Danger, Komonus, great danger."

He held her to him as she drank the cup, and the next when he refilled it. Her shivering subsided, she gave him the cup back.

"Fix your dinner," Mneme said. "I am fine. Nothing will happen tonight."

He did, watching her over the flames. She stayed with him that night, even with his snoring. He was warm and solid, and she needed that now.

~

Two days later they stood at the banks of the Asopos River. She could smell the thick mud, hear the cough of lions in the forest on the far side of the river. The mere sight of the water made her feel hopeful. Mount Helikon rose up from the plains in the distance, a long dark green and gray hump crowned with fluffy clouds.

"I'm coming home," she whispered to the mountain. "Soon, I will join you."

Komonus scuffed the dirt behind her, impatient to cross.

But she would not be hurried in this moment. She felt the strength of the current, the life it supported, the god's power incarnate.

"Asopos," she called. "I come to beg a boon."

The water stirred at the center where it was the deepest, roiling and twisting as froth rose up to reveal the river god. He had a full head of foaming silver hair, and a long, cascading beard that swirled like the current of the river.

"What brings you here, Mneme? And why do you come begging boons when you could command me and my water?"

She acknowledged him with a graceful swirl of her hand. "Because you are still the lord of this river. And I will not insult your sovereignty over it."

He settled the water around him, mollified by her respect.

"The gods are fading, the mortal world is changing," she continued. "It is not safe for one such as I to be abroad in it. I am going home to find a place for myself."

Asopos flicked his hand, and water rose up and slapped down with a loud crack. "I hope Zeus was rent into a thousand pieces and harpies fed on the bits."

She shrugged. "I know Zeus stole your daughters and threatened you with a thunderbolt when you tried rescue them. But I have no fight with you, Asopos. Komonus and I wish only to cross. Will you allow us safe passage?"

The god stared at her, and at the satyr, who stood behind her at a respectful distance.

"This Jesus," the river god said, continuing to grouse, "he knew the power of water, he respected it. Perhaps his words can bring the unruly mortals to heel."

"This Jesus is no different than any other god that arrives divinely," Mneme said bitterly. "People flock to the new message, boiling with the call, the rapture of agape. Until the heat of the teaching cools and they lose the awe. But perhaps you are right. Perhaps they will love his words to death. Perhaps they will fight over the meaning of his message."

The river god stared at her for a long moment and nodded sadly. "Zeus erred when he let Deucalion and Pyrrha survive the flood and start the mortal race over again. Some are okay, but most I would drown without hesitation."

She had to agree, but wondered what her life would like if the mortals had all perished. Without their thoughts, their attention, the divine ones would have perished as well. And she needed the creative spark the mortals provided, finding a partnership in their artistic endeavors. And they needed her to drive them to new heights.

How would she live alone on the mountain? Komonus had been a good friend, but he would die eventually. He had no children of his own, and even if he had she could not, would not, demand that they commit their lives to her service.

He sighed deeply again. "Come on then."

She pushed down the wave of despair that threatened to drown her and nodded deeply in thanks, motioning to Komonus to follow. Asopos gestured and the water lay down flat, the river bed showing under a shallow, clear sheet of water that they could cross easily. Little fishes came to greet her and she blessed them as they flitted about her, flashing in the sun. After Komonus gained the other side, she turned to the god.

"May your waters run ever strong and clean, Asopos," she said, although she saw in that moment that they would not. She tossed a silver coin and it caught the sunlight, flashing as it spun end over end, landing in the river with a tiny splash.

He bowed. "You are kind muse, Mneme. I hope you can find a home. I think we are all going to need a haven before long."

So, he had his own portent of the future.

"Thank you."

Mneme and Komonus walked for another day, straight through a forest that lay like a veil falling from the Helikon's crown down to its feet.

They traveled until they found a quiet place with a spring bubbling up into a pool. It looked familiar, and she thought she and her sisters might have taken their leisure here on long ago warm summer days.

When Komonus went to hunt, she made her way down to the edge of the pool. Transforming herself into her smallest aspect she found a leaf and lay down upon it, pushing out until she could float into the center of the pool, reveling in its cool peace.

Komonus returned and started to make a camp. She left the water, flicking water off of herself that glowed golden silver as she assumed a larger size. The droplets landed on the lilies and clumps of willow brush on the banks. By tomorrow, the plants would have grown lush under that benediction.

As he spitted the doves he had caught, Komonus said, "This is a nice place. There's plenty of game and a small grotto through the trees. You could do worse than this."

"Perhaps." There would only be the occasional shepherd, and they were not known for their artistic endeavors. It would be safe and comfortable, but lonely and sterile.

Mneme settled down on the green sward and partook of the Earth's breath, drinking in the sweet nectar. Komonus ate one of the birds, and they settled in for the evening.

He leaped up as they both heard rustling in the trees beyond the pool. Mneme stood.

A young boy stared out of the trees, his eyes wide as he took in Komonus' ears and lashing tail.

"Well, boy, come out where we can see you," the satyr said.

The boy crept toward them, making obeisance as he came.

"What is your name?" Mneme asked. He didn't look like a shepherd. His hair was shaved to protect him from lice, with a single forelock hanging over his brow. His clothes were patched but clean, his fingers scrubbed, although his bare feet were dusty.

"Prodekes, your grace," he said.

"Where do you live, young Prodekes?"

He gestured over his shoulder, his eyes going back to Komonus and the huge erection that tented the satyr's breechclout. "A ways up the mountain. We cut and carve limestone for Romans."

"We?"

"My father and mother and her family."

This was full of possibilities. Carvers often called upon the muses for inspiration for their art.

"Will you join us, Prodekes?" She gestured to Komonus, who squatted at the fire, tore a leg off the remaining bird, and held it out. The boy came forward, his eyes glued to Komonus as he took it.

"Are you a satyr, good sir?"

"I am. I am the descendent of Krotos, the milk brother of the muses of Helikon."

"Ah," the boy said, sucking the marrow out of the bone before tossing it to the fire and licking his fingers. "I have seen others in the forest. Are you going to live at Pegasus' springs?"

"Perhaps," Mneme said, ignoring Komonus' look. So, some of the satyrs had escaped. Relief made her breathe lightly for the first time since they had left the acropolis.

"Will you come see my father on your way?"

She decided that the boy was not asking her as a supplicant, rather more curious about her plans.

"Perhaps."

A shrill whistle cut through the air, a curling note that died out before being repeated.

"Oh, that is my father. I have to go. I hope to see you again."

Mneme nodded graciously as the boy bowed deeply before turning and disappearing into the forest.

"You should not have said that," Komonus said. "What if his father is one of the Christians and betrays you?"

"I don't know, Komonus. But I'm not good at lying, especially to boys. And you were the one who took off your turban and tunic."

Komonus grumbled as he cleaned up the fire and rolled the remains of the bird in a piece of linen. He curled up and Mneme shrank herself so that she could nestle in the crotch of a willow sapling.

The night was brilliant. Hera's milky spray glowed against the backdrop of stars. The moon was a thin sickle riding a cloud across the sky. A susurration of insects and scurrying night life provided a lullaby that carried her to sleep.

~

She woke to shouting and a pair of black figures struggling, backlit by the fire.

Mneme scrambled down from her perch and hid behind some

brush. She recognized Komonus' war howl, which was answered by the other figure, the same figure she remembered from her vision. Komonus cried out and fell. The apparition stood tall, the same impossibly long, sharp finger pointing down.

Just as the apparition stabbed, the moon came out from behind a cloud and she saw silver flash and realized it wasn't the apparition's finger at all, but a sword. She screamed, "No!", long and high, the sound seeming to carry forever on the night air.

In the dull light of the flames and the silver gleam of the moon, she saw blood on Komonus' chest. The man, for that was what the figure was, turned to look at her, and she leapt forward, growing taller as she moved.

He stepped toward her, and she recognized him for the Roman who had threatened them. He smiled, a predatory grin, and she realized she was naked. Fury long buried burst its bonds, and Mneme called to the water in the man, called it to come forth, *demanded* that it come forth.

She took satisfaction when his smile turned to confusion and then horror as he beheld her in all her glory. The water in his body obeyed her in a sudden gout, exploding from him, tearing a howling, burbling shriek from him as he died.

She didn't wait to enjoy that victory, but knelt at Komonus' side. He was still breathing, a gurgle that made bubbles in the blood pooling around the sword lodged in his chest.

"Komonus, oh, Komonus. Do not die." She looked around and saw the Gentle Ones gathering on the far side of the fire, ready to take him to Charon's boat.

"No," she moaned, terror and despair churning in her breast. "You are not ready to be Hades' guest. Thanatos may not have you. I am not ready."

She demanded the blood stop pouring from the hole in his chest and it obeyed, but that did nothing for the great wound. She cast about frantically, and saw her bag with its silver goblet and the small vial of nectar.

She could make Komonus immortal by having him drink the nectar.

She paused. Father Zeus had held that right to himself.

The Father god was gone, though, gone on the wind that brought the Christ. *We immortals who are left must make our own way as best we can*, Mneme thought.

She could live without Komonus, although it would give her no joy. And she knew the wind that had taken Zeus would be more appealing to her with every day she lived without her friend.

She didn't want to live without him. The satyr had been faithful, loyal to her from more than the command of his ancestor Krotos, her milk brother. And she loved him even more than she had her milk brother.

She scrambled for the pack, tore the contents out, and pulled the cork from the vial, pouring the precious contents into the cup.

Making her way back to him, she lifted his head, cradling him.

"Drink, Komonus," she said, pouring the silvery-gold nectar into his mouth. Some dribbled out of his mouth, sliding down his chin.

How much did it take? Zeus had never shared the secret, and she had never asked Dionysus when he gave Ariadne the divine nectar.

She glanced back at the Gentle Ones who stood silently, waiting to bear her friend away.

Komonus groaned and waved his hand weakly. "Let me down."

She laid him gently on the ground. He grasped the sword in his hands and pulled. He couldn't get leverage, and she had to help him. Once the blade was out, she flung the sword to the side.

"What did you do to me, Mneme?"

She looked back to see the Gentle Ones turn and leave as silently as they had come.

"I saved you. Now rest."

"But—"

"But nothing. Rest. We will speak of this in the morning."

He obeyed, and she covered him with his tunic and himation. She dressed, wrapped herself in her own himation, and sat beside him, not moving until Apollo drove his chariot above the rim of the world, following Dawn's rosy fingers.

When the light reached him, Komonus stirred. Mneme could see nothing of the wound, but smiled at the erection that tented the woolen cloth. Living was as good a reason as any for a satyr's phallus to grow hard.

He pushed off the coverings and looked about at the spattered gore all around the camp, the sword where it lay in the dirt, the ragged remains of the Roman. He shook his head.

"You gave me the nectar, Mneme. Why?"

"To save you."

"Only Father Zeus can bestow immortality."

"Father Zeus is gone. Did you not hear the soldier raging against us? The Age of Gods is over. Now there is only the one god and his son."

She shook her head. "And you did not deserve to die like that."

"You mean you did not want to be alone or without the pleasure I give you." He laughed a bit to show he meant no hurt.

"I care for you greatly, Komonus. I realized how much when the Gentle Ones gathered to carry you off. But what you said is also true. I have no desire to be alone in this new world. Or," she said, smiling slyly, "without the pleasure you bring me."

Komonus let his smile fade. "And I care for you, Mneme, far more than any command my forefather could give. Whatever price there might be to pay, I will stand beside you. Always."

Mneme smiled and took his hand. He lifted hers to his mouth and pressed a kiss to it. She squeezed his fingers gently.

Trees rustled and Komonus stood, flexing his arms and legs, clearly reveling in the strength the nectar had given him, his erection proudly pushing its way out of the loin cloth. An old man peered cautiously out of the branches in front of them.

"My Lord, My Lady," he bowed. He saw the remains and blanched, glancing up to them with fear in his eyes.

"Come out, Grandfather," Mneme said. "We offer you no harm. A man attacked us in the night."

He stared at the body and back up to them, new fear showing in his eyes at the violence Mneme had visited upon the soldier.

"Who are you?" Mneme asked.

"I am Menidothes, the stone worker," he said stepping out into the center of the copse and dropping to his knees. He glanced about, seeing the bloody sword lying on the ground, and looking anxiously at both of them to see who was wounded.

"Was he a Christian?" the old man asked. "They are sometimes no better than the wild men of Lybia the way they attack anything that does not conform their religion," he growled. "I tell you, the old days were better. The gods were interchangeable wherever you went. Just a new name, a few new traditions, new stories to tell."

Mneme smiled at him. It was mostly true; the old gods had spread far and wide and answered to many names. New ways to worship were generally welcomed, new stories celebrated and treasured.

"Stand, Menidothes. The man has been vanquished and will trouble no one again."

"My son said you were going to the holy springs," the old man said. "We would be pleased to host you at our home along your journey."

"You are kind to offer hospitality to strangers."

He glanced at her and Komonus. "We honor guest rite. And I see a satyr, prince of the forest, and a beautiful woman who glows with a pearly light. You can only be a goddess and I offer you what succor I may. We are a small family, but true to the old ways and pleased to see more of the true gods take up residence near us."

More of the true gods? "Have there been more here?"

He nodded. "Another like you. She did not stop, but continued up the mountain. She glowed as you did."

It must have been one of her sisters. Mneme smiled at him, relief and gratification swelling her heart. "I am not a goddess, but the muse Mneme. Your offer is gracious, and I would be pleased to see your work."

The old man fell to his knees again. "Ah, we are truly honored."

"Get up, old man," Mneme said. "Save your knees and stand like the righteous man you are."

He stood. "If you will come to our home, we would feast you. My wife is preparing a ram and there is fresh bread," he said, his hands shaking with nervousness. "And I would happy to show you my work."

Mneme beamed at him. "We will be happy to. When Apollo reaches the top of his circuit, we will come to your home."

The old man bowed and walked backward into the trees, the branches cracking and swishing as he left.

Komonus looked at her. "Is this wise?"

She shrugged. "They understand the danger. They cleave to the old ways. Who knows how long before they will be forced to relinquish their ways and accept Jesus and his father? We have time to accept their hospitality, then see whether Melete or Aoide have come home as well."

He flexed his muscles. "Then I will be off to scout for signs of my cousins and her passage. I will find the path to this villa and see what it looks like."

She nodded. "I will clean the copse and consecrate it."

He turned to leave. "Mneme?"

"Yes, my friend?"

"Will I still be able to eat mortal food?"

"I ate at the feasts Dionysus held. Although you will need to drink nectar and eat ambrosia. I will show you how tonight."

He paused, his ears swiveling and his tail flicking at an errant fly. "Thank you. For everything."

"And I thank you. You defended us. I saw the vision, but didn't understand it."

He nodded once sharply and was gone into the trees.

Mneme began to work. She wove a large mat of grasses and moved all of the body pieces onto it, then pulled it far into the trees for the bears and lions to feast on.

When she returned she gathered water, coaxing it from the air, the soil, and some from the pool. Combining it into a dense, thick cloud, she set it to hover overhead. She spoke words of benediction and slashed her hand down. The cloud let loose its burden and washed the blood into the ground.

She stripped and shrank, going into the water's edge to bathe. The water glowed pearly silver-gold where it streamed from her and swirled out from the center, imbuing the pool with a pale glow.

The glow would fade, but henceforth the water would be richer, warmer. Animals and plants would find it more beneficial.

Mneme's heart was light at the prospects of working with an artist who recognized her divinity and welcomed her into his work. She would infuse him with creativity in gratitude.

Komonus returned and she turned to him, showing him her glory. "Now, my friend. Now is the time for you to show me the pleasures your immortality has granted you."

He smiled and took her hand, pulling her to him. She clasped him tightly, her own pleasure rising to answer his desire.

The future would wait long enough.

ABOUT THE AUTHOR

Thea Hutcheson's story in *Realms of Fantasy's* 100th issue prompted Lois Tilton of Locus say her work "is sensual, fertile, with seed quickening on every page. Well done..." She has appeared in the Beauty and the Beast Issue of *The Enchanted Conversation; Witches' Brew;* and *Recycled Pulp*, part of the critically acclaimed *Fiction River* anthology series.

She lives in an unscenic, nearly historic small city in Colorado with a 1000 books, four rescued cats and one understanding partner. When she's not working diligently as a Planning Commissioner to change that, she writes, and fills the time between bouts at the computer as a factotum and an event planner.

Find out more about Thea at:
theahutcheson.com

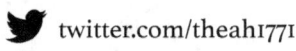 twitter.com/theah1771

bookbub.com/authors/thea-hutcheson

LEARNING TO SAIL

JAMIE FERGUSON

The air was calm, there wasn't a cloud in the sky, the water lapped gently against the sides of the little sailboat...and land was nowhere in sight.

John stood on the fiberglass hull of the two-person craft and scanned the horizon. It felt as though icy fingers were running down his neck and back, in spite of the fact that the temperature was in the upper eighties. He wiped his hands on his white T-shirt and squinted, first in one direction, then another. Maybe there...no, there to the left. No...

He balanced on the gently rocking boat for some time before conceding he was screwed. Utterly and totally screwed. He'd only closed his eyes for a minute, not nearly long enough for his boat to go out of sight of land. He'd been right off the island coast of Jost Van Dyke.

Okay, maybe a little more than "right off the coast." He'd gone further away from the Caribbean island in order to get out of earshot of yet another boat full of drunk, screeching college kids. Once he'd found a quiet spot, he'd been at peace for the first time in ages. He'd been alone. Away from people. Away from work. Away from technology. Away from any reminders of his crazy, stress-filled life.

He'd maneuvered himself into a reasonably comfortable position, sitting in the cockpit with his feet up on the hull, his head resting on his jacket. He remembered looking staring up at the full sail, wondering if he should furl it, and then...

He'd woken up in the middle of the ocean.

Leaving the sail unfurled had apparently been a very, very bad idea.

John squeezed past the blue-and-white sail and sat down on the edge of the hull. He rummaged in the storage area in the back of the cockpit for the seventeenth time, but a GPS unit continued to fail to materialize. He'd made the brilliant decision to leave his phone in his hotel room so that he wouldn't accidentally drop it in the water. All he had was a life vest, a warm bottle of grape Gatorade, and a waterproof jacket. Other than the life vest, the safety equipment he'd been assured was stowed in the boat was nowhere to be found.

He took off his flip-flops and wiggled his toes, then rested his head in his hands. Even if he knew what direction to go in, there wasn't even a hint of a breeze. At least the sound of the water was soothing. If he weren't going to die at sea it would have been quite pleasant.

He closed his eyes and listened to the waves as they gently slapped the sides of the boat.

Slap. Slap. Slap.

Thunk.

John jerked out of his daze and leaned over the hull. There was nothing there but water, but he'd felt something solid bump into the port side of the boat. Or had he fallen asleep and just dreamed it?

He snorted and shook his head. He was stranded in the middle of the ocean because he'd taken a nap in his boat, and he'd been napping *again*?

He looked into the distance, but the line between the sea and sky remained a mere demarcation separating the two different shades of blue. He sighed and rubbed his eyes, and then grimaced as the trace of sunscreen on his fingers made his eyes burn. Of course, that wouldn't be a problem for much longer, since he'd neglected to bring any sunscreen. Pretty soon he'd be as red as a lobster. The tops of his feet already had that tingly, pre-sunburn feeling, except where the straps of his flip-flops had protected them.

He settled back down and wondered how long it would take him to die. A day? A week? He'd probably die of thirst before starvation. The thought made him thirsty, and he eyed the bottle of Gatorade. Might as well drink it all now and get the process over with sooner. He reached down into the cockpit and grabbed the warm plastic bottle.

"Hello."

He froze, one hand on the cap. The female voice was warm and mellifluous. He had to have imagined it—there was no one else for miles and miles, and this time he was definitely not napping. It seemed a mite early for it, but he was clearly going crazy. That might at least make dying of thirst a little easier.

He set down the bottle and peeked over his shoulder just to be sure.

A beautiful woman floated in the ocean, her hands resting on the stern of the boat. She smiled up at him. She had curly, dark brown hair that clung to her neck and to her bare shoulders, which was as much of her that he could see. Her eyes were a brilliant emerald green. The water droplets clinging to her skin sparkled in the sunlight.

"Uh. Hi." He ran his hand across his forehead. A mirage. That's what she was. His rapidly progressing insanity had created her to distract him from his impending doom.

He scratched his chin. Perhaps going crazy wasn't such a bad thing after all.

"What are you doing out here?" she asked.

"I, um, fell asleep. When I woke up I was here."

She raised an eyebrow. Her eyelashes were long and dark.

"Have you ever sailed before?"

Great. He looked like an idiot to his mirage. His face grew hot.

"Yes, but it's been a while."

He refrained from mentioning that "a while" was twenty–three years, that he'd been a kid at the time, and that almost everything he'd done today he'd only known to do because he'd looked it up online before leaving the hotel. He hadn't lied to the boat rental place —he really did have the required 30 hours of sailing experience. He just didn't remember most of it.

"What's your name?"

"John."

She surveyed him for a moment. Her hair had begun to dry in the warmth of the sunshine. Tiny little curls had sprung up around her forehead. The larger curls seemed full of energy, almost as if they were alive.

She took a deep breath and hoisted herself up onto the boat.

John caught his breath as he realized she wasn't wearing a top. He stared at her wet breasts as they were jostled about by her movements, then pulled himself together and scooted to one side of the boat so that she had enough room to sit. He dragged his eyes to meet hers, but they quickly wandered back to her torso. She wasn't real, so it wasn't rude. Right?

He was so distracted by her breasts that it took him a moment to notice her bottom half.

"Hey, what the—?" He pulled away from her, lost his balance, and barely managed to keep from falling overboard.

She grinned and smacked her tail fin against the hull. The motion made her breasts bounce, as if they too were happy.

From the waist down she was a fish; her tail stretched out across the top of the little boat. Her scales were a rich green with hints of gold. They shimmered in the sun. Water dripped off her fishy half into the cockpit, and pooled in a small puddle on top of his jacket.

"Eirene." She held out her hand.

John took it cautiously. Her skin was soft and smooth. Should he shake her hand? Kiss it? What was appropriate when meeting a mermaid? He tried to surreptitiously peek at her middle, where the human and fish halves converged. The transition was very swift, a band of tiny scales that changed rapidly from green to gold to flesh-colored, and then became skin.

"It's, uh, it's a pleasure to meet you, Eirene." His eyes kept wandering back below her navel. It didn't seem too disturbing, not after the initial shock. Having a tail looked right on her, somehow. Which made perfect sense, since his imagination had created her. Could she really turn her tail into legs, like in the myths and legends?

She squeezed his fingers, and then released them. She didn't smell like a fish, but of the ocean breeze by the shore, salt and sand with a hint of seaweed. He had an almost uncontrollable urge to touch her scales. Would it feel like touching a fish?

"You're a long way from the islands," she pointed out.

"Yeah, I know," he muttered. He fiddled with the hem of his T-shirt. "I didn't plan very well."

She tilted her head and gazed at him as if she were taking his measure. A light breeze sprung up and tousled her hair. The boat began to move slowly as the wind tugged gently at the sail. It could be going in the right direction.

Or not.

"I'm usually much better prepared for everything," he said. He wiggled his toes and stared at the blue-and-white sail. "I'm just so tired. I work too much, and it never stops. Never. There's always one crisis after another. I'm only here because the CEO decided he wanted to have a meeting on St. Thomas, but it's a total boondoggle for the executives, and the rest of us have work to do. I've spent every day this week on the phone and trying to keep my laptop online, but the network connection at the hotel sucks. This morning I just couldn't take it anymore, and I rented this boat. Which was obviously a stupid idea, since now I'm in the middle of the ocean, and I'm going to die here, and the only good thing is that I'm going crazy and my imagination came up with you."

He stopped babbling, took a deep breath, and gave her a sideways glance. He licked his lips; they tasted of salt and sunscreen.

Eirene looked up at the sky. Her hair had almost completely dried. It hung well down her back, and a thick lock covered the nipple on her left breast. His eyes wanted to focus on the right nipple, but he forced them up to her face. Her brow was furrowed and her lips were pressed together, as if she was thinking about something. The more he looked at her face, the more he wanted to keep looking at it instead of her more curvaceous bits. He found himself hoping she'd turn toward him so he could look into her eyes again. The breeze tugged a small chunk of hair across her face, and he found his hand lifting to brush it away.

She tossed her hair back into place with a shake of her head and he yanked his hand back, hoping she hadn't noticed.

"What, uh, what do mermaids do all day?"

She turned to look at him, and he cringed. This was starting to feel like a bad date, where every time he opened his mouth he said something more stupid than the last.

"I mean, do you just swim around and look for sailors who are lost?"

Yes, this was exactly like a bad date. He clamped his mouth shut and tried not to look as dumb as he sounded.

She chuckled. Her laugh was warm and infectious. He would have enjoyed it more if she hadn't been laughing at his ineptitude, but he couldn't help but smile.

"You're an exception." She poked him in the arm. "Besides, most people who sail actually know how."

There certainly was no arguing with that. His skin tingled where she'd touched it.

Eirene waved at the vastness of the ocean gliding by past them. "There's so much to do. We're stewards of the sea. We help the little creatures. Especially these days." Her eyes narrowed. "Humans are destroying the earth. So, no, I don't normally help people who get lost because they don't know how to sail."

He swallowed and glanced up at the sky. The sun was behind them, and the wind had picked up a bit. They were making decent time, if only further out into the middle of nowhere.

"I avoid eating fish that's overfished," he said. "But I can stop eating it altogether."

She rolled her eyes. "Don't be silly. Fish are tasty. Although at least you're paying attention to what you shouldn't eat."

John felt a brief moment of happiness at having done something she approved of, and then noticed her expression, which made it clear that there were plenty of other things he'd probably failed to do.

"The problems are much bigger than what you eat or don't eat." She rubbed a spot on her—leg? What was the right term? It didn't seem to make sense to call her entire bottom half a tail. Her scales had dried, and he wondered how long she could go without having to get them wet again. "Even if you never ate fish again, the ravage of the oceans would go on."

John bit his lip, and tried to think of a response that would help make up for the fact that he spent most of his time sitting in front of a computer instead of campaigning against environmental destruction.

Nothing sprang to mind.

"You're right," he said finally. "The problem is big. Way bigger than me, or than you. Even though you are a mermaid," he added hastily. "I don't know. I'm sorry humanity is stupid. We're destroying other parts of the world too, not just the oceans. It's not fair. I'm really sorry."

She studied him for a moment. He felt as though he'd just taken a test that he'd forgotten to study for. But it didn't matter. He was going to die out here anyway. She wasn't even real. And even if she had been real, then he would have deserved to feel bad, and probably die too, because he was human and therefore apparently part of the problem.

He hung his head and stared at the pale white stripes on the tops of his feet where his flip-flop straps had been.

"I like you, John," she announced.

The smile that brightened her face was like the sun coming out from behind the clouds after a weeklong rainstorm. He found himself smiling back.

"I like you too, Eirene. I'm sorry you're not real and I'm going to die of thirst out here. I would have really liked to get to know you better." Trite, but accurate.

She squeezed his arm.

"Are you always this much of a pessimist? We merfolk never stop finding ways to have fun." She grinned. "And that doesn't mean sitting around all day combing our hair."

She shielded her eyes and looked up at the sun, then back at him.

"Turn to starboard," she directed.

"What?" He blinked. He must have missed something.

"The boat. I want you to turn to—to the right." She giggled. "I could tell that you didn't know anything about sailing when I found you asleep so far from land. Do you know how to turn the boat?"

"Uh..." He tried to remember what he'd learned in the videos he'd watched that morning. "Yeah, you pull this thing. The uh—"

"No, you don't. And that's called the tiller. Here, hold the—this thing. And pull this—hey, not too hard or you'll tip the boat over!"

Water splashed over the hull and into the cockpit, drenching them both. Fortunately, the little craft wasn't going very fast, or it would have capsized. His morning studies were starting to come back to him, although it was clearly a good thing that Eirene knew more about sailing than he did. They both ducked out of the way of the boom as it swung around. The sail billowed, and the boat picked up speed as it headed on its new course to wherever they were going.

Eirene scooted closer and snuggled up to him. He put his arm around her and rested his hand on the scales on her hip. They were soft and warm, nothing at all like the skin of a fish. One of her nipples pressed against his chest—he could feel it through his now-soaked T-shirt. He swallowed and tried to concentrate on her hair, some of which had twined its way around his neck, like an aquatic form of ivy.

"Hey, is that land?" he asked. There was a faint smudge on the horizon. He blinked, but it didn't go away. Eirene wrapped her arms around him. The island grew larger and larger. They sat in silence as the white dots in front of it began to look like miniature boats.

"Is this all real?" he asked. He pulled back from her so he could meet her eyes. "Are you really *real*?"

"Don't I seem real?" she asked, and winked. She retrieved her hair from his neck and waist.

"I'm not going to die, and you really are a mermaid?"

She smiled, scooted over to the edge of the boat, and then flipped her tail over the side.

"Wait! Don't go!" He reached out and grabbed her arm. "Please. Please don't go."

"I can't stay here," she said. Her emerald eyes grew serious. "I can't allow myself to be seen."

"But—but *I'd* like to see you again. May I?"

Eirene ran a finger over her lips, and then leaned over and kissed him. Electricity surged through his entire body, as if he'd just grabbed a hold of a live wire. She turned her head, bringing her mouth close to his ear.

"The fifth of May," she whispered, her breath tickling his skin in a very pleasant manner. "At the lighthouse in San Diego."

She slid off the boat into the water and vanished.

"Wait!" he yelled, leaning over the side of the boat.

There was nothing there but the ocean.

John scanned the water, but she was truly gone.

He turned back toward shore, wondering which island he was approaching. The sunlight sparkled on something in the cockpit; it was one of Eirene's scales. He stared at it for a moment, and then picked it up and put it in his pocket.

What had she said?

San Diego in May. May fourth?

No, the fifth.

He was supposed to go to a conference in Boston that week, but his job had sucked away enough of his life. Perhaps it was time to make some changes.

And to take some sailing lessons. Just in case.

ABOUT THE AUTHOR

Jamie focuses on getting into the minds and hearts of her characters, whether she's writing about a saloon girl in the American West, a man who discovers the barista he's in love with is a naiad, or a ghost who haunts the house she was killed in—even though that house no longer exists. Jamie lives in Colorado, and spends her free time in a futile quest to wear out her two border collies since she hasn't given in and gotten them their own herd of sheep.

Find out more about Jamie at:
jamieferguson.com

facebook.com/jamie.ferguson.author

twitter.com/jamie_ferguson

instagram.com/jamie.ferguson.author

goodreads.com/jamieferguson

pinterest.com/jamieauthor

bookbub.com/authors/jamie-ferguson

THE SEA KING'S DAUGHTER

ANTHEA SHARP

The surface of the North Sea rolled and ruffled quietly beneath the May wind. In the sky overhead, gulls caught the eddies, calling in high, lonely voices. The rocky shore of Eire rose on the horizon, a dark blur of land before the water stretched away for thousands of miles to the west.

Beneath the waters, the calm beauty of the day mattered little. Pale sunshine filtered down, and further down, to the very halls of the Sea King, where the matters of the world above meant very little. His palace rose from the sea bed, whorls of shell and pearl glowing with iridescence. Four fanciful towers, one for each of his daughters, were decked with banners of woven sea grass that waved in the gentle eddies.

The open, curved halls were traversed by fishes and merfolk alike on their way to the throne room for the birthday celebrations of the king's youngest daughter, Muireen.

This was not any birthday, however, but the coming of age Muireen had been waiting years for. Finally she was turning seventeen and would be allowed to rise to the surface for her first glimpse of the mortal world.

Six years earlier, her eldest sister Aila had been the first of them to break the surface of the bright water and see what wonders the world above held.

"Tell us, tell us," her sisters had clamored when she returned, then listened, wide-eyed, to Aila's descriptions of the wheeling birds, the bright sun, the taste of air in her lungs instead of water.

She had even glimpsed a mortal ship riding majestic over the waves, all unaware of the kingdom they traveled over. Although her bodyguard had not allowed her swim any closer, for fear of discovery, Aila had heard singing, and a strange buzzing instrument not known beneath the sea.

The next sister to rise, Dagmar, had shaken her head dismissively upon her return.

"It's gray and cold," she'd said. "Water spits in cold drops from the sky, and the bones of fish float, rotting, in the waves. There is no reason to visit the world above."

"What of the mortals?" Muireen had asked.

"I saw no sign," Dagmar said, flat disinterest in her voice.

When the second-youngest sister made her trip to the surface, she proclaimed it "quiet and a bit boring."

Privately, Muireen vowed that she would swim toward shore. She would stay from dawn to dusk and do everything she could to catch a glimpse of the mortals who inhabited the world of air. Whether or not the guards that would accompany her would allow such a thing was a question she pushed away. Her determination was strong enough to succeed.

For years, Muireen and her sisters had scavenged the shipwrecks scattered on the ocean floor. But while her older siblings had lost interest, Muireen still was fascinated by the strange objects to be found in the detritus. She could not make heads nor tails of many of the items, but whether they were weapons or decorations or strange tools, they piqued her imagination.

"Why can we not visit the surface more than once a year?" she'd asked her father. "Surely we can learn things from the mortals above."

"No," the Sea King had said, his voice hard. "The only thing they may teach our kind is death and destruction. Our history is filled with tales of murder, the blood of our people staining the currents while they hunted us down without mercy. Once a year is danger enough."

Only the weight of law and custom kept her father from forbidding all merfolk from ever rising to the surface.

Today, though, was her day. Muireen's heart beat faster. Today, she would feel the mystery of the sun on her face, breathe the strangeness of air, hear the sounds of the birds.

And maybe, if luck was with her, she would set her eyes on a mortal.

∾

Eiric Airgead set his carefully folded nets in his small boat, checked that it was not taking on water, then stepped in and pushed off from the stone jetty. The sky overhead cupped the pearly pre-dawn light, and the village's small harbor was busy with fishermen heading out to make the day's catch. Half the fleet was already gone, their boats patches of darkness over the pewter water.

The sea wind blew Eiric's dark hair about his face, the breeze strong enough for him to raise sail. Quickly, his boat flew out, rocking up and down when he hit the rougher water outside the sheltering curve of the harbor. Behind him, whitewashed cottages glowed softly with the dawn over their shoulders. The stone-walled fields and lanes climbed up the hillside, and he could see a half dozen villagers striding up to tend the fields and flocks.

He'd never had the heart of a farmer, himself. The sea always called to him, the waves whispering his name. The village lived by the sea. And died by it, as well—as no doubt would be his own fate.

But while he lived, he'd ride his small boat over the waves, casting his nets beneath the surface to pull up silver shimmering wonders of fishes. He'd sing, and play the tin whistle tucked in his pocket to pass the time. Most of all, he'd know the freedom of the wind and water, the language of current and cloud.

Bright porpoises danced beside his boat, and seals watched him with their large, dark eyes. The huge *Ainmhí Sheoil* moved like a dark shadow below him, but he was wiser than to cast a line for the shark. His boat was too small, his arms too weak.

It took many men in a larger craft to be able to ride out the death run of such a massive fish. Once, one of the village's boats was gone for nearly an entire moon. When they finally returned, they told a harrowing and heroic tale of being dragged far to the north by the basking shark, at last overcoming it, and then making the long journey home. That winter, the village ate well.

Though Eiric fished alone, he contributed enough to the village's stores that he was considered a hard worker, and a good match for any of the lasses. Red-haired Biddy had made it plain she'd welcome him to come courting, but she had a hard edge that Eiric misliked. Perhaps he might instead woo Orla, who tended her flock of sheep, but she was a quiet girl. Too quiet, mayhap.

Eiric's mother was gone, and his father as well, leaving no one to push him toward a marriage he was not certain he wanted. And so he fished, and played tunes up to the sky, and was content to live alone.

~

Muireen's sisters combed out her hair and braided it with pearls. They burnished the silver-blue scales of her tail until it glowed, and told her she was as beautiful as the sun slanting through the midsummer waves.

When she was finally ready, her sisters accompanied her to the curved-walled, iridescent throne room. There, the king and all the court had assembled to bid Muireen a safe journey to the surface. After an eternity of toasts and speeches, it was at last time for her departure. The currents swirled, tugging at Muireen's hair and slipping over her scales, whispering *come, come.*

"Don't do anything foolish," her eldest sister said as she embraced Muireen in farewell.

"Princess." An older warrior bowed before Muireen, her silver hair braided tightly against her head. "I am to be your bodyguard today. My name is Ceilp."

"Well met, Ceilp," Muireen said. "And thank you for your escort."

The Sea King beckoned, and she went obediently to float before him. *Soon. So soon.*

"Daughter." The king's strong voice sent ripples through the water surrounding them. "Today you will breathe air for the first time and claim your birthright between the worlds. I call upon the blessing of the sun and moon to protect you. I command the tides and currents to carry you safely to the world above, and back home to us. Go now, and see, but take care not to be seen in return. The safety of our people rests in concealment and caution. Do you understand?"

"Yes, Father." Muireen dipped her head in consent, but she could not contain the racing of her pulse.

Of course she would be careful, but she would not return until she'd at least glimpsed a mortal. She'd waited her entire life to visit the surface.

The king lifted his scepter made of glimmering shells.

"Safe travels to you Muireen, daughter of the sea," he said. "And to you, warrior Ceilp."

The merfolk and water creatures let out a liquid cheer. Muireen clasped her finned fingers together and bowed to her father. Her escort bowed even lower, and finally they were free to go.

It took all Muireen's control to keep herself swimming at the sedate pace required by politeness. Although she wanted to give a mighty sweep of her tail to propel her through the pearly opening of the palace gates, the backwash would disrupt the onlookers. Only children and uncouth swimmers sent disruptive wakes when they swam inside the palace. Certainly no princess of the sea would behave so rudely—even though her blood bubbled through her like air, seeking to rise.

Up, up to the brightness above the waves.

When the palace was a glowing shell behind them, Muireen glanced at her guard.

"Might we swim a bit faster?" she asked, trying to control the impatient twitch of her tailfins.

Ceilp frowned slightly. "Very well. I can see you won't settle until you take your first breath of air."

Muireen didn't hesitate. Stretching her arms ahead of her, fingers spread wide, she thrust her tail up, then down and surged forward. The sea pulled past, strands of kelp waving wildly behind them. Small silver fishes scattered before them and Muireen laughed aloud.

Ceilp kept pace on her right, and though she was not smiling, some joy sparked in her eyes.

Far off and below them the water shaded to indigo, marking the territory of the sea witch. Muireen glanced down and shivered. No one ventured into the witch's domain without a very good reason, and even then such a journey was fraught with peril. She was an unsavory creature who wished nothing but ill upon the mer.

Legend held that once she had been the sea king's lover, but that her ill-humored nature had at last turned him against her. She'd been banished from court and left to dwell in the bitter shadows she preferred, stirring up mischief when she could.

Still, her magic was powerful, and sometimes merfolk in great need turned to her when all other hope was lost.

A shaft of sunlight sifted overhead, lightening the sea to a delicious greeny-blue, and Muireen banished all thought of the sea witch. Today there was no room for dark tales and darker waters. Not when the adventure of a lifetime awaited.

Eiric fished all morning, his nets yielding a fair catch. When the sun neared its zenith, he pulled out a hunk of brown bread and some dried fish to make a meal. As he finished, brushing the crumbs overboard, the breeze freshened from the west.

He shaded his eyes with one hand and looked to the horizon. Clouds smudged the line between sea and sky, and he frowned. Might be a storm brewing, or mayhap just a squall, but a wise fisherman knew when it was time to head for shore.

Glancing back toward the sheltering bulk of Eire, he realized with a stab of dismay that he'd gone quite a distance from land. Sometimes the currents were tricky out of the north, pushing small boats such as his from their paths and out to sea.

He'd been careless, focused on the good fishing and the sparkle of sunlight on the water and paying little heed to the wind and waves carrying him away. Quickly, he stowed his nets, then wrestled with the sail. The wind was stubborn, changing direction as soon as he'd caught it. The sail luffed, sounding suspiciously like it was laughing at him.

"Hush now," he said, trying to soothe the coarse cloth as well as his own mounting unease. "We'll make it to shore soon enough."

At that, the wind died down entirely. Eiric let out a breath. Why did the elements mock him so?

He didn't want to cast his nets or line back out, in case the breeze freshened. To pass the time, he pulled out his tin whistle, the metal warm from where it had rested inside his coat, and began to play.

Perhaps he could coax the wind to rise if he played something sprightly. Fingers flicking over the holes, Eiric spun the bright notes of a jig into the air. The slap of water against the boat kept an arrhythmic counterpoint but, alas, the sky remained still.

He played another jig, then a reel full of flurries and turns, and then a quieter tune, the melody of an old song about a lover lost at sea. He was not a singer, his voice too rough and low, but with the whistle he could sing out, the notes pure and aching.

Something splashed in the waves behind him.

Eiric turned, halting the music, but there was nothing to be seen except a white froth like lace, already dissolving into the blue green waves. Likely it had been a fish leaping, or perhaps a curious seal, drawn by the sound of his music. Still, that didn't explain the prickling between his shoulder blades.

He waited for several breaths, but whatever it was had gone. Still, he resolved to keep a sharp eye on the water. Fishermen who ignored their instincts went soonest to the bottom of the sea.

"Halt," Ceilp said when Muireen was only a few lengths from the enticing glimmer of the surface.

Impatience surging through her, Muireen did as her escort asked. Overhead, the bottoms of the waves beckoned.

"Why?" she asked.

Ceilp gave her a serious look. "You have never breathed air before. And although our mer magic should make air no different than water, sometimes the transition can be awkward."

"I know," Muireen said. "We must take in a long sip of seawater, then let it out in three quick puffs, then rise to the surface and not breathe in for three heartbeats."

"Indeed." Ceilp said. "Remember it well. Also, it helps to be touching someone who has breathed both air and water. It aids the magic for some reason. Wait." She held out her hand to stay Muireen, who could not seem to keep herself from floating up.

"I will rise first to make sure it is safe," the guard said. "Stay two tail lengths below. Once I determine all is well, rise and take my hand. Then we will break the surface together."

Muireen nodded, her pulse racing like a high tide under the mysterious moon.

With a last, stern look, Ceilp swam up, her tail strokes leaving swirls in the current. After what felt an eon, she descended to where Muireen waited.

"It is safe," she said. "A storm brews in the distance, but that will not concern us."

She held out her hand, the webs between her fingers a pale orange that echoed the burnished hues of her tail. Muireen folded her fingers around Ceilp's and, tails beating the water, they rose.

In her excitement, Muireen nearly forgot to suck in her seawater and let it out in three pulses. Still, she managed, releasing the last bit of liquid just before the top of her head touched that magical, permeable ceiling where water meets air.

Then her whole face emerged. Conscious of the change in her lungs, she held her breath. Her pulse thundered through her body. Once, twice, thrice. Then she opened her mouth and let the air come in, filling the places that had known only salt and the sea.

The world above the ocean was cool and bright. It felt strange to lose the comforting presence of the water against her skin. Her cheeks and lips and eyes felt bare in a way they never had before, as though something had been peeled away, leaving her exposed.

Her hair was stuck against her head, clinging to her shoulders instead of floating free. And the sounds! Everything was sharp and exciting: the hiss and rush of the water, a high whistling that must be the wind, a distant rumble of surf on stone. The cries of the gulls overhead cut through her.

"Ha!" She could not help her shout of laughter.

"Are you breathing correctly?" Ceilp asked, watching Muireen closely.

"Yes." The word trembled on Muireen's lips. Even her voice was different here, lower and husky-sounding.

"Good." Ceilp released her hand. "Welcome to the world above."

Muireen spun herself in a circle, taking it in. The birds overhead darted and wheeled like fish in the sky. Strange diaphanous whiteness floated higher in the blue. The sun was too strong to look at, the glossy, hard light on the waves enough to make her squint and blink.

"What is that?" She pointed in the direction the sun rose, where a long, dark shape lay low on the horizon.

"Land," Ceilp's said. "The place where humans dwell."

Muireen's new-found breath hitched in excitement. "Can we—"

"No." The older mer's tone was forbidding. "No good comes from anything mortal."

"And what is over there?" Murieen nodded in the opposite direction, where a dark haze filled part of the sky.

"That is the look of a storm blowing in. Fear not; we will be safely below before it arrives."

Muireen frowned. "But I want to see the stars, and the moon, without lengths of water between me and the sky. Surely that is not too much to ask?"

"My duty is to keep you safe, princess." Ceilp emphasized the last word, reminding Muireen of her station, and responsibilities. "For now, you ought to practice changing from breathing air to water, so that your body may become used to the sensation. I will keep watch."

With a sigh, Muireen dove beneath the surface. The water wrapped about her like a blanket, comforting, yet almost smothering. She longed to throw it off, to rise and feel the excitement of air about her once again.

What would it be like, to live as a human, wholly above the

surface? To be unable to breathe water, to move about on two ungainly stalks, trapped against the ground?

She would never know.

Instead, she distracted herself with chasing a nearby school of porpoise in and out of the waves. Ceilp even joined in as they leaped and dove. Each time Murieen broke the barrier between water and air, she took in great breaths, tasting salt and cold and, once, a hint of something wild and green blown off the land.

"What is the land called?" she asked Celip, once the guard seemed in a better mood.

"I've heard it is called Eire," Ceilp said.

"Air?" Muireen laughed. "It is a fitting name."

Ceilp shook her head, but there was warmth in her eyes. "It has a different spelling, and a different nuance on the tongue. It is the name for an ancient goddess of the land, and the mortals have called their home accordingly."

Once again, Muireen glanced at the dark length of the island and silently rolled the name on her tongue. Eire. It seemed a little closer than when she'd first glimpsed it upon the horizon, and she was determined to edge closer still.

After a time the porpoises tired of playing, but under pretext of the chase Muireen had managed to maneuver herself and Ceilp nearer to the land. She sculled idly in the waves, letting the breeze explore her face. Then something tickled the edge of her hearing—a bright, breathy fall of melody that tugged her soul. Music?

"Do you hear that?" She lifted her head. "Oh, Ceilp, might we go a bit closer?"

The older mer set her hands on the two forked daggers belted about her waist, as if to reassure herself of their presence. She glanced up at the sky.

"Music means humans," she said. "It is too dangerous."

"Please?" Muireen tried to keep her yearning from showing in her voice. "We'll be careful. Just—can't we see where it's coming from?"

This was her chance to see a human! She could not turn away from the opportunity.

"No." From Ceilp's tone, there would be no changing her mind.

Muireen shot a regretful glance at the receding porpoises. They would not provide cover any long, which meant she must seize her opportunity now.

Before her guard could guess what she was about, Muireen dipped beneath the waves and sped in the direction the music had come from, using every trick of speed she knew. Behind her, Ceilp called for her to stop, but Muireen ignored the words.

Closer, closer, until she could hear the notes even beneath the waves, wavering and distorted, falling down like tarnished coins. She shivered with delight. Such a sound, made of breath and mystery, was never heard in the sea kingdom. Just ahead, she saw the curved bottom of a small boat, a promise of adventure riding the waves. Barely slowing, she shot up to the surface.

She rose above the waves long enough to glimpse a slender, dark-haired man leaning against the thin mast of his boat, a length of metal held to his lips.

Then Ceilp grabbed her tail and tugged her down with a splash.

"Foolish girl!" The guard glowered at her from the safety beneath the waves. "It's time I took you back to the palace."

"But—"

"No argument."

Under Ceilp's watchful eye, Muireen reluctantly turned her back on the bright glimmer of the world above. Her trick would not work a second time.

As they descended through the waters, the greeny-blue quality of the light seemed darker than before, the liquid murmur of the sea a poor echo of the dancing wind and calling gulls who owned the sky.

She closed her eyes, recalling the face and form of the human she'd seen. His cheeks were burnished bronze by the sun and wind, his dark hair worn short. He had seemed not much older than herself, and she wondered why he was all alone in a boat so far from shore.

"The storm's coming in," Ceilp said. "Feel it in the current? It's best we left the surface when we did,"

Muireen did feel it, the first tremor of turmoil and churn, and her heart squeezed in fear for the fisherman playing his music far above. He was some distance from land, and his craft was so small. But there was no use in begging to return to the surface.

Too late, anyhow—the pearly turrets of the palace rose ahead, glowing with luminescence as the water darkened.

At the entrance to her tower, Muireen pulled a long strand of pearls from her hair and turned to Ceilp.

"Thank you for your escort," she said, handing the guard the pearls. "I will always remember my first journey to the surface."

"It was an honor." Ceilp said. "I am glad no trouble came of it."

"Of course not, with such a capable guard as yourself." Muireen smiled. "I truly am grateful for your service today." Most of all, she was glad of seeing the mortal man. But small fishes had big mouths, and she dared not speak of that encounter. Nothing but trouble would follow if the king knew of it.

"Muireen!" her sister Aila called from the near tower. "You've returned safely! Come and tell us about your first breath of air."

Ceilp made Muireen a formal bow. "I will inform your father that your birthday journey is complete and you've returned safely. Good evening, princess."

"Fine swimming to you," Muireen replied.

As her her guard departed, she glanced up and up. Barely at the edge of her vision, a faint turbulence roiled. The storm.

Her heart clenched at the thought of the fisherman—but her sisters were expecting her. No matter how much she wanted to surge back to the surface, she could not.

At least, not yet.

Eiric ducked his head as another wave crashed against the side of the boat, the harsh spray coating his face and hands. The wind pummeled him, and he reefed the small sail close, trying to control his craft in the face of the raging elements.

Most of the afternoon he'd spent frustratingly becalmed. When he'd tired of playing his whistle he'd turned to mending the nets, though most of his supplies for such were back at his cottage. Still, it passed the time.

Finally, when the sun dipped low, racing its own reflection in the water, the breeze had sprung up. Brisk at first, then brisker still, until Eiric's boat ran before a fierce storm. No matter how nimbly he sailed, his heart clenched within him as the shadow of the clouds overtook the last pewter light shimmering on the sea.

All too soon, he'd been engulfed. Dark gray clouds matched the waves, and he lost all sight of the setting sun. Navigating by instinct, he prayed he was still headed east, and not out over the open waters, where death awaited with outstretched arms.

It took all his skill to keep his boat running upon the backs of the waves, and not directly into their hungry mouths. He did not always succeed. Fingers numb with cold, he fought the storm for what felt like hours. His ears were deafened by the rasp of the wind, his eyes stung nearly blind with salt.

Then he heard it—the crack and smash of waves breaking against stone.

He was near land, but not the sweet cove of the bay beside the village. No, he must have come in to the south where mighty cliffs rose, uncaring that a mortal life would be dashed to nothing against the rocks.

Aye, he'd wanted land. But not like this.

Forcing his hands steady, Eiric wove his boat through the water and wind, fighting to turn aside from the implacable cliffs. Hope strained his lungs as the sound of wave on stone began to fade.

Then he was pitched forward as the boat struck something in the water. Crying out, he grabbed for the side. Missed. A glimpse of black rock, splintered wood, and then the sea closed over his head, cold and relentless.

～

M uireen waited until indigo darkness filled the sea before slipping out of her tower room. The night guards were posted to keep watch for things coming into the palace, not sneaking out. Keeping to the shadows, she swam carefully until she was some distance from the pearly towers.

Then, with powerful sweeps of her tail, she drove herself up to the surface, angling for the place she'd seen the fisherman. The closer she rose to the ceiling of the sea, the more turbulent the water. The bottoms of the waves pulled at her hair and tried to unbalance her, the swirl of storm spinning her about.

Just before breaking into the air, she recalled her training, and prepared her lungs for the transition.

Harsh wind battered her face and shoulders, so much spray in the air that for a dizzying moment her body did not respond. She choked on salt, on the horrible emptiness above the waves. Shuddering, she thrashed her tail, lifting her high enough that her lungs finally responded.

Gasping, Muireen swept her sticky hair from her face and searched desperately for the fisherman's boat. How could he survive such a rage of smacking water and tearing wind?

There was no sign of him.

Surely he'd made for land at the first sign of storm, and was even now safely at home, far from the grasp of the sea. But even as the sensible part of herself argued that she ought to dive down to safety, something else pulled her on, toward the memory of where the island of Eire lay.

At length a strange sound came to her ears, a rhythmic crash and crack. Before she understood it, the storm threw her forward, and she smacked against the side of a rock jutting from the water.

Pain flashed through her, and she ducked down, away from the greedy hands of the weather above. The power of the storm was blunted beneath the water, and she drew in a steadying gulp, searching for calm. She should not be here, where the rocks waited to tear her body.

A bit of wood brushed her arm, borne by the sucking current. Then another.

It took a moment to realize what it meant.

The debris was new and sharp-edged. Some craft had hit the rocks and wrecked. Panic flashing through her, she turned in a circle, every sense alert.

There! Overhead, she saw the remains of a boat smashing up against the stone. And there...

Time slowed.

Muireen's blood beat stronger than the surge of the waves in her ears. She dove, hands outstretched, for the form of the man sinking to his death. It was the fisherman, and for an instant she saw a silver thread stretching from her heart to his, a path of starlight, of fate.

Then she reached him and wrapped her arms about him, pulling them both up, up, driving through the rough water until she reached the harsh air again. He was heavy against her, and cold, his head lolling. The waves beat at them like fists.

Desperately, she swam, steering away from the terrifying crash of sea on stone. Surely the land held more than the hungry rocks. Breath heaving, she scanned the shoreline. There! A bare crescent of sand beckoned, barely wide enough for a single body, framed by jagged black stone. She forced herself forward, her timing and agility slowed by the body in her arms. The tide threw her up against the side of a rock. She twisted, and the stone left a long, painful scrape down her tail.

Then she was through the worst of the surf, and felt the land rise up, pulling away from the sea. Teeth bared, she thrashed forward, for the first time cursing her tail. Ungainly against the rough grains of sand, she pushed the fisherman before her until he was out of reach of the waves.

He was not breathing.

Awkwardly, she turned him on his side and thumped his back.

"Come now, human," she cried. "Spit out the sea and live. Please."

As if hearing her, his body convulsed. A gush of water emitted from his mouth and he shuddered. Muireen laid her hand between his shoulders and willed him to breathe.

Another shiver wracked him. He coughed again, and then she felt the blessed pull of air into his body.

"Yes," she sighed.

His dark hair hid his face and she carefully pushed the sodden strands aside so that she might see his features. His cheeks were pale, but regaining color even as she watched. His lips were too soft for the rest of his face—the sharp nose and stern forehead, the black slashes of his brows.

As she hovered over him, his eyes opened. They were a wild, stormy blue. Muireen stared into those depths, and felt the hook set deep inside her heart.

"You." His voice was a whispered croak. "Saved me."

"Shh," she said. "Rest."

He closed his eyes and lay his head back down on the sand, but still he breathed. Beneath her hand, Muireen could feel his heart beating. Her fisherman would live.

But she refused to leave him alone through the night.

As the water pulled and pushed in and out of the little cove, she held him close and sang him the songs of the sea people in her low, husky voice. The storm quieted, and as the sky cleared she was amazed to see a shimmer of tiny lights overhead—the luminescence of the night that mortals called stars.

After a time, she realized the blackness was fading, nibbled away at one side of the sky by the approaching dawn. She could not stay, could not risk discovery, though it tore her in two to leave her fisherman.

"Farewell," she whispered, bending to lay her lips against his.

Their breaths mingled, and a salty drop fell from her eye to splash against his cheek. He stirred, and in a sudden panic, Muireen thrashed herself back into the shelter of the sea. The water took her in, cool and welcoming, concealing the secret of her tail.

She hid behind one of the rocks that had battered her. Her body rocked up and down with the now-quiet waves as she peeked out and watched her fisherman lying upon the beach. Watched as he sat up and rubbed at his face, then looked about him like a man who had misplaced something important. Watched as he rose, and winced, and cast a regretful glance at the splintered boards that had washed ashore in the night.

Watched as he turned his back on the sea and trudged away from her into the light of dawn.

~

Currents of cold water wrapped about Muireen as she swam into the dusky waters of the Sea Witch's domain.

She should not be there, venturing into the clammy kelp beds in pursuit of a vain hope, but for the past week she had been unable to think of anything except her fisherman. The sight of him walking away from her haunted her dreams, and her waking hours, until she could barely eat or carry on a conversation.

It will pass, Muireen told herself, but every day was worse than the one before. She could not help remembering the silver thread she'd glimpsed, tying them together. Was this the reason she could scarcely sleep?

A low moaning sound reached her ears, like the call of a whale, but full of menace, not melancholy. She shivered and swam on, toward a blot of darkness visible ahead.

The blackness resolved to a cave mouth. Muireen halted, her hair drifting about her. It was not too late to turn back.

Oh, but it was. The moment she'd glimpsed the fisherman, it had been too late.

With a steadying gulp, she dove forward, into the cave. It was even colder inside the black stone walls, and a faint greenish light emanated from the depths, a tunnel, leading her on. The sound grew louder, vibrating through Muireen's scales, until she could hardly think, let alone swim.

Then she emerged into a cavern, and the noise ceased. The green light illuminated pale fishes with bulbous eyes and a few sickly strands of waterweed growing from the cavern's sides.

But most of all, it showed the Sea Witch floating in the center of the space, her white eyes turned on Muireen. Hideous white eyes, white skin the color of dead things, suckered tentacles waving from her head, instead of hair. Where her tail should have been was only a swirl of blackness, as though a squid had ejected its ink and fled.

I should not have come. Muireen's chest tightened, and she turned to flee. Rough stone greeted her, slimed with the secretions of moon snails. The tunnel she'd traveled down was gone. Panic racing through her, she pivoted to face the witch.

"Sea King's daughter," the witch said, her voice carrying the memory of a thousand shipwrecks, "I am so very pleased to see you. Tell me, why have you come?"

For a fleeting moment, Muireen was tempted to say it was all a mistake. Tempted to plead that the Sea Witch release her, unharmed, that it had been nothing more than a foolish dare.

But her heart ached where fate bound her to her mortal man. There could be no simple escape from that snare.

"There is a fisherman," she said.

The witch opened her mouth and let out a keening cry of laughter. "Oh yes, yes. One of those. Delicious. Shall I tell you the terms of the bargain?"

"But you don't know what I want," Muireen protested.

The Sea Witch's blank eyes stared at her. "Of course I do. You want to take on the semblance of a mortal girl, so that you might seek out the fisherman you are so foolishly in love with."

"I'm not in love." Even as she spoke the words, though, a part of Muireen hummed in agreement. "How could I be in love with some ungainly human? I am a princess of the sea."

The witch held up a hand, black webs spread between her clawed fingers.

"I can see the strands of fate wrapped about your heart," she said.

"You were wise to come to me, for I can give you what you desire. For a price."

"What is the price?" Muireen's lips felt numb, as though she'd swum through the poisoned strands of a jellyfish.

"You must give me your voice," the witch says. "In return, I will be able to transform you into human form—but only for a year and a day. At the end of that time, you will turn back into a mer and re-enter the sea forever."

A year and a day. It was not long enough—yet it was far better than nothing at all.

"I agr—"

"Wait." The Sea Witch smiled, showing rows of serrated teeth. "When you return to your form, you will come to me to reclaim your voice. And you will give me one more thing—the bitter tears of your desolation. For in such heart-wrenching sorrow lies great power."

Muireen glanced away from the witch's horrifying countenance and thought desperately, but she could see no alternative. Distasteful as the bargain might be, she must take it.

"It seems I have little choice," she said.

"That is truer than all the pearls in the sea," the witch said. "Now, open your mouth and sing your favorite lullaby."

From somewhere, she conjured a glass bottle and held it over her head.

"Sing," she commanded.

Muireen began, and she could almost see her voice disappearing into the bottle. Slowly, the glass turned a translucent silver-blue: the exact hue of her scales. When the song ended, she glanced down to see that her tail was leached to a sickly gray.

Her gasp of dismay was only a breath. When she tried to form words, nothing came out but little bursts of warm water.

"It is done." The witch tucked the bottle away. "Go now, daughter of the Sea King. Rise to the land, and when you exit the sea, your tail will disappear and you will walk upon two legs. Or attempt to." She let out a harsh cackle. "I will look forward to your visit a year and a day hence."

The Sea Witch raised her hands and pushed, and a sudden dark current swept Muireen up. It bore her quickly through the tunnel and past the wavering kelp, through indigo waters to turquoise, and then pale blue.

With one final surge, it pushed her upon the shore—the same small beach where she'd taken her fisherman.

Muireen gasped and coughed, her lungs unprepared for the transition. Then fierce pain gripped her from the waist down. She opened her mouth, but had no voice to scream. She could only watch in mute horror as her tail disappeared, leaving two spindly stalks in its place.

Legs.

That she must learn to walk upon.

~

For five days, Eiric rested in the bed he'd inherited from his parents. The white walls of the cottage wrapped around him, the breeze rustled the thatch overhead, reassuring him that he was safe.

The villagers brought him broth and helped him rise to use the chamber pot. Biddy was there more often than most, but Eiric did not have the energy to turn away. Fevers wrung him, and a thousand aches from being tumbled against the rocks below the cliffs.

"It's a miracle he survived," the people whispered. "He is truly blessed by the gods."

He did not feel blessed, but cursed. Whenever he closed his eyes to rest, which was often, nightmares of the crashing sea sucked him under.

Again and again he fought to turn his boat, heard the sickening crack of the hull on stone, felt the hungry cold grasp of the waves. The only thing that made his dreams bearable was the memory of a young woman's face, looking down at him.

Her eyes were the warm blue of the sea at midday. Her long hair held brightness and shadow, tangled with sea foam. Her skin was pale, her hands upon his brow cool and welcome.

Each time he woke, Eiric was filled with a pang of loss. Had he imagined her, or had she rescued him from the storm's hunger?

A smaller, more urgent loss pained him as well, and that was the loss of his boat. He would have to go back to using the small leather coracle that had been his first vessel. No more venturing out into the deep deep waters, where the catch was best. No more room to stow his finest nets. He feared it would be a lean winter.

Biddy would feed you, his thoughts offered up.

He could not think of it—not when the pearl-skinned girl haunted his dreams. And his wakings.

A week unspooled past, and Eiric finally woke feeling…not rested, exactly, but well enough to get out of bed and see if anything salvageable had washed ashore in the tiny cove that had saved him.

He took a hunk of bread stuffed with cheese, a skin of water, and a stout walking stick that had belonged to his Da, and set out over the headland. The sun warmed his shoulders and the top of his head, and he felt as though his life might be worth living, after all.

It took him some time to reach the narrow path cutting through the bracken that led to the tiny beach. He'd had to rest often, and twice refilled his water skin from the small stream that crisscrossed his path.

His lunch called to him, but he'd be better off saving it for after he'd visited the shore. A reward for the hike back up the steep trail, which, in truth, he was not looking forward to.

For now, though, gravity aided him and soon the crash of the waves against the cliffs filled the air. It took all his concentration to keep his feet under him as he made the last descent to the sliver of sand below.

His boots hit the sand and he stood a moment catching his balance and his breath. Then lost them both when he saw he was not alone.

She was there—the maiden who haunted his thoughts, sitting huddled against a rock, facing the sea. Her long hair covered her like a cloak, but she was naked, the pearly skin of her limbs shining in the sun.

Heartbeat thundering in his ears, Eiric glanced about the little cove, looking for her clothing, or her selkie skin, anything that would help him learn what kind of creature she was. For though she appeared mortal, he knew deep in his soul that she was a magical being.

Sensing his presence, she spun awkwardly about and fixed him with her blue, blue eyes.

"Don't be afraid," he said, his voice a hoarse whisper. "I won't harm you, I swear it."

He could not bear it if she fled back into the waves.

To his relief, she gave him a tentative smile and made no move toward the shining water.

"I'm Eiric," he said, little caring that he might be giving his name to a faerie. Even if she were a fey maiden, he feared he'd already lost his heart to her. Anything more was a trifle. "Do you understand me?"

She nodded, and the beauty in her face made him weak at the knees.

"Have you a name you go by?" he asked.

Again she nodded. Then, with a stricken look, she brought her hand up to her throat and shook her head.

"You cannot speak?"

She opened her mouth, but no sound came out.

"Well then." Eiric settled on the sand. "Still, you and I might converse together in other ways."

A quick nod of her head.

"Where have you come from?"

She turned, hair slipping off one pale shoulder, and gestured at the sea. So, it was as he thought.

"Might I call you Muireann? It means 'sea fair' in my language. And you are very fair."

She blushed slightly and dropped her gaze to the sand. Eiric was hard pressed not to stare openly at her nakedness. Instead, he pulled off his shirt and handed it to her.

"You might put this on, if you like."

Giving him a smile as quick as a silver fish, she held the garment up, studying it a moment before pulling it over her head. She had difficulty with the arm holes, and he reached to help her, drawing one fine-boned hand through the sleeve, and then the other.

"You're not used to clothing, I take it."

He was rewarded with another of her darting smiles.

"I think..." He stared at the waves gnashing upon the rocks. "I think you saved me, sea-fair maiden. Was that you?"

In answer, she rose to her knees a bit unsteadily, then cupped his face between her hands. He held very still, as though she were a wild thing he did not want to frighten. Gods, but she was beautiful. And strong, and brave, by all indications.

Softly, she kissed him on the forehead.

Her touch was enough to undo him. Eiric gathered her into his arms and held her close. Her heart beat fast, and her skin was cool, but not cold.

Gently, quietly, they kissed, and his heart, at last, felt as though it had come home.

Muireen could scarce believe her luck. Her fisherman had come to seek her out! Joy surged through her in great waves, despite the awkard feel of her new body. And though she could not speak, they understood one another well enough.

She sat, nestled against his side, and marveled at the warmth of his human body. Together, they watched the waves come in, until the tide nibbled at their toes. With a sigh, Eiric turned to look at her.

"The sun's soon to be setting. I suppose you must return to the sea now, fair maid, though my heart weeps at losing you."

She shook her head at him.

"No?" His eyes widened. "Is it possible you might come live with me, and be my bride?"

She hesitated, but there was no way to explain that she must return to the sea in a year's time. That was a dim cloud on the horizon. After all, a year was a very long while.

She answered him with a kiss.

"Then, my love, we'd best away before dark. We can come another time to search for the wreckage of my boat—if any still remains."

She nodded, and let him pull her to her feet. For a moment she tottered, but with his help found her balance. Walking was more difficult, though, and she let out a little hiss of pain when she stubbed her toe on an outcropping.

"Sit here a moment." He guided her to a rock, then bent and took off his foot coverings.

They came in two parts, she was interested to observe. Mortal clothing was very strange.

"I fear my boots will be too large, and trip you further in any case. But my socks will give you some protection."

He held out the cloth wrappings, then helped her don them. They were warm from his body, and smelled rather strongly, but she was glad of the layer between her tender new skin and the ground.

"Now, Muireann, we must climb to the top of the headland and walk a fair bit before reaching my village. Luckily, it will be dark, so we can avoid the worst of the questions until tomorrow. Are you ready?"

She nodded. No matter what difficulties lay ahead, and she was certain there would be many, it would be worth it with her fisherman by her side.

~

A moon passed, and though the villagers still treated Muireen with suspicion, they had come to accept she was there to stay. All except the flame-haired Biddy, who spat and made the sign of protection whenever their paths crossed.

Together, Muireen and Eiric had managed to pull his wrecked boat from the rocks. Paired with another ruined craft, they'd cobbled together an ugly but seaworthy boat that could take the two of them over the waves.

For though Eiric tried to protest, Muireen was determined to go out with him upon the sea. She'd let him fish alone in his small coracle, and helped him gut and salt the fish he returned with, but she refused to waste their precious time by pining on land, waiting for him.

It was an advantage of not being able to speak, that she simply demonstrated her intent with actions. Though he pleaded, Muireen refused to leave her place at the prow of the boat, and so they set out together.

They worked well together, plying the nets and taking in the fish, And if once or twice Muireen spotted the trailing hair of a mer warrior beneath their boat, she was not alarmed.

No doubt her father had been full of wrath when he'd discovered her bargain with the Sea Witch—but such things could not be broken. Instead, it seemed he'd sent his guard to keep watch on her.

In the evenings, Eiric played his whistle as they sat before the fire in their little cottage. Muireen learned how to cook, though she was ever wary of the flames. She learned to sew, and to knit ungainly socks and sweaters that, while not lovely to behold, kept them warm as the night darkened.

After two moons, she was with child.

"Please jump the broom with me," Eiric said. "We should be handfasted. If not for your sake, then for the babe."

Muireen had refused each time he'd spoken of it before. She was far more comfortable going from cottage to sea and back, content in the simple life they'd woven for themselves. Putting herself on display before the villagers made the old fear rise, that they'd see her as a mer creature and kill her on the spot.

But for him, and the little creature now swimming in her belly, she agreed.

The day of the ceremony dawned bright and clear. Eiric and Muireen broke their fast, and then he turned to her, smiling.

"My love, I'll leave you now to make ready. Orla has kindly agreed to come help you prepare."

They kissed, and then a knock came at the cottage door. Shy, dark-haired Orla stepped in, carrying a dress the color of sea foam at sunrise.

"I brought you this. It's been in my family for two generations. I thought I might be wed in it, but..." She glanced at Eiric, regret in her eyes. "Anyhow, I'd like you to wear it, Muireann."

Muireen brought her hands together and bowed in thanks. It was very generous. Perhaps—the thought stabbed her heart—perhaps in ten months, when she was gone, Orla might take her place.

Or perhaps not. The love between herself and Eiric was a strong, true bond. She feared he might go mad from losing her, which was part of why she'd refused to wed him. But now there was the babe.

Smiling, she set her hand over her belly. At least there would be some part of her remaining when she returned to the sea.

The ceremony was held on the headland, the bright ocean shining beneath. Eiric said the words, and Muireen emphatically nodded her agreement. Together they let the priestess tie a braided cord about their clasped hands, then jumped the broom while the villagers cheered.

That night they feasted on mutton and ale, and Muireen felt, for a small time, part of the human world.

Despite her insistence on going out in the boat with him, the time came when Muireen's belly was too large for her to be of much use. Too, a melancholy had settled in her soul. Only three months remained until she must leave Eiric forever and return to the sea. Ah, and the Sea Witch would reap well her harvest of tears, for already the sorrow of parting felt unbearable.

Eiric attributed her moods to the state of her body, and was ever patient and kind with her. If he feared that the babe growing within her was less than human, he never spoke a word.

She worried, though, with thoughts that kept her awake and fretting into the cold nights. What if the child was born with fins, or a tail? What if she and the baby were cast out, or killed?

Be well, she thought fiercely at the little life inside her. *Be human.*

From one day to the next, spring came upon the land. The days grew longer and a warm wind blew over the sea.

And Muireen bore a baby girl, with no fins or tail, and her father's dark hair.

"We shall call her Brea," her father said, holding her up and smiling bright as the dawn.

Caught between great joy and great sorrow, Muireen smiled at him through her tears, and nodded. Now that her baby, her daughter, was born, she knew the pain of leaving would be doubled.

But for the month that remained to her upon the land, she could not let that shadow fall over her days. So, with great effort, she pushed it away. Instead, she concentrated on all the perfect moments: Eiric's smile and the scent of him, the soft skin of her daughter, the warmth the three of them made, curled up together in their bed.

The moon waned, and went dark, and that night Muireen dreamed of the Sea Witch.

"Tomorrow," the witch said. "Tomorrow you come back to the sea. If you are not in the water's embrace by sunset, your legs will disappear and you will be revealed for what you truly are. And you will be killed for it."

Muireen woke, shivering, and knew the witch spoke truly. Even if Eiric tried to protect her, he would not be able to stand against the villagers. In her mer form she would be too strange, too frightening. They would take her life, and little Brea's as well.

When Eiric woke and made ready to go out to his boat, she caught his arm and shook her head at him. *Don't go.*

"What's this, love?" He gazed down tenderly at her.

She touched her heart, then his, then glanced down at the babe sleeping in her arms. This was their last day together.

"Aye, I love you and our family with all my heart. But I must go out and fish."

She took his arm again, all her sorrow rising in her eyes, and he relented.

"Very well. But only for today."

She gave a small nod. Yes. Only that day—for tomorrow she would be gone forever.

She packed a lunch, put Brea in her sling, and they roved out over the headland. Eiric collected a bouquet of wildflowers for her, and she kissed him, wishing that she could speak of what was to come.

They ate, drank cool water from the stream, and she led him to the path down to the tiny beach where they'd first met. The first shadows from the lowering sun began to fall across the land.

"Should we not be returning home?" he asked.

She shook her head and started down the path. How comfortable her legs had become in a year, how deftly she stepped around stones, feeling herself balance upright in the air. Even carrying the small weight of her baby, it seemed a simple thing, to stride across the land.

When they reached the sliver of sand, she sat, facing the ocean.

Eiric settled beside her, one strong arm around her shoulders as she fed Brea for the last time. When the baby was finished, Muireen handed her to her father, her arms aching with loss.

The banners of the clouds were beginning to turn silvery orange. Heart aching, Muireen stood and stripped off her clothing: shawl, blouse, skirts and shoes. She unbraided her hair until it fell loose about her shoulders, brushing her back and belly.

Eiric watched, his gaze solemn.

When she went to her knees before him, a single tear slipped from his eye.

"Ah, beloved." His voice was choked with sorrow. "Is this our end, then? Must you return to the sea and leave me cruelly alone?"

She set her hand on Brea's head, then looked deep into the eyes of her fisherman. *Be strong, for our daughter,* she thought, even as her heart was breaking.

Their lips met. The sun dipped lower, kissing the horizon.

Then Muireen pulled away and flung herself back, into the arms of the sea. Pain ripped through her as her legs cleaved together. She gasped, and in that moment found her voice.

"Remember me, Eiric," she called. "You are my true love."

"As you are mine, sea maid." He rose, cradling their child in his arms. "Will I ever see you again?"

"Look for me in the bright dance of the waves. In the foam upon the shore. Where you go, there, too, my heart goes."

Uncaring of the pain—what was one more stab when her soul was shattering?—she hooked her fingers beneath one of the scales of her newfound tail and ripped it free. Even as a dark current swirled in to bear her away to the Sea Witch, she flung the scale to shore.

The last thing she heard was the sobbing of her husband, the thin wail of their child.

❧

"Oh, such bounty," crooned the Sea Witch as she captured Muireen's tears. "Not only mourning the loss of your love but of your baby. Such power."

At last Muireen pulled away from the witch, shuddering, her grief drained dry.

"A pity that's the last of it." The Sea Witch held up the vial containing Muireen's sorrow. "Or is it? Tell me—where is your missing scale?" She pointed at the gap in Muireen's tail.

"I threw it to him," Muireen said, defiantly.

"Ahh. Listen then, and I will offer you joy and despair in equal measure. Every year, upon this anniversary, I can use my magic to let you see the world of the mortals, via the scale you left behind. I hope your husband keeps it safe and close by."

"He will."

"Then you will be able to gaze upon him, and your child, for a brief time And when you say farewell and once again the anguish falls upon you, I will take it for my own uses. Do you agree?"

"Will he be able to see me, too?"

"Of course, for that will make the pain all the greater." The witch gave her a horrible smile. "Since your pain prolongs my life, I welcome it."

Muireen did not like to think she was helping the Sea Witch in any way. And yet, to be able to see Eiric and her daughter once a year, however briefly, was a chance she could not refuse.

"Very well."

"Good! And luckily you'll be out of the palace dungeons next year, just in time. Now go, back to your foolish father and worthless siblings, and give them my regards."

Again the dark current bore Muireen through the reaches of the sea, depositing her where the indigo water faded into greeny blue. Tiredly, she swam toward the pearly towers of the palace, ready to bear whatever punishment her father thought just.

Some day, though, she vowed she would make the Sea Witch reunite her and her mortal love.

The first time the silver scale lit with Muireen's image, Eiric thought he was dreaming. Gods knew, he dreamt of her constantly. But to his surprise, he could hear her, too.

"I have not much time, love," she said. "It is only through the magic of the Sea Witch that I may look upon you. Tell me, how do you fare? And our child?"

He showed her Brea, sleeping in her crib, told her all was well. Too soon, the light of the scale began to dim.

"When shall I see you again?" he cried.

"Next year." Her voice faded, and the cool silvery blue scale reflected back the light of his candle.

Ah, the pain was worse after seeing her face. And yet, knowing that she still lived, that she cared for him and their child, was enough to soothe the worst of the ache.

Every year, for a brief time, magic imbued the scale and Eiric was able to tell Muireann he loved her still. For he did, the flame of that love still burning fresh within him. He showed her how their daughter grew, and shared her milestones—first steps, first words, first swim in the sea which, thankfully, had not resulted in her sprouting fins or a tail.

"She is not a mer," Muireann said, "for never have our kind bred true with humans."

"I'm not certain she's entirely human, though," Eiric replied. "There is an odd touch of magic about her."

"Then perhaps she's a fey water creature of some kind. But she must find her own destiny."

Then the scale went quiet, and all other words must wait for another year.

It was not a pleasant thing, to bide so long, but it was enough. Eiric replayed their brief conversations in his head, traced her beloved features in memory, over and over. Their daughter grew into a lonely, quiet girl, and his heart ached within him for her solitude. He never spoke of her mother. That burden he would bear alone.

Many years passed, until one day while Eiric was out on his boat, the sky darkened with a sudden storm. He'd weathered storms aplenty but this one felt different—full of menace. He quickly stowed his nets, the memory of the fierce gale that had nearly taken his life shivering through him.

This storm tasted the same, the air heavy and metallic with the rising wind.

Then it was upon him, waves churning, spray blinding his eyes. This time, he was too far from land, fishing over the deep waters. There would be no escape from the ocean's wrath.

Still, he tried, fighting to keep his boat upon the waves and not under them, bailing when he could. Although Brea was nearly grown, he did not want to leave her an orphan, both parents lost to the sea.

But he was given no choice in the matter. A great, black wave rose over his boat, then smashed down, punching him to the depths.

Eiric floated, blinking against the salt water burning his eyes. Here, beneath the waves, it was strangely peaceful. The last of his breath left his body in a silver strand of bubbles, racing away toward the roiling surface. He let them go.

Then Muireann was there, floating before him. She pressed a bottle to his lips and he drank, then gagged on the foul secretion.

"Swallow it," she said, tears in her voice. "I cannot you save you, otherwise."

Coldness all about him, Eiric swallowed. Then screamed as the cold burned away. Something terrible was happening to him, yet his sea maiden held him close.

Finally, shuddering, the pain passed. He looked up at his beloved.

"Are we dead?" he asked, amazed to find he could form the words.

"No, my love." She smiled at him. "You are no longer human, however. There is no return to the surface for you."

"As long as I might remain here, beneath the sea with you, I care not. Wherever you go—"

"There my heart also goes," she finished the words for him.

Together, webbed hands clasped, they swam, tails flashing through the water. Away from the storm and darkness, away from the cold, to an enchanted palace in the far south, made of shining coral.

There they rule to this day, wearing crowns of pearl and mantles of kelp, the Sea Queen and her once-mortal love.

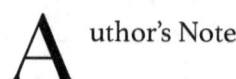

A uthor's Note

. . .

The *Little Mermaid* is my inspiration for this story. And while I wanted to incorporate some of the tragic elements from Hans Christian Andersen's original tale, I still wanted a fairytale happy ending for Muireen and her fisherman, no matter the sorrow it took them to get there.

To find out what happens to Brea, Muireen and Eiric's daughter, pick up *Brea's Tale* and discover the magic of Feyland.

ABOUT THE AUTHOR

Growing up on fairy tales and computer games, Anthea Sharp has melded the two in her award-winning, bestselling Feyland series, which has sold over 150k copies worldwide. In addition to the fae fantasy/cyberpunk mashup of Feyland, she also writes Victorian Spacepunk, and fantasy romance. Her books have won awards and topped bestseller lists, and garnered over a million reads at Wattpad. Her short fiction has appeared in Fiction River, DAW anthologies, *The Future Chronicles*, and *Beyond The Stars: At Galaxy's Edge*, as well as many other publications.

Anthea lives in sunny Southern California, where she writes, hangs out in virtual worlds, plays Celtic fiddle, and spends time with her small-but-good family.

Find out more about Anthea at:
antheasharp.com

facebook.com/AntheaSharp

bookbub.com/authors/anthea-sharp

THE SELKIE'S TREASURE

BRENDA CARRE

A crowd of locals usually filled the snugs and enjoyed the fare at the Selkie's Treasure on a rainy day like this one. If you could call ten narrow people a crowd. On an average day, there was a continuous cloud of steam and a series of off-tune (and sometimes off-colour) sea-shanties coming from Morag, the old Irish pub's grizzle-haired owner.

Today my only companion was the growly-mannered old guy sitting in the snug closest to the smoke-darkened kitchen. The old guy stared at me in a way not usual for him. His normal manner was to ignore me entirely, jabbering in Gaelic with a couple of other locals: a narrow paddy named Tom O'Groats with a pushed-in face and broom-straw hair, who smelled like a plug of chaw, and a russet-headed, red-eyed young woman named 'Nell Caterwaul' whose enormous nose might even vie with mine.

Now I can talk about hideous.

My nose is huge and my jaw is tiny, my ears look like "Bat Boy's," and my teeth rival those of an angler fish. I look like my head is on upside down. The experience of being 'out' from behind my camera is a lot like being a crustacean separated from his shell. Having that old guy stare at me so intently made me nervous.

His name was Roger Dhu, which means 'Black Roger', and a more appropriate name I couldn't imagine. He looked like somebody with a plan to creep up behind you in a dark alley and knife you for a piece of haddock.

In fact, most of the locals in 'Ogma-flanderdango' (or whatever this Irish village was called) looked like rum-runners and smugglers.

Black Roger's face was weathered like an old log, and his coal-coloured mustache and eyebrows looked ready to leap right off his face. He wore his usual outfit, thick cords, a heavy gray fisherman's sweater, and a green tweed old-guy hat shoved so low on his head his seal-colored hair stuck out in stiff tufts.

"What?" I snapped at last, tired of him ogling me.

"Do y' mind if me and my Guinness join you, Ozmosis O'Hara?"

I shrugged. The last thing I wanted was him joining me, but I raised my tankard anyway and said "Knock yourself out, my name's Oz, by the way, *only* Oz. The 'Moses' part has never suited me."

"Why would I want to knock meself out?" Roger asked, sliding himself into my snug.

"It's an idiom," I said, and buried my snoz back in my drink.

The locals were a nuisance and the weather was not only dismal, it seemed to have a mind to foil my pursuits. I'd been trying to take a certain picture for the entire two weeks since I'd arrived here, but the constant rain and wind and the heavy, hard-to-understand brogue of the locals was about to win the battle. My money was running out and I wanted to go home. I missed my partner James and all my familiar haunts in British Columbia. If I wanted rain, I could find it there and be tucked in front of a fire that didn't smell of peat and wet, farty wolfhound.

Here in Ireland I felt entirely a fish out of water—or a seal out of water, if you considered the 'haul out' of seals lazing in the sun on the beach down the hill in the rocky little haven. If only James had come along. If only...

"Morag tells me you've come to Mears M'Og to take photos of the wee folk, at the bequest of your Grannie's will?" asked Roger Dhu.

I tried not to look surprised. "How newsy of Morag," I said.

I'd said I was here to do photos for an article in the Kitsilano Courier. Morag must have been snooping into my things, otherwise how would she know about the will locked away in my bedroom? My tiny attic door might be more peel than paint, but the padlock still worked, ancient though it was.

Now, I didn't doubt the whole crazy tribe of locals would be trooping in here to gawk at the "foreign Canadian feller" who wanted pictures of the wee folk so he could win his old grannie's fortune. All Mears M'Og would be giving me directions.

No thank you. I'd squelched through too many bogs already. This is why I was drying out my hiney in the snug with my muddy Fluevogs off and my argyle socks in a filthy mess. I'd already decided to give up and head home in the morning.

"I'm sorry you're so down-hearted, my lad," said Roger Dhu

scratching his whiskery jaw—a fine scrapy sound like mice running through grass. "Don't mind my saying so, Ozzy, your Grannie P would never have given up so fast on us."

I stared at him, gobsmacked. "You knew my Grannie P?"

He winked at me, and took a thoughtful slog of his Guinness.

"Och, I knew her well lad. She was a true beauty, inside and out. Peasewater took the sunlight with her when she left. I do swear she shone when she walked."

I snorted. "Now that's stretching it a bit far, Rog. Grannie Peasewater was my favorite person in the whole world, but she was dottier than the back of a sparrow. She believed in piskies and elves, to the point I might add that I have been commanded by bequest to take a photo of the Fey. Ridiculous! There are no piskies, Roger Dhu, and photo-shopping one in to a picture's cheating. Though I must say I've been tempted.

"Grannie P's fortune would set us up, me with my photography, James with his staging business—and yes, I will admit, I want a nose reduction. I'm tired of making stupid jokes about it."

Roger Dhu grinned. "Morag, lass, we're dry!" he said, emptying his tankard and banging it down. He added a few words in Irish Gaelic that sounded like Ginny Whiskers coughing up a hairball.

"Now that reminds me. Let me mention that cat as well," I said.

"Ginny Whiskers you mean?"

"Yes, the—Akk!"

I jumped as Morag appeared beside us—well not really appeared, but she had this uncanny skill of creeping up on a person without being heard or spied until she was nearly breathing up your nose.

"Here y'ar, lads!"

She put her tray on the pitted table and exchanged our empty pint glasses for full ones. My pint was topped so the foam made a nice head. The beer inside smelled like a peat bog topped with honey. The fullness of Morag's on-tap beers and the unctuosity of her deep-fried domesticities were among the few things I was going to miss about this place—a kind of Shelob's lair with fish-sticks. But whatever that was in Roger Dhu's pint right now, it didn't look like Guinness. In fact, it didn't look wholesome at all. It smelled strong enough to put between stones with a trowel.

Roger caught my scowl and threw me a beatific grin. "Want a try?"

"I'll pass," I said.

"Would ya be liking yer dinner now, Mr O'Hara, while you and Roger are having your little heart-to-heart? Sure, and you must be peckish?"

"Er' not just now, Morag. Maybe after—whatever."

"Could be taties and mash or a nice frumenty puddin'?" she said, trying to tease me with something I was certain to regret if I ate it. Ah, she could cook like a jinni, but just yesterday she'd given me something called Black Pudding which I'd forced myself to eat even after she'd told me with pride how much pork blood had gone into it.

"Isn't 'Frumenty' some kind of sheep's brain?" I said warily.

Roger Dhu laughed. "Frumenty's made from wheat and milk and eggs and broth, sometimes almonds, currants, orange flower water and meat if you've a mind. Could be venison or even porpoise if you're seafood inclined."

"That's ok. I prefer my porpoise living. I'll let you get back to whatever you were doing, Morag. Haven't you got a seventy-person banquet to prepare for?"

I was trying to be funny. Even ten people plus the odiferous wolfhound were a squeeze in here, but Morag beamed like I'd just said something profound.

"Ook no, lad. I don't need to cook for the whole seventy until Samhain."

"I didn't think there were seventy people living in this whole forsaken, peat-raddled county," I said to Roger Dhu, as Morag waddled back into her lair with our empty mugs.

"Oh, aye. There's more than that, but a lot of them are too passing shy to appear without reason. Like this one here. She tells me she's taken a shine to you?"

Roger Dhu gave a chirrup and Ginny Whiskers hopped onto the bench beside him, her brindle tail quirked and her whiskers twitching like stiff little wires. This was the same cat I'd started to mention just before Morag appeared. Ginny Whiskers had been making daily visits to my room since I'd come here. She seemed to think it amusing to up-chuck happy deposits onto my pillow—fish I think, because of the scales, but well-digested.

The big cat drove her ugly little head under Roger Dhu's weathered old hand for a stroke, and began to purr like a miniature tractor as he gave in with a chuckle. Not satisfied yet, she squirmed wantonly under his arm and into his lap to present her belly for a scratch.

"Ah there's my wee lass, and whither did thou fare today my pretty?"

She answered by making air biscuits with her paws.

"I might be several corks into the wind right now, Rog, but I doubt there's much she can tell you but *miaou*."

I drank deep, belched, and thumped down my tankard. "Now before Morag appeared, I was going to tell you about that cat..."

I heard a thud as Ginny Whiskers hopped off Roger Dhu's lap and hit the floor. She gave a soft *mirrupp* as she leaped up onto the hard bench beside me. She bumped my arm with her head, demanding I stroke her. Almost as if she wanted to make amends.

"You little hussy," I said. Her fluffy throat vibrated under my hand. The satisfied slits of her eyes glinted like ruddy gold as she crawled into my lap and yielded her orange belly to my fingers.

"See there now, lad. Keep doing that, and before long our Ginny'll start to tell you what she wants of you."

"That's blarney!" I chuckled and took another long guzzle. My third tankard of ale was working a treat. It was loosening my tongue and I was starting not to care about anything anymore. "So where are the cronies you usually come in with, Rog?"

Ginny Whiskers' agitated tail beat the bench board. Alert to the ways of cats, I stopped scratching.

"They're about somewhere. 'Tis not like we're joined at the hip."

"Now that would really be a sight worth a photo— Ouch!" I shoved Ginny Whiskers off my lap and onto the floor. "She bit me!"

"A love bite?"

"That was no love bite!"

"*Awwoohrrr*," Ginny Whiskers growled, glaring up at me from under the table.

"Morag! Come over here and settle something for us, me darlin'. Tell Ozzy here he's got too much venom in him. Tell him it's not his schnoz is getting in his way, but his bad humour."

"I have too much venom? Who bit whom?" I snapped, glaring down at the cat.

"Hunk, huh, haak!" came an ominous and familiar noise from under the table.

"Aaak!" I yelped.

Before I could yank my feet out of the way, a *splat* of something warm and solid hit my stocking foot. Ginny Whiskers streaked off and squirmed like an eel through the chink between door and doorpost. What had been a reasonably dry left instep was now dolloped with some kind of membrane pate.

"She's done it again. Twice in one day? Cat, really?"

"Ook, she's blessed you," said Morag, making a delighted return to our table.

"Blessed me? Are you kidding?"

"Well, if you don't believe me, just look through the window. The sun's come out."

Weirdly, amazingly, Morag was right. Bright sunlight flooded through the dusty squares of the bull's-eye windows, over the wide stone sills, across the buckled slate floor, across Dog Madog and the ceiling-high hearth. Sunlight kissed the fire, flooded the tables, turned Morag's grizzled crown to brilliance, whitened her pinny, and sparked the brew in the pitcher she'd brought. Sunlight wrapped Roger Dhu in a golden aura, so he looked less like an old reprobate and more like Darby O'Gill.

He began to sing in a wheezy voice that sounded a lot like a whistling tea kettle. "Ah, there once was a colleen from Clyde. From eating green apples she died. It could not be prevented, the apples fermented, and turned into cider inside her insides, her insides."

That was it. I closed my eyes, threw back my head and laughed until I was whooping for air and beery tears dripped out of my eyes.

When I opened them again, Roger was beaming at me and tapping a jig on the table with his fingers. I took a deep cathartic breath. My head felt light and untroubled. I wiped my eyes and my nose on my sleeve and nodded.

"Ok. I think you just broke me."

Morag laughed and put down a new pint, but she didn't leave. She pushed her pear-shaped body next to Roger's, and gazed at me fondly while I endeavored to peel off my sock without getting cat barf on my fingers.

"It's lovely to see you smile, Ozzy. You'd given up, you poor little chicken. Now we can all go on with what's next to come," said Morag. She clasped her hands around my empty pint.

"Well, I know what's next to come." Needing to capture this moment, I reached for my camera. I aimed it at Morag and Roger Dhu and took a photo. The shutter clicked. The two of them looked startled.

"I'm going out, guys. Forget the piskies. I'm going to put on my shoes—without my socks—and go take some photos. Then I'm going back home to my lover. If I can get some good pictures I'll send them to you guys. I'll send them to a travel magazine too and give the Selkie's Treasure a good write-up. Atmospheric old inn, romantic attic bedrooms, traditional food, a decent shot at some tourists."

"Not yet," cried Morag. Her broad, crestfallen face regarded me from the codger side of the snug.

"What's the problem?" I asked.

Roger Dhu cleared his throat.

"Morag means it's not commerce we're wanting. That's the *last* thing we're wanting. What we do want is a child, and that's where you come in."

"Where *I* come in?"

"You need to have a child to carry on the Peasewater line. Girl or boy, doesn't matter. What does matter is it has to be yours," said Morag wringing her hands.

"Ummm, excuse me, you *do* know I'm gay?"

"Well that doesn't matter," said Morag with a sniff.

"Yeah, I kinda think it does."

Roger Dhu sighed and pushed his hat way back on his head. It made his thatch look even wilder than before. "Well no, Ozzie, it doesn't. Not for the Fae. You see now?"

I didn't. I scratched in confusion, right where my hairline met the bulge of my forehead.

He patted the hand holding my camera. "I see now we'll have to prod you a little bit more. Yer da was a Selkie."

I looked at Roger Dhu's tattooed hand on mine, at the mass of blue and green spirals all over his wrist. "My dad was a what?"

"A man who can don a second skin and become a sea creature."

"I know what a Selkie is! I mean, you're kidding, right?"

Both Roger Dhu and Morag chuckled together like brooks.

"And yer mother's a Lorelei and a bloody rotten one to have misled you so. We know how she hurt you. Grannie P wrote us a letter or two. I warned Connor—your da—but he wouldn't listen."

"Oh God," I said.

"Aye, there's a god but that would be Lir. He has dominion over the sea folk."

"You're telling me I'm a *Selkie*?"

"Not yet, not fully, we have to get you to see your own kind first. That takes a potion. After that you do the rite and take the change, Ginny Whiskers can help you with that. Change the once and you can do it again as often as you want. There's a wee catch, but Ginny Whiskers can take care of that too."

"A wee cat?" I said thinking I'd heard him wrong.

"Ha, no! A wee *catch*. We'll be needing a favor, but that comes last. Your mother was supposed to leave you here with us, but she stole you away."

"My mother?" I didn't know whether to play along, or run for the hills. It seemed now all I could do was repeat the last thing he'd said.

"Aye. Your mother. Face of a goddess after she took on her power. Do you think she always looked that way? Not so much. Who do you think you got that shnoz from, hey?"

My hands started to shake. This couldn't be true.

"They're all about glamor, the Lorelei. Their voices bewitch and the unwary don't even know they're being seduced. We can give you the Sight back, Ozzy. It's no doubt the real reason why your Grannie P sent you here. She wanted you happy and complete."

~

"For what we are about to consume, oh lord, make us truly disgusted," I said.

I gazed at the floating bits in my ale and made a face. It smelled like bitters laced with linseed oil. Beyond this and the crushed herbs Morag had pulled out of the bib pocket in her apron, they'd actually taken a piece of the membrane (eeww) the kitty had coughed up onto my sock, and put that in too.

"You'll be able to see the very things Grannie P wanted you to see. You'll be able to take your blessed pictures and go home to the lad you love."

"This is nuts."

Even so, a madness seized me. I pinched my nose shut so I wouldn't be able to taste much, and chug-a-lugged the whole mess.

"Ahhk! That was...just...uhhh!" I shuddered with reaction.

"There's herbs in there to keep you sober as well," said Morag proudly.

"As well as what?" I said. My scalp was already prickling like goblin fingers were raking through it. The room went double for an instant, then there were four people sitting opposite me in our snug. Two Rogers and two Morags. Both looked younger, and not really human. The Treasure itself was vast, like the nave of a cathedral, and it smelled of ancient oak leaves and mysterious power. Then only Roger Dhu and Morag sat in front of me once more, in an ill-lit, dumpy little pub.

But all of a sudden I got it. The stuffy snugs, the farting dog, the smoking peat, the rain. It was all illusion. I'd just had a glimpse of the real Selkie's Treasure.

"What about my own appearance? Is it real, or not?"

This was a rhetorical question, but Morag answered it anyway. "What do you want to see, lovey? What do you want your James to see? What do you want the world to see?"

"Wonder," I said.

~

We left Morag back at the Treasure getting ready for her seventy-person dinner. In a pub the size of a cathedral, that now didn't seem so impossible.

I followed Roger Dhu down the rocky road between houses so old they looked less like houses and more like big loaves of bread covered with haystacks. Amazingly spry, Roger Dhu took the downward way better than I did in my fancy shoes. My insides were fizzing like champagne. Something was going to happen. I was afraid to ask what.

The low October sun was a photographer's dream, mellow as a honey-colored filter. It set the entire place in a new glamor of light and shade. The whole world felt sharper, harder, more real.

I flapped my arms like a ninny and waxed poetic. "Oh, Yeats," I sighed, staring downhill past a series of bright shamrock-green hummocks. "Now *this* is Ireland."

A sweep of rocky prominences, cobalt sea, and a rugged bay lay below us. A dozen round little fishermen were putting out to sea in their equally round little boats. The air smelled of kelp and smoke and ancient stone.

Way down the beach, the tiny figure of Ginny Whiskers darted after crabs, doing that back-arched spidery thing cats do when they're "playing" with something.

"We need to get down where the tide is flowing," said Roger Dhu. "Morag's herbs won't last forever, and if you lose the Sight before we're done, that'll be it."

I stifled a giggle. "I have the Sight? I have it now? I thought I had the *drunk*?"

"Aye, you have the drunk too, but it's mainly magic you're drunk on, lad."

"Ok." I chuckled.

I turned to pan around the village, putting the camera in video mode. The occasional lace curtain twitched aside from tiny, dark windows. Ghostly faces peered out at us, then nodded and withdrew when Roger gave them the "thumbs up." We squelched past my little rented electric blue Prius. It was parked in a deep rain-puddle. I wanted to stop and get a montage of my car and the old stone building reflected in the puddle, but Roger cleared his throat.

"Ok, ok," I said, stumbling after him.

Time telescoped into itself. I could not say how long it took us to get down the high hill to the sea. I saw that what had looked like a load of boulders down there weren't boulders at all, but seals. Grey, pinkish, spotted, and torpedo-shaped, they lolled about and barked at us. But their eyes were not the eyes of seals.

Then we rounded a huge outcrop of stone and the shingle beach lay before us. Nor were we alone. A tall, orange-haired girl stood before us. The wind seemed to pull me toward her. That was all my mind registered.

My body, on the other hand, was experiencing a reaction no woman had ever given me before. She was striking and unapologetically naked. It was the potion—it had to be.

Her body was lush, and her russet skin was striped like a tiger's. She stood poised and waiting, wicked and feline, one hand on her strong, bare thigh, shoulders arched back, chin tilted proudly, orange hair wafting up like a cloud of down. "Took your sweet time getting here, now didn't you?" she said. There was more than a spark of mischief upon her.

"Ozzy. This is Nell O'Shea. Or Red-Eye Nell as you named her up the hill. She's one of the *Sidhe*, and she's here to help us."

Of course she was. First Selkies and now *Sidhe*.

Nell stepped forward on those strong bare feet—sleek, long-toed feet made for running. Her teeth were small and white, the canines pointed. "Would you be wanting to take my picture now or later, after I've gone and had my way with you?"

I swallowed, trying to bring some moisture to a mouth gone dry as last year's bread. There was no way I was going to get a picture of anything right now. My hands were shaking way too much.

"Come now. Surely Roger Dhu, told you what we need more than life?"

'This is going to kill me,' my wits told me. 'I'm going to die.'

At least the me I'd known before was going to die. The flighty, bitter, ugly, insecure Oz who'd come down the hill—the one who'd given up on magic—*he* was going to die. This Oz breathed magic. *This* Oz wanted to create, embrace creation so fully he'd never be the same again. And this *Sidhe* woman was creation. She stroked my jaw with a long sharp finger. Her touch was silk and steel and filled with hunger.

'A child,' they'd said.

This would not be a human child. This child would be got in an ancient way, as I had been. He or she would be the result of a deeper, more primal rite. James had understood, bless him, even before I did. He'd sent me here. This wasn't love or passion. These were the Old Ways my mother had forsaken when she'd denied me my past and hers. I had been a somber child, and then a bitter man, but now I had a chance to do something.

"I understand," I said, taking Nell's hand. "It's how we keep the Magic from dying, isn't it?

"I'll be leaving you then, with this," said Roger Dhu. He took out a knife from his jacket pocket—a primitive thing with a blade of obsidian.

~

What passed between the *Sidhe* woman and me I will not say, for these are the Old Ways, and the People do not talk. I will say this: without Morag's herbs and that inhuman frothing of my spirit,

I'd not be living now. There was blood. A lot of it. A river of it, and it soaked into the shingle and the sand. It soaked in deep to sustain the mortal world, and I rose transformed. I now have the rippling marks of Roger Dhu's knife on my body to prove I am a Selkie.

And my son shall be one as well.

Nell walked with me afterward up the hill to Mears M'Og. If I could write a song about the two sides of magic, the dark and the light, the terrible and the wonderful, that would be Nell.

She'd donned the glamor she wears for the world again. She looked the way she does most days at the Selkie's Treasure: Red-Eye Nell with the scarred face and the bent body, clothed in a drab shirt and dungarees. Even like this, wearing the glamor of ugliness to throw off the tourists, she was still beautiful to me, she and the new life I'd put in her.

"So will you be taking that picture of me now, Ozzy, so you can collect the money from Grannie P's will?"

"You'd let me take your picture?" I said.

"No catch." She faced me and stood with the boiling sea behind her.

I lined up my shot and gasped.

There was nothing in front of me, but the rugged Irish coastline and a bunch of seals. Then I pointed my camera downward and took the picture.

Sweet Ginny Whiskers sat there licking her paws, a witch's smile upon her.

"It's a cat—you're a cat. Oh, Lir!" I put my camera down and there was Nell once more.

She laughed with me. "Aye. Silly you. You could have seen the Fey at any point this week. Your Grannie P. told you true, Ozzy, the Fey are all around us, but it's good to be wary of letting folks take our picture. It might be better maybe to keep that ugly mug of yours and a bit of a crust to keep folks distant. Do you still want to keep that picture of me, now you know what I am?"

I shrugged like a doofus and deleted the picture. "It's only money." I said.

"Oh, and sure it is, so let's get it for you," Nell said with enthusiasm. I want you to have your Gran's money, but I'm not the Fey you want. Take up that silly contraption and take a selfie, my dove."

"But I don't look magic, Nell, not to anybody without the Sight."

She kissed me softly right on my snoz. "You are a love, me darling, and you thought ye were magic before? What have I already been telling you? Does that bloody matter? You're a Son of Lir. Your dead Grannie will know. She had the Sight. Truth will know, and for all the rest you can photoshop something in that looks convincing for the lawyers can't you? Find a picture of a leprechaun somewhere and photoshop that in. Everybody thinks they know what a leprechaun looks like, but *whatever* you do, don't use our village as your background—use the Hill at Tara or something. We don't want tourists here."

"What do leprechauns really look like, Nell?" I asked her, grinning.

"Anything they want to," she said.

I laughed. "As Lir's my witness, Nell, you're a delight."

So. Did I use the money to get a nose job? No. It's a good nose, a useful nose, a wonderful glamor of a nose. I'm used to the silly old thing. It's become my trade mark. I called my company *The Nose*, and I put it on my business card.

I used Granny's pots of gold to buy us a house on Vancouver Island with a rocky beach and a good place to swim, and I turned my photography business into a successful enterprise. We call our house the Selkie's Treasure in honor of the place where I had my beginning.

James, bless his own dear soul, has accepted what happened to me like Jack accepted the beanstalk. He completes me as no one else ever has. I swear he's more of a Selkie at heart than I am. He and I have gone back to the Selkie's Treasure once or twice, and he's met Nell and Roger Dhu and Morag all the locals at the Selkie's Treasure. They may not like the common run of guests, but Morag always has a place for us.

Little Sheamus is more his mother's child than mine. It's fair, I guess. There's always a cost to magic, isn't there? To know my son is happy means more to me than having him close. I think of him every day when I look at that photo of him on the lap of Roger Dhu. It sits on our bedside dresser, next to photo of James and me pretending to hold hands with a pixie on an Irish billboard. Both photos are in scrolly silver frames, and the dresser's a mid-century modern affair that belonged to Grannie P.

By day, I am James's, and most nights we're content to walk together hand in hand under the stars. But then there are those full moon nights when my magic grows strong within me—nights when I slide out of my human form and into another element deeper than time and passion. My kindred come to our beach and they welcome me as one of them. I consort with water horses and *sisiutl*. I go beyond countries—beyond the ken of an earthly sun and moon. The children of the *Sidhe* swim Canadian tides, they remember the songs of a distant shore, perhaps the Hill at Tara, or perhaps the coast of Tierra del Fuego. What difference is there between a few leagues of sea for a People who can cross through the thin spaces of the world?

I pray to two Gods now. To Yahweh, that my James might live as long as any human may. But most of all, I pray to Lir that when my James is gone and I must stay, that the sea will take me down to its heart.

Then I will swim forever, beyond the Sun, beyond the Moon, deep and abiding and into the froth of Power.

ABOUT THE AUTHOR

Brenda Carre writes long and short fiction with a dark, mythic twist. Her short fiction has appeared in the Magazine of Fantasy and Science Fiction, and Fiction River, to mention a few. Her indomitable character 'Gret' was the cover story in Pulp Literature Magazine's issue 15. She is currently working on a big book mythic/epic fantasy series she calls: 'Lara Croft meets a Wizard-of-Earthsea in the Pacific Northwest'. She also writes spicy romance under the name Tess Cornwall. Brenda is a visual artist and educator, and teaches a workshop on mapping through story.

Find out more about Brenda at:
brendacarre.com

[f] facebook.com/carrtell

[twitter] twitter.com/brenda_carre

[g] goodreads.com/Brenda_Carre

[BB] bookbub.com/authors/brenda-carre

BLOOD AND WATER

ALETHEA KONTIS

L ove.

Love is the reason for many a wonderful and horrible thing.

Love was the reason I lived, there in the Deep, in the warm embrace of the ocean where Mother Earth's loins spread and gave birth to the world. Her soul was my soul.

Love is the reason she came to me in the darkness, that brave sea maiden. I remember the taste of her bravery, the euphoric sweetness of her fear. It came to me on wisps of current past the scattered glows of the predators.

The other predators.

Her chest contracted and I felt the sound waves cross the water, heard them with an organ so long unused I had thought it dead.

Help me, she said. *I love him.*

The white stalks of the bloodworms curled about her tail. We had a common purpose, the worms and I. We were both barnacles seeking the same fix, clinging desperately to the soul of the world. Their crimson tips brushed her stomach, her breasts. They could feel it in her, feel her soul in the blood that coursed through her veins. I felt it too. I yearned for it. A quiet memory waved in the tide.

Patience.

My answer was slow, deliberate. *How much do you love him, little anemone?*

More than life itself, she answered.

She had said the words.

I had not asked her to bring the memories, the pain. There is no time in the Deep, only darkness. I could but guess at how much had passed since those words had been uttered this far down. Until that moment, I had never been sure if the magic would come to me. Those words were the catalyst, the spark that lit the flame.

Flame. Another ancient memory.

The empty vessel that was my body emptied even further. I held my hands out to her breast, and there was light.

I resisted the urge to shut my inner eyelids to it and reveled in the light's painful beauty. It shone beneath her flawless skin like a small sun, bringing me colors...perceptions I had never dared hope to experience again. Slivers of illumination escaped through her gills and glittered down the abalone-lustered scales of her fins. Her hair blossomed in a golden cloud around her perfect face. And her eyes...her eyes were the blue of a sky I had not seen for a very, very long time.

She tilted her head back in surrender and the ball of light floated out of her and into my fingers, thin, white and red-tipped, much as the worms themselves. I cupped her brilliant soul in my palms and felt its power gush through me. So long. So long I had waited for this escape. I had stopped wondering what answer I would give if I should ever hear the words again, ever summon the magic. When the vessel was full, when my dead heart beat again, would I remember? Would I feel remorse? Would I have the strength of will to save her, to turn her away?

You will see him, I told her.

She smiled at me over the pure flame of her soul.

I was a coward.

I pressed her soul into my breast. The moment the light filled me I became her. I could see my body through her eyes – translucent white skin marred by jagged gills, blood red hair tossed up by the smoky vents and tangling about the worms, black eyes wide, lips parted in ecstasy.

I could see him in the back of her mind, the object of her affection. He was tall and angular, with sealskin hair. There had been a storm and a wreck, and she had saved him. She had dragged him onto a beach and fallen in love with him as she waited for him to open his eyes. She had run her fingers through his hair, touched his face, traced the lines of the crest upon his clothes. He was handsome and different and beautiful. When he awoke, he took her hand in his and smiled with all his heart. And when he kissed her, she knew she would never be able to live a life without him in it.

In that small moment, as the glow of her soul dimmed into me, she told herself it was worth it.

Once the transformation began, the pain pushed all other thoughts out of her head. Water left her as suddenly as her soul had left her, her gills closing up after it. The pressure that filled her chest made her eyes want to pop out. She clamped her mouth shut, instinct telling her that she could no longer breathe her native water. She beat furiously with her tail, fleeing for the surface.

Halfway there, the other pain began. It started at the ends of her fin and spread upwards, like bathing in an oyster garden. The sharpness bit into her, skinning her, slicing her to her very core. Paralyzed, she let her momentum and the pressure in her chest pull her closer to the sky. Part of her hoped she could trust the magic enough to get her there. Part of her didn't care. It wanted to die, and knew it could not.

That price had already been paid.

Her head burst above the waves and she opened her mouth, letting the rest of the water in her escape. Her first full breath of the insubstantial air was like a lungful of jellyfish. She coughed, her upper half now as much in agony as her lower half, not wanting to take that next breath and knowing that she had to.

She lay there on the undulating bed that was once her home and let it heal her. She stared up at the sky until it didn't hurt so much to breathe, until her eyes adjusted, until rough hands plucked her out of the sea.

She was dragged across the deck of a ship much like the one from which she had rescued her lover, right before it had been crushed between the rocks and the sea. The man who had pulled her up clasped her tightly to him. He was covered in hair, more hair than she had ever seen in her life, and in the strangest places. It did not reach the top of his head, but spread down his face and neck and onto his chest. Perhaps it liked this upper world as little as she did and sought a safer, darker haven beneath his clothes. She reached out a hand to touch it, and he spoke to her. The sounds were too high, too light, too short, too loud. She did not understand them. His breath smelled of sardines. She ran a finger through the hair on his face, and he dropped her.

Misery shot through her and she collapsed on the deck. Her hair spilled around her...and her legs. She stared at her new skin. It looked so calm and innocent, but every nerve screamed beneath it.

Another man stood before her now, wearing more clothes than the hairy man and shiny things on his ears and around his neck. His bellow was deeper than the first man's but still as coarse and profane, and still foreign to her. He crouched down before her and brushed her hair back from her face. He cooed at her. She touched the bright thing around his neck that twinkled the sun at her, and he grinned. His teeth were flat. She wasn't threatened. Braver now, she pulled at the necklace. He let her slide it over his head and put it around her own neck.

He picked her up and carried her to a place that hid her from the sky and set her somewhere softer than the deck. She liked this place and this man who now worshipped her. He had given her a gift, and now he would take care of her. If only there was a way she could tell him why she was there. She was sure he would help her. Perhaps he could see into her heart and just know.

The man removed his shirt, and she relaxed even more. He wanted to put her at ease. By looking like her, he would make her feel like she belonged. He took off the rest of his clothes and came up beside her. He patted her head, ran his hands down her hair. He touched her breasts, her belly and her legs. Still sensitive, she brushed his hand away. He put it back. She tried to push it away again, but he was stronger. She frowned. He smiled all those flat teeth at her once more. She wondered if she might have been mistaken. He moaned, parted her knees and entered her.

The misery she had felt before was nothing compared to this anguish. She inhaled the excruciating air and screamed a hoarse cry. She clawed at him, pushed at his weight on top of her, but she could not move him. Agony ripped her body apart again. A tingling sensation washed over her and the light in her eyes began to dim. Somewhere in that darkness, through the pain, she could feel his heartbeat. The emptiness in her cried out. He had something she needed.

She reached up, pulled him to her, and sunk her pointed teeth deep into the skin of his neck. She drank him down, consuming his soul, filling the barren places inside her. He collapsed on top of her and still she drank, until there was nothing left.

The door burst open and the hairy man entered. He pulled the naked man off of her. He could tell what the man had done from the blood between her legs. He could tell what she had done from the blood she now licked from her lips.

"Siren," he whispered.

She gasped. In her brain there was an avalanche.

Words flooded her, images and thoughts, smells and sounds. Knowledge. She cried out again and slapped her palms to her head. She had taken the man's soul, and his life right along with it. She watched as the shafts of her golden hair turned deep red, filled with the captain's blood.

The first mate had named her. He knew what she was. She was death, the shark, the thing to be afraid of. She lured men to their graves with her beauty.

In one swift motion he pulled the knife from his belt. She did not flinch as he approached her. There was nothing left to fear.

The knife swept down and split the captain's throat open, hiding the teethmarks in the cut. He stared deep into her eyes as he pulled a large ruby ring off the dead man's finger and put it on his own. The knife, streaked with what little crimson was left in the captain's body, he brandished at the crowd of men gathered at the door.

"Eddie Lawless, what's goin' on?" the man in front asked. The men behind him whispered low, words like "magic" and "evil" and "witch" catching in her ears.

"It's Lawson, Cooky," the hairy man responded. "Cap'n Lawson. An' don't ye forget it."

"Yessir," the men mumbled. "Yessir, Cap'n."

"Leave me," Lawson ordered.

"But sir, what about Cap'n—"

"I am the cap'n," he told them. "Ye can collect the carcass later. Leave me now." He slammed the door in their faces.

The mattress shifted under his weight as he sat down across from

181

her. She did not want to look at him, concentrating instead on the ends of her new hair and the line across the dead man's throat.

Lawson shoved the body onto the floor. "Siren."

She looked up.

"So. Ye can understand me then."

She nodded once.

"Good." He pulled the sheet down and wiped his knife blade with it. "Understand this. I know what ye are, what ye need and what ye do. If ye do exactly as I tell ye, I won't kill ye."

If she had known how to laugh, she would have. It was unsettling. She knew what laughter was, what caused it and why someone did it, but she didn't have the slightest idea of how to make her body perform such a feat. It was the same with the words – she could understand them, but she couldn't get her tongue around them and speak back. She would have laughed at the thought of this man killing her, for she would have welcomed death. But she there was one task she meant to accomplish before that happened. She had to find her lover.

She nodded her head once more.

"Excellent." He left the bed and went to open a trunk on the other side of the room. He rummaged through it for a moment, and then tossed a bundle of burgundy material into her lap. She stared at it, marveling in the slight difference between it and the color of her hair. She reached out and stroked its softness, drawing patterns on it with her finger.

His chuckle brought her out of her state. "Ye 'ave no idea what to do with it, do ye?" He took her by the hand and gently eased her off the bed. "Come on, stand up."

She placed one foot flat on the floor, then the other. Then she pushed up with all her might, locking her knees and propelling herself forward into him.

He caught her before she hit the floor. "Woah. Easy. Ye 'ave to get yer sea legs." He helped her balance enough to stay upright. Surprisingly her feet held her without too much trouble.

"Now," he said, grabbing the bundle off the bed, "ye're lucky I 'ave a daughter an' I'm used to doin' this." He spun her around so that she faced the wall. "Six years ago I only knew 'ow to <u>undress</u> a woman." He pulled her hands up above her head and eased the material down around her. He moved her hair to one side so he could button up the back.

"There." He turned her back around. "It's a bit large an' it'll probably be a tad warm. But it'll keep the sun off ye, and the...my...men away from temptation." He looked her up and down. "Not that they'll need much warnin', mind. But ye get enough rum into a man...well... stranger things 'ave 'appened."

He looked down at the former captain's body. "Ye won't need to... eat...again for a while then?"

She shook her head.

"Right. Best if ye only do it when I tell ye." He shoved the knife back into his belt.

Her eyes widened.

"Oh, don't worry," he chuckled. "Ye're aboard a pirate ship, darlin'. If there's one thing we've always got more than our share of, it's blood."

He wasn't wrong.

They encountered a ship three days later. There were blasts from cannons spread amidst the cries of men. She lost her footing when the ship lurched sideways, hooks pulling the losing ship close enough so that men might cross over. She peeked through the windows at the smoke of the guns, swords clashing as the blood flew.

Lawson came back to her room when the battle had died down. He opened the door and threw a man down at her feet. His clothes were ripped and his face was a bloody mess. Gray eyes looked up at her from the red-stained face and filled with terror.

"No...oh, God, no" were the last words he spoke.

His fear was intoxicating.

She closed her eyes when she was finished and let the magic wash over her. It wasn't just the blood she craved; it was everything. She needed the senses and the feelings, the emotions and the pain, the good and the bad. She needed his life, his soul.

Rejuvenated, she tossed her hair back and peered up at Lawson. He cupped her cheek and wiped a spot of blood away from the corner of her mouth. "There's my girl." He threw open the door and kicked the man's body over the threshold. "There's yer cap'n, men," he bellowed. "Seems 'e got into a spot of trouble. Any of ye want the same trouble, just cross me."

Crews were mixed and booty was swapped, and then they were off in search of the next victim.

The second ship they burned. It was spectacular. She ran to the railing and held her hand out to the beautiful, live thing that danced on the sea as it consumed sails and timbers and bodies alike. She had seen candles and lamps, but this was a beast, wild and hot and bright as the sun. Hands grabbed at her clothes to keep her from falling over the rail, and they pinned her down when the magazine finally exploded, taking the rest of that ship's crew with it.

On the third one, she found him.

The battle this time was a long one, and by the time Lawson brought her the captain of the other ship, he was half dead. She drank him anyway. And somewhere in the memories of this man was the someone she had been looking for.

She gasped when his face came to her. She drew back, her teeth disengaging from her meal, blood running down her chin and staining her dress. This man knew her lover. Not well, but he knew him. She tried to make sense of the jumble of images that flowed through her, but nothing connected. She searched his body for a sign, a hint, something. She found it on the smallest ring he wore, a gold band stamped with the crest she had traced over and over on the beach that day.

When Lawson returned, she pointed at herself and then held up the ring. He smiled and patted her on the head. "O'course ye can keep it, darlin'. Ye can 'ave all the trinkets yer little 'eart desires."

He didn't understand. How would she make him understand? She slid the ring over her red-tipped thumb. She would save it until she thought of a way.

The fourth ship was a long time coming.

She spent most of that time at the bow of the ship. The crew didn't grumble much about having a woman on deck. Most of them apparently didn't consider her a woman. Lawson made it plain that he enjoyed having her there. Word was getting around about Bloody Captain Lawson and the Siren. They struck fear in the hearts of men and made quite a profit as a result, so if anyone had disagreements, no one made mention of them.

Lawson called her their figurehead. It was an apt description, based on what she had seen on the prows of other ships. She would lean against the rail, arms spread, red hair trailing behind her in the breeze. She liked letting the wind slip through her fingers. It reminded her of home. The currents of air were not that different from the currents of water. Men did not have the freedom of movement that her kind enjoyed, but the principles were the same. They walked among it, breathed it in, let it give them life. It brought sounds and smells to them. They did not see it or think to taste it, but it was always there in them, touching them, surrounding them.

She stood there, day after day, until the salt encrusted her lips and her hair was a burnished orange. What little red appeared in the tips of her fingers had been burned there by the sun. The men avoided her and prayed hard for another ship. They tread lightly around the captain. No one wanted to be the Siren's next meal.

Lawson finally bade her return to the stateroom, and she was too weak to disobey. The table was covered in maps and charts. She walked past them on the way to the bed and glanced down at the area Lawson was plotting. A symbol caught her eye, and she jumped back. She waved at Lawson. She pointed to herself, and to the ring around her thumb. She pointed to herself, and to the same symbol down on the map.

"There?" he asked her. "Ye want to go there? Why?"

She could not answer, so she just kept pointing to herself and the map.

"That's 'ome," Lawson told her. "Where Molly is. I promised never to go back until I 'ad a ship full o'riches. She deserves no less." He shook his head. "No, darlin', we can't go there. Not yet."

Frustrated, she closed her eyes. Disjointed thought flashes skipped through her mind. She tried to remember the man with the ring, tried to bring his soul to the surface. But it had been so long, and she was so weary...and there was a port...

Her eyes snapped open. She moved her finger on the map to an island just off the coast of the country bearing her lover's symbol. She pointed at Lawson, and then stamped her finger back down on the map.

"There? What's there?"

She threw her hands up in exasperation and scanned the room. She held up the medallion of her necklace to him.

"Gold?"

She nodded and kept searching. She found his knife on the table, picked it up, and then shook her head.

"Swords?"

She shook her head again.

"This?" He removed the pistol from his belt and held it out to her. She nodded emphatically.

He cocked his head and grinned. "Siren, if ye're right about this, I'll take ye anywhere in the world." He strode out of the room and hollered to his first mate. "Hard to port, matey!"

"Cap'n?" the first mate asked.

Lawson hooked his thumbs in his belt. "We're goin' 'ome."

The greatest tale of Bloody Lawson and the Siren is the Massacre at Windy Port. Legend has it that their ship, cloaked in dark magic, slipped by the watchmen unnoticed. Once docked the crew cut a gruesome swath through the town, led by Lawson and his Sea Witch. Lawson brandished a rapier in one hand, a pistol in the other. The Siren, dressed in fine burgundy velvet, marched through town before him, seducing men to their grisly deaths. Her eyes were as black and cold as a shark's, her hair a mass of ebony fire waving about her. They left none living in their wake, took what they wanted and stole back into the night as invisibly as they had arrived.

Like most legends, not a word of it was true.

They sailed into Windy Port under a royal flag they had appropriated from a previous hunt. They docked without incident, the crew scattering to the winds to pick up intelligence, hefty bar tabs, and the occasional whore.

The moment Lawson set her down on the dock, she fell. The hollowness inside her throbbed. She could not believe anything could have been so still as land. There was no life in it. The air was not strong enough to keep it fluid. It was rock. Still, empty, dead rock. She was but a shell, a humble reconstruction of the world upon which man walked every single day. How did they survive without a connection? She hugged her stomach, doubled up and gagged, only emptiness escaping her dry heaves.

"You okay, honey? Take it easy. It'll pass soon."

The words spoken to her had a cadence she had never heard before, and it surprised her so much she didn't understand them at first. The hands that pulled her hair back away from her face were small and delicate. The woman had on a black dress. Her hair was pinned up on her head and decorated with shiny black beads. She smelled...soft and nice. And she was gentle when she accepted the Siren's embrace.

"It's all right," the woman said as she patted her back. "Everything's going to be all right."

She didn't scream when pointed teeth pierced her flesh.

Everything was going to be just fine.

Suddenly conscious of her appearance, she pulled her dress over her head and began tearing at the woman's clothes. Lawson knelt beside her and motioned for his men to surround them so as not to draw attention to the scene. "Discovered vanity, 'ave we?" he chuckled as he helped her undress the woman's corpse. Once she had changed, the men weighted the body and rolled it into the ocean.

Lawson helped her stand. He tossed a dark cloak about her and covered her hair with its hood. She was glad he didn't force her to wear shoes – it was hard enough enduring this much separation from the water. She didn't know how much more she would be able to bear.

The inn they went to almost pushed her sanity over the edge from sensory overload. The room was filled with people of all shapes and sizes. There were smells from the food, the ale, the dogs in front of the fire, the fire itself. Men and women talked and shouted and joked and laughed. A scrawny youth crawled up beside the dogs at one point and sang for his supper. She was mesmerized. These were so different from the songs of the water, the flash of fish in the currents, the mating of whales in the deep. Some were slow and soft; some were fast and loud. And when the rest of the room joined in, she clapped her hands in merriment.

The crew dropped in one by one to report and consult with Lawson throughout the night. There were nods and low whispers. She watched as papers were signed and money changed hands. Thus Bloody Lawson conquered Windy Port, without ever leaving his seat. When the festivities ended he paid for his meal, tipped heavily and left, dragging his cloaked companion behind him. It was the sailors and merchants that returned to their vessels the next morning and found them empty or missing who took their anger out on the citizens of the port. Lawson and his crew were miles away before the massacre even began. Bloody Lawson and the Siren were never heard from again.

Several months later, Edward Malcolm opened a waterfront inn in the capitol city named The Sea Lass. He purchased the house next door as well. It had a master suite and a nursery and a very large kitchen that could be used to supplement the inn's in case of overflow. One of the rooms in the house had a door with seven locks. They were installed the day before Molly's return from school.

Molly's homecoming was a grand event. Lawson, now called Edward, had covered every flat surface in the house with sweets and cakes and flowers. He had hired a seamstress to take Molly's measurements for a whole new wardrobe, the only one that didn't seem overly preoccupied with the Prince's upcoming wedding. Paper-wrapped packages of all sizes littered the largest of the tables. A doll and a rose waited on the chair for his princess.

The Siren sat on a stool in the corner, cut off from the sun and the earth, the water and wind. She waned as she watched the miniature cherub-faced human run through the door to embrace her father. Her mop of dark brown curls disappeared in her father's coat as she hugged him, right before he picked her up and twirled her around the room. There was something about this strange apparition, this child, and she could not decide what it was.

Molly giggled as she snuggled her doll. She reached out to the rose.

"Be careful," her father warned her.

"Yes, Papa," she said smartly. "I will watch for the pricklies and the thornies." She buried her nose in the crimson petals and took a deep breath. When she opened her eyes, Molly saw the Siren there in the shadows.

The child set her doll down carefully on the table. "Who is she, Papa?" Molly whispered.

"She's..." he started, twisting the ruby ring on his finger. "I saved 'er," he said finally.

"She's so pretty," Molly said. The child came around the table and held the flower out to her. "She's just like the flower."

"Yes," he said. "Just like the rose. She's got pricklies and thornies too, Molly. You 'ave to be careful around her."

Molly took another step forward, still offering the flower. The Siren took it and grinned, being careful not to show any teeth. Before her father could stop her, Molly launched herself into the Siren's arms.

The child's skin was softer than the woman's at the pier. Her hair smelled of sugar and...something...indescribable. She took another deep breath. There was life within this little bundle, so much life she all but vibrated with it.

Edward wrenched her away. He took her by the arms and held her tightly. He sank down to his knees, so that he could address Molly eye to eye.

"Don't ye *ever* go near 'er again," he said sternly.

"But Papa, she's so sad," Molly cried.

"She is dangerous," he admonished. "Just be a good girl and do as yer papa says."

Molly bowed her head. "Yes, Papa."

"We'll even call 'er Rose, okay? So ye don't forget." Edward chucked her under the chin. "Now, what are ye gonna name yer dolly?"

Molly's eyes brightened again and she rushed back to the table for her doll.

The Siren sunk her nose into the flower and inhaled sugar and sweetness while she watched the child open the rest of her gifts.

That night as he escorted her to her room, he said to her, "Ye touch my daughter, I'll kill ye." Then he shut the door and turned seven keys in seven locks.

Each day after that was much the same. She was not allowed to leave the house, and the third time Edward caught her staring out the windows, he forbade her that too. Each night he would take her to her room and give her the same warning about his daughter before turning the seven keys of her prison.

She would sit on her bed and stare into the darkness, wondering what she had done wrong. Had she not given him the riches he desired? Had she not paved the way for him to return home to be with his daughter? She had made him happy – why should she suffer as a result?

She edged closer to the window and watched the moon move across the sky. Somewhere not far, the reflection of that same light was skipping across the waves. Somehow, she would escape from this prison. Someday, seven locks would not hold her.

Every few nights he would bring her someone, long after Molly was asleep. He would wake before the dawn and take the body away. She learned all she could from these poor souls, but it was never enough. They were whores or cheats or liars, people whose absence in some way benefited Edward and whose minds were such a jumble of unreliable information she could never discern anything that could help her.

She waited. She waited while he scolded her every night. She waited as he shoved each of the seven bolts home. She waited as he fed her, sparingly, enough to survive. She waited for him to get comfortable, to slip, to let something get by him.

Like the snitch.

Edward bent over and the unconscious man fell from over his shoulder and onto the bed before her. "Small, but 'e's all ye'll get, understand?"

She opened her mouth, throat contracting. "Yeth," she managed to say.

"Good. 'Cause if ye touch my daughter, I'll kill ye." He shut the door. She counted slowly to seven before pulling the man into her lap and feasting.

Her heart pounded with a foreign pulse.

He was there.

Her lover.

He was everywhere inside this man's head. He sat at the head of a table, talking sternly to a group of older men dressed in black. He sat in a large chair at the end of a hallway. He rode a horse down the path through the garden and along the beach. He rode in a carriage beside a beautiful, golden-haired maid and people threw flowers in the street before them.

He was the prince.

And he was getting married in a week.

Edward fell ill the next day. He did not come to let her out of her cell. The first two days of isolation weren't bad. The third day, the snitch's body began to smell. The fourth day, she tried to feed off it again and gagged. There had not been much in him to begin with, and whatever was left in him now was gelled and rancid. The fifth day, she began to shake. She pounded on the door and the walls and the window until the skin of her fists shed. The sixth day, she began to scream. It came out of her as a long, keening wail. It echoed her hunger, her desperation, her emptiness. Her voice gave out as the sun rose on the seventh day, his wedding day.

She spent the hours curled up against the door, hoping to hear something. Any sign of movement at all would have been welcome. She played with the ends of her faded hair, teasing them in and out between her toes. The shadows moved, lengthened, and eventually, the sun's light died. Her hopes went right along with it. She placed her palm flat on the door beside her head.

It was warm.

She closed her eyes and could feel the energy radiating from the other side. She could hear small, shallow breaths. She could taste sugar on the air.

Molly.

She knocked two times on the door.

"Rose?" the tiny voice called hesitantly.

She knocked two times again.

"Daddy's sick and he had to go away." Skirts rustled against the floorboards. "I'm lonely. Are you lonely?"

Two knocks.

"Do you want to play with my dolly?"

She spread her fingers against the door. "Yeth," she croaked.

The warmth faded, and there were sounds of a heavy chair being dragged across the floor. One, two, three, for, five, six, seven keys were all slowly turned in their locks. The chair was pushed aside, and the door opened.

Molly flew into her arms, the momentum pushing her back onto the bed in her weakened state. She cradled the frightened child in her arms, felt the porcelain head of her dolly poking into her side. She soaked up the child's energy, willing it into her empty body. She bent her head and smelled the sweetness of her. She nuzzled her nose in the softness of her, like burrowing into the petals of a newly-opened flower.

She shouldn't. She knew she shouldn't, but he had caused her so much pain, and she had nothing left to lose.

Molly screamed and fought, but every bit of her gave the Siren the strength to hold her down, to fill the abyss inside her with this soul of pure innocence. It was so beautiful. The sensations did not wait until she was finished. They exploded into her mind every second. There was fear, yes, sweet fear, but then came sadness and betrayal. There was happiness and laugher, anger and tears, but most importantly, she finally realized the whys. She knew why a person felt joy and why they felt pain. She learned the elation of seeing something for the very first time, and the despair in losing it.

Loss. She knew now what she had been dealing out all this time. There was no way she could have ever known the impact of death without knowing what it was like to live a life. The weight of all the souls she had consumed pressed heavily upon her. She learned consequences. She realized that the things she did affected people other than the person she was killing. She understood that all the pain she had felt before was nothing to the pain these people would feel for the rest of their lives. She felt regret, and love.

Love.

It spread through her. Unconditional love tickled her down to the red tips of her fingers and toes. Love was trust. Love was faith. Love was believing in the impossible. The rainbow of Molly's soul filled her with love until the last drop. She held Molly's limp body in her arms...and she laughed.

She laughed and laughed, her voice echoing through the dark, vacant house. She laughed until she cried, tears flowing unchecked down her cheeks. She cried for Molly, for all of them. She cried for all the things she had done. She cried for herself, for everything she had lost, for nothing.

Or was it nothing?

She had to hurry. She had to leave this place and never come back. She gently laid Molly's body out on the bed and curled her arm around her dolly. She smoothed back the dark curls and kissed her forehead. She covered herself in the black cloak and fled into the night.

She was glad again to be in the air and running over the earth, despite what little support they gave her. She followed her heart and the dim memories of the snitch up to the castle gates.

She strode up to the guards there and threw her hood back. Those that knew of her let her pass. Those that didn't know of her learned.

The myriad halls and stairs and rooms made the castle a giant labyrinth, but she knew where she was going. Up and up and up...to the balcony suites of the Prince's bedchamber. She did not stop until she was at the foot of his bed, staring down at his sleeping body. She wanted to shake him awake, wanted to explain everything to him, wanted to scream her love for him to the rafters.

But she couldn't.

If he awoke now, he would know what she had become. He would see the evil inside of her, the mark of it in her hair and on her skin. She had saved his life, true, but how many others had she taken on her path back to him? With love came regret. She knew what she had to do. She knew that the only thing she had to offer him now was her absence. If she could just touch him one more time...she reached out a hand to him and stopped herself.

No.

It would not stop at a touch, she knew that from what had happened with Molly. She could never be with him, truly be with him, because eventually she would consume him. His soul was not bright enough for her to survive alone outside it, nor was it strong enough to sustain him once she had consumed it. If she stayed beside him, it would mean his death.

She was a monster.

She forced her hand back to herself and placed it over her heart. She hoped that it spoke enough in the silence for him to hear it, to feel how much she loved him. If it had been water and not air between them, she knew he would have felt it.

He stirred and opened his eyes.

She gave herself one moment, one tiny, blessed moment of looking into his eyes before she turned and ran.

She tripped down the stairs and cut her feet on the stones. The cloak caught on something and she unfastened it. She was sure that soon they would come for her. They would hunt her like the beast she was. She tasted the tears that streamed down her face and knew there was only one refuge.

The cold beach sand kissed her feet like a prayer. The salty spray mixed with her tears, chasing them away. The first tiny wave reached up and licked her toes. Waves rumbled in a cadence she had almost forgotten how to translate.

Come, they pulled.

Home, they crashed.

She took small steps forward. The sand slipped out from beneath her if she stayed too long. The force of the waves pushed her backwards in opposition to the call she felt.

Come, they pulled.

She stumbled, and the tide ripped her sideways along the beach. Gasping, she managed to regain her footing and continue walking out to sea. The current grabbed at her clothes, and she tore them off. The tips of her hair mingled with the foam. Flotsam swirled around her waist.

Home, they crashed.

She walked until the undertow took her and dragged her out to sea.

I lost her sometime before that, back when the moon shone off her white skin and blood red hair. But I didn't have to live inside her anymore to know where she was headed.

She would grab the first sharp object she found – maybe a crab's claw or a clam's shell – and rip gills into herself so that the water could flow through her again. The first one might have been straight, but the rest would be ragged and flawed. She would make her way to the Deep, her body drawn to the never-ending call of the soul of the world. She would make a home there among the bloodworms and the warm vents and the other predators.

She would take her love and regret with her. She would heal in the balm of the ocean, away from the complexities of mortal life. She would tell herself that if the day came, if the words were spoken and the magic came to her, she would turn them away. She would not let evil back into the world. The suffering would end with her. She would stew in the self-affliction until it became a dim memory, tucked away in the recesses of her mind like sight and sound, air and fire. Time would fade her lover's face, his name into nothing, and then time itself would melt into darkness. She would ebb and flow and never die.

And when that day did come, ages and ages from now, she would choose the light. She would choose the escape. She would let the evil out one last time just to feel it all again, to live.

As I had.

Strong arms wrapped around me, brushing my satin bedclothes against the small jagged scars on either side of my chest. I leaned back against him, feeling his heartbeat through his chest.

"I just had the strangest dream," he said. I felt his deep voice rumble through the skin of my back. "You came to me while I lay in bed, only your hair was red and your skin was different. You stared at me like you wanted to say something, and then you ran. You looked so...sad."

He turned me around to face him. "The day you saved me was the happiest day of my life. And this day should be the happiest day of yours. Don't be sad."

I smiled and shook my head.

"Good." He kissed me then, long and slow and deep. He hugged me tightly before pulling away. "Come back to bed?"

"Yeth," I whispered, the words still foreign to my tongue. He kissed me once more and left me. I looked out over the moonlit water once more and said my goodbyes before following him, my prince, my soulmate, my love.

Love.

It was the reason I lived.

ABOUT THE AUTHOR

New York Times and *USA Today* bestselling author Alethea Kontis is a princess, a voice actress, and a force of nature. She is responsible for creating the epic fairytale fantasy realm of Arilland, and dabbling in a myriad of other worlds beyond. Her award-winning writing has been published for multiple age groups across all genres. She is the host of "Princess Alethea's Fairy Tale Rants" and Princess Alethea's Traveling Sideshow every year at Dragon Con. Alethea has narrated for ACX, IGMS, Escape Pod, Pseudopod, Cast of Wonders, Shimmer, Apex Magazine and Clarkesworld Magazine, and she contributes regular YA book reviews to NPR.

Alethea's YA fairy tale novel, *Enchanted*, won both the Gelett Burgess Children's Book Award and Garden State Teen Book Award. *Enchanted* was nominated for the Audie Award in 2013 and was selected for World Book Night in 2014. Both *Enchanted* and its sequel, *Hero*, were nominated for the Andre Norton Award. *Tales of Arilland*, a short story collection set in the same fairy tale world, won a second Gelett Burgess Award in 2015. The second book in The Trix Adventures, *Trix and the Faerie Queen*, was a finalist for the Dragon Award in 2016. Alethea was nominated for the Dragon Award again in 2018, for her YA paranormal rom-com *When Tinker Met Bell*. In 2019, the third in her Harmswood Academy trilogy–*Besphinxed*–was nominated for a Scribe Award by the International Association of Media Tie-In Writers.

Princess Alethea was given the honor of speaking about fairy tales at the Library of Congress in 2013. In 2015, she gave a keynote address at the Lewis Carroll Society's Alice150 Conference in New

York City, celebrating the 150th anniversary of Alice's Adventures in Wonderland. She also enjoys speaking at schools and festivals all over the US. (If forced to choose between all these things, she says middle schools are her favorite!)

Born in Burlington, Vermont, Alethea currently lives on the Space Coast of Florida. She makes the best baklava you've ever tasted and sleeps with a teddy bear named Charlie.

Find out more about Alethea at:
patreon.com/princessalethea

facebook.com/AletheaKontis

goodreads.com/AletheaKontis

bookbub.com/authors/alethea-kontis

VERBENA DRAWS FIRST BLOOD

LOUISA SWANN

Verbena Crumb, deadly sorceress and powerful necromancer, drew in a breath of air that scarce qualified as *air* and glared down at the lake that dared shimmer in the early morning sun.

As far as Verbena was concerned, *shimmering* was a state best left 'til later in the day, after night-loving sorceresses had properly processed the beginning of the sun's new cycle. As for the thin air—whatever god had determined that air should be thinner as one climbed had as much sense as the mule beneath her. Climbing was a form of exertion and common logic dictated that the more one exerted oneself, the more air one needed.

If *she* had been present during the making of this world, Verbena would have assured the air was distributed properly.

Or heads would have rolled.

"Is them the ones yer seekin'?"

Verbena turned her glare on the man who had spoken. Though she had grown accustomed to the stench of death and decay through the years—raising the dead tended to dull one's sensitivity to foul odors—Carson Reid, the bootless twit, made her nose wrinkle in disgust.

"Ya see 'em down there?"

For the better part of three days and most of the previous night they had been winding their way along trails barely wide enough for the mules, scrambling over boulders, winding around bushes and trees, struggling up inclines and down abrupt slopes. The lake had remained hidden for what seemed an eternity, surrounded by towering firs and pines as thick as cows were long.

They had spied the enormous lake surrounded by snow-blanketed mountains just as dawn lightened the skies, though the trail maintained a good distance from the water's edge, winding through a seemingly endless supply of oversized trees.

After another rather arduous scramble over rocks and boulders, they'd found themselves on a promontory with the entire lake at their feet—or hooves, if one expected the mules might be impressed.

Verbena studied the vista with a critical eye.

Mer de l'Ouest, the "Sea of the West." Or so some had called it. Though the name was highly inaccurate.

She released the buttons on her canvas overcoat, letting the cool air brush her neck, and thought about a map she had once seen. It had depicted an enormous body of water that began, or so the man with the map had claimed, in this location, spreading both north and east. Others claimed the Sea was further east; some said further north. East or north, one thing was crystal clear—

This wasn't the Sea of the West. It wasn't a sea at all.

No matter its size, the lake was too clear, too *pure*, to qualify as a "sea." The surface was impossibly calm, reflecting both mountains and surreal blue sky as precisely as mirrored glass . . .

Verbena squinted at the calm surface and frowned at an object about a ship's length from shore. What *was* that?

If the object had been closer to shore, she would have discounted it as a rock, but a rock would have to be enormous to show that far out. It would likely be a darker color as well, not the color of dead flesh.

"Let's take a look, shall we?" She flicked her left wrist, triggering the vessel on her bracelet to release a short stream of a water-like substance into her palm. The liquid pooled like quicksilver while maintaining the transparency of water.

Verbena was constantly amazed at how well magic could be melded with science. She had spent most of her life devoted to the practice of necromancy. Since her mentor had succumbed to the torments of time, however, she had discovered that specialization limited her. Although her mentor's voice still haunted her on occasion, insisting she focus only on necromancy, if she wanted to become the most powerful sorceress in the world, she needed to learn to control *everything*.

Wind had been fairly easy to bend to her will. Water, not so much. She'd spent the last year learning various spells and refining her technique, but water continued to prove troublesome. So, she'd had her gadgeteer—a young man eager to put his talents to good use —create a device to aid in her endeavors. It had taken several attempts—the first bracelet leaked so badly it had ruined her favorite gown.

Verbena had been proud of the way she restrained her impulse to burn the gadgeteer to a crisp that day. He'd promised to do better.

And he had.

Hidden beneath the sleeve of her overcoat, a sturdy silver tube stretched from the middle of her forearm to her wrist. The tube was fitted with a bracelet at each end, one around her forearm, the other around her wrist. The bracelet at her wrist was hollow, with an extension that wrapped partway around the base of her thumb.

It had taken a day to get used to the sensation of having something that snug about her wrist, but the adjustment period had been worth the aggravation. She had infused the water contained in the tube with properties that gave it more viscosity.

And now all she needed to do was command it.

With a light touch of power, she coerced the water in her palm into a spinning oval, then rolled her wrist—a skill she'd only just mastered—moving the oval into position between her thumb and forefinger. Carefully, she widened the gap between thumb and finger until the water shimmered, resembling the soapy film a child would blow into a bubble.

With a sense of triumph, Verbena lifted her hand and peered into the shimmering circle, studying it as one would study their own face in mirrored glass.

Verbena didn't see an image of herself, however. The combination of viscous water and power magnified objects at a distance, allowing her to view an object as if it were directly before her. She scanned the lake below in anticipation that slowly turned to burning frustration.

Though it only felt like a moment had passed between triggering the water to flow into her palm and bringing the televiewer—a term coined by her gadgeteer—into focus, the object she'd wanted to view was gone.

"Yer lookin' in the wrong direction," her guide said. "Take a gander at that strip a sand down yonder."

Verbena's mood darkened even further at the tone of the man's voice. Carson sounded like he was explaining something to a child. 'Twould serve justice well if she turned the man into a bespectacled mule or an eagle without wings—

"Just comin' outta them pines, see?"

—or a rotten turnip. Did the man think her blind?

Verbena bit back a snarl, cleared her mind of bespectacled mules and rotting turnips, and shifted the televiewer from the lake to the "strip a sand" indicated by her guide.

At first, she believed the twit mistaken; there were no people in sight. Perhaps he needed new eyes. The fingers of her right hand twitched. She could help with that—

Movement at the base of a pine bordering the sandy spit caught her attention. She tightened her thumb and forefinger, focusing the televiewer on the man who had just stepped clear of the trees.

Verbena's mood shifted from sour apples to near jubilant in the span of a heartbeat.

Xander.

The mad sorcerer.

A thrill of anticipation tightened her skin and Verbena grinned. Time to begin settling old scores.

"Them. The. Ones?" the guide asked again, carefully enunciating every word.

Verbena nodded sharply. "Yes—"

She froze at the sight of a wolf-sized dog that seemed to materialize right before her. The televiewer made the beast seem so big, so threatening, so *near*, she almost dropped the liquid in her hand and leapt backward. Dropping her hand without returning the water to its container would have been a waste she could ill afford. It took time, magic, and skill to make the form of water needed for the televiewer to work.

Through sheer force of will, Verbena kept her focus on the liquid between her fingers, gradually turning away from the shaggy beast to scan deeper into the trees. She took a deep breath and stretched thumb and forefinger further apart, widening the image.

Three men, dressed in the flannel shirts favored by miners

around the world, strode out onto the sand, pausing beside the sorcerer as a wagon rolled out of the woods behind them. She didn't recognize the men, even when one of them removed his hat. Verbena closed the space between thumb and forefinger, tightening her focus, and tried to read the man's lips as he spoke—

"What in tarnation is that?" Carson sounded rather incredulous.

With a silent curse Verbena let her focus fade, using her power to carefully return the special water first to her palm, then back into the container. When the liquid was safe in its tube, she returned her attention to the group—and immediately saw what had Carson so excited.

Verbena couldn't hide a smile. Of course, he'd be incredulous. A creature made of clay and stones bound together by magic should not exist according to those unfamiliar with magic. And the golem pulling the wagon was indeed made of clay and stone.

Twice as tall as a man and as broad as a water barrel, the golem leaned into the broad leather straps bound about its chest and shoulders, dragging the wagon to the water's edge. Verbena's vantage point revealed there was nothing of consequence concealed within the wagon's high walls, though the way the wagon rattled—loud enough to hear even at this distance—had already told her the wagon was mostly empty.

Somewhere in the distance an eagle cried, the sound surreal in the crisp early morning air.

All so...natural, so...*primitive*.

As if on cue, the air around her exploded with sound and activity: birds twittering and tweeting incessantly, bushy-tailed gray squirrels squabbling amongst themselves, racing up trunks and leaping through the branches, not seeming to care if the tree bore the sharp needles of vanilla-scented pine or the soft leaves of whispering aspen —or that their *activities* rained bark and needles alike onto the unsuspecting humans standing below.

It would be a simple matter to cleanse the trees of their annoying inhabitants, Verbena mused, plucking a chunk of bark from her hair. But she hadn't come to annihilate the local wildlife.

She had come to thwart her old nemesis.

The golem represented an obstacle she hadn't anticipated. Not that she couldn't handle the magical creature, but the golem's very presence meant Xander's power had increased.

She needed to put Xander to the test somehow. See just how strong he'd become.

Time to rethink her strategy.

Verbena turned to her guide, her mind busy sorting through options and discarding them almost as rapidly as they popped into being. "Be a dear and fetch me a cup of tea."

If she didn't get the dust from her nose and the dry from her throat, she was liable to go full-blown lunatic. While the very act of lunacy provided both entertainment and stress release, she couldn't afford the distraction. Not until she had—

"Ya know we ain't got tea," Carson said with exaggerated patience. He pulled off his hat and scratched his head. "Got some beans in the saddle bags. Roasted 'em misself. Ya want, we kin sit for a spell and I'll brew ya a pot a coffee jus' like I done the past few days."

Verbena snarled. She despised this so-called New World where the inhabitants—colonials and natives alike—were all savages. She longed for the anonymity of London, a place she had not graced with her presence for a number of years, not realizing until embarking on her latest *adventure* how much she missed the cobbled streets and alleys and, most especially, the tea.

No one west of New York knew how to brew a proper cup of tea, and she abhorred the black dreck the colonials called "coffee."

Carson, the twit, could choke on his blasted beans, roasted or not.

The notion pleased her so intensely Verbena raised a hand, intending to implement the vision. Dark magic burned within her, burying any sign of patience—or humanity. The magic strained like a leashed dog yearning to be set free—

Do not waste yourself on such a pitiful creature.

The words hissed through her mind in a tortuous whisper, accompanied by a surge of power that seemed at odds with the command. Startled, Verbena barely managed to throttle the urge to strike the man dead, and stabbed Carson with her gaze instead, coiling the power within her like a venomous snake.

She pressed a finger to the tiny scar in the center of her brow, using the pressure to ease the pain accompanying the words. Where had that voice come from? It wasn't her mentor's voice or an "outside" voice, from the mind of another creature. She had the distinct feeling she should recognize the source, but the more she tried to bring the memory into focus, the quicker it slipped away. She finally put the matter aside, dropping her hand to her side. Both pain and voice had vanished.

For now.

She studied Carson's face.

The twit had no concept just how close he'd come to being changed into something more suitable to his demeanor.

Why did the man always put her in such a foul mood?

She'd been too long without tea, she decided. That mud he called *coffee* always turned her stomach sour.

Profound silence surrounded them as if the birds and squirrels—even the wind—had sensed her abrupt change in mood.

"Feels like we gotta cat on the prowl," Carson said, his voice filled with ominous warning.

Verbena glared at him. "Whatever do you mean? We are too far out in the wilderness to encounter someone's cat."

Any cat worth his mice would be back on the docks in San Francisco hunting rats, not out here in the absolute middle of nowhere.

Carson held up his hand. "Ya feel that? Like something's 'bout ta happen? That's the same feelin' I get when there's a big cat close by. Them things is cold-blooded as they come. Eat they own grandmas if'n they could."

She glared at him, completely befuddled.

"You know. A mountain lion. A really big cat."

She'd heard of lions, but they had all been in Africa with zebras and giraffes. Mountains and lions didn't go together, so what was the fool on about?

Merely an excuse, she decided. The man simply wasn't prepared.

A voice at the back of her mind grumbled that there was no excuse for not being able to prepare a proper cup of tea.

The mule beneath her shifted restlessly, reminding Verbena just how sick and tired of riding she was. A week-long mule trip—riding sidesaddle the whole way—had been a poor choice. A carriage would have been much more to her taste.

But carriages were not an option. Though 1850 was just around the corner, carriages had not yet made their debut in the colonial wilderness. The west was a region still mired in the primitive throws of fresh discovery—both of fertile lands and glittering gold.

A pox on this entire colonial wilderness, she decided. If the inhabitants of this strange land couldn't prepare a proper cup of tea, they simply should not exist.

"No lion in his or her right mind would traipse through an area infested solely with birds and squirrels," Verbena said. She forced herself to relax and let her power fade.

A moment later, the birds started their infernal racket back up.

"You see?" She waved a hand vaguely in the air at the birds. "No. Lion."

After taking a long look around, Carson nodded. "Looks like yer right, Miz Verbena. I'll get the coffee brewin'."

It took all of Verbena's willpower not to smite the man from his mule.

"We're not stopping that long," she said. "Water will suffice for now."

She gritted her teeth and calmed the power within her. No need to alert the sorcerer of her presence. She had taken a risk using the televiewer to see Xander and his crew up close. Any use of magic not only left residue behind, such use was detectible to anyone with the gift. Though she'd used scarcely enough power to feel its drain on her energy, it was likely that the sorcerer knew someone with magical abilities was close.

He wouldn't know it was Verbena, however. She'd keep herself hidden from Xander until she was ready to make her move.

By then, it would be too late.

Carson had already dismounted and was unhooking the canteens from his saddle.

Leaving Verbena to dismount on her own. She ground her teeth, disengaged her leg from the high pommel, and allowed herself to slide to the ground.

Fortunately, she had become adept at both mounting (using nearby boulders and logs) and dismounting by herself. It was immensely impolite for Carson not to offer assistance, but she'd decided on their first day of travel that she'd have gone through a full dozen stable boys if she'd meted out punishment to every soul who'd demonstrated a lack of manners since she'd departed San Francisco.

And he'd been the only man willing to lead her to this magnificent mountain lake by the shortest means possible—via old Indian trails—cutting at least a day off her journey.

A day that meant the difference between success.

And failure.

Verbena clung to the saddle, assuring her feet and legs were awake and functioning properly before releasing the leathers. At her insistence, they had left camp after the night was half gone and the moon had risen high enough to light the way, descending precarious slopes along boulder-strewn trails in order to reach the lake just after dawn.

It was imperative that she be at the lake before the sorcerer departed.

Just as her plan dictated.

Her plan had *not* included dusty trails, recalcitrant mules, and idiot guides.

The state of her parched throat and dust-riddled nose was not improved by the stench of sweaty mule. Verbena turned her attention to the leather satchel attached to her saddle. She carefully unlaced the satchel's flap, lifted the flap over the mule's rump, and let the inner wall of the satchel drop toward her.

Revealing the tools of her trade.

A sound split the thin air, one of the most heinous noises ever to assault Verbena's ears. Starting out as a groan, the grating cacophony escalated to somewhere between a donkey's bray and a horse's neigh before dying off with a grunt.

"Ya already had yer breakfast," Carson called to her mule.

"You are more than welcome to my portion of whatever concoction that man brews up next time we stop for food," Verbena whispered. The mule's left ear swiveled backward, listening to her.

"Mules don't drink coffee," Carson said. "We'll let the mules drink once we reach the lake." Once again, the man sounded like he was explaining something to a child.

One more time and she'd turn the man into a rotting turnip and feed the turnip to the mule.

The mule snorted and turned its ear forward. Its dark hide twitched as a fly landed on its withers.

"Go on then," she commanded, waving a hand at the fly. She didn't need her mule getting upset because a fly had taken up residence.

Verbena wasn't what anyone would call "a sensitive soul." Animals of various types were made for one purpose—to serve her. She and the mule (she refused to use its name) had butted heads their first day together. Verbena had taught the beast a "lesson." Though the mule raised an objection every now and again, the beast now obeyed without question. Mostly.

In return, Verbena kept the flies from bothering it. Mostly.

Quickly, she sorted through the things in her satchel, fingers flying over an assortment of colored stones, straps, and precious metals until she found what she was looking for. Without hesitation she pulled the contraption—a silver bridle of interesting proportions —from an inner pouch and held it up to the sun.

She almost hadn't brought this particular tool. The bridle was beyond precious, but its uses were extremely limited. The instinct— no, the *compulsion*—to carry it with her had proven greater than her reluctance not to expose it to danger.

If the creature she'd seen in the lake was what she thought it might be, binding said creature to her will might prove useful. This bridle was the key to that binding—

"That's some right purty gear," Carson said.

Verbena almost dropped the bridle. She'd been so intent on what she was doing, she hadn't heard the man approaching.

Carson shook his head. "Petunia here don't take ta getting all fancy."

Petunia. The poor mule should thank her for not using its name.

"This isn't for...the mule," Verbena said, hanging the bridle over the sidesaddle's high pommel. She sighed as Carson handed her the canteen he'd allocated for her use, used a tiny bit of power to cleanse the canteen's mouth, and sipped just enough of the stale water to wash away the dust.

The beast glared at her and snorted, dampening the front of her gown.

"Didn't you hear the man? You'll get your water when we reach the lake," Verbena said, handing the canteen back to Carson.

One more day.

She only had to bear her primitive circumstances one more day.

Once she'd accomplished the morning's task, she would return to San Francisco and set the stage for her next "adventure." Becoming the most powerful sorceress in the world was not an easy task. It had taken time, planning, and ruthlessness to reach this stage in her development—

"Ya want I should go down first?" Carson asked. "Announce yer presence or some such?"

"No!" The word came out more vehemently than she intended. Verbena softened the response with a smile. "I want to surprise my... brother. You see, it's his...birthday."

Her plan did not include socializing. If all went well, she would pay the camp a surprise visit, procure the items she had come for, and leave without incident.

She chewed the inside of her lip for a moment. "My brother and I always made a game of seeing who could scare each other the most when we were young..."

She brushed her fingers over the blue sapphires embedded in the bridle dangling from her pommel. She hadn't really expected to find a creature of myth and magic in the lake, but if the creature turned out to be what she suspected it was, achieving her next goal could prove to be much easier than she had anticipated.

"They be preparing for somethin'," Carson mused. "Though what they 'spect ta find there at water's edge is anyone's guess."

Verbena turned her attention to the strip of sand. At first, she thought the men were setting up camp, but they were all pacing back and forth along the shore, apparently searching for something—

"Perhaps they look for gold?" Verbena suggested, though she knew better. Her source had told her the men and wagon were there to pick up cargo being shipped across the lake.

She hadn't seen sign of a boat. Not yet.

Which gave her time to set the next stage of her plan in motion.

"Is there a way to get down to the shore?" she asked. "Without alerting those men to our arrival?"

"More'n likely," Carson said. "You gotta particular place on yer mind?" He watched her curiously.

Verbena tapped a finger to her lips, trying to recall exactly where the *lump* had been in relation to the shore.

She pictured the shape in the waters...to the *north* of the men maneuvering the wagon in the sand. So intent was she on what she thought she'd seen, Verbena almost missed the boat that had finally come into view.

"A riverboat?" Verbena studied the craft thoughtfully, noting the dripping paddlewheel and the translucent steam rising from the central stack. Could this possibly be the boat the sorcerer was expecting?

She had assumed whatever vessel Xander had hired to haul his cargo would be more...*practical*. This riverboat looked like it should be chugging up and down the Mississippi, not carrying illicit goods in the middle of the godforsaken wilderness. Riverboats were for gamblers and transporting people, not the type of cargo she suspected might be on board.

How had it even gotten here?

There was no sign of any other boats on the lake, so—riverboat or not—this must be the vessel Xander was waiting for.

Verbena's heart fluttered like a trapped bird as she led the mule to a knee-high boulder and mounted.

"Let's head for that sandy area north of the men, just beyond that group of trees," she said.

Xander and his men wouldn't be able to see her back in that little cove.

She looked Carson over from head to toe and picked up the mule's reins. "If you think you can get us there."

Carson tied the canteens back onto his saddle and adjusted his gun belt on his hip. "Wouldn't be worth what yer payin' me if'n I cain't find that bit a sand."

The nearer they drew to the shore and the sound of lapping waves, the more intensely Verbena felt the pull of...something. At first, she had thought the sensation mere anticipation—plans failed so often it seemed unreal when one finally succeeded.

As the sensation grew stronger, she realized what she was feeling wasn't success.

It was the creature in the lake.

Verbena shook her head. That was impossible, wasn't it? She hadn't even come near the creature, had done nothing but set eyes upon it the once, and still she felt drawn—

Something burned against Verbena's right thigh. With a start, she realized she had completely forgotten the bridle. She'd sat right on top of the thing.

If she was to use the creature against Xander, she'd need to get the bridle free—which would require her to dismount and remount. She wasn't skillful or agile enough to free the bridle from its current position without risking bodily harm in the process.

You've yet to find the creature, she reminded herself.

She needed to be prepared, especially if the creature turned out to be what she expected.

Hooves scraped on stone as the mules scrambled over another section of rock at the edge of an aspen grove.

And then they were crunching through sand.

Verbena caught her breath. The lake spread before them, its vastness greater than any other lake she'd seen. The snow-capped mountains cradling the waters thrust into an impossibly blue sky. A soft scent of growing aspen and damp soil tinged the air.

And the bridle beneath her thigh burned like a bed of coals.

Verbena yanked her mule to a stop and quickly unhooked her right knee from the pommel. She slid from the mule's back, sinking slightly in the sand, and stepped toward the lake—

And immediately stepped back. The force drawing her to the water was strong, she realized. *Almost* irresistible.

Drawing in a deep breath, she turned back.

"I need you to sp...to do some reconnaissance," she told Carson before he climbed down from his mule. She didn't need the twit nearby if the creature decided to show itself. "Keep an eye on my brother. See what he's really up to."

The guide raised a bushy eyebrow. "Ya goin' ta make tea er some-thin'? Should I leave my bags?"

Verbena just glared at him. "Your humor is *not* appreciated. I'll be readying the surprise I'm going to spring on my...brother."

Carson nodded. "I'll take a quick gander—"

"Take your time. I want to clean up a bit."

That garnered another bushy eyebrow raise. "Good 'nuf."

Carson touched a hand to his hat brim, turned his mule, and ambled back into the trees.

Fighting the urge to plunge heedlessly into the water, Verbena carefully unhooked the bridle from the saddle and looped it over her arm.

:*That does not belong to thee.*:

The strange voice slammed into her mind, almost knocking

Verbena to the sand. She blinked and put a hand to her head as pressure began building inside her skull.

She had experienced many things, including voices in her mind, but she'd never had someone get inside her head the way this—*thing* —had just done.

"Of course it belongs to me," Verbena said through gritted teeth. "I paid good coin for it—"

:*Such things are not to be sold for blood nor coin!*: the voice roared.

Tears burned in Verbena's eyes as she forced herself to look beyond the pain and study the water's calm surface. She had known it wouldn't be easy binding a magical creature with the bridle, but she hadn't really known what to expect.

"What...what are you?" she asked. She had to know for certain before she attempted to use the bridle. If the creature was something other than a kelpie, the bridle would not prove as effective as she needed. Yes, the bridle had attracted the creature's attention, but was the creature truly a kelpie?

She'd heard tales during her travels about a kelpie's volatile nature. Shape-shifting water horses were known for being devious. They would do practically anything to lure unsuspecting victims into the water so the beasts could devour the poor victims at their leisure.

Nothing had ever been said about a kelpie's ability to mind-speak or that they possessed the type of magic generally reserved for sirens, magic that could compel someone to their death—

With a start, Verbena realized she stood at the water's edge, one foot poised for another step, a step that would take her into the water.

Into the kelpie's control.

Instinctively she knew if she took that step, she would be lost.

The silver bridle burned through the fabric of her overcoat. The ornate filigree glowed so brightly it made the sapphires seem dull in comparison.

She had purchased the bridle—at an unspeakable cost—then set the uncut sapphires herself, laboriously carving runes into the sapphires, then affixing the gems to the headstall. The bridle would reportedly bind the kelpie to the one who held it. Though she hadn't known when or where she might need such an item, when the time finally came to put the bridle to use, she had the suspicion there wouldn't be time to waste on casting spells.

Verbena didn't trust the tales told in either legend or myth. She had added the rune-carved sapphires to ensure the bridle worked as promised. The sapphires could be activated with a single word, a word that would bind the kelpie to her command.

A word she, of course, could not—at the moment—recall.

Verbena rolled her eyes, exasperated by her own lack of discipline —how could she forget a simple word?

Was the kelpie to blame for her memory lapse?

"Show yourself," she called, in a bid for more time. "When we've been introduced—as is proper in polite society—then we can discuss what it is you want."

A dark, serpentine form broke the water's surface. Verbena's heart stood still as the figure continued to rise until it seemed it would blot out the sun. A horse-like face the size of a hot air balloon glared down at her. All that showed was the head; the body remained below the surface.

No one had told her that kelpies could be so...enormous.

Or that they had enormous whiskers resembling those of a catfish.

Would the rest of the creature resemble an enormous horse or would it be more serpent? Cautiously she opened her senses, sending a thread of power questing toward the being. The thread caressed the creature, the touch light as a feather against her senses. Though the creature's form remained vague, the light touch verified what she had suspected—the creature was indeed a kelpie.

Their gazes locked.

Alarmed, Verbena dissolved the thread. "My name is—"

:*It matters not who thee are, witch,*: the voice thundered. :*Return that which thee stole. Mayhaps I will let thee live.*:

"I'm not a witch," Verbena said in exasperation. "I'm a sorceress."

:*Thee stink of death.*: The kelpie snorted, sounding more like the horse it resembled than a creature of the depths.

"I specialize in necromancy," she admitted. How on earth was she going to bridle this creature? Her neck got a crick just looking up into its eyes.

The lore that accompanied the bridle said one merely had to hide until the kelpie showed itself in horse form, then slip the bridle on when the creature passed by. That particular task was generally fraught with danger, but Verbena had played the scene out over and over in her mind.

In every instance, she had used magic.

And the creature in her mind had not only been on land, it had been the size of a large horse, not a small ship.

"Someone is going to pay for his lack of clarity," she muttered under her breath. The man who had sold her the bridle would never withhold information again. Louder, she said, "It is proper to exchange names during an introduction. Let's begin again, shall we? My name is Verbena Evelyn Crumb."

:*I go by many names.*: The kelpie's voice grew so soft she almost couldn't hear, no matter the voice was in her mind. :*Nixie, wihwin, bunyip, tangie, nuggle, ceffyl dŵr, cabbyl-ushtey and more. As I have already informed thee, names do not matter. The bridle does not belong to thee. Return it and I shall release thee.*:

Verbena held back a very unladylike snort. Release her indeed. Though her water magic needed practicing, she had mastered enough skill to call on the very waters themselves if need be.

Though controlling an entire lake might prove more difficult than controlling the water in her bracelet.

No, the kelpie was hers. All she had to do was place the bridle over the kelpie's head—

:*I sense trickery in thee; deceit of the highest order,*: the voice roared. :*Leave the bridle in the sand and get thee gone before I change my mind and devour thee where thee stand.*:

A shot rang out from somewhere behind Verbena. She threw the bridle over her shoulder and whipped around, hand raised and ready to defend herself. The power fed on her anger as she sought a target—

Carson galloped out of the trees, his mule's ears flat against its head. He held a smoking pistol in his right hand and was fumbling to reload.

"Run, Miz Verbena," Carson called. "I'll hold the beast off."

Was the man utterly daft? Did he think wielding such a pitiful weapon against a magical creature would really save her? Verbena might have laughed—if the kelpie hadn't chosen that moment to snatch Carson in its jaws.

The mule screamed, a sound so shrill and filled with terror it nearly made Verbena's heart stop. Then the animal turned on its heels and ran.

Without hesitation, Verbena's mule followed.

Carson's cry was cut off as the kelpie effortlessly tossed the man in the air.

And swallowed him whole.

The stench of fear filled the air along with a fine pink mist.

Blood, she realized. Verbena shook her head. She shouldn't be startled by the blood or the smell of death accompanied by the requisite voiding of bladder and bowel. Her line of work involved a lot more stink—and a lot less noise.

No screams of the dying—her victims were already dead. On the few times she'd actually had to put someone out of his or her misery, they'd been too far gone to protest...

Stop! Verbena told herself. *Focus on what is before you.*

The rage within had gone cold and the power—without her conscious effort—had dissipated to a reasonable level, allowing her to think.

Truth be told, Verbena had no idea what precious cargo was on board that riverboat. All she knew was that Xander had traveled all the way from New York. When she had heard of his *travels*, she had determined he wouldn't have what he coveted so dearly, no matter what the item was.

Xander was mad. He was also determined to rule the world.

Verbena had no such delusions of grandeur. Yes, she wanted

power. Her greatest desire was to be the world's most powerful sorceress.

But ruling the world? That was best left to fools and idiots.

That did *not* mean she wanted someone else to rule in her stead.

Verbena held the bridle up, scarcely daring to breathe. "It appears to be in my best interest not to argue with you."

Tricking the creature was not going to work. As much as she despised bargaining with anything remotely fae, such a bargain was the next best option. She could use her magic, but instinct told her using magic against the creature would only worsen the situation.

:*Thee thinks to bargain then,*: the kelpie said.

The sound of shouts and the churning paddlewheel made up Verbena's mind.

"Let's call it an exchange," she quickly said. She would have to word her request very carefully. "I've brought the bridle to you—at considerable cost. All I ask is aid in protecting what is mine."

:*Very well. Relinquish the relic into my care and I will see it returned to its proper place.*:

Proper place? She'd purchased the bridle in the Scottish Highlands. How did he propose to take it back?

Verbena bowed her head. It was no business of hers what the creature did with the bridle—as long as he lent his aid. She had always used whatever tool was closest at hand. The kelpie was another tool.

Moving with care, she laid the bridle on the sand and took a step backward. The kelpie bent down and gently lifted the bridle in its teeth. Then it tossed the bridle in the air—

Time held its breath as the bridle slowly rose, then descended, straps spreading wide...

The kelpie caught the bridle on its nose and shook its head, settling the bridle into place. A stable boy couldn't have done a better job.

Did this mean the kelpie was under her control?

:*Just try to control me,*: the kelpie growled.

Verbena sighed and turned her attention back to her current

dilemma. The kelpie had only to hold the riverboat at bay while Verbena got on board. She would quickly incapacitate the crew with a few well-placed spells. There was no longer need to deal with the men onshore—with the possible exception of the sorcerer.

"There is a boat approaching," she said, surprised at the note of wistfulness in her voice. It might have been fun to ride on a kelpie…"If you could assure the boat does not reach shore, I will—"

:What is this boat *of which you speak?:*

With a start, Verbena realized the creature was serious. This was likely the first time it had seen a large vessel plying the lake's waters.

Verbena pointed at the riverboat. "That is a boat. Not a living creature, a—" How did one explain a machine to a kelpie?

It wasn't important, she decided.

"It must not come any closer. If you use your tail to prevent it from moving further, that should suffice."

Nothing went as planned, of course.

The kelpie moved into place near the riverboat—and chaos broke loose.

Firebolts shot from the shore—likely Xander protecting his precious cargo. Though Verbena couldn't see the sorcerer, she could picture the rage purpling his face.

The man never could keep his temper.

Gunshots accompanied the firebolts.

The kelpie twitched as if it had been struck, then flipped its tail—sending riverboat and cargo to the bottom of the lake.

Over the splashing and gurgling that accompanied the boat's demise rose a growling snarl that could only have come from Xander.

She quickly called the kelpie to her side. A scorched-hide stench rose from a palm-sized patch near the middle of its neck, but otherwise, the creature appeared unhurt.

"Are you able to lift me into the air?" she asked, turning her intended command into a request. Better to be on one's best behavior when dealing with an injured beast. "I need to deal with those men. Then I can tend to your wound."

The kelpie lowered its head until she looked into its eyes. Panic froze Verbena for a brief moment. She took a deep breath, shoved the panic away, and raised her hands, preparing to use her power if need be. Then the kelpie turned, exposing a spot just behind its ear.

Did it expect her to mount?

Mindful to keep her feet from the water, Verbena stepped carefully onto the kelpie's head, glancing around for something to hold to.

The kelpie's hide, which appeared utterly devoid of color from the ground, shone with tiny rainbows up close. A light stench of fish and water plants filled the air—

The kelpie moved and Verbena grabbed at the mane—rather unnerved to find the strands were, in actuality, thin, ribbon-like snakes instead of hair. Her stomach plummeted as the kelpie lifted its head.

Verbena settled herself between the snake-like strands of mane, arranging her skirts so she could hook her right leg around a handful of snake-hair.

Then she brought up the dark magic, feeling the power churning within. The power burned in its intensity, demanding to be released, but she held it to her, coiled and ready.

"Take me to the sorcerer," she shouted, wind whistling in her ears.

The kelpie complied, carrying her into the stream of firebolts. A bolt struck the creature's neck near Verbena, eliciting a deafening bellow. The stench of freshly scorched leather stung her nose.

"Hold fast," she said, biting her lip. She blocked everything from her senses—the stench, the sound, the men on the ground pointing rifles her way—and focused on the sorcerer standing in the wagon.

She thrust out her hands, releasing her power in a powerful wave. "*Pavo!*"

The sorcerer froze, caught in the power of her spell before he could release another firebolt. The snarl on his face resembled that of an angry dog, lips drawn back, teeth exposed. The other men and the wolf-dog also froze, resembling statues in various positions of attack.

"Xander, my sweet," Verbena purred. "No need to get nasty. Just admit I have won this little battle."

She relaxed her spell on him just enough to let him speak.

"You," Xander snarled. "Have not won anything. My property now resides at the bottom of a very deep lake."

"Of course, I've won." Verbena purred, stroking the kelpie's neck. The creature stiffened beneath her touch as if affronted by the gesture. Perhaps that was taking their partnership a bit too far.

Verbena lifted her hand and gestured at the smooth expanse of water the riverboat had so recently occupied. A stream of bubbles broke the water's otherwise calm surface.

"Can you retrieve this *property*?" she asked in a low voice. "More than likely, it's in a trunk—a large chest or box or—"

:*I am familiar with treasure,*: the kelpie snarled. Its head dipped and for a moment, Verbena thought the creature about to drop her in the water where she would be at its mercy.

:*I honor my bargains,*: the kelpie said in that low voice she could barely hear. :*See that thee honor thine.*:

The kelpie lowered its head to the sand and waited, moving away as soon as Verbena stepped off.

Then the kelpie vanished into the watery depths.

Where had it—

Before the thought could fully form, the kelpie's tail lifted high into the air, revealing a man-size chest wrapped in a serpentine tail.

Answers my question about the shape of its body—while in the water, she thought.

Kelpies could shift into several different forms, preferring an equine form while on land, though she'd heard tales about kelpies who shifted into a child's form or a woman's in order to lure their prey in close. But she'd always wondered how such forms fared in the watery depths.

Water rained from the kelpie's tail and chest as if a cloud had just burst directly overhead. The kelpie's head broke the water's surface and the creature paused, studying her so intently Verbena felt her skin start to crawl.

:*Thou art one who travels side by side with trouble.*:

Verbena wasn't certain what the kelpie meant, but it didn't really matter. She had Xander's precious cargo, though maintaining the spell holding Xander and his men was taking its toll. She could feel her energy slowly draining.

She motioned at the wagon. "Set the chest in back, if you please. Crush the sorcerer if he gets in the way."

Xander gave a soft curse. He couldn't even glance up, she realized. Couldn't see his death sailing in on the wind—or being dropped from a kelpie's mouth.

Though crushing the sorcerer probably wasn't wise. If the chest actually did fall on the sorcerer, it would render the driver's seat completely unusable. Though the sight of such an occurrence would be worth the inconvenience.

Verbena grinned. She could have the golem help clean up the mess if need be.

The golem stood still as a statue in the traces of the wagon as the kelpie lifted the chest into the wagon, settling the enormous chest behind the sorcerer with scarcely a sound. Xander didn't even twitch, though the hatred glimmering in his eyes would pierce stone if given physical form.

Gently lapping waves blended harmoniously with birds twittering in the trees, the natural sounds belying the strange scene taking place on the sand.

Verbena nodded at the kelpie. "My thanks. If you will be come close, I'll heal your wounds as promised."

Between the small uses of magic and the larger spells, she'd used up most of her power—power that pulled directly on her physical energy. Healing the wounds would likely drain the rest of her power, but she had given her word.

And she always kept her word, be it to the good or to the bad.

:*Beware the treasure*,: the kelpie said. :*And the sorcerer.*: It slid beneath the water without a whisper, leaving behind only the tiniest of ripples. So much for healing its wounds.

Xander mumbled something and Verbena felt more of her energy drain as the spell holding him begin to weaken. The sorcerer was counteracting her spell, moving more quickly than she had anticipated.

There would be no face-off today.

She quickly went to the golem, pulled two gems—one hematite, one sapphire—from the pocket of her overcoat, and pressed them both into the golem's body. She quickly whispered the words of unbinding, set the hematite to work releasing the sorcerer's spell on the golem, then activated the sapphire, binding the golem to her.

Exhaustion swept over her and her knees threatened to buckle.

The golem looked down at her, patiently waiting for a command.

"Remove him," she said, pointing at the sorcerer.

Xander opened his mouth. Before the sorcerer could utter whatever curse he intended, the golem turned in the harness, grabbed Xander in one enormous hand, and hurled the sorcerer into the lake.

The men on the beach started to move.

"Get us out of here!" Verbena scrambled into the wagon and gathered up the reins as the wagon rolled forward in short, jerky motions. She settled herself in the driver's seat, grabbing the edge of the seat in one hand to keep from being tossed around. The golem found his stride and the ride smoothed—a bit.

A voice echoed off the trees.

She glanced over her shoulder to see one of the men moving. But he wasn't headed for her.

The man charged headlong into the lake.

After Xander.

The tiny scar on Verbena's forehead burned. She touched it lightly, stroking a finger around the scar's edges. Not only was she exhausted, another headache was starting up.

The wolf-dog snarled and lunged at her, attempting to hurl itself into the wagon. The savage jaws snapped just shy of her arm.

"Go, go, go!" She snapped the reins against the golem's back and the wagon surged forward. The trees blurred around them, swallowing lake, men, and wolf-dog from view.

~

She found the mules just as the rutted wagon trail—if it could be called a trail—turned southeast, following the lakeshore. They were back among the firs and pines, grazing.

Verbena pulled the golem to a stop before the four-legged beasts took off again. The golem smelled rather pleasant to her—of magic and turned earth—but the mules might not appreciate the scent.

Besides, she needed to think and the wagon ride was *not* one of the smoothest she had ever experienced.

She needed time to renew her energy, her power. But she didn't have that time. Not yet. The sorcerer and his men wouldn't be far behind.

Carson had said there were several roadhouses along this route. She could hire a guide at one of those roadhouses, but she had the . golem to think about now, and—

Verbena sighed. She might as well find out just what this cargo was. What Xander had been so obsessed by. What Carson had given his life for. Without hesitating, she reached back and fumbled with the lock holding the chest close. After a moment, the lid fell open, revealing hundreds of black and red stones.

Stones? She had gone through all this—given up the kelpie bridle —for *stones*?

Unable to believe what she was seeing, Verbena grabbed the nearest stone.

As soon as skin touched stone, her whole world changed.

Verbena had never experienced the type of power emanating from the stone in her hand. It was as if both heaven and earth pulsed in the red veins woven through the black matrix. The power promised strength and power, power that surged through her exhausted body—

She dropped the stone back in the chest with a gasp and clutched her hand to her stomach. Not only had the stone promised to give power—it had threatened to drag her into its depths.

Quickly, Verbena dropped the lid and snapped the lock closed. She'd spell that lock when she was capable. Make the contents inaccessible to anyone but her. There had to be a way to utilize the power within the stones without being absorbed by them in turn. Otherwise, Xander wouldn't have gone to such lengths to possess them.

Would he?

No matter. She needed to get the stones somewhere safe. Only then would she have time to delve further into their mystery.

Unease rose within her along with the sense of impending disaster. She needed to get moving. To get as far from Xander as she possibly could. Then she could decide what to do with the stones.

The road to the southeast was too predictable, she decided. Too easy. Xander would assume she had gone that way. She craved a bath and sleeping on a real bed again. But the roadhouses here in this godforsaken wilderness had proven as primitive as their patrons. She could do without such questionable comfort for a while longer.

Verbena studied the golem's sturdy back. The creature was strong enough to carry the chest.

She guided the golem off the trail, deep into a stand of trees. A light breeze tickled her cheek.

There wasn't much in the wagon besides the chest and some odd lengths of rope. Rope was what she needed right now. She looped several short pieces in one hand, climbed down as gracefully possible from the wagon, and went back for the mules.

Catching the mules was her first priority. That went smoothly enough.

Getting the stubborn beasts to maintain their calm when she led them back to the wagon—and the golem—didn't go smoothly at all. Carson's mule would have none of it, ripping its rope from her hand and galloping off.

Her own mule was more tractable. Barely. The beast rolled its eyes and erupted in a tirade that would leave her deaf for months.

All that racket would surely attract attention. Verbena clenched her jaw and dug deep inside, seeking a trace of power. Something she could use to calm the mule—

And found it. The tiniest ember still burning, so deep she hadn't known it existed.

Verbena tapped on that power, laying a soothing spell over the mule. Her legs trembled as the power left her. She clung to the mule's saddle. What was the beast's name again?

Petunia.

That would not do. Not at all.

"Penelope," Verbena said. "I'll call you Penelope. Not nearly as ridiculous as that other."

Penelope didn't argue. The mule had become as tractable as the golem.

Fortunately, it took only a few moments to find a place to leave the wagon—among the trees, well off the trail they'd been following. She'd thought about rigging some sort of harness so the golem could carry the chest on its back, but the golem simply picked the chest up and rested it on his left shoulder, then waited for instructions.

Penelope stood still while Verbena mounted. She turned and guided the mule back along the trail, back to civilization—of a sort. The town where she'd hired Carson had been little more than an overgrown mining camp.

As soon as she reached a telegraph office, she would summon her gadgeteer. She'd have him bring his equipment and the makings for tea. Together they would figure out the mystery of the stones and ways to put the power they contained to good use.

:*You should find out if there are more stones,*: a voice whispered in her mind. A voice not her own. Nor was it the voice of her mentor.

Most likely her imagination, Verbena decided. She tended to hear voices that weren't there when she reached the stage of utter exhaustion.

In the branches overhead a bird of iridescent blue with an odd crest on its head took exception to her passing, screeching in protest and leaping from limb to limb, as if its scolding could hurry her little expedition along.

Verbena rolled her eyes.

"You are fortunate my power is depleted," she told the bird. "Else I would fry you like a chicken and eat you for supper."

When she reached civilization, she would consume an entire chicken, she decided. She'd earned it, after all.

Xander would come after her. Verbena was counting on it. By the time her gadgeteer arrived, she would be rested and fed. All she needed was a good cup of tea.

Then she'd be ready for anything.

Even that blasted sorcerer.

ABOUT THE AUTHOR

Growing up in the wilds of the Sierra Nevada mountains, surrounded by deer and beaver, muskrat and bear, Louisa Swann found ample fodder for her equally wild imagination. As an adult, she interweaves her experiences with that imagination, creating tales of fantasy and science fiction, mystery and thrillers, steampunk and historical fiction. Her short stories have appeared in Fiction River anthologies, including Reader's Choice; Mercedes Lackey's *Elementary Magic* and Valdemar anthologies; and Esther Friesner's *Chicks and Balances*. Novels include light-hearted mysteries (*It Ain't No Bull*, *The Trouble with Bulldogs*) and her new steampunk/weird west series, *Abby Crumb and Myrtle Creek* (with Brandon Swann).

Find out more about Louisa at:
louisaswann.com

 facebook.com/swanngang

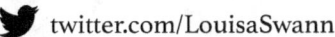 twitter.com/LouisaSwann

BB bookbub.com/authors/louisa-swann

THE ROAD BENEATH
INDIANAPOLIS

BRIGID COLLINS

There are no ships in the expanse of the Pacific Ocean between Guam and the Philippines. It is a wide blue field, a plane of salt and heat on the surface. The sun is an inferno overhead. Everywhere the stench of fish and seaweed and salt hangs like a wet rag over the mouth. The waves roar and bellow all the damn time, but the ocean's grumbles can't cover the moans and wails of some six hundred US Navy sailors slowly dying.

It's been three days since the Japanese torpedoes hit the USS *Indianapolis*.

Three endless days.

Lieutenant Gordie Thomas was so damn happy to get shipped out of Guam, him and Frankie Calloway and the rest of his men who are either drifting elsewhere on the water or dead and bloated already. The Japanese still swarm over that whole island despite how the US liberated it from Japanese occupation almost a year ago. Gordie had quite his share of dealing with the holdouts. He'd been enjoying the brief near-vacation of his posting on the *Indianapolis*.

Gordie clings to the corner of the faded orange flotation device that has become his entire existence over those three endless days. The material that covers it is rough and abrasive, but Gordie is long past being able to feel it. He's numb all over, his top half burnt to the point of peeling and oozing, his lower half stiff with the cold of the water. He wears no life vest, just his duty uniform soaked through and crusty with salt. His tongue cleaves to the roof of his mouth. He and the six other boys holding onto this floater found a tin of water in the flotsam yesterday, and managed to share it, which meant not a one of 'em got enough to make any damn difference. Commander Kerry died last night while the rain was hammering them and making all the boys scream as if it were flaying the burnt skin from their faces. But the commander had gone quiet, and when Frankie Calloway nudged him off the floater, nobody blamed the kid.

But Calloway's drunk the ocean water, and now he's talking like the other ravers and swatting his hands at invisible things. Gordie can't do a thing to help, but he sure feels responsible anyway.

Calloway keeps slipping deeper into the water as he talks, then catching hold of the floater and making it jerk. The sea's high today, and with the sun blazing up top, it all makes keeping hold of the float hard.

Gordie licks his lips, grimaces at the taste of salt and blood on them. "Calloway, cut that shit out."

Calloway flings a hand up, sending drops of water flying. "Just asking the pretty gal for a dance, Lieutenant. She won't dance with me! You tell her how I shot that Jap yesterday, would you?"

He loses his grip on the floater and slides back until the water sloshes over his chin.

Beyond Calloway, another cluster of men scream. The water around them turns foamy with activity, then the foam begins to turn pink.

"My leg!"

"*Ohh* God," moans the man to Gordie's right. Another lieutenant. Gordie doesn't know his name. "Oh, God, I don't want to die."

Calloway giggles and adjusts his grip. "Oh *now* she wants to dance."

He plunges his hand down into the water. When he draws it back, it's slicked with blood. "Oh, no..."

To Gordie's left, David Burrows begins to cry.

Gordie flexes his fingers against the floater, which is about all he can do. He can't much muster the energy to squeeze out any tears, though his heart thumps hard enough he thinks he'll be sick.

None of these men are under his command except Calloway, but he still feels his duty to do something for all of them.

But the sun's fried his brains. Most he can think of to do is to die alongside them.

Calloway barely has his head above water. He holds onto the floater with only his bloody hand. The floater jerks hard under his grip, erratic. His eyes go glassy and wide, and he looks at Gordie like a sinner come to make confession.

"I don't—don't wanna d-dance no more—"

Gordie tries to lift himself, hoping to reach out or something. "Cal—"

But Calloway is gone, the pink foam closing over his head, and Gordie knows that image of his face, sunken with starvation, sunburnt, the skin flaking off in strips, lips cracked and running, so so young, just a kid, just a god damned kid dying in the middle of the Pacific fucking Ocean—

That image will stay with him for the eternity that remains of his likely very short life.

He doesn't know what makes him duck under the water once Calloway is gone. He can only possibly replace that final image of the kid with a far worse one. But he does it anyway, just lets go of the floater and lets the ocean swallow him up. His upper half blazes with pain as his tortured skin meets cold, cold salt, and he lets a lot of his air escape as bubbles in the bloody water.

He can't move his legs too good, but he tries to point himself towards the place he knows Calloway went under. A shadow thrashes there, surrounded by a deeper cloud of red.

The shadow turns, comes closer to Gordie, and Gordie curls his stiff fingers into a fist. He'll go for an eye. Won't be enough to kill the shark that ate his subordinate, but it'll be something.

The shark emerges from the cloud of red, only, Gordie discovers it isn't a shark at all. The creature that comes for him has the face of a woman, pale as death even through the streaks of blood. Her features are angular, pointed like a shark is pointed, but beautiful and terrible all at once. No hair flows from her smooth skull. She has arms like bones, covered in the rough, green-gray skin of a tiger shark, and although the back end of her still lies within the concealment of the cloud, Gordie makes out the shape of her shark tail.

Her eyes are black black black, black as tar and just as soulless.

But there's intelligence there, something more than instinct and the drive to devour. She looks at Gordie, pauses in the water. The blood swirls around her, a dancer's veil that provides not a scrap of modesty. Her fish-belly white breasts sway in the rhythm of the rising sea.

Gordie's lungs burn, he needs to breathe. But the thought of going back up to the surface without getting some kind of vengeance for Calloway burns his heart, and so he forces his legs to work, dammit, work, and kicks toward the shark woman, fist outstretched.

A smile stretches the shark woman's lips apart, revealing rows of pointed teeth stained with blood and jammed with floating strands of viscera.

Bits of Calloway, or others.

She stretches out with her gray fingers, faster in the water of course than Gordie. Catches him up in her arms and crushes him against her breast like a lover.

She kisses him. He tastes—

Her teeth cut his lips. He can't push her away. Her sandpaper skin scrapes his hands and lets the sting of the ocean in deeper. His whole body stings, tingles, pulses with the power of her and the sea and the death happening all around him.

Then she pulls back, but she doesn't release him.

He breathes.

He sees. The blood still clouds the water, but he sees.

Limbs. Entrails. A boot floats by, empty.

But the shark woman is pulling him by the arm down down down into the depths and the darkness below the sun-drenched surface. The cold grows, the pressure builds, but Gordie doesn't grow more sluggish. The deeper they go, the more strength floods into his body. The pain is still there, burning, freezing, but he is strong enough to swim.

Not strong enough to break away from the shark woman.

She brings him down to the lowest depths of the sea, to the sandy seabed fathoms and fathoms beneath the surface where he belongs. Corals are there, and dark creatures with waving tendrils affixed to rock formations worn smooth by millennia spent underwater. Long, thick strands of kelp wave in the current. They are dark green and translucent and shadows dart behind their broad leaves. The colors are muted, washed with gray and the dimness of depth. The sea creatures here scuttle out of the way at their approach, and the approach of other shark women.

The shark woman who holds Gordie's arm points to the sandy bottom.

<look>

Where she points there is a pattern in the pale sand, a line gouged by the passing of many creatures, and it is lined with algae-covered shells of all kinds. The shark women swim near it, but do not travel along it. They avoid it, recoiling if they get too close.

<the road to my home. the road to faerie>

The other shark women stir as she pulls him closer to the road. Gordie is bleeding, from the lips, from his hands. They are interested in him, but they've all just feasted on the sailors floating above. How many are still alive? Gordie doesn't know, but he can still hear them screaming, moaning, dying.

<come>

She takes them both down to the road, and they skim, low enough that their passing swirls the sand around them. It rasps against Gordie's face, stings in his eyes. His arm hurts where her gray fingers dig in.

They follow the road, alone. None of the other shark women have come with them, and no other sea creatures dare to come close.

It grows darker, but Gordie can still see.

Up ahead, a rock formation looms. It's an archway, like a giant eye of a needle, the kind Gordie remembers his mother using to patch up the knees and elbows in his clothes when he was a boy. The rock is pitted as if acid has eaten parts of it away, and the water here takes on a strong, corrosive tang. It looks so much like a doorway to somewhere terrible, someplace where horrors happen, worse and worse still than what he's already experienced. On the opposite side of it is a gorge filled to the brim with blackness that Gordie can't see past, even with the enhanced vision the shark woman has forced upon him. He doesn't want to see it.

All around, on either side of the road, huge pieces of metal lie on the sea bed. Gordie makes out the rivets on sheets of siding, the piping from an interior mechanism. The gray paint that defined the look of the last place he called home.

A sliver no larger than a Bowie knife lies in the middle of the path, but when Gordie looks at it he can tell it came from the hull of the *Indianapolis*. He just knows. It's thick and gray and sharp on the edges, and there's a curve on one end like it used to bump up against a rivet.

The shark woman draws to a stop with some distance still between them and the stone arch. She swings him around so he's between her and that doorway.

He looks in her eyes, as he has no choice, and sees the etchings of pain that jag down her whole body.

<the metal piece. it blocks our way home to faerie. a mortal must remove it>

And she shoves Gordie toward the arch then withdraws a few body lengths back.

Gordie feels her hold on him still. His arm burns where she held him tight, and the spot pulses as if she's still pushing him towards the object that lies ahead before the arch. Unable to do anything else, he swims along the road, feeling clumsy without her to guide him. His hands drag in the sand.

His fingers rasp against the shard as he picks it up, and the sand dances in little whirls before settling back down.

The shard has a good heft to it.

And when he holds it close to his heart, the shark woman's phantom hand lifts off of his arm. The cold of the ocean washes over him, and the darkness closes in.

Gordie pushes himself towards the shark woman. Her black black black eyes stare at him, no longer with any hint of the intelligence he saw earlier. She is all cold and consuming, but cautious still. He holds the metal, the iron she cannot touch.

Gordie's heart thuds hard and his lungs burn again. The shark woman throws her hairless head back and sends a cry through the water, a cry that shakes the rocks and vibrates through Gordie's bones, that sets the eye of that giant needle glowing with a fey, dark blue light.

The shark women come. They writhe down the opened road,

frenzied in their need to get along it, snapping their vicious jaws at each other and drawing blood that clouds the depths as the blood of the sailors clouded the surface.

The shark woman who took him twists towards the doorway, but Gordie won't miss his chance to get revenge for Calloway. Not all of the fey strength she imbued him with has drained away yet.

He knifes through the water towards her, his shard of the *Indianapolis* held tight in his hand. The edge cuts into his palm. It is sharp enough, he thinks, and he is right.

When he catches her, the shard plunges easily into her heart. She screeches like nothing else he's ever heard, her death inhuman in every way, and the sound stirs his empty stomach until he's certain he'll be sick. The blood that blossoms forth is black, thicker and colder than the water. It tastes like molasses and copper amidst the brine of the sea.

She writhes around the iron, gnashes her many teeth. Then she falls still, floating unmoving in the current the same as so many good Navy boys.

Gordie pulls the shard from her heart. He hopes her sisters will eat her, but they are too caught up in their homeward frenzy to notice one death amongst them.

His lungs burn, and the darkness closes in.

He's going to die down here.

But suddenly, he doesn't want to die. He's got the shard, the sliver of the *Indianapolis* that he used to kill the sea monster that ate one of his men.

If he lives, he can take it home to Calloway's parents. He can tell them that their boy is avenged.

And so Gordie holds that shard close to his heart, fights the burning in his lungs, and kicks until he reaches the surface. The waves roar and bellow all the damn time, but the ocean's grumbles can't cover the moans and wails of less than six hundred US Navy sailors slowly dying. Everywhere the stench of fish and seaweed and salt hangs like a wet rag over the mouth. The sun is an inferno overhead. The ocean is a wide blue field, a plane of salt and heat here on the surface.

But on the horizon, in the expanse of the Pacific Ocean between Guam and the Philippines,

There is a ship.

ABOUT THE AUTHOR

Brigid Collins is a fantasy and science fiction writer living in Michigan. Her short stories have appeared in Fiction River, The Uncollected Anthology Volume 13: *Mystical Melodies*, and the *Chronicle Worlds: Feyland* anthology. Books 1 through 3 of her fantasy series, Songbird River Chronicles, are available in print and electronic versions on Amazon.

Find out more about Brigid at:
backwrites.wordpress.com

 twitter.com/purellian

bookbub.com/authors/brigid-collins

OF DROUGHT AND HARSH MOONLIGHT

DEANNA KNIPPLING

Look you, the worm is not to be trusted but in the keeping of wise people; for, indeed, there is no goodness in the worm.

— SHAKESPEARE, *ANTONY AND CLEOPATRA*

It was the year 1934 in the month of May when a sweet-faced, dark-haired, whistling man named Anson P. Martin came to town. The second he stepped off the train the whole town brightened. It didn't happen suddenly, like turning on an electric light, but like sunrise, so that you hardly knew it before you were holding up your hand to shade your eyes. Some of the women who came into Roethler's Dry Goods to tell Claudine all the gossip said he looked "like a Greek god!"

The profound dark mood that had existed in the town before his arrival—a town which shall remain nameless, except to say that it lay somewhere out in the prairie states at the confluence of a river and a railroad—was a condition that had been created by drought and poverty. The banks were calling in their loans like animals with a leg caught in a trap, one day to demand every penny you had, the next to themselves to lie down and die. Scavengers picked the bones clean before you even knew the beast was dead.

Those who remained in the town were the stubborn sort who took pride in outlasting tornado season every year, and then winter. Winter out on the plains was a kind of haunting that called to you, especially in those years. To live was to resist the call of the void.

Claudine Roethler was a childless spinster who had inherited her living from her father, Price Roethler, who had established the store in 1905. Born at the turn of the century, she was no longer pretty, although she would probably never quite stop being beautiful, her mother having been a great beauty. Her mother had drawn the business of ladies all 'round the area to buy her hand-mixed cosmetics, which Price had proudly sold at a separate counter. Claudine's mother had been a witch of sorts, and cosmetics were not the only things she sold, until she ran off with a traveling salesman for New Orleans and subsequently was murdered, a fact which both Claudine and her father still mourned when they heard.

But that was neither here nor there; Claudine herself had neither the taste nor the talent for her mother's work. She had taken too much after her father, sharp-eyed but with a pleasant enough tongue, and practical. She was able to support herself in good form, even during such times, although she had to let go of her two assistants and cut down on store hours. She kept a ginger tomcat named Scarecrow who kept her company in an ill-tempered, elderly sort of way. She used to say that all she needed to start all over again was her cash-box and her cat, and both of them went with her down into the storm cellar when tornadoes threatened.

But then she got a glimpse of Anson P. Martin. He was some sort of god, all right, for although he was pleasant enough to the eye, he should not have affected her as severely as he did. And she could tell, with that same glance, that there was no goodness in him, only vanity and impulse.

But there it was.

Mr. Martin settled into one of the rooms at the Opera House. As the days after his arrival turned into weeks, it became clear that he was a man of means. He had been in all the shops, showing his funds about. He had even bought soap and a shaving-kit from Claudine. He attended the Methodist church every Sunday.

In his presence, Claudine felt awkward and tongue-tied. He seemed to want to have nothing to do with her, watching her sidelong out of the corner of his eye and laughing at her when his back was turned. She told herself, again and again, to stay away from him, and she did.

For the most part.

He tore through women's beds like there was a pocketful of silver dollars under each of the mattresses. What did he care what wreckage he left behind? He hired a car and would drive women around through the countryside after church, sometimes more than one at a time. As blatant as that.

What was he in town for?

To play poker, he said, and amuse himself for a few weeks before he moved on to Omaha. He told people he was a liar and a cheat, and then he lied to them and cheated them, and then he told them how he had done it, to rounds of applause.

Claudine could feel him coming closer to her, closer every

minute, like the sun about to crest over the horizon, but she could not keep from staring, waiting to go blind.

But then he did not come.

Instead he parked outside the one bank that had any money left, an establishment that was directly across from Claudine's dry-goods store, and went inside to make a deposit. She looked up from the counter, where she was serving a pair of local ladies, and all three of them stared as he got out of his hired Chevrolet Eagle and went into the bank, only resuming their business a few minutes later.

While he was inside, he told the bank manager some kind of story about how he was going to start up a leather goods store. Midway through the discussion over Mr. Martin's funds, another pair of cars came up to the bank, and four masked men ran in and held it up.

Claudine spotted them as they drove up, and reached under her counter for her shotgun, but she had left it upstairs. In a calm voice, she told the other two ladies to come behind the counter and crouch down. Then she ran out the back door and kept running until she reached the Sheriff's office.

Meanwhile, the robbers cleaned out the safe, the drawers, and even the customers' pockets.

Then they took Anson P. Martin with them as a hostage, singling him out because he had tried to sweet-talk them out of hurting anyone and convinced everyone else to stay calm. The bank robbers roared off in their cars, taking Mr. Martin and his hired car—why not? it was just out front—with them.

The sheriff and deputies took off after them, but had no joy. After that the Pinkertons were set on them like hounds. It was established that the robbers had crossed state lines; some Bureau of Investigation agents came out to talk to the tellers, manager, and customers who had been at the bank at the time. The four bank robbers had been seen in Missouri.

"Four?" asked Claudine. "Not five?"

She had made up her mind that Mr. Martin was a compatriot of the robbers; it was all awfully convenient, especially when you considered that cash for a couple of payrolls had just come in by armored car earlier that morning, and that Mr. Martin's room at the Opera House, when searched, was suspiciously empty of personal belongings, although he had left behind a couple of wrapped bars of French soap and a shaving kit.

Then the hired car was found near Omaha, Nebraska, with blood on the seat. A week or so later, the owner of the Opera House was asked to identify a body which had been found along the bank of Carter Lake on the Iowa side. The body was too far gone to be sure. But it did have curly dark hair, and the right kind of hands, with long fingers. That much at least she could tell.

Claudine offered up a prayer for him at the Catholic church and lit a red candle, reminding herself not to be too quick to judge.

I n the town was a beggar whose real name had been forgotten, if anyone had ever known it. He was called Old Duke and he lived down by the river in a shack that bothered nobody much. The piece of land he was on was always flooding out in the spring, which washed away the shack. In fact, that very spring it had just washed away and Claudine had helped cook for the men who rebuilt it. Old Duke was soft in the head, and everyone half-expected him to get too drunk and drown himself in the river, or be bitten by a rabid skunk and get killed that way.

But he was also a kind of good-luck charm. The town had hung on where others had failed. And the ones who had moved off hadn't fared as well as the ones who stayed, although that might have been due to it being the less advantaged folks who had left, versus the ones who had stayed. It didn't hurt much, to fuss over him a bit now and then, and it made them all feel a little better. Claudine herself had given the old man her dead father's coat, tucking sweets inside the pockets, and ordered him special a pair of half-decent shoes just last year. Before she had run off, her mother had always been bringing him something or other of a summer afternoon. Other beggars and hobos had passed through the town, but Old Duke was the only one who seemed to stick. In the winter he shored up his shack and used it to go ice-fishing on the river, and disappeared somewhere to sleep. Nobody enquired too closely about the details.

With the bad drought had come a lowering of the river; Old Duke had moved his camp down the new bank to stay close to the water. Usually in the summer he did not beg, or did not beg for much, but with the lower water came less freshness to what was there, and the fish began to die back. They were harder to catch. And Old Duke began turning up at doors, covered in dust and smelling not so much like the stink of old leather.

Claudine began walking down to the riverside, early in the morning, to bring him fresh water. The July heat had begun to nose its way all the way into the crack of midnight, keeping the air from ever truly turning cool. Old Duke always thanked her, but it was wordless, the bob of a head.

Then, a few days after the body which might or might not have been Mr. Martin's had been found, he said, "Make sure to keep that cat inside, or it might get et."

"You wouldn't eat my cat, would you?"

"Don't like gingers," he said, grinning at her with a handful of rotting teeth. "Like me a nice gray."

"All cats are gray in the dark," she said, and he whooped with laughter. She promised she would keep Scarecrow inside at night, and he thanked her for the water.

Then, the next day, he asked her, "Been down to the new bridge yet, ma'am?"

The Public Works had been surveying to find a place to build a new bridge. A good bridge would save time driving for a lot of folks, and time was money—especially when it came to the trucks that brought in grain to be shipped along the rails.

"Not yet, sir, not yet," she said. "Have they started work yet? You aren't packing up and moving over there, are you?"

"Not likely," he said. "I don't like to get too close to that place, and nor should you."

"What's wrong with it?"

He gave her a look with a pair of startlingly blue eyes, buried deep in his thick and cracked skin. "Didn't your Momma teach you nothin'?"

She shook her head. "I was never much up on that stuff. I always got along better with my Pa."

"I knew Price," he said. "And I knew your Momma. She was the curious sort. A little curiosity might do you some good."

"Why's that?"

"But not too much curiosity," he said, after a moment's hesitation. "Never you mind about being curious. You people would bust a hole in a dam just to see the water leak out."

And that was all he would say on the matter.

The heat increased and storms came and went, and one day a tornado was spotted. Claudine brought the cat and the cashbox downstairs with her, then thought about Old Duke. She cursed herself for caring, but there was no help for it: she had to head down to the river and see if he would come with her.

"And stink up your storm cellar?" he asked, when she reached him. He refused to go. Finally she had to take refuge in another house's cellar at the bottom of the bluff, to keep from being battered all the way back to the store by the branches and other trash being thrown around by the storm. She banged "shave and a haircut" on the door of a storm cellar and they let her in. The folks who lived there, the Shipleys, owed her money on credit, which a lot of people down at the bottom of the bluff did.

They looked at her strangely when she told them Old Duke was still out on the riverbank. After a long, thick moment, they praised her for her conscientiousness, then said no more on the matter. They pretended to be more worried about her cat than anything else.

Above them, the buildings groaned in the awful wind. A window smashed. It felt as though giants were marching drunkenly through the town, clumsy and coarse.

~

Upon her return to the store, Claudine discovered that one of her windows had been smashed and the contents of her shelves had been overturned and flung about everywhere. Her cat and her cashbox were both intact in the cellar, but that fact only comforted her briefly: the entire town had suffered. And suffering meant fewer sales, even after the mess had been cleaned up and the window repaired. The worst of the damage was on the far side of town. Poverty had protected, for the most part, the people who lived below the bluff.

The new bridge had been completely torn up, though. The PWA men would have to start all over again, if they were to continue at all.

Claudine paid a pair of men—opportunists, but she was grateful nonetheless—to nail up plywood over the broken window, which seemed to raise the temperature indoors about a hundred degrees. She began to set things in order.

She continued late into the night, only stopping when she nearly fainted from heat, hunger, and exhaustion. Taking inventory, she was irritated to discover that all kinds of items had been blown out into the storm. In addition, much of the new cloth would have to be shaken out, at the very least, and might have to be sold at a discount. The new-made clothing was almost all torn to shreds.

She supposed she should be grateful for the fact that her store, crouched down tight among a row of red brick buildings on Main Street, had survived intact. Even the bank across the street had a couple of plywood boards up over its windows.

She fixed up a sandwich of day-old bread and cheese, then tried to settle herself down to sleep.

It was impossible. Besides the heat, there were just too many things undone. And much on her mind was the fact that she felt the town was at a tipping point against the drought and the bank failures. She had been hanging on, and hanging on, and hanging on, cutting her expenses down, milking the value out of every last penny already, and could hardly bear this trouble on top of everything else. She could only imagine how the rest of the town was doing. The bank robbery hadn't helped, and she suspected that one morning she would wake to find the building closed up and the bankers fled.

Was it time to close up her daddy's dry-goods store, sell what she might of it, and turn tail? But where else would be better? And what on earth could she do with herself when she got there, with no property and little capital? She was too used to being her own master, too proud.

She gave up on sleep and stepped outside to check the weather. The sky had cleared as though the storm had never existed, but the smell of it lingered in the air. The night was cool, and alive-smelling, and thick with dampened prairie dirt still hanging in the breeze. She wiped her eyes. Her lungs still felt raw from having been out in the storm earlier. It hadn't rained much after the twister had passed, and the heat had already dried up most of the mud. The moon hung overhead like an audience holding its breath at the theater.

It was only then that she remembered that she had left Old Duke down at the riverbank to fend for himself. A chill crept over her skin. She turned her boots toward the road that led down the bluff and started walking.

The road wound downward among some old, gnarled oaks, the kind of trees that seem like pagans dancing some strange ritual. She had left the store without a light, food, water, or bandages. She chuckled under her breath. If she had consulted Old Duke on the matter, he would told her that a flask of whiskey was the most important thing—and she hadn't even brought *that*.

She walked faster, then started to jog down the road. She caught herself thinking that if he was gone, if he was *dead*, then the town would fall. If he was all right, then there was still a chance.

She made it down to the bottom of the hill. The houses down here were in better shape, with most of the windows still in one piece, although some of them had to be taped up with brown adhesive tape to keep the cracked glass from falling out. She turned onto the side road that led down to Old Duke's spot on the river. She was running now.

The old man's shack had stood next to some cottonwood trees by the river. Their upper branches had been stripped clean or torn away, the broken ends jutting jagged in the moonlight.

An enormous cottonwood branch had speared clean through the shack, like a dagger.

She called to him but heard no response. The door had been ripped away, and inside the darkness was deeper than she could peer through. She cursed herself again for not bringing a light. The smell was about enough to make her gag.

She squatted down and reached inside, felt something wet. She crept forward a little, and put a hand on a body, still warm but not warm enough, and sticky with blood. She felt around a little, and found an arm, followed it out to the wrist, and checked for a pulse. There was nothing.

The fingernails of the hand trailed against her wrist and caught at her skin. They were sharp to a point, and hooked like cat's claws, only heavier—like a mountain lion's claws, she supposed. Old Duke usually kept his hands in his pockets, or behind him. Maybe he had some kind of nail fungus that he was ashamed of.

She started pulling on his arm. She was afraid to go any deeper into the shack, afraid that it would fall on her.

When she had his upper torso almost out into the moonlight, she got her arms up under his shoulders and started pulling that way, thinking that it would be gentler. His head lolled loosely against her shoulder. He had sticks caught up in his hair, heavy ones.

He was out of the shack now, but still in its shadow. She dragged him a few steps further, then put him down, panting.

The moonlight lay full on his face.

Its face.

What she saw before her was not human. It was dressed in ragged clothing, all right, but the face that gazed upwards into nothingness wasn't Old Duke's. It was a wolfish kind of face, more or less hairless, but with a jutting jaw. At its temples were the stub ends of heavy horns that had been broken clean off. The stumps were dotted with blood. Its blank, open eyes were sheep's eyes with hourglass pupils, and the glint had gone out of them.

The ends of its hands *were* claws. Its legs bent more like a dog's hind legs, or a deer's, and its feet ended in split hooves. With a shaking hand and a perverse sense of curiosity, she checked its jaw and found a row of sharp teeth.

And under its chin was a clean cut that opened as broad and sure as the stroke of a paintbrush, all the way through the flesh to a bone that shone almost gold-colored in the moonlight.

"You shouldn't be here, little Claudine," said a voice behind her.

She spun around.

It was Old Duke behind her. She was relieved to see him, and recognized his coat as the one she had given him. He smelled the way he always did, dry as dust, and she almost leaped forward to embrace him, in her relief.

Instead, she laughed. It sounded a little crazy in the night.

"Oh, hello," she said. "Am I glad to see you! I was worried that a tree fell on you."

He shook his head. "It was trying to save *me*," he said. "I'm sorry that it got hurt."

"What happened?"

He said, "Long story short, this feller tried to murder me during the storm. He must have thought I would be distracted." He grinned, showing his terrible teeth.

"Good Lord," Claudine said. "Why?"

"Sump'in I did a long time ago."

"Who is he? *What* is he?"

The old man's mouth tightened. "My son."

The next morning, after not a lick of sleep, Claudine re-opened the store at the usual hour. She had stopped in earlier at a café further down the street for breakfast and coffee. She had carefully weighed the expense. On the one hand, she needed to cling to every penny. On the other hand, goodwill required that she did not. It was going to be a long period where people bought on credit or not at all.

She had decided to stay put, seeing as Old Duke had made it through the storm, and that went into her calculations, too: as long as it did not force her to take a loan from the banks, she would give credit as long as she could. And that meant she needed to get the word around. And *that* meant breakfast and coffee out where she could be seen, and heard.

No one came into the store at first. That was to be expected. But slowly a few people trickled in—shop owners' wives and children, mostly—to commiserate. She repeated her intention to give credit, although none of the shop owners' wives or children bought anything on credit. One little girl, fiercely clutching her mother's hand, even paid for some candy with a nickel. Claudine gave her extra, and nodded at her mother: they understood each other.

Then even that trickle died away. Claudine cleaned, cursing every time she found yet another shard of broken glass. She was going to have to order another window, but thinking of the expense made her cringe.

Finally, as if she had been waiting for it without even knowing, the bells over the door rang, and in walked a sweet-faced, dark-haired man that she immediately recognized as Anson P. Martin.

The supposedly *dead* Anson P. Martin.

He still made the room light up. Everything seemed fresher, newer, and in better repair. Claudine put a hand up to check that her hair wasn't a fright.

Mr. Martin had had a haircut and wore a beard now, had changed the style of his clothes and added a pair of spectacles, but she knew him still. She was that kind of woman. Even as she blushed to see him, her hackles went up.

"Mr. Martin," she said. "What brings you here? Aren't you supposed to be playing dead?"

He bared his teeth at her, to show willing. "I'm sorry, you must have me confused with someone else."

She shook her head. "Oh, I know you. I stared at you like a schoolgirl enough the last time you were here, didn't I? I said a prayer for you over at church, to atone for thinking you part of a—"

But there was no one else in the store, and she was speaking her truth to a man to whom life and death were casual matters.

"You must have me confused with someone else," he said, this time more firmly.

She stared at him, willing herself to answer him with a shake of the head and words of pleasant agreement. But her eyes and voice, she knew, would have betrayed her. And so she said, and did, nothing.

"I'd like to buy some soap and some hair oil, ma'am."

She packaged them up for him, then rang up his bill. He paid up, in cash, while telling her the story that she was supposed to remember: that his name was now Harry C. Pooler, that he was from New York State, that he was passing through town to survey the damage to the new WPA bridge that had been destroyed by the twister.

She kept her mouth shut, electricity running through her fingertips, making her feel like sparks were about to jump out of them, while at the same time making them numb. It must have been no longer than a hymn sung at church that he was in her store, but it felt like an eternity before the door closed on his back. Fortunately she hadn't had her window replaced yet, so she didn't have to watch him walk away, or look back at her, or any such thing.

He was supposed to be dead.

She did not, not for a moment, bother to doubt herself; his voice was the same. Even if he had had a twin brother, the voice would not have been the same, not as close as that. A beard and glasses to disguise himself! Really! He was acting like a villain from a film.

And who else would have picked out the same type of French soap? It had been an unusual choice for a man in the first place. To run into two so similar men, so near in time, of similar appearance and identical voice and manner, was to strain credulity past the point of breaking.

Why was Mr. Martin here? He didn't work for the WPA. Although he might have pretended his way into a position with them, it was, in one way or another, a lie. He was no honest man. Therefore, he had come here for his own dishonest purpose. And yet he had known that the bridge was out, and even before the local paper had come out, it being only a weekly and the building having been much damaged in the storm.

So while Harry C. Pooler and Anson P. Martin *might* be two different men, and Mr. Pooler *might* work for the WPA, and he *might* therefore have a legitimate reason to be in town, it was far more likely that Mr. Martin had returned to town for some purpose related to the bridge...or to the storm.

Claudine chewed on her lip all the rest of the day. Business, if selling on credit to folks who probably would never repay her could be called that, picked up. She closed late, putting it off as long as she could, but finally it had to be done. She went back to her rooms at the back of the store and fed both herself and the cat, then sighed and filled up a canteen of cold well water, fixed up some meat and bread in some waxed paper, and walked down to the river.

~

Old Duke was not anywhere near his shack by the river. In fact the damaged shack had been pulled down and its pieces had been dragged up near the road, to be removed by crews. Likewise, the body that had lain in the shack was gone. Claudine called for Old Duke for a few minutes, but she knew he was nowhere near.

He had gone to the site of the new bridge. She just knew it.

She felt time sliding away under her hands. Old Duke had cautioned her to stay away from the place. He had a son who was a monster. It had been no mere matter of misfortune or injury that had caused his son to appear so, but a complete separation from the human form. Her inexorable reasoning took her a step further: if the son was completely separate from her own species, so must the father be.

If there were such creatures in the world, then the world was not what she had thought it in the first place.

She shivered at the thought of it. The sun had not yet set. Her feet were already taking her toward the bridge. What was on her mind, she found, was her mother, mixing up cosmetics.

I knew your Momma. She was the curious sort.

Claudine knew herself for no curious sort, only a stubborn one.

The road out to the new bridge site didn't require much of a walk, no more than a mile or so. The sunset was a long flare of light that seemed to hang on forever. The wind rustled the leaves in the tall cottonwood trees until they sounded like the flow of water. She could smell a spark in the air that was like the freshness after a storm, but the sky was clear and lazy-looking, completely smooth from one side of the world to the other. She still had the canteen on a strap over her shoulder and the wax-paper package of bread and meat in her hands.

She did not want to be like the Shipleys, huddling in their storm cellar while a man waited it out aboveground. She was too proud to turn back. Too proud even to be terrified.

She approached the construction site cautiously, trying to keep her footsteps silent.

The roadbeds on either bank had been built up and packed down, but no road had yet been laid over them. The base of the bridge would be cement. A couple of the supports had already been poured. They jutted up out of the water, steel rods poking out of the top. The metal rods looked as though they had come alive, twisted every which way by the storm. Construction materials lay everywhere.

She looked out over the bridge. No one was to be seen anywhere. She saw movement on the other side of the bridge, but it was only a half-hidden deer picking its way along the bank. It disappeared silently, almost as though it had never been there.

"Hello?" she called out. But no one answered. She had felt so sure that there would be a tragedy here. She had thought it all out.

She waited until full dark, then turned around and walked back into town.

～

She had finally fallen deep into sleep, all the way past even dreaming, when she was awakened by a sound below her. At first she thought it was the cat. But then something large fell over in the store downstairs and she was wide awake. She threw on a robe and grabbed her shotgun from beside the door of her bedroom. She didn't like the thought of firing it in her store, but she wasn't about to let a burglar steal from her, not while she was working so hard to be generous.

She checked the gun, grabbed her light, and opened her bedroom door slowly, on quiet hinges.

An animal whined in the darkness, too deep to be the whine of a dog. From behind her, the cat hissed. Claudine shoved him backward with one foot, then slipped out of the door and closed it behind her. She still had the hallway and stairs to face. As a girl, she had made a game of going back and forth without letting the boards creak—but she had been younger and lighter then, and the boards had had more give.

The whining continued. The first thing she imagined was a rabid-bit dog, but she couldn't see how it could have got into the building. A raccoon might be clever enough, but she had never heard one whine.

A man with a dog, maybe?

She made it halfway down the stairs before she made the first creak. The whining stopped.

"Who's there?" she shouted.

There was no answer.

She walked down the last few steps quietly but swiftly, unlatched the door, then kicked it open.

The room was pitch black in front of her.

"Move and I'll shoot," she said. Nothing moved.

She braced the shotgun under one arm and turned on the flashlight, shining it around the room.

On the floor underneath one of the racks was a man's body. She recognized the coat, dirty though it was, as well as his scent as Old Duke's. When she stepped closer, she was unsurprised to see that he had taken on the same appearance as the thing that had died in his shack: antlers, hooves, claws...teeth.

She prodded him with her toe. "You awake?" she asked.

He grunted.

"Bleedin'? In some kinda trouble?"

He was lying on his side, curled up around himself. She shone the light onto the floor underneath him and saw a spreading pool of blood—it looked dark under the beam of light, but not quite the same color as blood, more of a dark blue or green.

She walked swiftly to the front of the store and checked the door. That one was all right. The back door had been left hanging open, though. The lock was twisted, like the metal itself had crawled away from the frame. She pushed it shut and wedged it with a wooden chair that she kicked under the handle.

Then she went back to Old Duke and put the gun and light down. She rolled him onto his back and pulled apart his layers of coats until she reached a layer of flesh and fur, not quite warm enough to the touch but warmer than the floor. She found the wound easily enough. He had been shot in the side at an angle. The bullet had gone in right in front of the hip and came out on the same side of his backbone. She rolled him back onto his side and used the light to check for bullet fragments. Not seeing any, she tore one of her last calico day-dresses off the rack and used it to help staunch the flow of blood, which was flowing but at least not pumping.

Old Duke started mumbling, his same voice as ever. "Tea...tea," he said. "Your momma's special tea."

Claudine pressed her lips together. She supposed he ought to know best—and he surely did not want her to run for a doctor. She placed his claws atop the wound in his side. "You have to hold that," she said. "Hold it tight and don't faint."

Then she dashed upstairs to the big steamer trunk where her mother had kept her things—supplies for her cosmetics shelf, and supplies for other things, which she never displayed but always had on hand.

Her momma's special tea wasn't meant for healing, but for

women who found themselves in a family way but without means of supporting the child. She found the little cardboard box of it in its drawer. She would have to boil water on the stove to steep it. She busied herself, lighting the gas and filling the kettle. The cat was nearly frantic trying to get downstairs. Finally she shut in him a closet, knowing that she would come back to claw marks and cat urine, but at least it wouldn't be on her mattress.

While she was waiting, she went back downstairs "Found the tea, boiling some water. It's old stuff, though. I don't know how much good it'll do you."

"Good enough," he grunted. The claws on his wound were weaker than they had been before.

"What else can I do right now?"

He shook his head, the antlers on his brow turning back and forth.

"Who did this to you?"

He shook his head again.

"Not your son?"

Old Duke started coughing, blue blood coming up at his lips. "Not this time."

"Why?"

She expected him to go silent again. But he said, "Others hunt me too. On the run...two different worlds." He coughed again. She realized that he was trying not to laugh.

The kettle whistled and she went to answer the call.

Claudine was bringing the tea down the stairs in her largest mug when she heard the back door crash open. The damned shotgun and the light were still on the floor next to Old Duke. She crept down to the bottom of the stairs and peered through the cracked door.

Booted feet marched into the store, then stopped. A chuckle

echoed around the room. "No witches here to help you this time, Old Duke," said a voice.

She recognized it, of course, as belonging to one Anson P. Martin, or whatever his name was.

The smart thing to do would be stay put and let fate work itself out as best it could. She heard the sound of footsteps again, and the sound of dragging. Mr. Martin was dragging Old Duke toward the back door.

She set the mug of tea on the floor and eased herself through the door. Even though the lights were on now, she didn't think she'd been seen or heard. She crouched down behind a large shelf of bolts of cloth and tried to get a peek at the floor where Old Duke had been.

The light was still there, still lit, but the shotgun was gone. She made a face. She waited until Mr. Martin had dragged Old Duke out the door and the screen had slammed shut, then dashed across the store. Her shotgun was nowhere to be found, but underneath the counter was an iron crowbar. She took it up and slipped on a pair of new house shoes from their rack.

A trail of blue blood led to the back door.

If she yelled for help, how long would it take for someone to come? Longer than she liked, this far past midnight. She could run to the Sheriff's, but that was more or less the same problem.

But across the street was a *bank.*

The same one, as a matter of fact, that had been robbed so recently, and upon whose fate the town depended.

And there she was, with a perfectly good iron crowbar in her hands.

She turned around and tore off toward her front door. She went out, closed it, then pried her own front door open with the crowbar, making sure to split the wood.

Then she ran across the street to the bank.

With one big overhanded swing, she smashed the crowbar into the glass of the bank door. It had wire embedded in it, and the glass shattered and fell out. She took the crowbar to the bank's big, plate-glass window then, dancing back out of the way as soon as the glass cracked. It fell out in shards that looked as though they would have liked to kill her.

She belted it back through her store and out the back door.

A shout came from the other side of the building. Good. The bank had an alarm, although she hadn't been sure if she'd set it off. But someone had noticed. That was the important thing.

The trail of blood led down the alley, but neither Mr. Martin nor Old Duke were to be seen.

That was just as well. She walked softly to the end of it and caught sight of movement further on. Mr. Martin was moving at good speed down the next block's alleyway, Old Duke's hooves dragging along behind him.

She knew where Mr. Martin was going: out to that bridge.

She smashed a couple more windows, then turned away from the alley. No matter how quickly Mr. Martin dragged Old Duke along, it wouldn't be as fast she as she could run.

Not that she would be able to do any good when she got there. She didn't even have the pennyroyal tea with her. The prybar she had left behind to help frame Mr. Martin for the bank break-in. Mr. Martin still had her shotgun.

How was she going to get through this? Any of this?

She hadn't been inquisitive enough. She had let the surfaces of things trick her into thinking that she knew everything there was to know about running a store and living her life, independent of any man. How ill-prepared she had been, she hadn't even imagined.

∾

She arrived at the bridge with time to spare. Overhead the moon lingered. It was well past midnight, and yet there the full moon was, directly overhead. It wasn't quite right, the moon. It seemed to waver in place. Looking at it made her eyes water.

The low riverbed seemed to drink up the light, reflecting nothing. The water stank from weeds rotting in low, stagnant pools. She hid behind one of the bridge supports and waited for whatever was about to come next.

If there's anybody listening, I don't know what to do next. But I'm prepared to learn.

It was the only prayer she had left to offer up.

She heard the sound of footsteps coming along the road, loud in the night. No dragging, though.

Then she saw Mr. Martin's shadow. He had picked up Old Duke and slung him over his shoulders. The shadow flickered. It was there and it yet wasn't—the strange moonlight had twisted it. Mr. Martin stepped up onto the new roadbed. Where he was going, she couldn't imagine. The bridge wasn't yet complete.

Then she realized that he was going to throw Old Duke into the water. Why, she didn't know—it wasn't barely deep enough to drown in.

The moon shimmered even worse than before, and then something rubbed up against her hand, cool to the touch.

She looked down at it: a piece of metal had come up out of a pile of supplies near her, and was nuzzling her hand like a cat. It was a section of rebar. She patted it without thinking, then crouched down next to it and whispered, "Sure would be a shame if that there man up there found himself tripped with his arms and legs wrapped up tight together."

The piece of metal seemed to consider this, and butted at her hand again. She patted it again, and then it slipped off, a few more of its kind following along behind it, as though it was the most natural thing in the world. The sections of rebar seemed almost liquid in the moonlight, oozing up the sides of the dirt roadbed like worms.

She crawled up after them, keeping quiet. She wasn't sure what else to do.

Mr. Martin had reached the end of the bridge. He dropped the shotgun and hoisted Old Duke off his shoulders and onto the packed dirt.

"Can't believe it took so long to find you," he was saying. "Can't believe I was in the same damned town as you for *weeks* and didn't find you."

Old Duke didn't answer. His form was quiet and still: a thing used up, or almost.

"Not taking you all the way back to San Francisco. Here's going to have to be good enough. Like to drop you right into the hole you dug for us all."

He was panting and leaning on his knees. The shotgun lay beside him.

"They really did me over in Omaha. Supposed to be dead now myself. That's where I got the idea you weren't really dead. Told your son. Did you know I knew him? We could only agree on one thing, and that was how much of a bastard you were. Has he come a-visiting yet? Wouldn't be surprised—"

The rebar had arrived at Mr. Martin's feet. It wound around them. Other sections of it pinned his arms to his sides. He yelled and struggled, but it was no good.

Claudine climbed the rest of the way up the roadbed and picked up her shotgun, which she then checked to make sure it was loaded, and aimed it at Mr. Martin.

"Hello," she said, blushing and teeth chattering. "Mr. Martin, or whoever you are."

He rolled from his back to his side, looking at her. "You don't know what you're getting into. Go home. And pray that this bastard doesn't call down trouble upon your house."

"He's this town's good-luck charm," Claudine said stubbornly.

Mr. Martin laughed. "Good luck charm?" It apparently struck him as funny enough that he could barely breathe—but that might have just been the rebar digging into his sides. "Good luck charm?" he whispered. "He'll send us all to hell, that's how much of a good luck charm he is."

Old Duke moaned. Claudine left Mr. Martin to stew in his own juices. Old Duke's fur felt even colder underneath his coats, and soaking wet with that strange blood of his.

"Water," he said.

She didn't have any. "Shh," she said. "I'll run back to town and get help. As long as those rebars stay put—"

One claw came up and grabbed the front of her dress, tearing the cloth and scratching hard. "Push me. Over. Into the water."

"But..."

But that was what Mr. Martin had wanted to do. So that couldn't be right.

"The water! Don't...think about it. Just do it."

Well, she hadn't come all this way to pretend that she knew what was going on. She put the shotgun down and began dragging Old Duke to the edge. She got as close as she could without herself falling over and stopped to catch her breath.

Mr. Martin was watching her, looking as puzzled as she felt.

"What now?" she asked.

"Wait," she thought she heard the old man whisper.

A sound was rising from upstream. A delicate sound, but one that seemed to thrum through her feet.

She shuddered as she realized what it was: water.

"Get ready," she thought she heard. But Old Duke's canine face was lolled open, eyes empty. He was gone.

Nevertheless, she stepped around him and scooted him closer, bit by bit, to the edge. It wasn't going to be a straight fall, but an awkward roll down a steep slope to the water. The moonlight made her head hurt. She straightened up, looking upstream for the flood she knew was coming. Then, at some movement, looked across the river.

An enormous beast watched her. The horns that sprang from its brow seemed to be covered in pearl, and its white fur shimmered in the moonlight. It was the brother, at the very least, of the empty old monster lying at her feet.

Then the water came rushing down the riverbed and the earth shook so hard underfoot that she dropped to her knees. Someone grabbed her from behind. It felt like her skin burned at the touch. She was slung away from the edge and had to scramble to keep from sliding off the roadbed into the water.

Mr. Martin had freed himself somehow. His clothes were falling apart and smoking, only blackness underneath. He began to drag Old Duke away from the edge—he must have changed his mind.

The sections of rebar lay on the roadbed, twisted and steaming. It looked as though acid had burned through them, and they flopped around weakly, dying. Claudine took up handfuls of dirt and rubbed them into her shoulder, shouting at the pain.

"Almost tricked me, old man," Mr. Martin said. His face didn't look like much of a face anymore, but a face-shaped candle melting in the heat. "You almost had me that time."

The water thundered around the roadbed. Trash piled up around it. And the water was still rising. Claudine, teeth chattering, walked down as close as she dared to the broken tree branches and said, "I don't suppose any of you could see to helping Old Duke out, could you?"

But there was no response. She was on her own. Oh well. At least she still had the shotgun. She knew all about *that.*

Mr. Martin had picked up Old Duke and slung him over his shoulders again, and was staggering toward her. In the moonlight, his sweet face seemed slack, and his eyes pitch-black.

She stood in front of him, aiming the shotgun at his chest.

Mr. Martin chuckled. "You don't want to be in my way just now, Miss. Step aside."

"I can't let you do this."

He paused. "Why? What has he ever done for you?"

"My momma liked him," Claudine said. "But if that's not enough reason for you, let's just say that when you came to town, it felt like life had come back to the place. Then it turned out you were nothing but a dirty bank robber."

"Me?" Mr. Martin said incredulously. "You're doing this just to spite me? Damn old broad, what did you think, that I was ever going to get around to *your* bed?"

Claudine shrugged. "Take him back to the water, or I'll put a shell in your chest."

"No." He began to stagger toward her. "You don't know what the hell is going on, yet there you are, digging in your heels just because you can. Can't you see that this is for your own good?"

"If it was for my own good, you wouldn't have mocked me," she said, and shot him.

He fell down, and Old Duke fell from his shoulders. Mr. Martin was bleeding but it didn't look like right. She had another shell, so she fired it into his head at point-blank range. His head melted into a puddle of black goo.

She didn't think it would hold him long.

She tossed the shotgun down and dragged Old Duke to the edge of the roadbed. The water was about a foot past the edge. She got behind him and shoved.

The water took him away downstream, subsiding almost as soon as it had him in its grasp.

On the other side of the river, the great beast reared up on its hind legs and roared. Then vanished.

She felt a breath of air against the back of her neck and spun around, expecting the thing that had played at being a Greek god to rise up and do something terrible to her.

But it was gone.

S he staggered back to town. Everyone was in an uproar. The story was, someone had busted into the bank and tried to steal something, but had been chased off before he could get into the safe. He had run directly across the street and broken into Claudine's dry goods store—

She broke in to tell them that she knew that part. She had come downstairs to find Mr. Martin in the store with some kind of dye all over his hands. What dye, *she* didn't know, and how he had survived being killed in Omaha, she wasn't sure of either. Maybe it hadn't been him in Omaha—she was sure he had been in her store, however. She had threatened him and he had knocked her down, breaking down the back door in his haste to get out, and had run down the alleyway behind Main Street, trying to break into other shops as he went.

She had followed him all the way out to the bridge with her shotgun.

Did she shoot him? they wanted to know.

She had shot *at* him, but she wasn't sure if she had hit anything. She hoped she had. Then the flood had come and...

The flood.

They led her to the bluff. Past the trees she could see where the flood had wiped out everything down there. Houses, electric lines, everything was a swirl of mud and broken branches. She saw a dead cow float by and turned her head to the side. The Shipleys were gone, along with at least a hundred other folks.

For a couple of moments, at least, she didn't feel anything but shock.

She hadn't known—

Then it all started to crash in on her.

It wasn't that she hadn't known. She hadn't *thought*.

Old Duke had spun her around his finger from beginning to end. He had used her—she had let herself be used. A battle between *whatever* those things were, and she had picked sides like the damn fool that she was.

The fact was, neither one of those sides gave a damn about the people down at the bottom of the bluff, or about her either. Just about themselves.

Old Duke was gone, they told her. No one had seen him since before the flood.

He had damned well better be, she thought. He had damned well better be.

ABOUT THE AUTHOR

DeAnna Knippling is always tempted to lie on her bios. Her favorite musician is Tom Waits, and her favorite author is Lewis Carroll. Her favorite monster is zombies. Her life goal is to remake her house in the image of the House on the Rock, or at least Ripley's Believe It Or Not. You should buy her books. She promises that she'll use the money wisely on bookshelves and secret doors. She lives in Colorado and is the author of the A Fairy's Tale horror series which starts with *By Dawn's Bloody Light*, and other books like *The Clockwork Alice*, *A Murder of Crows: Seventeen Tales of Monsters & the Macabre*, and more.

As always, this story is dedicated to Lee and Ray,
without whose love none of this would be possible.

Find out more about DeAnna at:
wonderlandpress.com

f facebook.com/deanna.knippling
🐦 twitter.com/dknippling
BB bookbub.com/authors/deanna-knippling

AWAKENING

LINDA JORDAN

Merial stood on the shore. The wind off the sea blew her knee-length green hair in a swirl around her. Rope-like strands battered her tough, naked skin. The wind curved around Merial. Playing.

The slate-colored sky roiled with clouds. Rain was coming. She didn't care. The seals just off the point barked at her to come play. She stood firmly on the rocks. Unwilling to move.

Her mother's words rolled through her mind.

"Your father's a dryad."

A dryad!

All her life Merial had seen herself as one with the sea. Her mother, a naiad. Merial assumed she must be too. Even though she swam more slowly than the other young ones. Wasn't as flexible. She had a much more difficult time doing water magic than any of them. The others flowed and she struggled. Which made her stronger.

She'd just assumed water was her element.

Now to find out that her father belonged to the earth, to the trees and the forest.

She'd never met him. Her parents had parted soon after she was born, before her memories. They'd decided that Merial was more water than earth, before she was too young to have any say in the matter. So mother had raised her and father returned to the forest.

She should go find him. Talk to him. To see if she was meant to be somewhere else. Her fists clenched as the sea splashed cold salt water on her face. As if it was telling her to wake up and go away. Go to the forest.

She'd never met a dryad. And she didn't want to. She just wanted to fit in the world somewhere and be happy. Be helping the sea. As if she'd ever been any help to anyone. As if she belonged anywhere.

A gull swooped past, shrieking over the sound of the crashing waves. The white and gray feathers ruffled by its flight. The bird landed nearby, picking at the exposed mussels on the rocks. The tide was going out, leaving the shore behind.

She should go find the others. They were harvesting purple dulse today. Thinning out the seaweed and casting it up on the shore.

Humans would come and collect it, to eat it as well, Uaine the elder said. The land here was shared by humans and Fae.

Merial had only seen one once. The thought of the human made her shiver, such a frightening creature.

Her bluish skin oozed water. How could she not be of the sea? Dryads probably didn't leak water like she did. Their skin was probably rough, like tree bark. Her father must be monstrous. How could mother have loved him? Why had they thought it was a good idea to cross those elemental boundaries?

Merial smelled the seals now. Their particular musky scent, mingled with that of fish and salt. She licked her lips, tasting the salt water there.

Still she stood, her webbed feet gripping the sharp rocks. The wind threatened to blow her off the outcropping.

Finally, she turned and climbed down. Her mind made up. She must go find him. Otherwise she'd always wonder. Always feel like she belonged elsewhere. She must know before her sixteenth summer. There would be a proving then. Uaine was looking for students. Those who would carry on the wisdom after she faded and gave her body to the sea. Students willing to devote their lives to making Faerie grow.

Merial had always thought she would be one of them. Even though she was slower and less talented than many water spirits her age.

Her bare feet felt the rock which stuck out of the sea and melded into a small strip of sand that merged with the grasslands. The forest lay beyond.

Merial didn't know where her father lived. Eoin, that was his name. She supposed there were many different forests, but she'd keep going until she found him.

She tried to find a path to pick her way through the sharp, thick-leaved grasses towards the nearest clump of trees. There didn't seem to be any paths. The beginning of the forest was made of pine trees mostly. She didn't know much about trees, but Merial did know the difference between pines and yews and holly. She could tell an oak tree from an ash. And Hazelnuts, she knew those too. Often they grew along streams, dropping their ripe nuts in the water. Once water-logged, the nuts were quite tasty.

Whatever would she do for food? It was winter, there probably wouldn't be much. She should find a stream and walk or swim up it. There might be some grasses in them. Perhaps some snails.

It took most of the day before she scented water. It was a small stream. She sat in it, washing off the dirt from traveling. Soothing her bruised and cut skin. She'd unwisely traveled through a clump of wild roses. She'd gotten gashes while trying to get out. Merial found quite a few wizened rose hips, which were tart and tasty once she chewed them for a while.

She sipped the fresh water. Then wet her hair. It would drip and keep her skin moist. A few trout swam past quickly, alarmed at her presence.

"I won't hurt you my friends. I don't eat fishies."

They returned and eventually swam between the tips of her webbed fingers.

The stream flowed through the middle of ash and yew trees. Merial sensed no other Fae about. Perhaps she wasn't in Faerie any longer. She didn't know where the boundaries were, but Faerie was a very large place. Perhaps Fae didn't live everywhere in Faerie.

She swam up the shallow stream. It was barely deep enough to pull herself along. Grabbing at tree roots and large rocks in the stream bed. The water grew colder and Merial realized she was traveling uphill.

She'd never been this far from the sea and the pull of it unnerved her. She didn't belong in the forest.

The sun had set and Merial found a deep pool to spend the night in. She wrapped her arms and legs around a log which had fallen across and into the stream. It formed a dam, creating a deep pool behind it. Several large fish lived there, but she didn't recognize what kind they were. They weren't going to come near her to find out what she was either. They clumped at the other end of the pool, staring at her. She slept anyway.

When Merial woke, the sun had just climbed above the trees. Its warmth lit up the dark places of the forest. It warmed her too much with no sea breezes to cool her. She dropped beneath the surface of the water, wetting her gills and the large fish scattered in panic. So as not to alarm them anymore, she swam farther upstream.

The water felt cool and was deep enough for her to swim. She made good progress all morning. Then she came to a deeper spot, filled with grasses. Grabbing a handful, she chewed it. It wasn't salty like sea grass, but would sustain her. She ate several small snails, which had a mild fishy flavor and thin, crunchy shells.

The day had grown quite warm for winter. The forest had changed to yew trees and a few oaks. Many of them very old. She could hear them speaking to each other, but couldn't understand what they said.

Two does entered the clearing near her and she said, "Hello."

They looked up at her in alarm and almost fled.

"I mean you no harm. I'm looking for a dryad named Eoin."

The largest doe said, "I know of no such dryad."

"Where are the dryads? Perhaps I can ask them."

The smaller doe looked shrunken with age. Her fur, rough and mangy. She said, "There have been no dryads around here for a very long time. Just humans."

"Am I still in Faerie?"

"Can you not even tell?" asked the smaller doe.

"No, I can't. I belong to the sea. I've never been this far inland."

"Faerie weaves in and out of these hills. If you follow the stream you will go back inside it," said the large doe.

"How far is it?"

"A day's walk," said the smaller doe, chewing on her leg.

Probably an itchy spot, decided Merial.

"Thank you," she said.

Merial swam farther upstream. Through patches of shade and dappled sun and then much later, rain. The stream passed near a group of stone dwellings. Smoke came out of the tops and the smell of humans lay heavy in the air.

Merial couldn't see any humans, but left quickly. She didn't want to meet any humans. They were dangerous and frightening. The things they did to Fae they caught were difficult to think about.

By night Merial still didn't think she'd made it back to Faerie. Her arms ached from swimming without resting. She huddled beneath a bridge, sitting in the deepest part of the shallow stream. Only her head sticking out. In the middle of the night a human came and made a nest beneath the bridge. It didn't even see her. Just drank liquid from a bottle, then curled up and slept.

Merial didn't sleep any more that night. She just watched the human and rested. Early in the morning a clanking metal thing went over the bridge. It was one of the human inventions, which she'd heard they rode. Smelly, metal things.

After that Merial fled farther upstream, beginning her day. She swam and swam. Cold rain streamed down. It was a dark day, the sky filled with deep gray clouds and the sun never came out. Was this her destiny? To go on searching for her father forever? Maybe she should just turn back and return to the sea?

But she didn't.

She passed many ducks and even a couple of swans before finding her way back into Faerie. Merial felt it when she swam through the boundary this time. It shimmered and she could reach out and touch the energy. The water coming out of Faerie tasted fresher and had a vitality to it that was lost farther downstream. It gave her a small burst of power that relieved her exhaustion.

When the stream spread out and became shallow, Merial stood and walked. She could smell the forest surrounding her. It had an earthy moistness to it that the forest downstream lacked. The trees still talked to each other, but this time she could understand them.

"Well, it's been a long time since one of you has been around here," said an ancient oak."

"What is it?" asked a young hawthorn.

"It's a water spirit, to be sure. I don't know what kind. Definitely from the sea."

Merial stood and looked at them.

"Well, what are you?" asked a hazelnut.

"I don't know. My mother's a naiad. My father's a dryad. What does that make me?"

"Ah," said the oak. "I thought I sensed something earthy about you. I would say that it makes you a very complex creature."

"But am I dryad or naiad?"

"I don't have the answer to that question," said the oak.

"Who does?" Merial asked.

She'd never talked to a tree before. It was said that trees knew everything because they were all connected by their roots. That they shared their wisdom between them.

"Only you can know the answer to such an important question. And you are very, very young to learn such an answer, even for a Fae."

Merial snorted. She certainly didn't know.

"Do you know a dryad name Eoin?"

"He has passed this way," said the oak, its bare branches waving in the breeze blowing through.

"Where is he? I need to talk with him," she said.

"Keep following the stream. He is farther that way." The tree pointed upstream with all its branches.

"How much farther?" asked Merial.

"For your kind, probably days."

"Thank you," she said, and kept walking up the stream.

How long would this take? Already she longed for the sea. For the taste of salty kelp. And mussels, clams and oysters. The few tiny snails she'd eaten yesterday hadn't been enough. Her empty belly rumbled.

She walked upstream, the rain pouring down and lubricating her skin. It was dark here in the forest even though the sun was still up, because it was hidden by clouds. The water continued to be shallow. Finally, the forest grew even darker and she found a pool to sleep in. The water came up to her neck if she sat on the gravel stream bed. At least it would keep her gills wet.

Merial woke to the sun shimmering through the bare tree branches. The night had grown cold and ice crystals formed on the branches, making the sun's light split into a million different rays. It looked so beautiful.

On the bank beside the stream sat a centaur.

"Stunning, is it not?" he asked.

"Yes." She stared at him. She'd never seen a centaur before. Hadn't really believed they existed. A melding of Fae and horse. How could such a thing be?

His skin was a luminous gray and he had Fae ears. A strip of red and gray hair ran from above his forehead and over the top of his head and neck. It continued down his back and ended where the Fae part of his body ended and the horse began. His tail was also red and gray. The horse fur was red with gray dapples throughout it. From his knees down to the hooves hung a long gray fluff of hair. He was quite the most beautiful creature she'd ever seen.

"You look puzzled," he said, his warm golden eyes looking at her as if he could see into her very soul.

"I've never seen a centaur before," she said, looking away after realizing how rude she was being.

"Neither have most Fae. We are some of the oldest beings ever to exist in Faerie, but there are not many of us left."

"What happened to your kind?"

"We got tired of living. Of seeing the bickering between different kinds of Fae. Then there were several Luminaries who took power and they did not take kindly to us. Called us inferior beings. We were persecuted for a very long time. When that ended those of us left kept to ourselves. We live at the fringes of Faerie. Unwilling to take part in life with other Fae."

"And yet, you're talking to me."

"You too are not among the other Fae," he said.

"I'm just far from home. When I'm in the sea, I'm never alone."

"Who is with you in the sea?"

"The mussels, clams, fish, urchins, sea stars, other naiads, merpeople, there are so many beings that live in the sea. Seals, otters, whales."

"You are not alone here. The moss I sit upon on is alive. The trees, that briar over there, the rocks in the stream. The flock of birds perched in those trees. The hare who has her head stuck out of her burrow over there. She is listening to our conversation. If it were summer, there would be bees, butterflies and countless insects surrounding us. Many of them are resting now, others waiting to be born. There is so much life here."

Merial looked around, realizing he was right. She'd always viewed the land as barren while the sea was a rich living place.

"Still, why are you talking to me if centaurs are solitary creatures?" she asked.

"We were not always solitary. I am lonely and you seem lost."

"I am. I've never been on land before, not this far inland."

"You are still not on land. You are sitting in a stream." He cocked his head as if amused at her.

"But I'm not in the sea. I've never been as far from the sea as this."

"Why are you here?"

"I'm looking for my father. A dryad named Eoin."

"Your father is a dryad? Well that makes sense."

"Why?"

"You do not look like the water Fae I have met before. Your hair is thick like dryads' hair, not thin and silky like most water Fae. Your eyes are large, oval and green like dryads' eyes, not pale and squinty. And the water Fae who I have met are more tall and slender than you are," he said. "You are more muscular, like dryads."

"I know. I don't fit in anywhere."

"Nonsense. Everyone fits in or they would not be here. You are no exception."

"I don't suppose you know where my father is."

"No, but I can take you to where most of the dryads live. At least the ones I know about. There are so many beings in Faerie and Faerie is such a large place. She changes so much and so quickly that one is never in the same place twice. Ever."

Merial wasn't sure she'd like company. She felt a sense of relief that the centaur would show her the way, but she didn't really want anyone to witness a meeting with her father. Surely he'd reject her. If he had wanted a daughter he would have come to visit at least once in her sixteen summers.

She said, "When do we leave and which direction should we go?"

"Whenever you are ready. Do we need to stay near water? Can you walk on land?" he asked.

"Water is easier. Do the dryads live far away from water?"

"I am not sure, it has been a long time since I met them and I was not looking for water at the time. Following the stream will be difficult for me. Sometimes I can walk near it. In other places the shore is filled with downed trees and too much shrubbery."

"I can swim and meet you at the clear places."

"That might work," he said.

"I'm Merial. What's your name?"

"Merial, what a lovely melodic name. It has been so long since anyone called me by name, I can barely remember. I believe my name is Embarr."

"Well Embarr, let's go. I was told that the dryads were days away. There's still a long way to go."

Merial swam upstream through the icy water. Where the stream ran deeper there were warmer pockets. She spotted Embarr moving alongside the stream, but a ways off because of all the willows growing near the bank. She could almost swim as fast as he moved. But maybe he wasn't going at his fastest speed.

She swam until the sun rose higher in the sky. The farther upstream Merial went, the warmer the water grew. Ice had long since vanished. She could feel and hear Embarr's hooves thundering on the ground just off to her left. He was hidden by the bushes and downed logs.

Once she came to a place where the bank was clear, Merial stopped and stood up in the stream. It came up to her thighs here. The water became deeper as the stream grew narrower.

Embarr leapt over a small log and came over to the stream. His torso bent over and he took a handful of water and sipped it.

"That was a grand run. I have not run in a very long time. No need to, really."

Merial nodded. She felt a bit tired. She hadn't swum fast since she'd left the sea. Always unsure where she was going.

They rested a while and then took off again. The bank was clear for a while, then another section of forest drew close to the water. Embarr moved off to where the trees grew less thickly. Merial continued to swim upstream. Grasses massed near the edge of the water. There were more fish hiding in it than she'd seen downstream. The water tasted sweeter, richer and more alive.

At the next clearing Merial stopped. She had swum twice as far as the day before. Her arms ached from tiredness. She stood up and waited. After a time Embarr walked into the clearing, breathing hard.

"I am really tired," he said. "It is getting warmer out."

"So am I. Shall we rest until tomorrow?"

"Yes, the sun is going down."

It *was* getting darker, she hadn't even noticed. There were hazelnut trees bending over the stream ahead. She walked beneath them, looking for some last nuts of the season. There was one floating in the water, caught in some grass, but when she went to pick it up, it fell apart. Too rotted to eat. She let it drift downstream for those creatures who would enjoy it.

Embarr was picking some withered berries off a bush and gave her two. They were tart and chewy, but she had no idea what they were.

"That is it for dinner, I fear," he said.

"I don't need to eat very often," Merial said, her stomach rumbling.

"Neither do I. Perhaps there will be more food where the dryads are."

"That would be wonderful."

She sat near the edge of the stream. The water there came up to her neck. Embarr stretched out on the grass, his torso still upright.

They didn't talk, just watched the sun set and the moon rise in silence. Listening to the chatter of nearby birds. A red fox came through the clearing, gazed at them and continued on. Later a group of deer wandered through and stood staring, probably trying to figure out what Embarr was.

Merial slept and presumably so did Embarr. When she woke in the middle of the night, he was lying flat out on the grass near the bank, snoring. The nearly full moon was high in the sky. She went back to sleep until the sun rose in the morning.

After snacking on more tart, dried-out berries, they set off again. The day stayed sunny and grew warmer.

When they stopped for a rest, Merial spotted yellow flowers blooming.

"Those are daffodils," said Embarr.

"Do they usually bloom in winter?"

"No. They normally flower in early spring. But we are approaching the heart of Faerie. Oft times, the temperatures are moderated here. Some Luminaries have even kept this part of Faerie in summer year round."

Even the water in the little stream grew warmer. Fish flourished here, as did snails, tadpoles and frogs.

Finally, Embarr told her she needed to get out of the stream.

"Just a bit farther, over that way, are some dryads." He pointed away from the water.

She got out and walked with him. Her webbed feet clumsy on the uneven ground. The forest smelled of damp earth and fresh green growth. She felt relieved when they came to a place where the forest floor was covered with soft moss, and no branches littered the area beneath the trees.

They walked past bushes of all sorts: shiny, spiky, and even one filled with beautiful white flowers that had thick, flexible petals and a golden, yellow center.

Beyond that stood three dryads. They were cutting apart a dead and decaying tree. Cutting it into smaller pieces with magic. Then stacking the pieces into piles.

"Hello," said Embarr.

The three of them turned and astonishment lay on their faces.

"Hello," said a dryad, whose long green ropy hair reached her knees, even though it was tied back in a thong.

"I am Embarr, and this is my friend Merial. She is searching for a dryad name Eoin."

"I am Ash, this is Pine and Willow. Eoin is nearby. Shall I call him for you?"

"Yes, please," said Merial. "I can't seem to walk very far on dry land."

How could she have ever thought she could be a dryad? She couldn't even make it through the forest with ease.

The dryads continued to shoot magic into the air. Cutting branches off the tree and catching the falling pieces. Then trimming the branches down to size and stacking them. The three dryads worked together in a graceful dance. They worked on the same tree until it was done.

The dryads were all strong and muscular. Their skin colors were varying shades of green. They all had the same ropy hair, but one had brown, the other black and Ash's was green. All their hair was pulled back and restrained, probably so as not to get in the way of their work. Willow wore a strip of fabric around her hips, fastened with a metal brooch. The other two were unadorned, as most Fae she'd met were. Unless it was a celebration. Then Fae wore elaborate costumes.

Merial sat beneath a large oak tree, on a patch of particularly soft moss. Embarr lay down next to her.

When the dryads had finished, Ash came over to them and sat.

"Eoin will be here shortly. I have lived thousands of summers and yet this is the first time I have ever seen a centaur. It is said that your people left Faerie."

"No," said Embarr. "We have just retreated to the edges, where most Fae do not go anymore. We dislike politics."

"And there has been far too much of that," said Ash. "The fire Fae and sylphs have too little to do. The stone Fae continue to build. The dryads care for the forest. And the naiads tend the water and its creatures. But the others. ..."

She held up her hands in frustration.

"Why are you cutting the tree down?" asked Embarr.

"It is past its time. We are hastening its decay somewhat. So we may plant more trees here."

Behind Ash, five dryads entered the clearing. This group was as varied in skin tones and hair colors as the first. Leading them was a tall Fae with dark green ropy hair and skin the same color. The only male in the group, he wore a leather string around his neck. From it hung the small, pink and white shell of a scallop.

Merial stood and stared at him.

"Who wanted to see me?" he asked.

"Are you Eoin?"

"I am."

"I'm Merial. Ileanna's daughter. Your daughter."

His eyes opened wide.

The other Fae went over to speak with Embarr, fascinated by the presence of a centaur.

"Come, let us talk," said Eoin.

He held out his arm for her and she took it, feeling the strong muscles. They walked a ways away, into a sunny meadow. He sat on a downed log and she sat nearby on a smooth, warm boulder. The sun felt good on her skin.

"I always wondered who you would turn out to be. Ileanna asked me to leave when it was clear you were more naiad than dryad. How is she?"

"She is fine. Busy weaving baskets of kelp when I left. But why did you leave?"

"I was so restless. Missed my forest. I was living along the shore, alone mostly. She spent much of her time underwater, acclimatizing you to the sea. I was unnecessary. And we dryads like to keep busy. I could only plant so many trees there. The sea coast isn't hospitable to trees. I still miss her, every day," he said, fingering the shell.

Merial said nothing. Her mother never spoke of him. Did she miss him at all?

"How old are you?" he asked.

"Sixteen."

"Ah, then the choosing comes for you this summer, does it not?"

"Yes. That's why I'm here. I don't fit in with the naiads."

"You look like a naiad to me. Well, except for the hair. And your eyes. And your build. Your skin weeps water and is the color of the sea. Your fingers and toes are webbed. You have gills. You have a watery feel about you."

"I'm slower than the naiads. And not as powerful. I'm stronger. And I have to work much harder to swim the same speed. My magic barely exists."

"Perhaps your magic has not arrived yet."

Bees buzzed past her, looking for pollen. Spring must have come to the heart of Faerie. There would be no bees near the sea at this time of year.

She could smell the sun on her skin, salt water oozing from her pores and drying. Merial finally answered him with the obvious, not wanting to seem rude.

"Of course it has. Everyone gets their power by five years."

"Dryads do not. Sometimes their power doesn't come on until their in their twenties. Before that magic just comes in trickles. We get what we need to survive. You probably have a bit more than most dryads your age. Survival in the sea is more difficult than in the forest."

"Really?"

It gave her some hope that more power might be coming. Beyond just the little trickle she already had.

"Dryads often have to go through a challenge of some sort, an initiation before their power comes in fully."

"I'm challenged at everything. How much more challenge do I need?"

"An initiation then. I know naiads have them."

"They do. There are contests. Races. Treasure hunts of a sort. Finding things the elders have hidden."

"Well, perhaps that is what you need."

"I've never entered them. They're just a reminder of how slow and clumsy I am compared to the rest."

He shifted on the log, lifting up one leg to put an ankle over his knee. She looked at his face. He was very handsome. No wonder her mother was attracted to him. Merial recognized the sharp cheekbones as her own. Her mother had a rounder face.

"I think you should begin entering them. That might set in motion what you need to bring your magic on. For dryads, sometimes we need to put ourselves in dangerous situations to push things along. Perhaps a fear of failing would be dangerous enough to find your magic."

Merial pushed a dead seed stalk over with her feet.

"I nearly always feel like a failure."

"Well, you must change that. You will never find your power if you think you will always fail."

"Why?"

"It is the way the world works. If you do not believe in yourself, then the magic will never come to you."

"It is so," said a deep voice behind her. Embarr. "Excuse me, I could not help but overhear you. You must believe in yourself. You believed you could find your father, am I right? Otherwise you would never have set off on this journey."

"I guess so. But it's hard to believe I can defeat naiads at water magic and basic swimming skills, when they've been beating me at them ever since I was born," said Merial.

"That is because you do not understand how important it is to believe you can accomplish things. That belief is a sort of magic. It helps us push through when we would give up in defeat," said Eoin.

Merial shifted on her stone.

"It's not like I give up," she said. "I swim harder and more than any of the naiads. I practice all the skills we use, every day. It's just that it doesn't seem to matter. They still out swim me, out magic me. Every time."

"By saying that, I can tell you have given up," said Eoin. "Your words define you. You must change the thoughts in your head. I was like you once. I could never keep up with the other dryads. Never had as much power as they did. But I learned how to believe I did anyway.

A yew tree taught me that. By looking at my life from the outside, he could see what my problem was. I changed the way I thought. It was not easy, but it worked. And my life changed completely."

Merial snorted. "So you're saying if I just change my thinking, everything else will change?"

"Yes," said Eoin. "What have you got to lose? You have been disappointed before. Have the courage to believe in yourself and change your life."

"I suppose I could try, but how do you change every single thought?"

"With great determination and discipline," said Eoin.

"And kindness," said Embarr.

"Definitely kindness," said Eoin. "When you hear a thought that says you cannot do something, replace it with a thought that says you can. It will sound untrue at first. It will take time."

Merial looked at her feet, spreading her webbed toes.

"I guess you're right, I have nothing to lose. So, you really think I'm a naiad? Not a dryad?"

"Do you have an urge to serve trees, or the forest?" asked Eoin.

"No. I'm not drawn to trees. Or the forest. It's a strange place to me. I've never been this far from the sea in my life."

Embarr said, "Sometimes, I have seen Fae change their element later in their lives. Sometimes, I have seen Fae who carry two elements and feel at home in both. Perhaps this will happen to you. However, those Fae were fully at home in one element first."

"And I'm not, you're saying?" asked Merial, feeling a breeze move through the clearing and lift her hair, drying her skin.

Eoin said, "If your magic has not come in yet, then no. You are not at home yet. Give yourself more time. Wait until your magic appears. It will arrive no matter where you are."

"What do I do while I wait? I've been waiting for sixteen summers. The other naiads have all had their magic for at least ten summers."

Eoin said, "Go home, grow stronger. Keep training. Enter the proving this spring. Spend your spare time working towards believing in yourself. Telling yourself you are as good as the others. That will be your greatest challenge until the proving. You must work for your magic. Dryad magic doesn't just appear like that of some of the other elements."

Merial groaned. Those were not the words she wanted to hear.

She and Embarr stayed with the dryads for two days. Merial tried to do the dryads' magic with even less success than water magic. She stuffed herself on dried berries and some of the awful tasting, starchy roots the dryads dug up to eat.

On the third day, she set off for home.

Embarr had decided to spend some time in the forest, so they parted. Somehow, it was easier to say goodbye to her father than to the centaur. Her father had just waved and wandered off into the forest.

Were all centaurs as large-hearted as this?

"Goodbye, my friend," Embarr said, finally. "You better get swimming. It is going to take you a few days."

"At least I'll be swimming with the current, rather than against it."

She waded into the stream and set off. Merial found a new type of large water snail which tasted meatier than the tiny ones she'd eaten on the journey upstream. The small snails hadn't satisfied her hunger at all.

Then one evening where the stream ran past a human settlement, three boys sat with their legs overhanging the bank. They were laughing and drinking out of a bottle they passed around.

She felt afraid to swim past them. They felt menacing. The boys poked a stick in the water. Jabbing it at the fish.

She didn't have much magic, but hoped it would be enough. It was almost dark out. A ways upstream of them she rose from the water, making herself look large and terrifying, like a banshee shrieking and screaming. The boys scrambled up from the bank and ran away, leaving their bottle behind. She sniffed at it. The liquid smelled strong and horrible. Only humans would drink such a thing.

Merial hurried past the place, hoping they wouldn't return again. She'd done what could be done for the fish.

It took only two days to swim downstream and Merial didn't stop, even to sleep. She smelled and heard the sea before seeing it. She could feel its power in her bones. Yes, this was her element.

She was no dryad. The forest hadn't given her anything like this feeling.

Merial swam right into the sea where the stream met it. She sensed all the living creatures nearby. Salty kelp made her mouth water. Sea urchins and stars moved among nearby rocks. An octopus hid in a crevice. A group of mackerel swam just on the other side of the group of rocks.

She swam deeper and away from the rocks, where the waves didn't pound quite so relentlessly. Down to where the naiads currently lived. They'd only been in this area since last fall. Winters were easier here and this had been a stormy winter. Come fall, they'd probably move on and nurture another part of the sea.

Her mother, Ileanna, had sensed Merial and swam out to meet her. They hugged as naiads did, slippery wet skin to wet skin. A full embrace. A mark of respect and trust.

"I'm so glad you've returned safely. I knew you'd have to go one day. To find him, but I thought you'd tell me."

"I'm sorry. I didn't think. I just felt a need to go and left," sent Merial.

"Did you get what you needed from him?"

"Yes. I belong here. And he told me dryads didn't get their magic until later. I still have time."

"That's wonderful," sent her mother, obviously relieved.

The other naiads who were Merial's age, clustered around. They embraced her as well. Which surprised her. Merial always thought they disliked her. Saw her as the outcast she felt like.

There was a feast of raw clams, oysters, mussels and dulse. The food tasted salty, meaty and rich. Just like Merial loved it. No dried, withered berries or starchy roots that tasted like dirt.

A group of seals swam nearby wanting to eat the food, and were chased off. The naiads protected their space.

For the following months, Merial trained every day. Swam as fast as she could for half of every day. Challenged herself to collect the most mussels in the space between waves. Mostly she focused on thinking well about herself. Every time she thought something was impossible for her to do, Merial forced herself to rethink the thought. To rephrase it into something she could do.

Changing her thinking was very difficult at first, but as winter ended and spring began, she found it came easier. Then, one the day when daylight and night were equal, the naiad elders called a proving.

Merial was as ready as she'd ever be.

Anyone could enter a proving, but they only competed against those of their own age group. Two strange water elements had come to enter. One was a young river spirit, the other one much, much older. Perhaps even an elder. Fuath was the name a couple of older naiads sent to each other. Their sending felt tinged with revulsion and fear.

The river spirits were thin and had shorter green hair that reached past their upper bodies only. Their hair was tied back with woven reeds. They looked strong, but somehow stunted. Not flexible and graceful like the naiads.

Merial hadn't met any river spirits before, so she had no idea what they were like. But these two scared her. They were predators and she felt they carried a sense about them that they were in this to win. Merial didn't think they'd be very particular about what they did to win. The younger one radiated power as if she couldn't control it, or perhaps she didn't care. The older one seemed weaker.

The other younger naiads weren't sending. They kept their thoughts to themselves, worried about the proving, Merial knew.

She took a long slow stream of water in through her gills, calming herself. Merial waited for the older naiads to have their contest first. She braided her long ropy hair and used the thick strands of her own hair to tie the long bundle together, remembering the dryads' hair. It reached her lower thighs now.

The older river spirit won her age group, collecting what she needed to and fighting her way back to the elders who judged the contest. Because they had to fight their way back through warrior naiads, the older groups were allowed to use bags woven from kelp to carry their catch. Merial's age group would not be fighting and did not have the luxury of a bag. At least she had large dryads' hands, not slender naiads'. Her hands could hold a lot.

It seemed to take forever before the elder came to her group. There were six naiads, the younger river spirit, and herself.

"You will be looking for three creatures each. They are: a prawn, a small conger eel, and a jewel anemone. I will take you each to a section of the rocks and you will work that section until you find your three creatures and bring them to us, completely unharmed. No matter how long it takes. You will be judged on your speed, if you return unharmed, as well as the creatures being safe and healthy, as we will be transferring them to new homes."

The elder took each of them to a different section of the rocks. When they were all in place, the elder sent, *"Begin."*

Merial swam down the rock face, letting her senses search the crevices. A group of sea stars filled one. Mussels lined another. She moved quickly, trusting her intuition and letting her senses do most of the work. Finally, she felt the presence of shrimp. Poking her hand in, she pulled a shrimp out quickly, before it could swim away. She calmed the creature as best she could.

One down.

Finding the jewel anemone was faster. Farther down the rocks in between two jagged boulders, she found it and gently convinced the anemone to pull up from the rock it was attached to.

The only thing left was the eel. They were fast and wary. She'd never been in this section of the rocks before. She kept going down, knowing they often fed on bottom dwellers.

Then she found a cave. Inside the cave was a feeling of power such as she'd never felt before. Merial swam inside. The interior of the cave was lined with urchins and anemones. There was a large snail on the roof of the cave. It was dark purple with spines longer than her fingers. She'd never seen one before. It drew her.

She mesmerized the shrimp and anemone, setting them down on a bare spot. Willing them to stay.

As she reached out for the snail, Merial was shoved aside by a large, dark shape. It was the young fuath. Merial recognized her power and intent.

Merial punched the river spirit in the belly.

Why was the fuath attacking her? Was this part of the proving?

She quickly kicked out, shoving the fuath with her feet. The fuath hit jagged rocks. Merial sensed pain on the river spirit's back. Merial picked up a sea urchin and jabbed the creature into the fuath's face, then moved to the side, releasing the urchin. The fuath screamed at Merial. Then dove at her.

Merial spun out of the way and reached for the spined snail, holding it gently in her fist, most of the long spines sticking out between her fingers. She swam to the fuath, ready to attack when the fuath kicked her. Merial rolled to avoid the rough rocks, but her arm hit the rocks and she impaled her palm on some of the snail's shorter spines.

"That wasn't smart," Merial told herself.

She watched as the fuath picked up a small rock and swam towards her. Merial pivoted, grabbed her shrimp and anemone. She swam out of the cave with great speed. Out into the open water where it was murky. She couldn't see the fuath, but sensed the river spirit's rage.

Merial found a reef of rocks and hid. Sticking out of a crevice was a small eel. She used her magic to send calming energy to the creature. Made herself invisible and grabbed it with the hand holding the anemone and shrimp. Then swam quickly towards the elders.

Just before she got there, the fuath grabbed her foot. Merial shot a blast of energy out her foot with the intent of causing pain. She'd tried it before and it had never worked. This time it did. The fuath let go and Merial sensed her agony.

Merial wasn't the first one back. But she wasn't last this time either. And all her creatures were unharmed. She put the three of them in separate bags which one of the elders held. Then she opened her right hand, which still held the snail, her palm impaled on its short spines.

The elder opened her eyes wide.

Merial didn't know what that meant besides astonishment.

Merial's hand was bleeding. Both where she hit the rock and on the palm where the snail's spines had pierced her skin. She hoped the spines weren't poisonous, although she felt too warm. Energy raced through her from the fight.

In the space of a fish streaming past, all the elders crowded around. Merial sent them a description of being attacked by the fuath. They looked at each other in concern, then back at the snail and Merial's hand.

Several of the warrior naiads swam off to find the fuath.

Uaine, the oldest and wisest of the elders gently pulled the snail and its spines out of Merial's palm. She held the snail with reverence, looked at it and sent, *"Do you have any idea what this is?"*

Merial shook her head.

"It's a spiny sea snail. I've only seen one of these in my life. This creature is very, very special."

"I sensed that. It's very powerful."

"Yes, it is. And it has conferred some of its power to you, I believe," Uaine sat the snail on Merial's painfully wounded hand. She could feel the creature sticking to her palm with its suckery foot.

Two warrior naiads swam up, holding the fuath between them. Her face was bleeding, urchin spines broken off in the wound. She snarled at Merial. Four other warrior naiads came, holding the other fuath.

The elders sent to both fuath and Merial shrank back at the screaming.

Uaine took her aside and sent, *"While these two are restrained I want you to take this snail and hide it where no one will find it. That's why they came here. They sensed it, but couldn't find it. We will take them back to their river and they will never enter the sea again. You will let this snail go about its business. This creature has transferred its magic to you, it has no more left. Perhaps that is temporary or perhaps it is forever. We do not know much about them. Tell no one where you put it. Do not visit it again lest you give away its place. It has honored you beyond measure. At our feast tonight, I will tell the story of Gulla, the last naiad who was so honored, then you can begin to understand what has happened today."*

Merial swam towards the cave where she'd found the snail, just to make the others think that's where she was going, but she wasn't. Once she got to the cave, she swam out to the reef where she'd found the eel. Then past it to another reef. This one was large and convoluted. Filled with crevices, caves and life.

She tucked the dark purple snail into a beautiful cave filled with anemone, urchins and sea stars.

"There, you are a jewel among jewels."

The snail replied, *"Thank you and bless your way through the water."*

Merial marveled that she could hear the snail's thoughts. She'd not been able to reach creatures that small before. Her senses were becoming more finely attuned.

Merial swam past the reef, hearing the myriad of thoughts. A small squid swam up to her, its eight arms waving. Its body, the size of her hand. She held her right hand out to it and it wrapped its arms around her, gently exploring the wounds with its tentacles. Then it shot off into the water, as if it had news to spread.

Her hand throbbed, but the snail's slime seemed to have sealed the wounds on her palm. She wasn't bleeding anymore. She found a patch of kelp and cut a section off, wrapping it around her hand. It would help protect the side she bashed against the rocks and aid in the healing. Every naiad knew this.

Merial swam around the inner reef, feeling the energy vibrating through her. She'd never felt like this before and wanted to be alone with her thoughts.

What had the snail done to her? Had it awakened her magic? Was that what she felt?

She felt powerful enough to win any contest, even one where she had to battle warrior naiads, even though she hadn't been trained for that yet. The younger naiads were just given the basic techniques that allowed them to defend themselves. She'd watched the older ones train, though.

Finally, Merial returned to the others and watched as they prepared the feast. Her mother came over and embraced her.

"I'm so proud of you."

"Thank you," said Merial, unused to praise from anyone.

After the dinner of sweet kelp, sea lettuce and raw crab, everyone gathered around Uaine. She floated in front of them and began. The first sendings were all about those who had won the proving. And about the two fuath. There had been no strangers who had come to a proving beyond anyone's memory. The two had been returned to the mouth of their river with a warning they would be killed if ever found in the sea again.

Then Uaine began to tell her story.

"I was very young, barely fifteen summers, when the last spiny sea snail was found. It was found by a naiad who no one expected much of. She was thirty summers old and had never had a young one. She wasn't terribly fast or powerful. Her name was Gulla, which means divine sea. Divine sea, what does that mean anyway? Well, on this dark, stormy spring day, Gulla showed us. She found her ten creatures, raced her race and fought off four naiad warriors armed with spears. She returned to the elders with a spiny sea snail, as well. That one was dark green, unlike the purple one Merial found. It was beautiful and during the battle, even with Gulla shielding the creatures in her sack from the four naiads trying to steal it, the snail was unharmed. It had however, pierced Gulla's leg, which dripped blood. The snail's venom was moving through her body, doing its work. At the time only one of the elders knew what that meant. It had been millennia since anyone had seen such a snail, let alone been touched by one. There were only tales that no one believed anymore."

Uaine put her hands together and blew a vision for everyone of the snail, and then Gulla's leg and the energy coursing through the naiad's body.

She continued, *"Gulla tried to explain it to me once. She said the snail allowed her to see not one creature's thoughts, but all of them. She could choose which ones to listen to. It helped her see danger, but it also let her see which areas of the sea needed the naiads' help most. It allowed her to see which naiads were struggling, but unable to send to anyone. I was one such naiad. Feeling alone and abandoned after my mother was killed by a shark. I was being pulled down by my grief. She saved my life then. She went on to become one of the wisest of our elders. Such was the spiny sea snail's gift to her. And to all of us."*

Merial sighed in contentment. For that was what she felt. For the first time in her life she felt held and supported by the sea. By all its creatures.

Even though she had a lot to live up to.

She could do it.

Merial felt sure of that now.

ABOUT THE AUTHOR

Linda Jordan writes fascinating characters, visionary worlds and imaginative fiction. She believes in the powers of healing and transformation.

She's fascinated by nature's peculiarities, mythology and spirituality, what makes humans (and aliens) tick, political systems and the creation of music and art. She loves including all this and more in her stories.

In another lifetime, Linda coordinated the Clarion West Writers Workshop as well as the Reading Series for two years. She also spent four years as Chair of the Board of Directors during Clarion West's formative period. She's worked many other jobs, more than she cares to count. Eventually, she fled the city to live out among the tall cedars.

She lives in the rainy wilds of Washington state with her husband, daughter, four cats, a cluster of koi and an infinite number of slugs and snails.

Find out more about Linda at:
lindajordan.net

facebook.com/LindaJordanWriter

twitter.com/LindaAJordan

bookbub.com/authors/linda-jordan

SELKIES IN PARADISE

DEB LOGAN

My name is Artie Woodward-Kendrick, and I'm the luckiest woman in the world. I'm married to my very best friend, Jed Kendrick.

Who could've guessed I'd ever find someone to love; that I would ever marry? Certainly not me!

You see, I'm a seer. I see things normal people don't, things they couldn't see, even if they wanted to ... which no one in their right mind would. I mean let's get real; even I don't want to see the Fae. But I don't have a choice. I was born with this strange ability to see the unseen, to know the unknowable.

I thought I was alone. Thought I'd be alone my entire life. I knew I'd never find love.

Sure, my mom and dad loved me, but even they thought I was weird. They worried about me constantly when I was a kid, dragged me to more shrinks than I care to remember. None of them helped. After all, everyone assumed I was imagining things.

Only I wasn't.

So I learned to hide.

By the time I made it to high school, I was adept at hiding. I hid my knowledge from my parents. I tried desperately to hide my weirdness from the kids at school. But most importantly, I hid the fact that I could see what I'd named *the terrors*, that I knew they existed, from the terrors themselves. And as long as I hid, I was safe.

Lonely ... but safe.

So how did I manage to find a man who not only befriended me, but who grew to love me? How did my life change from hidden and lonely to fulfilled and glowing with contentment?

Jed Kendrick moved to my hometown in Colorado.

We recognized each other, and our loneliness ended. We were both seers, and on our first day at McKinley High we became a team, but that's another story. Suffice it to say that over the last six and a half years we've fought terrors and other forms of Fae from Colorado to Ireland.

And somewhere along the way, we fell in love.

Now, I'm glowing with happiness because just a few days ago, on a glorious late November day — Thanksgiving Day to be exact — I became Jed Kendrick's wife, and he became Artie Woodward's husband. The Woodward-Kendrick team became official in the eyes of the world.

What's next, you ask? Who knows! But whatever it is, we'll face it together.

Right after we get home from the awesome honeymoon our family and friends arranged for us ... in Hawaii!

~

O n a crystal clear day in late November, our plane landed in paradise. Aside from a fateful trip to Ireland to meet Jed's Grannie O'Toole, I'd never been beyond the borders of Colorado, so when I stepped from the plane into the open-air terminal at Lihui Airport on the Hawaiian island of Kauai, I was overwhelmed. I stopped in the midst of a throng of people, clinging to Jed's arm, and inhaled the exotic mixture of sea salt, tropical flowers, and lushly green growing things.

Jed squeezed my hand and smiled down at me. "We're here," he said, his voice tinged with amazement. "We're actually married and on our honeymoon."

I nodded, momentarily lost in the love and wonder shining in his eyes. There had been moments in Ireland when I'd despaired of ever seeing Jed's handsome face again, and now here we were ... married and on the island of Kauai.

Before I could answer, a pretty young woman with a waterfall of shining black hair and sun-kissed skin stepped up to us. She wore a sleeveless red dress patterned with huge white flowers, and her arms dripped with brightly colored flower leis.

"Aloha," she said as she placed a lei around each of our necks. "Welcome to Kauai. We hope you'll enjoy your stay."

I smiled my thanks, but my attention was caught by the beauty of the flowers that made up my lei. I'd never seen, or smelled, anything like them. I recognized white carnations in the necklace of flowers, but the other varieties were a mystery.

I glanced up and met her gaze. "Thank you. These are beautiful, but what kind of flowers are they?"

She held up another of the leis she carried and indicated a white, star-like flower edged in delicate pink. "This is plumeria. Most of the fragrance of your lei comes from it. You'll see them often here in the islands. Sometimes in pink, often in yellow." Pointing to other flowers in turn she said, "We also use tuberoses, carnations, orchids, and jasmine, but you'll see many other types of leis during your stay." She smiled again, and with a little wave, turned to greet another couple.

Jed fingered the lei around his neck — his was made up of darker, more bold colors than mine and featured quite a bit of greenery — and said, "Wow. I didn't expect to be given flowers just for walking off a plane."

"They look good on you," I said, grinning up at my tall, lanky husband. I'd nearly lost Jed in Ireland. He'd been ensorcelled and held thrall by the Fae, and I'd almost given up hope of finding a way to rescue him. But Grannie O'Toole and Laird Angus had helped me and ... well, that was a tale I didn't want to think about right now.

It was enough to have him here with me, to be able to watch him examine his lei while I admired his more-than-six-foot frame, his tousled black hair, and his gentle gray eyes rimmed by long and lovely dark lashes. His full lips twitched as he noticed my stare.

"Like what you see?" he asked, his eye color darkening to a smoldering, smoky gray.

"Always," I replied, my heart beating faster as memories of our wedding night crowded my mind. "Let's find our luggage."

"Yes," he agreed, licking his lips. "I think we need to check out our accommodations." He swallowed, his Adam's apple bobbing. "Soon."

～

Our hotel suite was stunning. The laird had gone all out for us after our Irish misadventure. He'd booked us into a luxury resort on Kauai's north shore and made sure we had all the amenities. I wandered through the sitting room and stepped through the sliding glass door onto the ocean-view lanai, while Jed tipped the young man who'd brought our luggage up.

A soft murmur of voices, the muffled thump of a closing door, and a moment later Jed was beside me, his arms sliding around my waist. We gazed at the picture postcard view of palm trees, white sand and impossibly blue water and then turned to each other.

"Welcome to paradise," Jed murmured as he drew me close and bent to kiss me.

His lips were soft and warm, and I melted into his embrace. Jed loved me. He understood me. He was my partner in life, my equal. And now ... right now, he was my lover.

Our kiss deepened, became more passionate, and when the spark it kindled grew to a flame, he pulled away. The light in his eyes echoed the smoldering heat growing in my core. In one quick movement, he bent and, moving one strong arm behind my knees, swept me off my feet and into his arms. Without a word, my lover carried me across the sitting room and into the bedroom ... to the perfectly arranged and very enticing king-size bed.

"You're wearing too many clothes," he whispered as he placed me gently on the pillow-soft mattress.

"So are you," I answered in voice so husky I barely recognized it as my own.

We remedied that little problem and spent the next few hours doing what newlyweds have done since time immemorial: exploring each other's bodies and discovering new depths of our love.

Our first day on Kauai was drawing to a close when we emerged from our hotel suite in search of food. We opted for dinner on the terrace overlooking Hanalei Bay. I watched the sun sink into the darkening water, marveling at the vivid shades of red and gold as I savored firm, sweet flakes of mahi mahi flavored with mango sauce and delicious coconut rice.

Jed caught my free hand in his, stroking my fingers with his thumb. We didn't speak. No words were needed. We simply drank in the moment, appreciating the tranquility and peace of this beautiful place.

After dinner, we wandered through the open air hotel lobby and down a stone-paved path to a pristine white sand beach. The rolling waves of the bay beckoned us with their froth of white lace.

We strolled hand-in-hand in the moonlight, serenaded by the susurrus of water on sand, cooled by a light sea breeze that lifted my long dark hair and ruffled Jed's black locks. As we rounded the curve of the bay, I noticed a woman in a long white dress sitting in the sand at the edge of the water. Her knees were pulled up so that her chin rested on them, the gentle waves kissing her feet with each inward flow. We walked a few steps closer, and she raised her head and glanced at us. Moonlight shimmered on her face, and I saw that it was glazed with tears.

I laid my free hand on Jed's arm to stop him, disentangled my fingers from his, and stepped nearer to the woman. Closer now, I saw that she was young, not much older than me, with lovely dark slanting eyes. But the moonlight played tricks with her hair, making the nearly waist-length sable waves appear to have a silvery sheen.

"Are you hurt?" I asked, just loudly enough to be heard over the waves. "Can we help you?"

And then Jed was beside me, pulling me back toward the resort. "Come away from her, Artie," he whispered urgently in my ear. "Can't you see what she is?"

I looked again, and saw what my love had seen.

The young woman had risen. She stood with her feet in a froth of water, her long white dress wet to the knees, one hand held out to us in a gesture of supplication. An unearthly glow surrounded her, one not detectable by normal human eyes ... but neither Jed nor I were normal humans. We were seers. And right now our sight showed us a woman of the Fae.

"Please," she said, making no move to approach us. "Please, can you help me?"

Jed pushed me behind him, but made no move to flee. "What could a mortal do to help a Fae woman?"

She gasped and stumbled back a step. "Y-you know what I am?"

I stepped to Jed's side, despite his annoyed glance. "Not precisely," I said. "Only that you aren't human."

Nodding, she moved closer, hesitantly, like a wild animal. Curious, but cautious. And always with her feet in the waves.

"I'm a selkie," she said, her dark eyes wide and full of pain, "but I can't return home to the sea. Someone has stolen my skin. I'm marooned here, with no one to tell my kin what has become of me. Can you help me? Can you at least carry a message to my colony?"

A selkie. One of that ancient race of shape-shifters who live in the oceans of the world, appearing to human eyes as seals in the water, and transforming into human form on land. But the transformation required a catalyst. To become human, a selkie had to shed its skin, which was then carefully hidden. Very carefully, because without its skin, the creature was powerless to shift into its true form and return to the water.

"We've learned to distrust the Fae," Jed said, his voice low and menacing. "My wife may be sympathetic, but I won't risk her on what could be a trick."

Tears streamed across her cheeks as she shook her head. "It's no trick. I'm desperate, and you're the only ones who can possibly understand my plight. Please, help me." She wiped her cheeks with trembling hands, took a deep breath, and continued. "If you won't seek out my kin, at least tell Maris where I am and what has happened."

"Who?" Jed and I asked simultaneously.

"Maris Grainger," said the selkie woman. "She lives on Maui. I have no money and I can no longer swim, so I can't reach her. Go to Maui, to Maalaea Harbor. Look for Captain Bill's Island Cruises. Her father works there. He'll tell you how to find Maris. Tell her Serena needs her help. She'll go to my family. Maris will know what to do."

I frowned. "Is she a seer?" I asked, confused. "How can this Maris Grainger help you?"

"Maris is special," she said. "Different. Neither Fae nor human, but she's kind and cares for all who inhabit the sea. She'll help. She'll know what to do. Please, tell Maris Serena needs her."

Jed and I exchanged a glance. We'd planned to do some sight-seeing on Maui anyway, and an island cruise sounded lovely. I quirked an eyebrow at him and he shrugged his shoulders in a *might as well* kind of way. I grinned and stood on tiptoe to kiss his cheek.

"We'll see if we can find Maris tomorrow," I said.

The selkie nodded. "Thank you."

Jed and I turned and practically ran back to the resort.

"Well, that's a first," Jed said quietly when we were safely back in the open air lobby. "A member of the Fae asking for our help."

I nodded. Every other encounter we'd ever had with that race of supernatural creatures had been hostile. As we took the elevator to our suite, I wondered what manner of being this Maris Grainger might be. Not Fae. Not human. Then what exactly was she?

Evidently a being who was kind and cared for sea creatures.

How intriguing!

The next morning we caught an island hopper flight to Kapalua Airport on Maui, rented a red Jeep Wrangler, and drove to Maalaea Harbor. What a wonderfully adventurous start to our day! Flying over the emerald jewel of Kauai and the diamond-tipped sapphire of the Pacific before landing on Maui's northwest coast. We drove south along Highway 30, the open-topped Wrangler giving us clear views of the ocean to the west and the stunning West Maui Mountains to the east.

We arrived in Maalaea Town a little before noon and went in search of Captain Bill's Island Cruises. The young woman manning the ticket booth told us that the Graingers sailed on the Sea Princess, which was currently on a whale watching run, but that we could book seats on the Sea Princess for its 2:00 p.m. snorkeling cruise.

Jed pulled out the credit card Laird Angus had provided and paid for our afternoon adventure. The young woman advised us to be back by 1:30 to board the Sea Princess and grab choice seats.

Pushing his wallet back into his pocket, Jed turned to me. "Shall we find some lunch? We've got a little over an hour to kill."

As if on cue, my stomach growled, loudly.

"I'll take that as a 'yes,'" Jed said with a laugh, and we turned and strolled across the street and down a block to King Kamehameha's Crab Shack. Snagging a table on the patio overlooking the bay, we studied the menu, a large chalk board hung above the serving window.

"I think I'll try the crab cakes," I said, mouth watering in anticipation.

"Yeah, those look good," Jed answered, eyeing another patron's plate briefly before looking back to the menu, "but I'm going for the coconut shrimp." He glanced at me, smiled, and said, "You sit still and enjoy the view. I'll go order."

The view was certainly worth savoring. The deep blue waters of Maalaea Bay; the dark outline of hills around the curve of beach; the neat masts of ships in their slips along the dock, as well as the full-bellied sails of those returning from their errands on the ocean's deep water. All covered by a sky so clear and blue it felt unreal. I'd always thought my little corner of Colorado enjoyed clear skies, but that was before I came to Hawaii.

Jed came back carrying plates loaded with delicious smelling food.

"Wow," I said, accepting my lunch. "That was fast."

He nodded, sat down, grabbed a piece of breaded shrimp and dragged it through a deep red sauce. "I didn't expect to be handed our plates as soon as I paid." He popped the shrimp into this mouth, chewed, swallowed, and grabbed another. "This is really good!"

I cut into my first crab cake with my fork, lifted it to my lips and sighed with contentment as the moist, flavorful tidbit hit my tongue. "Oh, yeah," I murmured between bites. "If we were staying on Maui, I could eat here every day."

We finished our meal, but lingered at the crab shack's table, sipping POG, a refreshing passion fruit-orange-guava juice drink, and alternately watching the bay and our fellow tourists. The number of people walking around in skimpy swimsuits and flip-flops made me feel positively overdressed in my khaki shorts and bright pink T-shirt. Of course, Jed and I both wore swimsuits too; we just wore regular clothes over them.

A little after 1:00 we saw the Sea Princess slip into place at Captain Bill's dock. Happy tourists disembarked, their necks slung with cameras, the afternoon sun glinting off sunglasses and binoculars.

Jed stood and held out a hand to me. "Shall we?"

"We shall," I answered with a grin. "I'm really anxious to meet this Maris person. I wonder how Serena expects the girl to help?"

"No clue. I just hope she's actually on the boat with her dad and not off having a picnic with friends or something."

I nodded. We'd made this trip to meet Maris Grainger, and one way or another, we would do so. If she wasn't aboard the Sea Princess, we'd just have to keep an eye on her father, Richard, until he led us to her.

We needn't have worried. When we boarded the Sea Princess, we were greeted by a teenage girl with short, curly red hair, dozens of freckles across her nose ... and a faint other-worldly glow outlining her trim young body. She was dressed much as I was, in neatly pressed khaki shorts and a T-shirt, but her T was emblazoned with Captain Bill's name and logo.

"Welcome aboard the Sea Princess," she said, taking our tickets and checking our names off on a clipboard. "Please find a seat. The mate will explain what we're about in a few minutes."

We walked on. No point it trying to talk to her now; she needed to get the rest of the passengers aboard.

Moving forward, we claimed seats along the bow rail of the little ship. A few minutes later a tall man wearing khaki trousers, a short-sleeved white shirt, and wrap-around sunglasses unhooked a microphone and called for our attention.

"Welcome aboard the Sea Princess," he announced. "I'm Richard Grainger, and I'll be your guide today. We'll be setting sail in a minute or two for Molokini Crater where you'll enjoy some of the best snorkeling in the islands. Our sailing time will be about an hour, so please pay attention while I give you some necessary safety information."

I listened to the man's speech, at least enough to take note of where the life preservers were stowed, but most of my attention was focused on Maris. True, we hadn't asked the teen's name, but normal human girls didn't have a glowing aura.

Frowning, I watched the girl as she moved quietly and confidently across the deck. Something was off. She definitely had a nimbus, but it wasn't as bright and clearly defined as that of most Fae. Hers was somehow softer, more misty than I'd come to expect.

Neither did I see the image of her true form upon her human body. When the Fae choose to be seen by mortal men, they wrap themselves in a glamour. They appear human, no matter what their true forms may be.

Because of our unique heritage, Jed and I see the Fae for what they really are. Our *sight* allows us to see past the image they project to their true selves. We see their human disguise superimposed upon their other-worldly forms.

Maris presented a soft Fae nimbus, but I saw no trace of another form.

"What is she?" I wondered quietly to Jed.

He shook his head and adjusted his sunglasses on his nose. "I don't know," he answered, just as quietly, "but her father is pure human." He nodded toward our guide. "I wonder if he's really her father, or just some poor schmuck she's ensorcelled into believing they're related?"

"No telling, but we've got an hour to find out what's going on."

Richard Grainger had ended his spiel by inviting the passengers to explore the ship, enjoy non-alcoholic beverages and snacks in the lounge off the galley, and watch for passing humpback whales, which he promised to point out if any were spotted by the crew.

With forty or so passengers moving freely around the decks, we'd be able to approach Maris easily.

"Let me talk to her first," I said, laying a hand on Jed's arm. "We don't want to scare her by ganging up on her."

He nodded. "Okay, but stay in plain sight. We don't know what she's capable of."

I patted his arm. "Don't worry. I won't underestimate her."

Maris stood against the wall in the lounge, presumably keeping an eye on the platters of food in order to restock as needed. I picked up plate, arranged a slice of pineapple, some bits of cheese, and a couple of crackers on it, and then moved to stand beside her while I nibbled.

"This is a nice boat," I said, trying to sound casual. "Is it a yacht?"

The girl smiled and her nimbus glowed a bit brighter. "The Sea Princess is a double-hulled catamaran, a very stable yacht."

I wiped my fingers on a napkin and held out my hand. "I'm Artie," I said, and nodding toward Jed, added, "that's my husband, Jed. We're on our honeymoon." I grinned, blushing slightly.

Maris took my hand. Hers was warm, her handshake firm. This close, I could see the ghostly image of long, slim fingers, webbed almost to the tips.

"I'm Maris Grainger," she said. "Congratulations."

"Thanks." I released her hand and, picking up a piece of cheese, nibbled a bite. "Grainger," I said, as though considering. "Are you related to the mate who's our guide?"

She dimpled. "He's my dad. We moved out here from Kansas about a year ago."

"Kansas? Really? And you're both working on a sailing ship? That seems a bit odd."

She shrugged. "Dad was a sailor before he met my mom. They lived in Hawaii for a while, but moved inland when I was a baby."

"How interesting!" I glanced around for more people in Captain Bill T's. "Is your mom on board too?"

Her smile disappeared, a deep sadness filling her eyes. "No. Mom died in a car accident in Kansas.

"Oh," I said quickly. "I'm so sorry."

We stood in silence for a few moments. I glanced at Jed, who met my gaze with solemn reassurance. He couldn't hear what Maris and I had said, but stood ready to assist if needed.

I took a deep breath and decided to take the plunge. The lounge held only a few people, no one near enough to hear what I said to her next.

"Maris," I said quietly, "Jed and I, well, we're what's known as *Seers*. We see things other people can't." She stiffened, and I placed a hand on her arm. "We can see that you're not, well, you're not exactly human."

She startled, tried to pull away. I tightened my grip on her arm.

"Please don't leave," I said, putting as much compassion in my voice as I could. "We mean you no harm, but we have a message for you."

She stilled. I knew she was ready to flee, but stood her ground, quietly wary. I dropped my restraining hand.

"What kind of message?"

"Do you mind if Jed joins us?" I asked. "We didn't want to scare you by both approaching you at once."

She glanced in his direction, moved a little to her left, giving herself a clear path to the door, and nodded. "All right. He can come over, and I'll listen, but if you try to hurt me, I'm screaming for Dad."

I beckoned to Jed as I said, "We're not interested in causing you any trouble, Maris. We just need to talk to you."

Jed strode across the room and stopped beside me. "You must be Maris," he said, holding out his hand and giving her his most charming smile. "I'm Jed Kendrick and I'm very glad to meet you.

She put her hand in his, a bit timidly, but managed a smile when he released her after a brief shake.

"I was just about to tell Maris about our encounter last night," I said.

"Great," he said. "Why don't we sit down at that table. We might as well be comfortable while we talk."

Once we were all seated, I told Maris our tale. "We're honeymooning on the north shore of Kauai, and last night while we were strolling along the beach, we met a young woman. Only she wasn't ... a woman, I mean. She was a selkie in human form." I paused and studied Maris's face. "Her name is Serena." Maris's eyes widened. She knew Serena.

"Someone stole her skin," I continued, "and she's stranded in human form. She told us about you. Asked us to find you and tell you that she needs help." I paused again, a frown tightening my brow. "The thing is, neither Jed nor I can imagine how you, a teenage girl, can possibly help her."

Maris exhaled the breath she'd been holding and said, "Oh! That's terrible. I may not be able to help, but I can let her colony know where she is and what's happened to her. They may be able to figure out how to get her home. At least she'll be with her family again, even if she is cut off from the sea."

"Her colony?" I asked blankly.

The girl nodded. "She's a member of a colony of selkies that lives on Ni'ihau."

"The Forbidden Island?" Jed asked.

"That's right," Maris said, nodding. "It's a private island and most of it is uninhabited. It's a haven for Hawaiian Monk seals, and the selkies decided to make it their home as well. They're related to the Monk seals, after all."

"They are?" Jed and I said together.

"Sure. The Hawaiian selkies are descended from a few Scottish selkies who decided to try their luck with human sailing. When their ship was destroyed in a storm, they managed to grab their skins, transform, and swim to safety. They joined a herd of Hawaiian Monk seals and eventually interbred and became the selkies of Ni'ihau."

"Wow," I said. "I had no idea."

"And how do you fit into all of this?" Jed asked. "What exactly are you?"

Maris glanced around the lounge, but we were the only occupants at the moment. The loudspeaker had announced a whale sighting a few moments before and everyone but us had raced to the port rail to see.

"I'm a siren," she said. "Well, technically, I'm only half siren. My dad, as you probably noticed, is completely normal. Evidently my mom was a real siren."

She shrugged. "I'm a little fuzzy on the details 'cause I didn't know anything about it until last year. Mom kept me away from salt water because she didn't know if my blood would be strong enough to allow me to transform, but she knew I'd be drawn to the sea. So I grew up in Kansas."

"And she never told you?" Jed asked, a little callously in my opinion, but then he hadn't been there to see the look in Maris's eyes when she spoke of her mother's death.

"She died before she got around to explaining," Maris said.

Jed had the grace to look uncomfortable. "Sorry," he said quietly.

"But now I know," Maris continued, her tone brightening, "and Dad and I live here now and I get to swim in the ocean with my friends every day."

"So, do you snorkel with the tourists?" I asked.

"No. I stay on the Sea Princess while everyone snorkels." She grinned. "Wouldn't want to scare away the tourists."

"Of course," Jed said with a nod. "You wouldn't need any equipment, and you probably change shape."

She nodded. "Not as much as a selkie, but it's noticeable. I can swim with my dad, but no one else. At least not in salt water. In fresh water, I stay human."

"Fascinating." I said, and Jed nodded his agreement.

Snorkeling at Molokini Crater was wonderful. The turquoise waters were crystal clear, with no sediment to impede our vision. We marveled at the many types of colorful tropical fish as they darted around us, and thrilled to the stately sea turtles that swam so close we could almost touch them. I was truly disappointed when it was time to board the Sea Princess and return to port. But Maris met us with towels and promised to introduce us to a pod of dolphins before we left, so I was content to act the compliant tourist.

As we drove the Jeep back to Kapalua Airport, Jed and I agreed we'd had a very successful day. We'd done the tourist thing, had a taste of snorkeling in paradise, and had fulfilled our promise to Serena. Best of all, Maris had promised to meet us the next afternoon at Hanalei Bay, where we hoped to give the selkie good news.

It was nice to know that not all Fae were evil creatures. Far from needing to protect humanity from selkies, it seemed that, in Hawaii at least, selkies needed protection from humans!

～

The next afternoon we strolled the white sand of Hanalei Bay again, only this time we had to thread our way past beach umbrellas and relaxed people resting on towels soaking up the bright Hawaiian sunshine. Swimsuit clad humans frolicked in the gentle waves, while the more adventurous could be seen adjusting their masks and fins before plunging beneath the surface of the salt water.

Jed and I meandered around the curve of the bay to a rocky outcropping where a lone figure sat staring out to sea, her dark hair billowing in the breeze.

"May we join you?" I asked Serena when we were close enough to speak comfortably above the susurrus of waves and wind.

She glanced up and nodded, a small, sad smile gracing her lovely features. "Of course. It's good to see you again."

I settled on a flattish rock beside her while Jed squatted at my other side. "We found Maris," he said, shading his eyes and glancing out to sea.

Serena sat a little straighter and stared at him, hope shining in her eyes. "What did she say? Will she help?"

I nodded, answering before Jed had the chance. "She said she'd meet us here this afternoon. I don't know when exactly, but..."

"There!" cried Jed, pointing at the water. "I think she's coming. That swimmer is too far out to be a tourist."

Serena and I both gazed in the direction he pointed, and after a moment's searching, I saw something bobbing in the water. Something that came closer and became more distinct as I watched.

"It's her," Serena said, excitement ringing in her voice, "and look! She's not alone. She's brought one of my colony."

A few moments later — faster than I would've thought possible — Maris emerged from the sea, like a red-haired, bikini-clad goddess. She was followed by a seal, who dipped beneath the surface and emerged again as a man with dark hair graying at the temples.

If I hadn't been watching closely, I wouldn't have noticed the unnatural elongation of Maris' hands and feet, or the webbing between her fingers and toes. Her transformation back to human-appearing teen was nearly instantaneous.

The man who followed her onto the rocky outcrop carried what looked like a wet ball of fur, held strategically since he wore no clothes. He didn't seem at all embarrassed by his state of undress. In fact, I had the impression that he held what was undoubtedly his seal skin in that precise location for my benefit alone.

Jed and I rose to our feet as Maris and the selkie approached. Serena jumped to her feet and ran to the man. He dropped his skin and enveloped her in a hug.

"Serena," he said. "We've been so worried. I'm relieved to find you whole and well."

"Father," she said with a sob. "I'm stranded. I can't come home!"

I glanced away from the selkies, feeling that I intruded on their reunion. I turned my attention to Maris instead, and saw that she too carried a wet ball of fur. Puzzled, I glanced back at the father and daughter. No, the man's skin lay at his feet, where he had dropped it to embrace his daughter.

Turning back to Maris, I quirked an eyebrow and nodded to the skin in her hands. But before she could answer my unspoken question, the seal-man cleared his throat.

"The Selkies of Ni'ihau are in your debt, Seers," he said with a formality that rang with Fae magic. The Fae rarely acknowledged obligation to humans, but when they did, it carried a binding geas. Jed reached for my hand, and we held tight to each other.

"We thought our daughter lost forever, but the message you carried has restored her to us." He inclined his head to us, his dark eyes shining with sincerity. "We acknowledge our debt. Word will be sent from dolphin to whale to seal until every one of our kind in the world knows of your deed. If ever you are in need and a selkie is near, we will render what assistance we can." He paused to stare directly into Jed's eyes and then my own. "Selkies do not forget. Never would we have expected such a kindness from a seer. You are unique ... and we will remember."

Chills ran down my spine despite the sun's heat. I knew I should respond, but no words came. My mind felt frozen by the selkie's words.

Fortunately, my husband has always been the socially adept member of our team.

"We acknowledge your gift," he said solemnly, "though we don't feel its need. What we did was a small thing. Carrying your daughter's message cost us little and gained us knowledge, not only of your kind, but of Maris as well. We value such knowledge. Let us part as friends ... with no debt between us."

I squeezed Jed's fingers in appreciation of his words.

The selkie studied us for a long moment. "You are gracious, Seer. We release the obligation of indebtedness in favor of friendship. May the Selkies of Ni'ihau and the members of your bloodline remember this day to eternity. Let there be friendship between our people."

He inclined his head to us, and Jed and I responded in kind.

"And now," he said, turning to his daughter, "we must get you home."

Serena sobbed and tears streamed down her cheeks. "But how? My skin is lost!"

Maris stepped forward, speaking for the first time. "Your mother sent you her skin," she said, holding out the dripping fur. "Wear it for your journey home."

Serena's eyes widened as she accepted the skin, stroking it wistfully. "Is this possible, Father?"

He nodded. "Only from a close relative can such a sacrifice be made, and only in extremis, but yes, you may wear your mother's skin for this journey."

He turned back to me and Jed. "We will take our leave now, Seers. Know that our offer of future assistance holds." He held up a hand when Jed started to object. "Not out of debt or obligation, but out of friendship. Farewell, Seers-Who-Are-Friends-of-Selkies. May your lives be rich and fruitful."

"Farewell, Selkies of Niʻihau," Jed responded. "May that which is lost be found."

And with that, Serena and her father slipped into the water, donned their skins, and swam swiftly into the depths of the blue Pacific.

EPILOGUE

Jed and I had been home from our Hawaiian honeymoon for less than a month when we received a letter from Maris. I opened it quickly and read aloud.

I just wanted to let you know that Dad and I contacted the police about what was stolen from Serena. Of course, we didn't mention exactly what was taken, only that thieves were preying on tourists on both Kauai and Maui, and that thefts had even happened on our cruises.

The thieves were caught and when the arrest was made, a seal pelt was discovered among the loot. The thieves claimed it was a magical artifact taken from a selkie, but no one believed them. The police saw it as evidence of the slaughter of Hawaiian Monk seals, an endangered species.

Dad says the judge will throw the book at them for that!

Now that Serena's family knows where her lost item is, they'll be able to get it back ... but not until after the trial. The family is anxious for those men to be imprisoned.

Hope everything in Colorado is great!

Your friend,

Maris

I folded the letter and smiled at Jed. "We're friends with a siren."

He nodded. "Not to mention a whole colony of selkies." He grinned and pulled me into his arms. "Who'd've ever guessed we'd be friends with any species of Fae?"

"Certainly not me," I said. "Life is full of surprises."

"Definitely," he said, hugging me even more tightly, "and I can't wait to discover the next one!"

ABOUT THE AUTHOR

Deb Logan specializes in tales for the young – and the young at heart! Author of the popular Dani Erickson series, Deb loves the unknown, whether it's the lure of space or earthbound mythology. She writes about demon hunters, thunderbirds, and everyday life on a space station for children, teens, and anyone who enjoys young adult fiction. Her work has been published in multiple volumes of Fiction River, as well as in *2017 Young Explorer's Adventure Guide*, *Feyland Tales, Volume 1*, and other popular anthologies.

Find out more about Deb at:
deblogan.wordpress.com

f facebook.com/deb.logan.750

g goodreads.com/deb_logan

BB bookbub.com/authors/deb-logan

A RECIPE FOR DISASTER

SHARON KAE REAMER

I think that the waves will devour
The boatman and boat as one;
And this by her song's sheer power
Fair Loreley has done.

— HEINRICH HEINE

Heiner

Threesomes. A recipe for disaster. As tired as the cliché was, a threesome never ended well. Everyone hated them. Heinrich was no exception, despite his being tangled in one.

He stepped nimbly down the rickety wooden stairs leading from the coastal path to the beach. The tide was receding across the Bay of St. Malo, leaving damp trails of braided sand behind. Heinrich stayed to the upper drier portion of beach and soon reached the far side, joggling along the paved path that paralleled the seawall houses. They were done up in an understated but flung-in-your-face floral finery, many blooms still fresh even this late in August.

The air smelled wonderful, fresh and salty, a conundrum that Heinrich would never be able to figure out. But this part of Brittany on the far west coast of France had always been a magical tonic for him. Time stopped and Life wore a bright coat of many colors. It was also a place where he felt close to his mother. She'd died just after giving him life in their castle near the Rhine, the result of an ancient curse. Thanks to Caitie, the curse was now rectified.

The few clouds and pastel blue sky promised a fine day. They should enjoy it rather than staying in bed.

They should, but Heinrich doubted that they would. A day alone with Caitie, sans children, sans Hagen, and Heinrich just returned from the Dreams two days ago. A perfect remedy for the sexual release he needed, the price he must pay for his journey through Ande-dubnos. He'd paid women in the past, had not wanted to seduce women solely for the purpose of preserving his sanity upon return to the waking world. But ever since they'd become lovers, Caitie was always there for him when he returned. And, loving her so desperately, he wasn't strong enough to turn her away. Never had been.

They might go down to the private beach to bathe by moonlight. They might. Before they left to drive to Lyon, where they would spend a very short night. Or, if he didn't tire, drive straight through and be in Quinson in the early morning. Heinrich wanted to deliver

Caitie to Hagen not a minute later than she would have arrived if she had gone directly by train.

They could leave earlier, but the drive through the night would be worth it for one special moment by moonlight. Caitie, her skin radiant with moonshine and ocean, relaxed and beautiful, was something he'd not seen before. The tide would be retreating by then, twelve hours from now, leaving room to sit on the sand and watch her. He could imagine she was a supernatural creature, a not-so-dainty mermaid, rather a nymph with a warrior's heart, come to enchant him.

The one mermaid he'd actually once briefly *tousled* with, the Loreley, had been anything but dainty. She had been both beautiful and terrible, a typical denizen of the Otherworld. Her legend was apparently not that old, the poems and ballads dated to only a couple of centuries, but Heinrich knew they had sprung from some other memory that *was* old; the Loreley is ancient. And powerful still, if mostly quiescent.

A river goddess, no longer worshipped—forgotten—the Loreley could have persisted and then, like so many Celtic deities, continued to exist by feeding on the Dreams of the people, reinventing herself to fit their images. Whatever her origin, the Rhine river entity was deadly to those she chose to remain with her in her watery domain.

Heinrich turned up a side street. He smelled the croissants and pastries before he saw the pâtisserie. After making his purchases he jogged back home, only a persistent black butterfly fluttering around his face.

He'd wake her again, with the smell of coffee and his kiss.

~

C aitie
I reveled in the quiet of a morning, one not too early, and one devoid of squealing, squabbling children: three first-graders and one second-grader. Brev was able, even with the superiority of being

a year ahead of the triplets, to hold his own with the squealing and squabbling.

I really hated to be gone from Burg Lahn, hated missing out yet again on a portion of my children's lives—the triplets' first week of grade school. I had promised the children's nanny, Gesine, to call later today—and every afternoon—to hear how things were going.

I'd been there for their first day at school to watch them with their handcrafted *Schultüten*, which no German first-grader would be without. I'd like to say it was a labor of love. But it was just labor. I'd never been very good at arts and crafts growing up. All the projects I tried to do ended up as sorry lumps of twisted materials. Like the wooden balance scale I tried to build in the fourth grade. Thinking about that disaster still made me shiver.

The *Schultüten* were made from gaily-colored construction paper, shaped (and sized) like ice cream cones for a (gentle) giant, and filled with school supplies and candy. Each of the ones I cobbled together had its own theme: a white cat with googly eyes (Theo), a bird of paradise with bright feathers (Jax), a fairy with gossamer wings (Jules). Those fairy wings had almost been my undoing. While trying to finish the damned things, I kept picturing the faces of my children on their first day, forced to carry grotesque *Schültuten* with pieces of glue showing, or misshaped parts falling off. That horrid vision was the only thing that fueled my efforts.

I snuggled down into the duvets, flinging them back to air my feet. Heiner had thrown the narrow French doors in his bedroom open wider, letting in a fragrantly cool coastal breeze. I doubted it would stay cool, but one could always hope.

The renovations to the house in Dinard were now complete, including the third floor for the children – each with his and her own bedrooms. The *en suite* bath for Hagen and me in our first-floor bedroom was not a luxury, not in the least. The few weeks we'd spent here, me with the children and Hagen overseeing the renovations, had been fraught with stress. I endured haughty looks of disdain from the well-to-do patrons of the Hotel St. George, just a short walk down the coast, where we'd stayed while the work was going on.

Our four children had shared a bedroom, and Hagen and I had a separate one, blessedly separate. But he'd left each morning to walk to the house, leaving me with a kiss and a smile. He was happy and engaged, and all was right in his world. I shepherded the children through the breakfast buffet (where the haughty looks came from) and then to the beach, followed by semi-chaotic coastal walks (Jules was forever distracted by creepy crawly things and slimy plants). Evenings were spent looking for a pizza place with a table for six.

On about the fourth day, I finally realized that all was right with my world, too. Beach with my children and pizza every night. The children were happy. Hagen seemed to be happier than I'd seen him in a long time. I relaxed and ignored the stuck-up fake people at breakfast. My family was the real deal.

Heiner had opted to stay at Burg Lahn during all this. I didn't blame him. Not one bit.

He had also opted to keep *his* 'floor' of the house in Dinard the same. Out of stubbornness. Or because he liked it that way (or both). His bathroom—not *en suite*—could also do with a make-over with its claw-footed ceramic tub that was losing chips off the finish. He didn't have to share the rooms on his floor with anyone, and he didn't intend to.

Except for me. Here and now.

I hadn't slept so soundly in weeks, months it seemed, this morning woken only by Heiner's tender kisses that tasted of crisp sweet apple. Now who could resist that? Not me. Not here and now. I tried to summon some guilt, but there was none at hand. I had long ago decided that if I was going to love two men, then I would have to stop feeling ashamed about it. Or guilty. Most of the time, I succeeded.

The smell of strong French coffee drew me out of the trance of this morning's remembered passion. The accompanying smile, a purely Pavlovian response to the aroma of freshly ground coffee beans brewing.

I threw off the duvet, blowing out a breath, and slipped on my sleeveless shift. My flip-flops had disappeared, and I vaguely remembered kicking them off before discarding the rest of my clothes last night.

Intending to dress decently for breakfast, I hadn't even got to my suitcase to rummage for shorts and a T-shirt when Heiner edged the door open with his elbows. The tray he carried held a carafe (it had a fancier name that I'd forgotten), two cups, whipped cream, and two croissants, one chocolate and one plain.

Heiner kissed me again after setting down the tray on the bed.

Just heaven. Here and now.

~

Hagen

Already at work for two hours, and the sun had just begun to creep over the cliffs at the top of the canyon. Hagen pushed up his diving mask, then tore it off. *Anger, much*? When the sun arrived, the water would take on the violent greenish-blue tint that this part of the *les Gorges du Verdon* was known for. And the place would be full of tourists with their electric rental boats, paddle-boats, and happily screaming children.

Hagen already missed his own happily screaming children. And his wife. He'd looked forward to picking her up at the train station in Manosque tomorrow evening. But instead of her boarding the train she was probably, based on the cryptic text message he'd gotten from her yesterday, lying in bed with his twin brother in the house in Dinard that he and Heiner had inherited from their mother.

Their threesome had always been an uneasy arrangement. The recipe went so:

Hagen loved Caitie.

Caitie loved Hagen.

Heiner loved Caitie.

Caitie loved Heiner.

Hagen married Caitie.

They'd married just six and a half years ago. Then the triplets were born. Lots of bad things happened. And then they renewed their vows a year later. That didn't change anything. The recipe was the same. But Hagen wouldn't change a thing. Except maybe the threesome part, even though Caitie and Heiner's relationship had progressed because of a love between them that he could not question. And because of his betrayal. It didn't matter that he'd had no choice. He'd betrayed Caitie, and now paid the price for it.

He'd marry Caitie all over again if she wanted to. Hagen didn't understand his anger. Or his dissatisfaction with life. He had everything he'd ever wanted, most of which he'd *never* thought he'd have.

The limestone walls of the canyon had their own distinctive rich limey scent in addition to the surprisingly fresh-smelling water. Bright blue sky promised a hot day of work for vacationers bent on amusing themselves. He'd go down again later in the evening when the tourists thinned out for the day. Dr. Anethe Babin, a French historian, his employer, and fellow treasure seeker, popped up from the water with nary a splash. He gave her a hand onto the skiff.

After Anethe and Hagen helped each other out of their scuba gear, they went to the monitors to see what they'd recorded this morning. Yesterday's search had revealed a small trove of artifacts, many broken, deep in the mud bank they'd been carefully dredging with suction hoses. Today they'd filmed everything *in situ*.

Anethe chattered to him in French, both asking and telling Hagen how they were to proceed next. She looked good in her 'neoprene lite' suit and showed off her well-toned figure by displaying the one-piece bathing suit that she had on underneath as she unzipped the neoprene to the waist. The move was calculated to get Hagen's attention. It worked.

He gave her figure a clinical and not-so-clinical appraisal and added a smile to go with it. Anethe seemed to enjoy the attention, and laid a hand on his arm as she pointed to what looked like a jeweled iron dagger embedded in the newly revealed section of compressed mud. Hagen ignored Anethe's hand as he zoomed in on the dagger, a jolt of excitement coursing through him at the sight.

"I think that one is yours," Anethe said, her eyes alight. They shone gray-green, in the bright daylight that reflected off the water. "Definitely looks Iron Age."

"Could be. What a wonderful find."

Hagen had never been a fan of archeological treasure hunts, or treasure hunters for that matter, but the opportunity to explore an area firsthand for evidence of its Celtic past was too good to pass up. He'd offered a German museum who'd contracted him for work in the past a share of his portion of the finds, in exchange for sponsoring part of the trip which would lend his finds legitimacy in the archeological community. It was a coup that gave him a lot of private satisfaction.

Even though he was 'officially' an amateur, Hagen was a recognized expert in a couple of areas, and the disdain some of the academic professionals showed him rankled. Most of the time he didn't care. But this—if they found something significant—would be like a slap with a white silk glove to their smug professor faces.

Anethe didn't need to know about his arrangement with the museum, and neither did her financial backers; a private French consortium, she'd told him. Anethe didn't tell him everything either, like who the consortium were.

What they would do with *their* finds was also not something Anethe had confided to Hagen. Nor had she confided *exactly* what they were seeking.

Hagen did have an idea, and it almost made him despair. He wanted to ask her, just to be sure. There were still those who thought the legendary treasure of the Knights of Templar really existed. Some had placed it in southern France, one of the reputed last strongholds of the Templars after they were banned in the seventeenth century, two of their leaders burned at the stake. The Gorge of Verdon, with its many caves, would provide good hiding places and was near Trigance, one of the supposed secret places for Templar treasure.

Maybe.

Maybe something had been hidden was one version of a myth that thriller writers and conspiracy-seekers assumed: the existence of a medieval holy grail. *Maybe there was hidden knowledge* was a version of the myth not-so-serious scholars (and believers) assumed. *Maybe it had been found centuries ago and plundered* was the likely version of the truth. Or *maybe it had never existed at all.*

But the treasure didn't interest Hagen. He was sure the thrill of discovery would be there should they find anything of that nature. Anything at all. But the secretive consortium funding the expedition were welcome to it. Hagen was here for the adventure and the promise of a few Celtic artifacts, for which he'd bargained and won the right to keep.

Nothing more of interest showed up in the videos. The knife, if it was as old as Hagen thought it was, would be worth the trip alone.

"One question, please," Hagen asked. They'd been conversing in French the whole time, but he switched to English for increased precision. It was his second-best language, and Anethe didn't speak German.

Anethe was changing out of her wet things into less wet things. She didn't have body shyness. Hagen turned partly away to avoid staring, even though he thought that was what she wanted.

"Your French is very good," she said. "Does it bother you to speak in French? We can talk in English if you prefer."

"No, but I think my French has become rusty again as of late, and I wanted this to be clear."

"Clear?"

"Why are we dredging here when there are so many caverns and tunnels, dry places to hide something for a long time? You *are* looking for something that's been lost for centuries?"

She nodded. "I agree with you about the location...but I had reliable information that we should look here first."

"Well, of course, if it's *reliable*," Hagen said and couldn't keep the sarcasm out of his voice. It irked. The mystery of their search and why she had chosen him, Hagen von der Lahn, an amateur expert on ancient inscriptions. This was just like a pulp action film, the kind he'd never much enjoyed.

She caught the edge in his tone and her cheeks colored pink, making her even more attractive. "What motivates you to look for Celtic artifacts? It is such a dead end."

"To some maybe. To me, it's—how can I explain it—a lifelong passion."

His bubble of irritation made her smile, one meant to reassure him. "I can understand that. You've fallen in love with a part of the past and can't let go, is that it?"

He nodded. But that wasn't the half of it.

The past hadn't let go of him.

Ever since he'd been lost-in-time and assumed the identity of one of his Iron Age ancestors, the (then) recently deceased Veneti tribal chief Iaun Reith, Hagen had a renewed, even obsessive interest in the continental Celts. The Iron Age folk were currently regarded as a network of tribes, some more warlike than others, spread in time and space over much of the Eurasian continent.

Anethe was right. No one except a few archeologists, linguists, neopagans, and a horde of fantasy buffs even cared about the Celts any more. That suited Hagen just fine. He didn't have a need for money; financially, they were set. Caitie didn't need to go back to work. Heiner was free to satisfy passions that included making his music and breeding horses. And managing the modest family fortune no longer occupied the majority of Hagen's time, leaving him free to satisfy his obsession by going on expeditions like this one.

What they'd found today was a knife that on first appearance was similar to one he'd brought back with him from his Iron Age sojourn. Caitie had rescued Hagen and traveled back home with him. How and why the knife had traveled with them, he didn't know. But it had been important afterwards, when Caitie's life hung in the balance.

So important that Hagen didn't believe the appearance of the knife had been a coincidence. And now a second knife had appeared.

Losing Caitie would have been hard for Hagen to bear, just as his father had lost his mother when he and Heiner were born. His father hadn't borne his loss for very long, despite having two children to care for, and took his own life. Hagen barely remembered him.

He waited for Anethe to finish changing before doing the same.

He didn't think it a good idea for them both to be naked at the same time, not in his current frame of mind. *Angry, some?*

They stowed their gear in the boat lockers, and Anethe piloted the skiff back to where they could secure it to one of the docks until later. They said their good-byes, each going in their separate vehicles to their separate accommodations. Anethe was staying in a privately rented room close to the gorge, but Hagen had chosen a hotel farther away from her because he wanted some distance between him and Anethe for when Caitie arrived.

Anethe was an attractive, accomplished woman and Caitie was sometimes crazy jealous. To minimize trouble, he'd booked a superior room at the three-star hotel *Le Relais Notre-Dame* in nearby Quinson. Without equipment, an easy walk to their rental boat. It was a beautiful, family-run hotel with a lovely enclosed garden, excellent food, in a quaint village. Because it lacked air-conditioned rooms, Hagen had his privacy from late-season tourists. The weather had been oppressively warm for early September. The hotel was nearly empty. After three decades of life in a non-air-conditioned castle near the Rhine, Hagen didn't mind.

Caitie was to enjoy herself as well as share his bed, a bed blessedly free of happily screaming children for a change. As she'd done in Pompeii and in Trieste. For him, a perfect arrangement, and it gave them some much-needed alone time. He wanted to pamper her and share his enthusiasm about something other than home and hearth. Hagen believed trips like this were important for their marriage, for them to stay happy-ever-after.

Caitie was his reason for happy-at-all, and he didn't know what he'd do if he lost her again. Even to Heiner. Especially to Heiner. Hagen had been the lost one until they met, and he still remembered the moment with perfect clarity, the first time she'd looked up at him with her clear golden eyes. He had denied the inevitability for a while since it had been foreordained, but then...sometimes you just can't argue with fate.

He hoped they'd be able to enjoy their stay without the complications of contemporary dead bodies in ancient crematoriums or angry

Roman citizens about to be disintegrated in a pyroclastic fury. But, in retrospect, he had to admit those had been worthy adventures.

Caitie told Hagen that she wasn't ready to go back to work, that she wanted to enjoy being a wife, mother, *and just herself*, for a while longer. When Hagen was honest with himself, which was fairly often, he hoped she'd never go back to work. He was enjoying the status quo of Caitie as wife, mother and *just herself*, even if that included occasionally *sharing* her love with Heiner. The status quo wouldn't last; nothing ever stayed the same with the two of them. As long as Caitie was committed to him, he'd weather any changes the future would bring.

Hagen continued to brood about his conversation with Anethe on the walk up to his room. *His* holy grail from this trip would be an inscription in Gallo-Roman text tossed in along with a pile of sacrificial daggers and helmets, gold torcs and knotted ropes. A curse tablet or three or four for good measure. That's what he *wanted* to find. Reality, of course, would be much less. But finding the dagger had been a good start.

After showering and changing into jeans and a linen shirt, Hagen was about to go down to confirm a reservation for dinner. His cell phone chimed. And then again.

The first message was from Anethe.

"Dinner? At my place? My cousin, the cook, has spent the day making bouillabaisse. *Fresh fish from Marseille. Must try. Will give us time to talk about the nature of our search."*

Bouillabaisse. A traditional Provencal specialty with wonderful complexity if done right. He'd had it once before in Nice. Caitie was not fond of fish, and this might be his chance to enjoy it again, although Hagen was suspicious of Anethe's motives. Was she trying to seduce him? He'd been right to anticipate that kind of trouble.

Hagen was about to decline the invitation...and then he saw that the second message was from Caitie.

"Heiner and I will be on the way soon. Should arrive in Quinson in the early afternoon. xx"

Hagen felt like throwing the phone across the room. *Anger, very much.* He clenched his fists and opened them, taking deep breaths. No reason to be upset. None whatsoever. He'd arrange for Heiner's room now, as far away from his and Caitie's as possible. And then...

He sent Anethe a message.

"Be there soon. Looking forward to it."

~

H einer
"You think he's upset? Why on earth would he be?" Heinrich couldn't keep the sarcasm out of his voice. He'd known they would incur Hagen's wrath with their unplanned and—this time—not-so-secret tryst. But it had been worth it. "What did he say?"

Caitie frowned and played with the braid Heinrich had just spent the last quarter of an hour plaiting. She tossed it over her shoulder. A few wisps had escaped. He kissed her neck. She still frowned. "He texted that he looks forward to our *visit* tomorrow. What did he mean by that? Is he sending us away again? Who is this Anethe? He said he's having dinner with her. Something about a traditional fish soup that he knew I wouldn't care for. He made it sound like dining with this Anethe was doing *me* a favor."

Heinrich shrugged. "Sounds to me like he's being treated to *bouillabaisse* by Anethe. I believe she's the one who hired him. He suspects a hopeless wild hunt for Templar treasure, but is also hoping to find a few Celtic artifacts. As for his mood, no, he won't send *you* away. He's just retreating into his Baron of Burg Lahn persona. He'll be fine by the time we get there."

She glared and waved her arms. "Why didn't he tell me all this about Anethe and treasure and...?" She scooped water and arced a stream of it out into the bay.

Heiner chuckled. Caitie didn't hide her possessiveness well. Or at all. "Because he knew you'd get jealous. And because you were making *Schultüten* and wouldn't let him help you but cursed like a mad pirate the whole time. And maybe now he wants you to be jealous. Think of it as doing penance."

Caitie just snorted. She sat in front of him, and wiggled her toes in the sand. She wore only a white cotton cover-up over her bathing suit. He began stuffing the bowl of his pipe, edging into a comfortable place on his favorite rock. The waves were compliant this evening, lapping around them, but when the tide came in, they would grow reckless and feral again. The Bay of St. Malo was not known for being mild. The sky had a milky pre-twilight glow, the water a dark green counterpoint. The air was mild and fresh, and Heiner was grateful they had this, this last private moment to themselves.

Caitie had turned up her face as if seeking the sun's warmth, even though it was well on in its downward journey into the sea. "Wonder what it would be like to be a mermaid."

"Wet, I imagine," Heinrich said.

She laughed. "You had that thing with the Loreley...and you never talked about it. What was it like?"

"Wet—"

"Heiner—"

"And fatal. Without using my Shadowcraft, I would have been a goner. But it was...interesting. She induced a temporary case of synesthesia."

"She made you sneeze?"

"Switching of the senses. Taste for smell. Seeing colors as sound, that kind of thing."

"Oh. Wow. That sounds intense."

He tamped down the tobacco and lit his pipe. The sweet taste mingled with the smell of the smoke reminded him of the sense-swapping effect in a strange way. And the drug in his lungs of the satisfaction of coupling with such a powerful entity. Heinrich decided enough had been said about the Loreley.

But Caitie didn't want to let it go. "How did you survive it?"

"I used one of my music spells to create a bubble of voice around me that blocked out the enchantment of the Loreley's song. And when the danger passed, I molded it into a shell of air until I surfaced in Ande-dubnos."

"Okay. So, the Loreley could—and can—access the waking world and the Otherworld. Even before the veil was opened."

"Correct. I imagine most of the water deities have that power. Water is..." He couldn't grasp the word he was looking for.

"A conduit. Where magic and reality merge, and also sacred. Like a confluence of rivers. And your...um, *interaction* with the Loreley aided the transition from here to there."

Heinrich reminded himself never to underestimate Caitlin von der Lahn. Her intuition was a force to reckon with. "An excellent way to think of it. And probably very near the truth of things."

"After you're done with your smoke, maybe we should get going," she said, her voice clouded over.

"Tired of my company so soon?"

She hunched her shoulders. "No, but...you know."

~

Hagen

The bed and breakfast where Anethe was staying was a two-story half-timbered house with a foundation of stone set back from the road. It had a Provencal charm about it, if a very simple one. But Anethe hadn't impressed him as the simple type. She had told him she lived in Paris for most of the year, and Hagen doubted she lived simply.

They sat outside on a sun-drenched terrace at a wooden table for two, with a view to the gorge similar to the one from Hagen's hotel. No other guests were in evidence. The sun strafed the top of the canyon walls, bestowing a final benediction for the day. A strong feeling of peace snuck up on Hagen, which contrasted sharply with the anger he had felt earlier. He'd hiked the gorge once equipped with a backpack and a tent when he was much younger, and it had been a time of welcome isolation in a spectacularly beautiful environment. He hadn't even minded the threat of snakebite. He'd been free from family strife or responsibility.

While they waited for the *bouillabaisse* to be served, Anethe and

Hagen munched on tapenade toasts with different toppings of a pecorino-like cheese, olive paste, and sun-dried tomatoes with fresh goat cheese accompanied by a fruity Provencal rosé. All of it very good, which added to the festive mood that was creeping up on him. Other diners had started to fill up the small patio. Most looked like locals to Hagen, always a good sign in a restaurant.

Anethe wore a loose, breezy peasant dress belted at the waist, and strappy sandals. He wondered if she was married, and if not, why. He couldn't imagine her without admirers. Her gray-green eyes sparkled in her heart-shaped face framed by short dark brown hair. Her smile was made even more pleasant by a sprinkling of freckles.

"Your cousin works here?" Hagen asked, and returned the smile. It had been a while since he had flirted with anyone other than his wife, and it felt as rusty as his French. Rustier. Out of necessity, he had spoken French earlier in the summer with the contractors during the renovations on the house in Dinard. But he'd also slipped into using Breton wherever possible. It came more naturally to him. Caitie always enjoyed it when he talked to her in Breton, even though she was not fluent in it. Her French was non-existent. He felt comfortable with both languages. But not so much with flirting with Anethe. He couldn't seem to stop thinking about Caitie.

"Michel is part owner. He was raised here. Has never left the area. His parents used to own a large inn in Trigance, but sold it after they got too old to run it any more. We spent a lot of time there, my family, when I was younger."

Hagen waited to see if she was going to add any more information. Instead, she lifted her wineglass to his. "Here's to the success of our search."

"Yes," Hagen said, touching his glass to hers. "The search...for?"

She smiled again and took a sip before replying. "Treasure, what else?"

He laughed. "Oh, I don't know. Maybe just a decent find. You don't expect to uncover a real treasure, do you?"

Anethe turned to stare out at the gorge. "Do you believe in truth of it all? Celtic priests—druids—and a warrior class. And bards? Is that what *you're* trying to find proof of?

Scholarly debate still raged over the existence of druids, and Hagen doubted he'd be able to contribute to solving that controversy. He also didn't care to. Caitie often called him and Heiner her 'wild-assed druids,' but the truth was, based on his own experience living with the Iron Age Veneti tribe on the western coast of Gaul, Hagen and Heiner (and Caitie) were descendants of a Celtic tribal aristocracy and not from the class of priests-judges-bards that might or might not have constituted the druids.

What interested Hagen most was answering a different question. Why were the continental Celts so easy to defeat by a single, incredibly gifted but not infallible, general named Julius Caesar?

He cleared his throat. "No, not really. But I am interested in finding something...anything...that would shed light on the defeat of the continental tribes. All we have, really all, is Caesar's account and a few others that were clearly a part of the Roman propaganda machine. It would be like, say, two thousand years from now historians reading Hitler's account of the Second World War...if he had won. And that being the only written account that survived."

"Interesting choice of analogy," she said. "You compare Julius Caesar to Adolf Hitler?"

"Of course not, no. There were atrocities on both sides during the defeat of the Celts. Caesar was highly motivated to have his version of events be the one that was preserved. The Romans were good at that."

The final failed campaign had clinched the defeat of a large but ineffectual unified Celtic force—a force that had opportunity and the advantage of numbers—under the command of a single not-so-intelligent general named Vercingetorix.

Pitted against the Romans with their orderly assault techniques, this massive force, skilled in Celtic skirmishing techniques, was utterly crushed. They then slunk home to lick their wounds and throw in the towel of independence. Just like that. But *something else* had contributed to the demise of myriad tribes – seemingly all at once – and those were the clues that Hagen yearned to find.

"You sound as if you were an eyewitness," Anethe said, watching him over the rim of her wineglass.

"Do I? The curse of the obsessed. But I'd love to have a time machine, to dial it back to specific moments and watch how things played out. Wouldn't you?"

Hagen was no prince, merely a member of an extraordinary, possibly unique, bloodline whose abilities to traverse the Celtic Otherworld allowed him to accrue power in that realm. And that sometimes included the ability to time travel. But it wasn't easy to pinpoint a specific time and place. He preferred to carry out his archeological research the old-fashioned way.

Hagen suspected, based on his experiences in Ande-dubnos, that supernatural forces had been at work to demoralize and possibly mislead the Celts. Maybe they had become enamored of having new Roman worshippers in addition to the Celtic ones. If so, then it hadn't gone well for most of the so-called deities. They'd faded as the empire waned and Christianity ascended.

Anethe put her wineglass down. "I would at that. I'd love to have that kind of *power.*"

Hagen, trying to swim out of the depths of his thoughts, snagged on the word Anethe used. Power. She had emphasized it. Only a little, but it was there.

"What kind of power?" he asked before he'd thought about it.

"All kinds, any kinds," she said and waved her hand as if irritated at the world and her place in it. "Healing power."

"Pardon me if I'm being forward, but are you ill?"

She shook her head and put her lips in a line and looked out to the scenery again, picking up her wineglass.

He thought it best not to pursue the topic of *power.* It had been his fault for mentioning time travel. He was saved having to extricate himself from that line of discussion, though, by the arrival of the *bouillabaisse.*

He waited for her to start. And then he took a spoonful. Thicker than a broth, the tan-colored soup with bits of white fish floating in it was complex, yes, and tasting very much of the sea, but without fishiness. Thyme and tomato, with a hint of fennel, contrasted the sharp flavors of garlic and saffron in the *rouille* they spread over more oven-roasted baguette slices and then dipped in the soup. It was an explosion of taste that was almost sexual in nature, deeply satisfying. This was the real thing. Hagen would never have guessed such a humble inn could produce such food. But that was part of the charm of Provence.

Hagen paid due reverence to the soup for a few minutes before he looked up. Anethe was studying him.

"You haven't asked me why I contracted you for this trip," she said.

Hagen sat back and wiped his mouth with the thick white napkin. He felt a sudden chill, even though the early evening air had remained mild with only the occasional stray breeze. "You told me I was recommended by a colleague of mine, Bruno Simon from Strasbourg. I didn't have a reason to doubt you. Should I have?"

"Possibly." It was her turn to lean back. "Would you like some more wine?"

"I've had enough. Thank you."

Anethe leaned forward, pushing her soup tureen to the side. "What if I told you that there is one incredible treasure in the *Gorges du Verdon*, and that I know where it is. I've already *seen* it."

Hagen placed his hands in his lap and schooled his expression to neutrality. "I'd say, 'Congratulations' and leave you to it. But then..." he paused and propped a finger aside his chin. "You don't need me, do you?"

Her smile was too quick. "Ah, but I do. You see, Hagen, I've heard some interesting things about the von der Lahn family. Or should I say, the Du Bois family, the other half of your lineage? Am I mistaken?"

Hagen sighed. "My mother was a Du Bois from a small village near Morbihan. She was cast out from the family when she married my father and moved to Germany. She used her inheritance to buy a house in Dinard, far from her family but still in Brittany since she didn't want to abandon her homeland completely. After my mother died, the Du Bois' and the von der Lahns never reconciled their differences. But I don't understand the relevance."

"What if you could have saved her?"

The anger Hagen had felt earlier returned. What nonsense was this? And why was she so interested in his mother's family?

She began to talk to him in Breton. Not only that, she used the dialect peculiar to Hagen's family, a dialect no longer existent. "My mother's married name is Babin, Hagen. Her maiden name was Du Bois. You and I are distant cousins."

Hagen smiled. The dinner was now proving interesting as well as tasty. Any inclination to flirt with Anethe Babin just evaporated. He answered her in Breton as well. "Estranged distant cousins. So that means your cousin Michel the cook is also part Du Bois?"

She shrugged. "He's a cousin on my mother's side. Yes."

The waitress came to clear the plates and asked if they wanted dessert.

"Just an espresso for me," Hagen said.

"Are you sure you don't want a *digestif*?" Anethe asked.

Hagen raised an eyebrow. "Are we not working this evening? All right, but just a small one."

When the snifters arrived, Anethe took a book out of the satchel she had draped over her chair. She handed it to him.

He took a sip of cognac.

The book was bound in a pinkish brown leather that was worn thin but still supple, and the pages were brittle and faded to a dark cream, which was not too bad if the book had endured years of sitting neglected on a shelf. The ink of the gothic script had faded. He paged through.

"It's bound in sheepskin," Anethe said.

There were also hand-written entries. The book was an antique and may have been valuable. But it wasn't really a treasure. Hagen's library back at the Burg had several books that were at least this old and in much better condition, including several first editions that would be worth thousands on the open market. And scattered throughout the castle, there were books that were even older.

The content seemed to be part travelogue and part folk tales and included recipes. Those were the handwritten parts.

"Intriguing," Hagen said and finished his cognac.

Anethe took the book and put it with the front cover face-down on her left palm. She then let it fall open so that the book rested in both palms. A desiccated four-leaf clover had been inserted as a page marker, browned and brittle. "Look at the recipe."

Hagen glanced at the French, not understanding all the words because of the old-fashioned cursive script, but enough to know it was a recipe for a fish soup, a *bouillabaisse*. He didn't want to mar the ancient page by touching it, so he let a finger scroll down the list of ingredients, holding it just above the paper. Rockfish, eels, *loup de mer*, and crabs were listed, nothing unusual there.

But he stopped when he came to the phrase, *queue de sirène. Sirène* had been crossed out and the word, *triton*, written above it. Sirène was the French word for a legendary creature, a mermaid or water nymph. But the addition specified *triton*, or tail of a merman, an even rarer entity.

He took a deep breath. "I'm sorry, Anethe. It's not personal, but, this...I thought you were a professional."

Hagen wanted urgently to leave the restaurant. He felt sluggish after the meal, and his head swam when he tried to stand. But it was time to go. His work here was *done*. Hagen hoped Anethe would let him keep the dagger they had found this morning, even though he doubted it now.

Hagen put the book on the table and tried to stand. Anethe drank her cognac in a single gulp.

Anethe picked up the book and walked over to him, taking his arm. "Oh, this has nothing to do with my *profession*, Hagen. At least not directly." She placed the book in his hand. "I have something else I want to show you."

They were in Anethe's room, which, it turned out, was not a regular part of the inn, but a spacious attic that had been converted into living quarters. Besides the four-poster bed in the middle of the room and a rack for clothes, there wasn't a lot of furniture. An oval four-paned window looked out on a sky that had faded to twilight.

It wouldn't be long before they would have to continue their work in the darkness. And Hagen didn't favor doing that. He'd rather wait until early morning again. Hagen also didn't favor sitting on Anethe's bed with her, but there weren't any other chairs or sofas at hand and he felt the need to sit again after the climb to the attic. He was unusually short of breath. Maybe a reaction to the heat or the strangeness of the situation.

There was a large wooden desk against a wall that abutted one of the eaves, with an old-fashioned wooden desk chair on rollers. She stood and motioned Hagen over to the chair. He had to duck down because of the low ceiling and slid awkwardly into the chair. She came to stand next to him and fished something out from a pile of papers. It was the knife they had found this morning. She must have gone back for it after he left. *Verdammt.*

He shook his head to clear the sound of bees buzzing. "Absurd."

She smiled, that playful flirtatious one she'd used on him this afternoon. "What part do you find absurd? Do you deny the existence of such creatures or would you be unwilling to eat one?"

"Both," Hagen said without hesitation, lying about the first part.

"And if I could show you one, of the masculine persuasion, right here in the *Gorge du Verdon*? A *triton*!"

He'd no doubt there were several remaining *exempla* of those entities bound to rivers and springs providing waypoints between the waking world and the Otherworld. He'd never come across one in France, but knew of the Loreley in Germany. Not to mention ocean deities, which were a completely different kettle of fish, so to speak. Hagen also had no doubt they were of the race his family called the *Tud* in Breton, the Folk, the so-called people of the Otherworld, although grouping them into such a broad species, like fairies, was being generous. Some were old, possibly older than the Celts, although Hagen had no knowledge of the truth of his speculation.

Many of them did have human blood, and most of them *fed* on humans. One way or another. Hagen had no intention of helping Anethe hunt down a male water nymph with an Iron Age knife.

There was a small clutch of nymphs, both male and female, in the Schattenreich. They lived in the River of Life and guarded passage to one particular entrance to Ande-dubnos. And they guarded it well. Their songs were beautiful. And deadly to those who couldn't resist, couldn't force themselves to swim to the surface after hearing them.

Through pressure from the Catholic church, such creatures had been reduced to the race of fairies. Some, like the Breton *morgens* were equated with demons and, perhaps, not without *some* justification, but were once revered and worshipped throughout all the Celtic lands, continental and insular.

Every sacred spring had once had its own water spirit. Many current river names still attested to such a past. In earlier, pre-Christian times after the defeat of the Celts, through *interpretation Romana*, some were also adopted into the Roman pantheon as well, with names like Grannus Apollo or Mars Condatis. Not all deities were accorded the dubious honor of becoming Roman deities through absorption...

Hagen had sunk into a near-trance and had to shake himself from his reverie. He tried to concentrate on Anethe. "What? Your cousin wants to add water nymph tail to his *bouillabaisse* recipe?

"Now you're being absurd," she said.

"Then why the cookbook?"

"It's an old book, over 200 years old. My uncle, the one with the inn in Trigance, gave the book to me. I'd read it often as a child."

"Don't tell me this is the recipe Michel uses?"

She laughed. "No, his mother came to Marseille by way of Tunisia and learned the traditional way of making the soup there. Michel learned to cook from his mother."

"Well, I wish you luck in your search. I had assumed you were looking for Templar treasure. That's what I get for not asking in advance." Hagen felt his words slurring. He took a few steps. The room spun. He swayed in place. "Although, I guess I don't get to keep the knife." Whatever it was they had given him, it must have been in the soup. "Most unpleasant."

"I know who and what you are."

"And you've apparently drugged me," Hagen said, his words slurring like a mouth full of oatmeal. Unable to stand any longer, he sunk to the floor. He put his head in his hands, trying to summon enough strength to leave, even if he had to crawl out to the street. His stomach felt like it was full of small sharp needles and felt tight and hot.

Had she poisoned him? Were these to be his last minutes, expiring in a dingy attic, not even able to see his last sunset? He'd wanted to go out a little more dramatically. At least Ankou would be there to greet him and escort him to his place. He'd earned that much from his rôle guiding the newly deceased only the Paths of the Dead, the duty he'd accepted from Ankou all those many years ago in exchange for a modicum of power. *Schattenwerk*. Shadowcraft. If only he could access it in the waking world.

Maybe he could still cross over to the Schattenreich, despite his grogginess...he closed his eyes and tried to take a deep breath.

And all thought fled.

~

C aitie
I trudged up the hotel stairs, not waiting for Heiner to follow. Hoping he wouldn't. If there was yelling, it was just going to be Hagen and me. I gripped the iron key to the room so hard, the metal dug into my palm. After the lovely drive through half of France in Heiner's Porsche, my mood had been elated and hopeful that everything was going to be fine. Now I crashed. A black mass of shame and anxiety growing inside me.

Hagen didn't answer his phone or his messages, had not left any messages saying why he'd been out. He wasn't there to greet us when we arrived at the hotel.

The hotel proprietor, a nice-looking young man with sun-bronzed skin and friendly brown eyes, and a well-trimmed beard, had said that he hadn't seen Hagen return to his room yesterday evening. And he hadn't come down to breakfast. It wasn't like my husband to miss a good breakfast, especially if he'd only had some fish soup the night before. With this Anethe. Had he even returned last night?

If I were in my red wolf form, my teeth would have been bared in a snarl.

I put the key in the door, and turned it, and felt a hand on my shoulder.

"About time—" I turned to confront my husband, but it was Heiner behind me, wearing a look of chagrin.

"Caitie, wait a second."

"What for? If he's not here, then—"

"Then, what? Are you going to accuse him of adultery?"

"If the cream is gone and the cat is licking his lips..."

"Take another deep breath. And then open the door," Heiner said.

"You're coming in with me? Do you think that's a good idea? Things could get messy. Valuable crockery broken."

A room service maid came out of a room down the hall, pulled her cart along and entered the next room closer to us.

"Let's go inside," I said.

I opened the door to a bright, well-appointed room, spacious and welcoming with a large four-poster bed—the duvets and pillows pristine and untouched. A whiff of lavender hung in the air. And the maid had not yet been in.

Hagen hadn't slept in his bed last night. His field pants and shirt were draped over the white wooden chair next to a small table that held his laptop. And his Range Rover was not in the hotel parking lot.

"That bastard," I said.

I pushed out a heavy breath, the pang of fear about Hagen's betrayal causing my chest to constrict. This was so not fair. But it was familiar. I'd been here before. My relationship with Heiner was also not fair to Hagen. And I was jumping to conclusions. Again.

Heiner's dark blue eyes, which had smoldered with a midnight passion early this morning, too early, in Lyon were now close to the color of a bruise, the pupils widened. "I sense something is not right. Don't you?"

Hagen's field boots were lined up neatly next to the bed. I went to the window and drew the white curtains aside. The window looked out on a lovely enclosed garden, which was awash in late afternoon sunlight; the perfect place for an intimate dinner. And there was a pool. Hagen had intended this trip as a romantic retreat for us for when he wasn't working. There was even a fireplace in the room. I sighed again.

Heiner was right. Something was wrong...it was a strong queasy absence of Hagen on all levels. Hagen and I were bound in the spheres that mattered—spiritual, physical, emotional—through his lynx talisman, an exquisite (and expensive) brushed gold replica of his spirit animal, which I wore around my neck on a smooth gold chain. I clutched it now, and sent all my love for Hagen gushing into it.

And got nothing in return.

Something horribly wrong. Hagen was either far away. Or sleeping. Or worse. Injury or death could also interfere with the sending. Heiner had stiffened, also sensitive to my emotional outpouring, which was to be expected since Heiner and I were also bound in the same way.

"You feel it, too?" I asked.

"Of course. Hagen and I have been attuned to each other since we were children."

"But why didn't we sense it before? Why just now?"

Heiner joined me at the window, his eyes seeing but he wasn't taking in the scene. "Maybe we did, but ignored it, thinking it was him being angry or sad."

I took Heiner's hand. Were we fools? Had passion misled us into ignoring Hagen's distress?

"What do we do now?" I asked. "I don't even know where to look for him. We can't just call the police and say, 'Hello, I have a psychic sense that my husband is in danger. Yes, officer, he is really a druid, and we have this spiritual connection.'"

"Why don't you talk to the proprietor again, see if we can find out anything else. I'll bring up the bags."

"My French isn't good enough."

"He speaks English. I'm sure of it. And he was immediately enchanted by you."

I laughed. "Funny. He's probably enchanted by M. Hagen von der Lahn's taking two of his best rooms for a week."

We walked down the stairs together. I took a deep breath and looked into Heiner's eyes, hoping for reassurance.

"*Très bon, chérie,*" Heiner said and patted my arm. "It will be all right." Then he loped out to his Porsche to get the luggage.

The proprietor, a Monsieur Pascal, tried to be helpful. He nodded and kept trying to reassure me with a charming brown-eyed earnestness, while we tried to reconstruct Hagen's day yesterday afternoon, the last time that M. Pascal had seen him. I leaned my arms on the wooden reception desk, while he recalled that Hagen had tentatively reserved a table at the hotel restaurant yesterday evening. That meant the invitation from Hagen's employer, Anethe whatever-her-last-name was, must have come at a later time.

Heiner passed through the lobby with the luggage and headed upstairs. I was just about to go through the day again, starting with breakfast, when an attractive young woman (was *everyone* in France good-looking?) strode up to the reception desk.

"I would like to leave a message, an urgent one, for Madame von der Lahn. Can you check to see if she has arrived?"

M. Pascal gazed at me, swallowing. That was too much of a pointer. I didn't have a chance to let him know with frantic gestures, not to give me away.

The woman turned to me. I knew it immediately. This was Anethe. Her eyes were the color of my father's, a gray the color of winter clouds laden with snow, but with a corona of green, which was interesting. She had a lovely figure and the cutest freckles. I felt my hackles rising. But I pushed everything down.

"You must be my husband's employer?" I asked, and added a neutral countenance.

She took me by the arm, nodding her dismissal to M. Pascal, and led me across the lobby towards the garden. I turned my head and smiled my thanks, hoping he wouldn't think me as arrogant as she was.

We stopped at a pair of facing couches. She nearly pushed me into one and sat across from me in the other one.

"Dr. Anethe Babin," she said and extended a hand.

I took it lightly with the tips of my fingers, as Hagen had taught me. The correct baroness greeting when you didn't know someone, and didn't necessarily want to know them.

"Caitlin von der Lahn. You are the historian working with my husband?"

"Madame von der Lahn, your husband needs your help. Can you come?"

I opened my mouth to say, "What the hell have you done with him," when Heiner came back down the stairs. He saw us and did an about-face, retreating into the stairwell. Anethe, facing the other way, didn't notice him.

I leaned back into the couch. I really wanted to go up to my room and hide and wait for Hagen to come back from wherever he was. But it didn't look like that was going to happen and this woman knew where he was.

"Is there something wrong?" I tried to be the aristocratic person that I wasn't, conveying a mild annoyance by folding my hands across crossed knees.

She waved a hand casually, managing to make it look elegant. "No, no, of course not. We were working...and lost track of time because of..." she glanced around and then whispered, leaning forward, "a spectacular find."

"I'm really happy for the both of you. But I don't understand why—"

"He's...sprained an ankle and needs help hiking out."

I jumped up. "Oh! I was so worried that he wasn't here when..." I almost said we. I gasped to hide my near-slip and sat down again. "When I arrived. Hagen hadn't left me a message. It was...worrying." I put a hand to my forehead, hoping I wasn't overdoing it. I didn't believe her that Hagen had sprained an ankle. He would still have had use of his hands and therefore his cell phone, which he always, always had with him. Unless connections weren't ideal in the canyon where they were working.

"He couldn't call. Reception is poor where we are working. It's deep in the canyon."

I wanted to believe her. There was something sympathetic about her. And familiar.

"You'll need sturdy shoes and long pants. There could be snakes," she said, staring at my on-the-road outfit of stretchy black linen pants and oversized white viscose top, her gaze lingering on my sneakers.

I made it a point to travel in comfort. My Gucci sneakers were comfortable and *très* chic, but not quite the thing for hiking canyon trails. Hagen bought them for me on a whim. I could have bought a whole store's worth of Keds for the price. But I did love them.

She sounded convincing. Maybe Heiner and I had overreacted. Snakes!

"Madame Babin, I think we should leave at once then. I've just arrived, but that's not important. Just let me change into more suitable attire."

"Just Anethe, please. With your help, we can get him out of the canyon." Anethe looked down as if embarrassed, but it seemed a calculated gesture. I knew a lot about those, even though I wasn't very good at them. "Hagen insisted that we not call for help." She lowered her voice again. "Because of the nature of our find. A true treasure!"

I held out my hand. "Caitie."

She took it and we shook, this time a genuine handshake. I wasn't sure she was genuine, but to get Hagen back, I would play along with her scheme, whatever it was. The treasure was definitely something that excited her. That Hagen would involve himself in a treasure hunt made me suspicious.

"How will we get there from here?"

Anethe nodded. "I'll drive us to the trailhead and then we hike down into the canyon. It is near a hidden beach on the Verdon river called *Baou Beni*, which means 'the End of the World' in the local dialect. The hike is only a little treacherous, not too slippery. It hasn't rained in a while."

I looked her over and wondered what 'a little treacherous' entailed.

She threw me a crooked smile. "You are plenty fit enough."

"I'll change and be right down," I said and rose.

"I'll wait for you outside," she said and glanced nervously at M. Pascal.

He busied himself at his reception desk, appearing oblivious to our conversation.

Heiner was waiting in my and Hagen's room. He had already changed into trail running shoes that he wore everywhere at Burg Lahn except for riding horses. He had his backpack slung across a shoulder.

"What next?" he asked.

"She says Hagen has a sprained ankle and needs help getting him out?" I asked rather than stated it.

"Where is he?"

"Deep in the canyon somewhere on a trail that might include snakes. Apparently, there is some sort of secret *treasure*."

I was already shedding clothes and rummaging in my suitcase for my cargo pants with a high amount of nylon stretchiness, and my Red Wing flex hikers. They were men's hiking shoes, but I loved them. And there wasn't a snake in the world that could get at my ankles with them on. "Anethe is driving us to the start of a trail and we're supposed to walk down into the canyon from there."

"I'll follow after you," Heiner said and quickly braided my hair. "Be careful. I don't believe in secret treasures."

"Thanks." I finished tying my boots. "Me, neither. But she did sound genuine."

Once downstairs, I looked around but didn't see Anethe. I didn't know what to tell M. Pascal, but I felt that someone ought to be informed that something potentially dangerous was going on.

He saw me and waved me over to the desk in frantic motions.

"Madame von der Lahn," he said, in a dramatic stage whisper and glanced towards the hotel entrance. "Madame, the one you were talking to."

I nodded. "Madame Babin. Go on."

"Her cousin, he has the *logé*."

"*Logé*, I don't understand."

"The small...inn. It is where she is staying."

"Oh. Okay."

"That is where Monsieur, your husband, went last evening for dinner."

I felt a tingling all down my spine, and my earlobes were burning."

"Monsieur Pascal. How do you know that? You told me you didn't know where he was."

M. Pascal's face turned scarlet and he folded his hands on the counter in front of him. "I...am sorry. But I did not want to be indiscreet. Before. But now that the cousin of Monsieur Du Bois was here to meet with you. *Bon*. I have to say it. I think there is something wrong. And I wanted you to know."

"Did you say that Madame Babin's cousin's name was Du Bois?"

He nodded. "We both grew up here in the region. My family knew his family—"

"Okay, thanks for letting me know. Where is this *logé* of Monsieur Du Bois?"

"Just down the road. I can show you on the local map." He pulled out a sheet with a kind of *general* map, the one *generally* given out in hotels, the ones that give a *general* location of a few roads and landmarks. He made an 'x' where the *logé* was. Just a few kilometers away.

I turned to go, now unsure what to do. Heiner stood in the stairwell. I quickly explained to him. "You need to go to the logé first. See if Hagen is there."

"And leave you alone? How will I find you?"

I told him about our destination, 'the End of the World'. "Oh, and Heiner...Anethe's cousin?"

"What about him?"

"His name is Du Bois."

"Not a coincidence?"

I shook my head. "Things just got weird."

"Okay. I'll go there first and then catch up to you on the trail. Try to slow Anethe down by being clumsy or scared or—"

"Just li'l ole me, trying to walk along this trail. My word, but I am really not fond of snakes," I said, pouring on my Texas twang.

"Perfect."

∾

Heiner

The Porsche slid to a halt in the parking lot. The so-called logé looked deserted. Heinrich took a deep breath and burst out of the car. He looked around first and decided to go around to the back before going in. The half-timbered construction with a base of stone didn't look run-down, but it didn't look inviting either. Around back, the dining terrace was deserted. Maybe they didn't have many guests or didn't do lunch.

Heinrich's stomach rumbled. Lunch would have to wait. His stomach clenched when he thought of Caitie alone with someone who might or might not be a long-lost cousin, one of the Du Bois'. He'd not spoken to any of them in over half a decade, and the last encounter he'd had with his distant cousin Ivonne Du Bois, at the grave of Caitie's mother, had not been welcoming.

The kitchen entrance was locked. Heinrich jogged to the front. The door was not locked, and Heinrich did not want to announce himself by knocking. He opened the door just enough to slide inside and waited in the dim foyer. Stairs were to the right and an empty parlor to the left.

When no one came running to confront him, Heinrich took the stairs up to the first floor. There was a long dark hallway with doors on either side that could have been rooms. The impression of dinginess grew stronger. Instinct made him continue up the stairs to the next floor. He could always explore after he was sure that no angry Du Bois cousins were lurking.

The narrow stairway ended on a landing with a single door. Heinrich paused to listen, but couldn't hear any voices. He tried the door, but it was locked.

Then he heard a cry.

He forced the door, a flimsy construction, and the frame splintered. Heinrich held his fists clenched and entered.

And there was Hagen. On the floor. His hands behind him, tied to a bed, and his legs bound in front. His hair hung limp and his forehead was covered in sweat.

He looked up when Heinrich entered.

"Heiner...how...where's Caitie?" Hagen rasped out.

"She's with Anethe. Supposedly, they are off to rescue you from a sprained ankle."

Hagen cursed. And a tear trickled down his cheek. Heinrich hugged his brother; Hagen reeked. They must have drugged him. And then Heinrich set about freeing him.

They did not have much time.

Heinrich parked his Porsche near Anethe's auto after Hagen pointed it out to him in the parking lot of the *auberge* near the start of the trail. They were high along the canyon wall, and would have to hike down to get to the base of the river. Hagen had told Heinrich that he'd been here once before, and the trail was adequately marked.

Heinrich hoped so. They did not have the luxury to get lost.

They had grabbed water on the way out of the inn. Heinrich made Hagen drink most of a liter of water on the drive to the trailhead. It seemed to revive him.

Hagen said he had heard Anethe and her cousin Michel arguing early in the morning. Michel had stormed off after and hadn't returned. Anethe told Hagen the restaurant and inn would be closed for the day. He could not expect help from anyone. Hagen had not believed her, but had slipped in and out of sleep. He had been too strung out to do anything but try to free himself in his waking moments.

The trail wound down the side of the canyon in a series of switchbacks that were not too steep, although in Hagen's weakened condition, Heinrich felt it better to pause every few minutes. Even with several short rests, they made it to the bottom in less than half an hour. Heinrich now set his hopes on Caitie's ability to slow her progress with Anethe enough so that they could make good time.

But first they had to pause. Hagen needed to throw up. Afterwards, he said he felt better, and drank more water. Heinrich tried to keep his impatience from edging into hysteria. Caitie was alone with the madwoman who'd drugged and imprisoned Hagen!

The trail went uphill to the left of a bridge that led to the other side of the gorge. They climbed steadily through scrubby forest of ash and aromatic juniper, and followed the narrow path that paralleled the river. Heinrich set a pace that might have been uncomfortably fast, but Hagen didn't complain.

Heinrich wished they could return under more pleasant circumstances. The canyon with its high walls and happily noisy river—below them now, its color a startling greenish turquoise—continued to carve its way through the layers of limestone. Even though not remote, Heinrich sensed that here remained a kind of wilderness magic that was missing in most highly traveled tourist spots. It reminded him of the Schattenreich, of the peacefulness in isolation that could sometimes be felt on the outskirts of the forest, near the River of Life. The Verdon Gorge smelled like life itself.

"What does she want with Caitie?" Heinrich asked after they'd just about reached an apex of the trail and come out of the trees. He paused to let Hagen catch up to him.

"Nothing good, I can assure you," Hagen said, his face grim. "I believe we may encounter something in the way of a river guardian."

"A guardian? You mean like the Loreley?"

"Something like that. But I fear not as pleasant."

Heinrich grunted and marched onward. He heard Hagen vomiting again behind him and paused, wondering if he should go on alone. They needed to hurry.

"If I recall, the way gets tricky for a bit until we reach the river again," Hagen said. "But there's a cable to hold onto on the way down."

Hagen's breaths were ragged, but he didn't otherwise appear in any worse shape than he had been. The liter bottle was empty. Heinrich stowed it in his pack.

After easy bouldering—easy for Heinrich, Hagen struggled a bit —they'd reached a needle-thin route along the river. The starkness of the white limestone contrasted with the riotous blue of the Verdon River. There was whitewater, not much, but Hagen said it could be more violent, depending on rainfall and time of year.

"This passage is called *le Styx*. You know, like the entrance to the underworld," Hagen said. "Sometimes it eats kayakers, although not often."

"It's beautiful," Heinrich said. "Too bad, though. We can't stop."

"Do you think they're far ahead of us?"

Heinrich paused to listen, taking a few steps forward. He did hear voices, faint, and they sounded feminine.

"No, I think we've almost caught them up."

"She'll have the knife," Hagen said. "*Verdammt.*"

Heinrich froze. "What knife?"

"The one we found yesterday...seems like a lot longer now... embedded in the river bottom. Likely Iron Age. Much like the athame Caitie and I brought back from the Veneti. Jeweled handle. That kind of knife. Perfect for a ritual sacrifice."

"Inscribed?"

"Don't know. I didn't get a good look at it."

"And why do you think—"

"Anethe went and retrieved it. The knife was what she was looking for. I'm sure of it."

"I thought she was looking for Templar treasure."

"Me, too," Hagen said. "But she's after a different prize. A mermaid's tail."

"*Merde*," Heinrich said and picked up the pace.

This stretch of the trail was a maze of limestone boulders. Even a giant could get lost in here. White paint marked the trail at regular intervals, or they wouldn't have had any idea which way was the right one. Hagen said this area was the product of a fault scarp that had collapsed.

They entered an arch that deepened to a small cave made by overhanging blocks worn smooth.

"The secret beach is just through here," Hagen said. "We're almost there—"

He stood erect and still, his head tilted as if he strained to hear distant music.

"What is it? Do you hear them?" Heinrich asked.

"No, but there's something else. We're in a nemeton. We can cross the veil here."

"You can sense it?"

Hagen nodded. "It's one of my specialties. Crossing in unusual locations, I've become attuned to places where it's possible. The nemeton makes it easy."

"I didn't know that."

Hagen smiled weakly. "Now you're one up on me since you've learned one of my secrets."

Heinrich nodded. "A direct passage from the waking world to Ande-dubnos? There's aren't many of those left."

"It's possible. Could also be the Between Lands. I suspect they've not gone to the beach at all. I'll bet they've gone in. I wonder if Anethe knows where it is she's taking Caitie."

Heinrich put a hand on Hagen's shoulder. "Shall we find out? I've got a few Shadowcraft constructions ready."

"I am not completely recovered from whatever it was Anethe slipped into my soup yesterday. In fact, I am feeling weak all over. But that shouldn't prevent me from engaging in a Shadowdance. I don't know with who or what I'll be *dancing*, but let's do it."

They crossed the veil together. The remarkably easy passage, like going through an automatic sliding door, led Heinrich to believe that it was meant to lure the unsuspecting traveler. Not a good thing.

Before them was a swiftly gurgling river that looked much like the Verdon River in the waking world, but wasn't as violently blue-green. It was crystalline clear blue with a few small whitecaps. There wasn't a canyon here, but a high grassy riverbank, the landscape perhaps reminiscent of a time before the gorge formed. An older time indeed.

The other main difference between this river and the Verdon was the masculine-looking creature floating between two flat rocks in the middle of the river; he deflected the water that tried to flow through the rocks. Other rocks on either side formed a stepping stone path that would enable one to cross the river without even getting wet.

If there weren't a supernatural obstacle in the way.

He had the head of a lion. Only a frill of fur defined the mane. The body below the waist consisted of a long, dolphin-like tail covered in iridescent scales the color of dried blood. The scales that continued up the creature's back were thicker and topped by short, sharp-looking iron spikes. The creature's two arms were thick and humanoid, covered in short golden fur, and ended in clawed hands, each with three fingers and a thumb. Several fingers were beringed with gold.

Those hands also now grasped an agitated Caitlin von der Lahn just above the waist. She straddled the two rocks to either side of the creature, the surging river water soaking her pants and shoes. She glared at the creature, her hands on her hips. Yes, she definitely looked pissed off—the kind of anger that carried a bite with it.

Anethe stood on the bank of the river, ineffectually brandishing a jeweled-hilt knife.

Hagen had disappeared. At least it appeared that way if you didn't know what to look for. He drifted in and out of shadow, using the insubstantiality of the veil to cover his movements and provide him with an extra dimension, so-to-speak, of movement. He neared the water, edging towards Caitie and the monster in an oblique way.

Hagen's *Schattentanz* arsenal included a short sword, and probably a fireball or three. And his body—in this form, an elegant and often deadly weapon. Heinrich had only seen him fight this way once against a monster out of shadow that just wouldn't live and let live.

The fight hadn't lasted long. It had been impressive.

Heinrich took a few slow, careful steps towards Anethe. She now brandished the knife at him.

Heinrich ignored her and spoke to Caitie instead. "Do you need help?" He couldn't resist a smirk.

She flicked back a braid dripping with water. "Heiner, darlin', do I look like I need help?" She cast a quick glance around. "Did you find Hagen?"

"He's not far away..." Heinrich produced a shock fireball and held it in his hand for a moment before tossing it, aiming for Anethe's knife-wielding hand. She screeched and dropped the knife, pulling her hand close to her chest.

The knife disappeared.

Heinrich saw a flash of Hagen taking a leap for one of the mid-river rocks before the veil swallowed him again in its shadowy embrace.

"Why don't you—hey, I told you to watch your hands," Caitie said when the river monster guardian tried to pick her up, sliding one arm between her crotch and placing the other on her butt. It looked like he either intended to wear her around his neck or force her into his mouth. Caitie pummeled his thick arms, but he didn't seem to notice. "Don't make me do something you might regret," she said, gritting her teeth.

Anethe had sunk to the ground. Her eyes shone with a morbid fascination. Had she wanted to feed Caitie to the creature?

"Can it talk?" Heinrich asked in the general direction of either of the two women.

"It can," the creature said in a cultured clear voice, speaking English with a French accent. "And it wants to know what brought you here."

"Put me down, and then we can talk," Caitie said.

Surprisingly, the fish-dragon-lion chimera obeyed, tossing Caitie into the drink. She surfaced, gasping, and hauled herself up to sit on one of the rocks that she had been straddling moments before. "That was uncalled for."

The creature tried, but didn't quite pull off, a shrug.

She wrung water from her hair and made a disgusted noise.

"You're marked," it said to her in modern Breton.

Caitie answered in the same tongue. "Yes, so I've been told. My name is Caitlin von der Lahn. And you are?"

"Names. They can be so ponderous. I have been called many. Not any of them nice."

"Sticks and stones," she said, in English. With a pronounced Texas drawl.

"Yes, I've had those thrown at me as well."

Anethe took the opportunity to interfere. "You cursed my mother, and now she is dying. Sticks and stones...you deserve death."

"Your mother?" the creature asked.

Heinrich wanted to echo the question. He'd not a clue about the situation, and rather thought they needed one. Or two.

Hagen appeared behind Caitie on the river stone. He kissed the top of her head.

"Nicely done," the creature said. "You move through the veil like liquid silver."

"Thank you," Hagen said. "You look very similar to a statue that once stood in the city of Noves until it was destroyed by the Romans. I believe you are referred to now as the Tarasque dragon. But you are reputed to have six legs and a shell like a turtle. And you ate a lot of people."

The creature laughed. "Of course. People are just too delicious.

Oh, and I was tamed by the holy woman, Martha, before the peasants killed me."

Hagen opened his palm and displayed the jeweled knife. "Anethe's mother was, I assume, the most recent owner of this knife?"

"Ah," the creature said. "That is a sad story. May I see it?"

Heinrich glanced at Anethe and took a step closer, wanting to make sure she didn't interfere. She glared at him. He didn't blame her. Shock fireballs left a nasty sting. He could have used a real one. He sometimes thought he was too merciful. She deserved worse. But things were just getting interesting.

Hagen handed the creature the knife without hesitation. "How may I address you, Ancient One?" he asked.

"Condatis works for me, although it is a collective name, shared by many of us. At least it *was* shared."

"It means the confluence, as in a merging of waters," Hagen said.

Caitie gasped. "Condatis! Before he died, your father told me Condatis healed him, although he had no power to cure a curse."

Condatis appeared to consider. "As I said, I am not the only bearer of that name. Although I have been known to heal those who are deserving. Curses are difficult to treat." He pointed to the knife Hagen held. "The curse on the knife—the blade is spelled iron—is not something I can rectify as it is compelled by the will and intention of the user."

Hagen doubled over for a few seconds but then righted himself. He looked even paler than before. Maybe crossing over had worsened his nausea.

"A curse of mediation," Heinrich said, and then louder, "our family has recently been freed from a centuries-old curse. We've no desire to be cursed again."

"Understandable," Condatis said. He turned it over. "The dagger is old by human standards. And it is the reason my scales are the color of blood instead of their original delft blue. Anethe's mother tried to eviscerate me. Hence, the curse. There is nothing I can do for her now."

"The poison inside of you," he pointed a clawed finger at Hagen, "that is something I can heal. But the healing comes with a price, and it may be too high for you to pay."

Hagen turned to Anethe. "You poisoned me? Wasn't drugging me enough?"

She laughed but it came out weak and sounded bitter. "One can never be too sure. I was going to use you to lure that...the abomination...so I could remove the tail. That, I was told, would have ended the curse that is killing my mother."

"And you believed that putting a river guardian's tail in a soup would end a curse?" Hagen had raised his voice, a rarity, and not something Heinrich enjoyed hearing when that voice was used on him. But he could well understand Hagen's ire. Heinrich felt his own anger rise within, churning his stomach. It was something Sebastian had always warned about. Never act from anger alone.

"No, of course not. The recipe was only to get and hold your interest. Obviously, it didn't work the way I intended it to." Anethe put her head in her hands and didn't say anything else.

"I believe I can clear up what is confusing you," Condatis said. He swished sideways in the water and hoisted himself onto the other rock, and faced Hagen and Caitie. "But I do think you should first make a decision about what you want to do about the poison."

"You mentioned a price?" Heinrich asked.

"Unless you can breathe underwater, the healing itself may kill you. But at least you won't die of poison," Condatis said.

Hagen bent his head. "If I die—"

"You'll go to the Dreams. Not a good idea, Hagen," Caitie said. "Not in a weakened state. And you've not gone for several years. I vote against you dying by either drowning or poison."

"I'll take my chances," Hagen said. "I'm really not feeling well at all."

Hagen's skin had tinged yellow in addition to being wan. His twin tended to underestimate any weakness. It was one of the rules of enemy confrontation. Don't let on, especially if you're about to die. "Caitie, I'm not sure we have a choice here. And the choice is Hagen's—"

"It is. Shall we proceed?" Condatis asked.

"I'm in favor," Hagen said.

Condatis placed the knife on the rock next to him. "We won't be needing this." Then he pulled Hagen into an embrace. They slipped under the water.

"Not without me, you don't," Caitie said and jumped in after them.

"Oh, hell," Heinrich said. And dived in after Caitie.

It was as Heinrich remembered with the Loreley. Down was up, and everything frothed blue and white with dark shadows mixed in. Hagen and Condatis moved through and within the veil leaving tiny typhoons in their wake.

Heinrich swam fierce, making an arrow of his body. He didn't know how he could work his Shadowcraft over himself as well as Hagen and Condatis. But he had to try—they only had a few short minutes before Hagen would begin to drown.

Caitie, just below him and closer to the frothing dance that included Hagen, Condatis, loose vegetation and everything else in the vicinity, swirled around in the water, her arms held close above her head like a ballet dancer in a tight pirouette. She sank faster until she was below the center of the water maelstrom that held Hagen and Condatis.

Heinrich blew out a breath in dismay and kicked his legs harder to reach her. He couldn't save both of them, and Hagen would never forgive him if he let Caitie die. She, too, would go to the Dreams, and it was at least as undesirable a result as letting Hagen go. Hagen, at least, had years of experience of getting through.

Heinrich was met with a blast of air moving outward through the water. It had to have come from Caitie. She made a walking motion with her hands and began to rise, kicking out, until she was level with Condatis and Hagen. The bubble of sound, a percussive acoustic wave, rose with her.

Heinrich smiled and pushed out a few more bubbles, kicking to join her. He put an arm around her waist, drawing her near, and released his own acoustic bubble, a Shadowcraft spell he always had on hand that he called Voice. His craft joined with hers. She turned to him in the water and smiled.

They breathed deeply of the melodious, pulsing air in their bubble, air that also reached Hagen.

Heinrich kissed her and she tasted how fragrant narcissus smelled. Her skin felt like a crisp sip of a chilled dry Riesling. Heinrich's song mingled with hers, echoing her deep passion; a fierce enduring love that coursed through him, for him, and for Hagen, and for the children, for all of those they loved deeply. It washed over and through him, becoming his core.

Heinrich didn't know how long the song lasted. Maybe it was already tomorrow, or they had traveled back to last week. They had somehow floated upwards and broke the surface at the same time that Hagen did. Hagen cried out and leaned back to float in the water.

Condatis was nowhere to be seen.

Caitie swam next to Hagen, fussing over him, until he murmured that he was all right. She kissed his cheek and pulled him in a lifeguard's grip towards the shore. Heinrich followed.

It was only when they had all pulled themselves out that they saw her.

Anethe lay prone, facing away from them. The jeweled hilt of the knife protruded from her side. Riverbank sand had already absorbed most of the blood that flowed from her wound, creating a gritty puddle as her life leaked away. Her hands were bright red from her efforts to pull out the knife.

Heinrich and Hagen went to her at once. Her face was pale, and her breathing faint. She was dying.

"I don't think even Condatis can rectify this," Hagen said, his voice a whisper.

"But why would she—" Heinrich asked and drew his lips in a line. He'd not wanted to be merciful before. He wasn't sure she deserved it now.

"She is of the blood. Her trial will be to survive the Dreams," Caitie said. "I did, that first time."

They lapsed into a short silence, their remembrance of Caitie's demise at another's hand still fresh. She'd survived the Dreams and returned, a living breathing woman.

"First, we have to see her off to the Dreams," Hagen said. "I'm sure she'll survive it. She's a very determined woman."

A circle of white froth, a soft cushion of liquid foam appeared next to them in the river. Condatis's voice came to them. "I'll see to it that she gets to the Dreams of your people. The rest is up to her."

"He's invisible and talking through the air now?" Caitie said, her hands on her hips.

Hagen removed the knife and tried to staunch the wound with his wet linen shirt, but it was no use. Anethe didn't regain consciousness. Heinrich held her hand and sang her down with a special song of Shadowcraft to ease her pain on the way.

The two of them picked Anethe up as gently as they could and lowered her to her funereal transport. The foam enclosed her within. A powerful strong tenor sang ancient words, the voice surrounding them even though they couldn't see its source. The mournful dirge was in a Celtic dialect no longer spoken in the waking world, except by a few descendants of one particular lineage, three of whom witnessed the ritual on the banks of the river. When the song ended, Anethe, within her frothy capsule, sank below, into the depths.

"I think," Caitie said, when Condatis's passage was only a ripple on the water's surface, "that if she hadn't lied to me and she hadn't poisoned Hagen, that I might have liked her."

"Maybe we can pay her a visit when she returns," Hagen said. "She'll then have a different perspective on things."

Her first trip to the Dreams. It could take a long while. They had months to prepare.

"She was trying to save her mother," Heinrich said. "I don't guess we'll ever hear the story now."

"Oh," Hagen said. "I can enlighten you. Condatis imparted it all to me during our Shadowdance."

We both stared at him.

"But I would really like to go back to the hotel and get dry first. It's quite a hike ahead of us, and the day...if it's still day...is going to fade fast in the canyon."

"But," Caitie said. "What...I mean. Oh, damnation." But she smiled when she said it. "Farewell, Condatis, wherever you are. And thanks for healing my husband."

~

H agen
The three of them could have had the dining room to themselves. It was late for dinner, but M. Pascal had been happy to see them again and agreed to keep the kitchen open. They were the only diners and had unanimously agreed to sit outside on the terrace.

Sweet-smelling nicotiana and lavender spiced the evening air in contrast to the elusive scent of peegee hydrangea. The sun had sunk, and the evening air was cooler but still balmy. Caitie had dressed in a white sleeveless sundress and draped a sweater over her shoulders, her reddish-brown flowing mane of hair a lovely contrast to the white of her dress.

Heiner seemed subdued as he sipped his *pastis*.

Caitie, as usual, brimmed with impatience. The questions hovered there, about to escape her lips. Hagen longed to taste their sweetness again, and was nearly overcome with his own impatience. She was here, and Heiner was here, and Hagen was so completely grateful for the both of them. For their love for him and for each other. He never thought he would say that—and he didn't want say it out loud—

But...

"Thank you both," Hagen said. "I don't know how to say this—"

"Me, too," Heiner said.

Caitie looked from one to the other and shrugged. "Goes without saying. But now we're here and we're talking and not drowning or poisoned or otherwise in a dire situation. How about a tale to go with dinner?"

"I'm *not* having the fish soup," Hagen said. "Even without a tail in it."

"I'm having a steak," Heiner said.

"Pizza for me," Caitie said.

Hagen decided on a shortened version of all that Condatis had imparted to him.

"I've managed to solve the reason, at least a partial one, for one of my obsessions," he said after the rosé arrived and he'd poured it into everyone's wineglasses. It would not be the only bottle they would share this night.

"The defeat of the Celts by the Romans," Heiner said.

"Betrayal from within," Hagen said. "One of the oldest stories."

"The Celts betrayed each other."

"In a most deadly fashion. The knife, the one I've secured in my suitcase, was used to eliminate the river guardians. It was a calculated betrayal and had to have come from—and I can't avoid using the term—the class of society known today as the druids."

"No way," Caitie said.

"The knife is spelled iron, and it can be used to destroy those supernatural water deities that were revered by all the continental Celts, both for their healing powers as well as their sanctity."

Silence surrounded them. It carried no solace.

"And so the basis of their beliefs was laid to waste from within," Heiner said after a few moments.

"The other side of the story is that the knife was cursed. By whom I don't know, but it must have been one of us."

"One of our ancestors?" Caitie asked.

"Had to have been. Someone who figured out what was going on. Powerless to stop the destruction, perhaps, the curse was laid down to make the betrayal costly. I assume the price that is paid for such desecration is death and that Anethe's mother is, in fact, dying."

"And what does Anethe and her mother have to do with it...oh. She attacked Condatis and almost killed him. But why?" Caitie asked.

Hagen poured their glasses full again. "That is still somewhat of a mystery, and maybe we can get more of the story from Anethe when she returns. If she's willing. But I assume it has to do with the Du Bois hatred of all things pagan and supernatural."

Hagen took a deep drink of wine. "The knife survived, along with its curse. And was apparently used. Again and again. Maybe with the help of the mermaid's tail *bouillaibase*. As much as I hate the truth of it, the church had a clear mandate to wipe out the competition from non-Christian sanctified beings. They only survive today in the collective memory as fairies and other kinds of fanciful beings, such as the horrid depiction of Condatis as the Tarasque dragon."

"A true recipe for disaster," Heiner said.

No one disagreed.

"Well, I wouldn't call Condatis ugly, at least not to his face, but his appearance does take some getting used to," Caitie said.

"I'll notify cousin Ivonne Du Bois of Anethe's temporary *absence*. She won't like it, but there's not a thing she can do about it," Heiner said.

Hagen's elation at Condatis's conveyed knowledge was tempered by the horror of its revelation. He'd never be able to publish the discovery, as par for the course when he found something out using supernatural resources, but at least he had a partial answer to his question. And Condatis had confirmed that the druids had existed. He'd ponder it all at length when they returned home.

But it was time to return to the here and now and that included Caitie. And his brother Heiner. And he wanted to show his gratitude. Heiner would love it. He hoped Caitie could be *convinced* to enjoy it.

"Excellent, Heiner. And now for the good news. Since I am no longer *gainfully* employed in the search for lost treasure, I think some relaxation is in order before we all go home. And thanks to M. Pascal, I've acquired wetsuits for all of us. Tomorrow we will go aqua trekking down the Verdon," Hagen said.

"Bravo!" Heiner said.

"Um," Caitie said. "What—"

"There are only one or two jumps," Hagen said. "And we'll be with you."

"Jumps?" she squeaked. "As in, from a height?"

"You survived *Schultüten*," Heiner said. "You'll be fine."

"I know," she said and sighed. "With the two of you by my side, it will be...fun." Her tone was hesitant, and Hagen knew she had planned it to that way to make them laugh.

And they did.

Hagen, Heinrich and Caitie touched glasses, embracing that they were here and alive and together.

A recipe for forever.

ABOUT THE AUTHOR

Now a full-time writer living near Cologne, Sharon Kae Reamer's speculative fiction is inspired by her participation in various archeoseismology projects during her twenty-something years as a senior scientist at the University of Cologne. Locations that include the Praetorium and medieval Jewish settlement in Cologne, ancient Tiryns in Greece, and Greek ruins in Selinunte, Sicily, provide perfect backdrops for creating fantasy stories rich with history and mythology, such as her *Immortal Guardian* and *Schattenreich Mystery* novelette series and her five-book *Schattenreich* novel series.

Her love for mixing and mashing science fiction and fantasy continues unabated. *Night Shepherd*, in the *Schattenreich* universe is a spinoff (one of many) of her soon-to-be-published first novel in *The Sundered Veil* series, a further conception of science fantasy.

Sharon plans to continue her pursuit of archeoseismology because the personal and professional connections she's made cannot—and should not—be deterred. She also cooks daily (German-English), gardens (chaotically, at best), knits (badly), does needlepoint (rather well) and reads (everything) all the damn time.

And, of course, she has cats.

Find out more about Sharon at:
sharonreamer.com

BB bookbub.com/authors/sharon-kae-reamer

A PROCESSION OF FAERIES

I f you enjoyed *Water Faeries*, check out the other volumes in A Procession of Faeries!

blackbirdpublishing.com/series/a-procession-of-faeries
facebook.com/a.procession.of.faeries

www.ingramcontent.com/pod-product-compliance
Lightning Source LLC
Chambersburg PA
CBHW071200250626
47159CB00001B/146